The Amazing Tales
of the Portal Pen

Written by Adelyn Rae

the amazing tales of the portal pen

Adelyn Rae

The Amazing Tales of the Portal Pen
Copyright 2019 by Luke LeFevre
ISBN 978-1-7342711-1-9

Written by Adelyn Rae
Cover Design by Luke LeFevre
Book Block Design by Whitnee Clinard
Edited by Mandy LeFevre, Rachel Knapp, and Jessa R. Sexton

A Woodfine Young Writers Guild Book

Published by
Hilliard Press
a division of
The Hilliard Institute for Educational Wellness

Franklin, Tennessee
Oxford, England
Abbeyleix, Ireland
www.hilliardinstitute.com

Dedication

I dedicate this book to my parents because they've supported me and encouraged me throughout this whole process! They've made my dream of publishing a book become a reality! THANK YOU, and I love you!

PROLOGUE

1967

A boy about the age of sixteen kicked his feet to the beat of "Yellow Submarine" by the Beatles. Papers fluttered anxiously as the ceiling fan whipped around. Stacks of books and CDs were piled all the way to the ceiling, and magazines scattered the boy's bed. Graffiti covered one of the walls of the room, and spray paint bottles lay sprawled out on the floor, their colorful liquid dripping onto the creaking wooden floor boards.

The boy's forehead furrowed as he furiously picked at a pen with tweezers. The pen was made of Turquoise Wood, with purple and golden accents. He was busy adjusting the hooks at the top of the pen, where he would later hook on keychains.

With one last tug of the tweezers, the last hook locked in place. "There," the boy muttered. He stopped his record player, gently lifted the pen to his ear, and shook it. The noise of sloshing liquid came from inside the pen, but another noise—the noise of sputtering sparks—filled his ears. With that, the boy jumped up in the air with joy. He whooped and shouted until his father banged on his door.

"Shut it, Billie! You sound like a wailin' hippo!"

But the boy just laughed and plopped back down on the ground. "Okay, time to test!" he whispered. He grabbed his misshapen notebook with bent pages and stickers from around the world plastered on the fading blue cover. He flipped it open to an empty page and began to write a story.

The next day, Billie sat in class while his teacher taught history on the board. The class was busy scribbling down notes while Billie was scribbling down stories. He was writing about a pirate with an eye patch and wispy, lime green hair named Captain Seaweed. He was the Captain of a ship called the Tsunami Cruiser and was the crankiest and meanest pirate anyone could ever meet.

Billie was just at the part where Captain Seaweed was making a traitor crew member walk the plank into the churning waves of the ocean when the history teacher slapped her ruler on his desk. Billie jolted upward and immediately stuffed his pen and paper in his desk.

"What was that you were writing, Mr. Mason?" the teacher asked, lifting an eyebrow.

"Nothing, Mrs. Sharp. I was taking notes," Billie lied smoothly.

"Is that so? Then, how come I saw the words *pirate* and *Captain Seaweed* on your paper?" Mrs. Sharp asked, practically spitting out the syllables with disgust.

The class began to giggle and snicker. But Billie wasn't fazed. "Why, yes. I was actually writing a story, Mrs. Sharp. I think you'll like it very much! It's about a pirate named Captain Seaweed and . . . "

Mrs. Sharp quickly interrupted him and spat, "Mr. Mason, I would much rather listen to what you've learned about George Washington today in class than one of your stupid stories." The class was so silent that all you could hear was the muffled voices of the class next door. Billie's fists balled.

The whole room was silent until Sparrow McFully shouted out, "Aww. Look at that! He's going to cry! What a stupid wimp!"

The class burst out in giggles, pointing and laughing at poor Billie while Sparrow pretended to rub his eyes and weep. Billie fumed. His own friend was his worst enemy, and Sparrow never failed to make him feel miserable. As the class continued to laugh, Billie suddenly heard a faint sizzling noise. He grabbed the pen from inside his desk and felt it rumbling. But he also felt a rumbling underneath him that he knew no one else could feel. It wasn't like an earthquake rumbling—it was like his body was almost shaking on the inside. He grinned suddenly at the realization: His pen worked perfectly. Billie began laughing along with the class. Maybe his childish stories were stupid. But little did they know an actual, living and breathing Captain Seaweed with an eye patch and wispy, lime hair was out there somewhere, riding his great ship over the churning waves of the vast sea . . .

CHAPTER ONE

Yeti Foots

I nervously pick at the corner of my paper. Ugh, my stomach is doing triple backflips. I then begin to fold and unfold the paper. Gigi, the stage manager, taps my shoulder. "Eva, sweetie, you're up next, okay? Be prepared to walk on when Phoenix Lopez walks off." As Gigi walks away, her frizzy, red hair bounces obnoxiously. I swear her hair is the same color as those fake cherry slushies that you buy at cheap gas stations.

I hear the muffled clapping and cheers and then the swoosh of the curtain as one of the contestants, Phoenix, walks off.

"You did great!" I whisper to him.

"Thanks! Good luck!" he says.

Oh, boy. My stomach feels like mush and my feet like Jell-O. I urge myself to walk up onto the stage. There are three big platforms—one for third, second, and first place. I nervously step onto the highest platform for first place. The stage lights blare in my eyes, so I squint and blink furiously. Even though I can't see them, I know there are hundreds of people sitting in the gym, eagerly watching and waiting. As I step up to the mic, everyone cheers.

"Hello and good evening," I say in my most pleasant but casual stage voice. Good. My butterflies have fluttered away. It always turns out like this. Once I'm actually on the stage, it's a piece of cake. Clutching the paper in my hand, I continue: "My name is Eva Mason, I'm in the eighth grade, and I won first place for this year's Creative Writing Festival." I'd practiced this so many times, and now it just flows out of me like water. The crowd claps and cheers. When they settle down, I say "This year, for my Creative Writing story, I decided on the genre of Fantasy. The inspiration for this story came to me when I was at the Orange County Fair in California last summer. My story is called 'Yeti Foots.'" The crowd respectfully claps, and I start to read:

"Yeti Foots" by Eva Mason

Somewhere, way up high on an icy mountain where the sky was always gray and the ground was always white and wet, a furry, white Yeti sat alone in a cave in the mountain. He made his bed from the padded snow on the ground outside, he ate special Chilly Soup from the snowflakes that fell from the sky, and he made furniture from the wood of the frozen trees. But he wasn't happy, because he was alone.

Somewhere, way up high on a flaming hot mountain where the sky was always orange and the ground was always brown and dry, a furry brown BigFoot sat alone in a cave in the mountain. She made her bed from the dry clay on the ground outside, she ate special Flaming Soup from the flaming lightning that fell from the sky, and she made furniture from the rocks of the dusty ground. But she was not happy, because she was alone.

One day, the Yeti was fed up with his cold and chilly life, so he decided to go somewhere new. He decided on the mountain across from him. I will build a new life there, *he thought. Meanwhile, the BigFoot was fed up with her sweltering and dry life, so she decided to travel to the mountain across from her.* I will build a new life there, *she thought. The journey was long for both of them. When the Yeti got to the dry desert mountain, he thought,* This is too hot for me! But my home is too cold! *When the BigFoot got to the cold, snowy mountain, she thought,* This is too cold for me, but my home is too hot! *BigFoot and Yeti sighed and decided it would probably be best if they headed back home.*

I pause for effect and glance up from my paper. The crowd looks dazzled. Is my story really that good? I look back down at my paper and continue to read:

In between both mountains was a little tiny valley that was neither hot nor cold. It had a light mist of snow, and a soft, warming breeze. The sky was a light lavender. On the way down, the Yeti realized that he was lonely. To have a friend with him, living in his home, eating with him, collecting snowflakes with him—it was a lovely thought. The BigFoot thought the same too. Yeti and BigFoot ran into each other in the valley.

At first, the Yeti and the BigFoot scoffed at each other, and the Yeti said, "Your place is too hot!"

And the BigFoot said, "Your place is too cold!" *And they marched on to their own homes.*

But then the Yeti realized, Maybe she can eat Chilly Soup with me.

And the BigFoot realized, Maybe he can collect stray lightning bolts with me!

And they rushed back down.

"Will you be my friend, Yeti?" BigFoot asked.

"Will you be my friend, BigFoot?" Yeti asked.

"Yes," they said together.

Together, they decided to live in the valley with the light breezes and little snowflakes and the lavender sky, and together they had two little children: Yeti Foots!

The crowd bursts into laughter, which melts into applause and cheers. I bow, fold up my paper, and stick it into my pocket. I thank the crowd, then wave and scurry off the stage. My heart is pounding in my chest, and I feel dizzy. I can still hear the crowd cheering. My mouth feels like sandpaper. My voice had swerved upwards when I said "thank you" so it had been more of, "thank youuu."

"Gigi, can I get some water?" I ask and sit down in one of the chairs backstage.

"Of course, sweetie," she says and jogs off, her cherry-slushy curls bobbing wildly. When I look up, I see my best friend, Romi, rushing toward me.

"Ahhhh!" she squeals as we embrace each other in a tight hug. "Wow, Eva! That was a great story! How do you come up with these?" she asks.

I shrug. "I guess I just get inspired really easily." We both giggle together.

"Come on! Let's go see your parents!" Romi urges.

I forget all about Gigi getting me some water as we jog out into the lobby where my parents and older brother wrap me in a hug.

"Eva, baby, you are so talented!" my mom gushes.

"Wow, Eva, that was so amazing," my dad says. His grin can't get any wider.

"How about some ice cream?" my older brother, Marty, encourages. He may be a sophomore in high school, and he may be a dorky teenager with spiky blue hair, but he still treats me like his awesome little sister. We all cheer at the thought of ice cream.

"Can Romi come too?" I ask, clasping our hands together.

"Of course!" Mom smiles.

We all pack into our van and drive off to my favorite ice cream place, Conner's Custard. On the way there, Mom's phone rings. "Grammy wants to FaceTime," she says, handing me her phone. That's what we call my dad's mom. Her real name is Georgia. My dad's dad was named Billie, but I never got to meet him. He vanished right before Grammy had my dad. I don't know the whole story, but I guess his life was hard or something— and then one day he was just gone. No one could find him, not even the police. Everyone was devastated. Still, neither my dad nor Grammy talk bad about him. And we call him Papa B.

I see Grammy's face appear on the screen. "Is that my little star?" Grammy asks.

I laugh. "I guess so!" I say.

"Your mom sent me the video, and I'm so proud of you!" Grammy says.

"Thank you! It was a little nerve-racking, but I think I did good," I say honestly.

"And you did!" Grammy says. "The story was very well-thought-out. I loved the idea for the Yeti Foots!" She laughs. I laugh too.

"Yes, thank you, Grammy!" I say.

"So, when is your next story festival thing?" Grammy asks.

"Not until October, Grammy. It's June now, so about five months away," I say.

"Well, great job, baby, and take care!"

"I will! Bye, Grammy!"

"Bye, sweetie pie!" Grammy waves. I wave again before clicking off and sighing happily.

Romi gives my hand a squeeze and rests her head on my shoulder. "I wish I could write stories like you, Eva," she says.

"Well, I've been doing it for a long time, R," I say.

"True," Romi agrees.

I reach into my backpack and take out my pen. It's shimmery with Turquoise Wood and has hooks to hang keychains on. It's my lucky pen. "This is a special pen that I always use when I write stories," I say.

"Wow, that's a cool pen, E!" Romi gushes.

"And look! It even has little hooks to hang stuff on! I put my keychains on them," I say.

"Aw, fun!" Romi laughs.

"My dad has always had this pen. He said Papa B made it himself," I gush.

"That's so cool! And look! Where did this Turquoise Wood come from?" Romi asks.

"He probably spray-painted it or something. But anyway, this is what I always use when I'm writing stories. And the super cool thing is, every time I finish a story, it makes a sizzling noise like sparklers almost, like it almost somehow knows when the story's done. Plus, it vibrates too," I say. Maybe I sound like I'm bragging. I hope not. "And the floor also rumbles when I finish a story. I think I just imagine it though." Ah shoot, why did I say that? Romi doesn't need to know that my brain pretends to make the ground shake. I *know* it doesn't. "I'm sorry, I know that must sound strange to you," I say.

Romi takes the pen from me and examines it. "This is so cool," she mutters. She plays with the hooks and fiddles with the keychains. "This is so cool," she says again.

"Yeah, it is," I grin.

"Does it ever run out of ink?" Romi asks.

I shake my head. "Weirdly, no. I've been using it for years," I say.

Romi's eyes go wide. "*Wow*, Eva," she grins. She seems super fascinated. Not jealous, just fascinated. I'm glad she's not jealous. She's such a good friend.

My dad pulls into a parking spot at Conner's Custard. "Alright, troops, ice cream time!"

We all scramble out of the car. I dash toward the front counter. But then I realize Romi isn't with me.

"Romi?" I call. I run back to the car. She's hastily fiddling with her purse. "Romi, you coming?" I ask.

She zips up her bag and hops out. "Yep. I was just . . . um, looking at your pen. It's so cool!" she gushes, climbing out of the car and handing it to me. Before I can open my mouth to say something, Romi jumps in, "What flavor are you getting?" She grabs my hand, and we dash up to the counter.

Okay. That felt weird to me but, eh, doesn't matter. What matters is ice cream! "Hmm, I think I'm gonna get the Rocky Road flavor!"

She squeals and says, "Me too!"

I squeal back.

CHAPTER TWO

Dawn Blossom Tea

I absolutely love my bedroom. It's not your typical girl's room. My brother and I both decorated one of the walls with spray paint and created our own graffiti together, just like my Papa B had done to his room when he was young. My ceiling slopes upwards and inwards, like a triangle. I have a large, lanky window and my bed is nestled below it, just under the lowest of the ceiling. It's really comfy with my bed under the low part of the ceiling, next to the window. All along the wall on the right side of my bed are bookshelves. But most of the "books" are binders full of stories—tons and tons of stories.

On the other side of my room is my desk. A giant bulletin board hangs over it. It has pictures, awards, clips of stories, and invites to birthday parties. Pretty much every day when I come home from school, I unpack my bag, do homework, eat dinner, and then rush upstairs to work on a story. It's not like I'm trying to win a prize for most stories written or anything. I just have this super serious urge to always have a story going. And believe me, I always have a story going. I guess you could say it runs in the family, since apparently, Papa B always had stories going too.

I dip my nachos in cheese dip absent-mindedly at lunch. Busy writing a story, I'm not thinking about eating. I always try to get to the lunchroom early before everyone else and get my food so I don't have to wait in line and waste writing time. As I scribble furiously into my notebook, my keychains on my pen clink together gently.

My current story is about a land called Lovely Valley where there's pretty much only pinks and lavenders and blushes and purples. This land is filled with rich scents and smells and loveliness and peace that can never be disturbed. But one day, a diseased Banshee wanders into this land and stumbles upon Lovely Valley and its little pink village that has bottles and bottles of any and every kind of medicine for any and every kind of cure.

The Banshee begs the townspeople for some way to cure her disease. The women of the Lovely Valley are willing to give her medicine if only she gives them her bright pink hair. The Banshee finally agrees, and her hair is cut off. (The Lovely Valley never gives away a medicine without a trade. And it always has to be a good trade.)

The Banshee is bald, but it ends up being for the best. She's now able to hide from predators because her bright pink hair had always made it impossible to blend in. Plus, it turns out her pink hair is what made her sick. The touch of her hair was too much for her delicate skin to handle, so it caused a skin disease. But luckily, the women cure her with a purple tea called Dawn Blossom Tea. As soon as the Banshee drinks it, she's cured! And suddenly, she turns into the most beautiful Banshee queen, even if she's bald, and all the women of the village bow down to her. The Banshee, now queen, lives happily ever.

"Whatcha writing, Sporky?" Phoenix Lopez, the second-place contestant from the Writing Festival and also my other best friend, plops down into the chair next to me with his tray full of Cheetos and pudding.

"That sure looks like a very healthy lunch!" I say, snickering.

Phoenix shrugs. "There's no such thing as junk food in my house like, ever, so I eat it while I can," Phoenix says, smiling and showing off a mouth of clear, metal braces. Everyone thinks Phoenix is handsome, but he is *way* more nerdy than charming. "Sooo whatcha writing,

Sporky?" he repeats, snatching the notebook from my hand.

We're always trying to compete for a better story. But in a friendly way. I even let him borrow my pen sometimes. I believe that there is tons of luck in that pen, so I let him use it. Phoenix's eyebrows scrunch together and he nods as he reads. "Mmm, I like it, Sporky!"

I sigh. Sporky is the nickname he gave after meeting me, claiming my head was round like a spoon and my fingers were long and skinny like forks. So he named me Sporky. "Not bad! But not great either. Too much purple and pink in my opinion," Phoenix says, clucking his tongue.

I laugh and elbow him. "It's never great in your opinion." I grin. Everybody thinks that we're a couple, and I guess we could be. We're both kind of quirky and love writing and get along well, but we're really better off as just friends.

Phoenix grabs a chicken nugget from my tray and munches on it. "Hey, Eva, remember when you let me borrow your pen a couple days ago? I finished the story I was writing with it." Phoenix takes out a slip of paper from his pocket and lays it out:

Once in a province called Spindle's Chase, there was a lovely palace called the Jewel Kingdom. A small town in this kingdom was made of gold and jewels. The people were made of gold, the livestock were made of rubies, and the grass and roads were made of jade. The king and queen were even made out of jewels: the queen was made of amethyst, and the king was made out of moonstone. The fountain in front of the castle was made out of turquoise gems, and the buildings in the marketplace were made out of Amber.

The king and queen had a son made out of quartz. He was small but adventurous and always loved to explore. One day, when his parents weren't looking, the Quartz Prince ran out of the kingdom, past the bronze guards, and past the ruby gate. He ran and ran until the grass wasn't emerald stone anymore, and he continued until he reached a large cave. The Quartz Prince went into the cave, where a family of homeless villagers were living. They were trying to cook a chicken but didn't have the right sticks for a fire. The prince felt sad and approached them. But as soon as he stepped from the emerald ground and onto real ground, his body froze and fell over, turning slowly into a quartz statue.

The Quartz Prince didn't know this, but a jewel creature from the Jewel Kingdom couldn't step off of the emerald ground and into the real world without forever freezing over into just a statue. The homeless family ran to the freezing prince, wishing they could help. But there was nothing they could do.

Before the prince took his last breath, he said, "You poor homeless family. Take my quartz body and buy all you need for a house, clothes, and food." Then, he froze completely into a statue and died. The family cried, but finally took his body to the closest kingdom so they could do as he said. They

*ended up in the Jewel Kingdom! The family was in awe of
everything—of how all of it was made of jewels and gold. The
family fulfilled the Quartz Prince's wish and traded his body
for a farm with lots of land, many animals, and a beautiful
house.*

*When the gold people realized the homeless family had
traded the Quartz Prince's body, they rushed to the king and
queen. Soon, the whole Jewel Kingdom found out how the
Quartz Prince had given the family a great fortune. They
ended up taking the statue of him and placing it in front of
the fountain so no one could ever forget him.*

I scan the paper again. "So, anyone from the Jewel
Kingdom dies if they're no longer in the Jewel Kingdom?
That's pretty harsh, Phoenix," I say, nudging him.

Phoenix shrugs, "Eh, I don't like cheesy stories, so I
just made it more intense." I shrug too.

Just then Romi sits down. Phoenix scowls and is
suddenly very interested in his chocolate pudding. I
don't know what he has against her. She's my very best
friend.

"What's up, Eva? How's it going, Pebbles?" Romi
snatches my apple from my plate. I wasn't planning on
eating it anyways.

Phoenix huffs. "My name is Phoenix," he spats.

Romi shrugs. I don't know where that nickname
came from, but Phoenix hates that Romi calls him
Pebbles. I snicker.

Just then, Chelsey Henrickson and Alexis Alec pass by the table. Ugh, I can't stand them. But I just do the ol' Mason family trick of telling myself their negative opinions don't matter. These two try to find every possible flaw ever existing in a person and blow it up like dynamite.

"What's up, oh great storyteller?" Chelsey says, running her fingers along my lunch tray.

"Nothing," I say. My mind goes blank like a white wall when people insult me. Alexis and Chelsey always hang out together. They are like a pair of drama queens, causing trouble and tearing others down.

Alexis slides her magenta fingernails across the table until she reaches my notebook. Her fingers wrap around it like a snake and soon she's lifting it up to her freckled face so she can see it. My blood boils. I don't let anyone read my story notebook unless it's my family, Romi, or Phoenix. Chelsey crowds around Alexis, and they open the cover. My throat feels like sandpaper, and my mouth won't move. I want so much to stand up to those two and snatch my notebook back, but I just can't.

Romi stands up instead. She grabs at the notebook, but Alexis swats her away. "Give it back to Eva!" Romi yells.

"No way," Chelsey says. Phoenix huffs and shifts uncomfortably. Ugh, I hate this. When Alexis's hand drifts down to the table, I snatch the notebook from her and stuff it in my book bag. "You're no fun," Alexis scoffs and the two walk off.

I fiddle with my pen. "I hate those two," Romi says as she sips her juice. I put my head in my hands and let myself sigh. The cafeteria ladies start to bring around the trash cans and the bell rings suddenly. All three of us lazily get up out of our seats and trudge to class.

The bus makes a turn onto Smithton Road and stops at the corner. My neighborhood is small, turning right off from the highway. It curves upwards, and my backyard is incredibly slanted. Our driveway is steep. The bus always stops at the very top of the road, and I'm always scared it's going to fall backwards and crash into the highway. I scramble out of my seat and hop off the bus. I run up the hill of our road and gasp for air. It's so hard to run up that road. I jog down the sidewalk until I get to the end of the road. We own a red brick town-house with a white roof, except it's just one story, so it's more like a condo. There's a rusty blue bench on our porch with gray cushions on them that say, "Hey, good-lookin'." It's kind of embarrassing.

I rummage around my pocket for the house key, then unlock the door and close it behind me. My parents aren't home from work yet, but Marty is always home before me.

"Hey, Eva!" Marty hollers from his room.

"Sup!" I yell back as I close the door to my room. I throw my backpack onto my bed and stretch. Oh, how I love coming home after school.

It takes an hour and a half, but I finish up my homework and finally get out my story notebook. Then I plop down in my desk chair, put on my headphones, and log on to my computer. No joke, my password is $TORIE$. There's this special website called The Writer's Circle, where kids up to age seventeen write stories and post them. It's super cool. I've posted exactly fifty-six stories of my own. Since I'm absolutely terrible at typing, I just write them out with my pen and take pictures of them.

I log in to The Writer's Circle, and the main menu pops up. It has advertisements for the newest stories. Oh, look! There's one of my stories underneath the top one! That's the story of the Yeti and the BigFoot. Wow, that's really taking off. There are five bubbles that change color at the top of the page: **My Gallery, Library, Group Chat, Log In,** and **Home Page**. I click on **My Gallery**. Immediately, a picture of my face pops up at the top, and then fifty-six light blue folders appear on the screen, each with the title for a different story. I click on my latest called "The Rainbow Catchers," which I posted four days ago. It's about how these secret spies go around and collect rainbows for their underground kingdom. It's pretty cool. Praises pop up under the story. Most of them read things like "Creative!" and "Good Work!" by random writers I don't know.

Romi and Phoenix have pages too. I click back to **Library** and search up Romi. She hasn't written a lot, but her stories are a lot different from mine. She writes about great empires and creatures in the night. Her most popular story is about a queen made of leaves. Everyone thinks the queen is small and innocent, but when someone decides to kidnap her, she creates giant root monsters that track her down, destroying the whole kidnapper's lair and setting her free.

An hour later, after scrolling through The Writer's Circle, I decide to get off. The garage door goes up, and mom and dad come into the house, loaded with groceries. I go over to a shelf next to my desk and pull out a huge notebook with stickers from around the world on it. This was my Papa B's. He used to write tons and tons of stories too with the very pen I use. I love that I get to read them, even though he's gone. They're all so cool! One of the best is about a pirate named Captain Seaweed who rode a pirate ship. My Papa B wrote tons of other stories too. One about a land with silver, floating bubbles with genies living inside. One about a town made out of food called the Spoon Kingdom. One about an adventurous jungle girl with a zebra dress and crazy, red hair named Dakota who slayed a tiger and rode a gigantic snake and tricked monkeys and swam with hippos. One of my favorites is about a forest with talking Tiki trees who possessed magic in their roots.

So, yeah, those are my Papa B's stories. They make me wish I'd been able to know him. They're all so amazing, and Grammy used to read my dad some of his stories when he was a kid. So, I guess writing runs in the family.

CHAPTER THREE

Mount Everest

Billie was stuck in a pickle. What to do, what to do? The girl he liked at that time, Alice McFully, was standing nearby in a clump of whispering girls. Little did he know that Alice McFully was a snob and a liar. Billie was backed up against the wall, Sparrow McFully's clammy hands keeping him there. Billie's eye was swollen and beginning to turn purple and green, and shiny, red blood trickled from his nose down onto his busted lip. He had been bullied so many times by Sparrow McFully about too many things to count, especially for writing stories. Billie didn't get what the big problem was, but Sparrow sure seemed to have one with it.

"Please, Sparrow!" Billie pleaded. "They're just silly stories!"

Sparrow grabbed Billie by the arm. "Billie, you and your stupid stories! You're such a sissy! You're in high school, you wimp. I thought you were my friend, but you've turned out to be an annoying and stupid loser who writes fairy tales instead of playing football! Now hand over those sissy stories so I can tear them to shreds!" Sparrow roared.

Billie quivered, but shook his head. Sparrow McFully raised his fist and Billie cringed, preparing for the worst. Just as Sparrow McFully was about to bring down his fist for the third time, a small hand pinched him hard. Sparrow McFully shrieked and spun around.

Alice McFully stood with a tight scowl on her face. "You put your fist down, mister!" she cried in her little voice. Sparrow just laughed. Alice huffed, "You better leave him alone, because . . . because . . . I like his stories, and they're none of your business anyways!"

Everyone gasped. Billie Mason was the outcast. He just had an inability to fit in. All he wanted to do was write all day and not engage in what the other kids did. He'd always get upset when Mrs. Sharp or any other teacher called him out for writing his stories.

"What did you say?" Billie sputtered, his cheeks a deep, beet red.

Alice sniffed. "That's right! I said I like 'em!" Alice blushed and Billie grinned. Sparrow let go of Billie and gave Alice a nasty look, but Sparrow knew what she was up to. Billie wanted to hug Alice. But poor Billie had no idea that she was setting him up. Alice smiled. "Billie? May I see your notebook? And your pen is so lovely too!" she asked in her shrill voice.

Sparrow McFully snickered. Filled with such glee, Billie practically skipped over to Alice and handed her his notebook and pen. Alice pretended to be surprised and fascinated, toying with the pen and flipping the notebook pages until she giggled and began to rip out some of the pages. She threw down the notebook and chucked his pen across the hall. Billie's eyes filled with disappointment and confusion as he scrambled to collect the papers.

"Poor Billie," Alice sang. "You fall for everything so easily!" With that, she dug the heel of her shoe into the pen and stomped on it.

"No!" Billie screamed. He dropped his papers and lunged at the pen, but it was too late. Sparks began to fly everywhere and the pen vibrated with such force that it began flying through the air. Luckily, the pen could never break. It sealed back up, and the sparks stopped. The pen flew through the air and landed in Billie's palm. But Billie's heart was still in pieces.

"What in the world?" Alice sputtered while Sparrow McFully just snarled.

"I shared my secret with you, Sparrow, but you turned out to be a bully and not trustworthy. And so did your sister. You McFullys!" Billie raged.

And with that, Billie grabbed his papers and pen and ran off. He ran past the school, he ran through the corn fields, and he ran past the busy streets of town until he found a little coffee shop called Mrs. Creamer's Coffee. Billie ran inside. No one was in the shop, so he decided to hide himself. He ran up the stairs of the shop and found that the second level was basically a storage unit. There, he cried and cried. Billie got out his notebook, all dirty and torn, papers ripped and loosened. He put his head against the door and breathed in a shaky breath. Then, using his pen, he began to write.

Once, he wrote, *there was a boy. And the boy was so miserable and lonely that he couldn't stand this horrible world. He was bullied every day for using his imagination, his family disliked him, he had no friends, and every day was even more miserable than the day before. So, he created a magical portal in an old coffee shop, not wanting to worry about bullies or any of the evil in this world. The portal was filled with magical fairies and creatures. The boy jumped into the portal and lived happily ever after.*

Suddenly, the pen began to vibrate and lept from Billie's hand. It rattled and shook and drew a large circle on the wooden floors of the storage room. Billie jumped back in amazement. Slowly the wood inside the circle began to bleed into blackness. Sparks flew out of the portal, and Billie felt his body begin to rumble tremendously. An actual portal had been created. Billie gasped and gingerly approached the portal. He knew it! The pen really did work! It wrote stories that actually appeared.

Billie realized that he'd just made a portal that was the door to the world of his own stories. "This . . . this is really . . . really it!" he breathed. He picked up the pen cautiously but then dropped it back onto the floor in horror. Billie was only seventeen! Did he really want to do this? Billie shook his head rapidly, tears beginning to form. He knew that inside that portal all his stories roamed free. He had made the pen from Turquoise Wood which could create anyone's deepest wishes.

The Turquoise Wood was from Mount Everest. It had slowly, over time, melted into one of the rock walls in a cave on Mount Everest. Only a few very clever archeologists knew it existed, but otherwise, everyone else thought of the magic of Turquoise Wood as a myth. Archeologists had searched every inch of land, even Mount Everest, but the magic Turquoise Wood stayed hidden until Billie had come along.

Billie and his family had gone up to Mount Everest for a family vacation. Billie had read about the Turquoise Wood in books, how rare it was and how it was the only evidence of magic from a long time ago. Eventually, some of the pieces disappeared until there was only one left. But Billie had been the one to find it on Mount Everest that day. After finding it, he brought it home and wished for his own magic—that his stories would become real, living creatures that roamed free in another land. But now, now that it was real, and the portal to enter his world of living, breathing stories was waiting for him, Billie couldn't go in. He just couldn't.

"I'm sorry!" he whispered to the pen. It felt hot in his hands. "I can't do it!" Billie cried. He found an old blanket and laid it over the hole. Then, he found an old desk that was large enough to cover the hole, so he moved the desk over the portal. He then draped more blankets over the sides of the desk, so no one could ever see the amazing creation. Billie sniffed, grabbed his pen and notebook, and ran home.

Chapter Four

Rumbling

Today I have a pop quiz in history class. Pop quizzes are the worst because you can't plan for them. Luckily, history is my favorite subject. We're studying the Boston Tea Party, which I happen to have studied a lot on. Well, I mostly just watched a video about it on YouTube and then took notes. But that's more than some of the other students did.

The clock's tick really can't be any worse at a time like this. I swear that thing is trying to drill its sound into your brain! I'm on question fourteen. Only six more questions to go! Ugh, is it A? Or D? It isn't C or B because those answers can't be accurate. Hmm.

Mr. Nelson walks slowly around the room, his slick black hair gelled back against his head. His shiny shoes click against the floor as he weaves between the desks. Mr. Nelson always has a stuck-up, snooty look on his face. He always reads over students' shoulders when we're testing, and every single time he clicks his tongue. It's so annoying!

Mr. Nelson's long nose peeks over my shoulder and I cringe. I carefully circle C to question nineteen. *Click* goes his tongue. Ugh. Is that a good sound or a bad sound? I hesitate, but Mr. Nelson moves on to the next student. I breathe a sigh of relief now that I'm out from under his stare and circle A to the last question.

Ah! Finally! I'm done with the test! Quickly scanning my answers, I flip over my paper so no one else can see. Mr. Nelson comes by and picks it up from me. Then I glance around the room. The majority of students are still testing. Poor Romi looks like she's about to cry in frustration. She keeps circling something, then erasing it in disgust. I crane my neck to look behind me. Phoenix's tongue is poking out and he's scribbling furiously. His eyes are darting all around the page as his nostrils keep flaring and unflaring. I know that behavior. It means he's in the middle of writing a story and it must be a good one. I wonder how long ago he finished his quiz, because he's obviously deep in his writing right now.

I glance back toward the front of the room. Mr. Nelson's writing our homework assignment which means that class is almost over. I quickly unzip my bag and slip out my story notebook and pen before trying to find a new page. Wow, I've written a lot. Sometimes I forget how many stories I've written. But my favorite part of a story is when you open up to a brand-new, vanilla-and-white page—and it's just waiting to be filled with a fresh new idea. Hmm, the hard part? *Thinking* of an idea for your story.

I look back at some of my other stories and start to think about Papa B. His stories are always so adventurous and fascinating and detailed. I love the way he describes characters too. Like his character Captain Seaweed: *With scraggly wisps of lime green hair and a frown frozen on his face, the great Captain Seaweed was a sight to see. The whole ocean cowered in fear when he and his ship approached, for with his tough, black eye patch, his fiery temper, and his gleaming sword always in hand, Captain Seaweed was the true King of the Sea.* Wow, right? Love it!

I twirl my pen around my fingers. I'm always trying to come up with new ideas. But this week I haven't thought of anything so far. Then it hits me—what if I did an extension to one of Papa B's stories? That would be something new for me. I'm always up for new things. Yes! I rack my brain for one of his stories and land on the one about a portal. It was so sad. How a poor little boy was so miserable that he created a portal to another world. He must have been super miserable. I wonder where Papa B got his inspiration from on that one?

It's settled. A grin stretches across my face as I grip my pen tighter and begin to write, the glistening black ink of the pen trailing across the page behind me like a gleaming snake. *Once,* I write, *many years after that strange boy created a portal to another world and made it his home, a girl discovered it many, many years later.* Hmm, what else should go with this story? I let my brain run where it wants and let my pen lead the way. *The girl wasn't sad and miserable, as the boy had been. In fact, she was very curious and adventurous and happened to stumble upon the old abandoned coffee shop where the boy had made the portal so many years ago.* Ah, now we're getting somewhere.

"Two minutes, class! Please finish up your quizzes and have them ready to turn in!" Mr. Nelson looks at me. "I hope you actually studied this time, Miss Mason, and didn't spend the whole week just writing another one of your stories."

Thanks for caring, Mr. Nelson. I wasn't writing a story and actually did study, I think. But I say nothing as my eyes slide back down to the paper and my brain refocuses. *The girl discovered the portal, and to her amazement, discovered that it was truly magical! She peered down the hole and saw gleaming stars and rainbow shadows dancing around, beckoning her to come in. How amazing it was! Yes, the stars and rainbows of the portal were so fascinating that she knew she had to explore what was down there. So, with one leap, she jumped into the portal where she fell down, down, down, until she was in the world of magnificent creatures. The End.*

I make a very satisfying dot for the period at the end of the sentence and smile. It isn't a long story with details like I usually do, but this is nice and simple. Suddenly, my pen begins to vibrate and the sizzling noise rings in my ears. I begin to feel the rumbling under my feet and cringe. I hate it when that happens. For some reason, my brain decides to make it feel like the ground is shaking after finishing a story. I went to a counselor named Mr. Pete once, and he said that sometimes our brains imagine things and that my brain is unique and likes to mark off when I finish stories. We didn't see him again after that, because he wasn't very helpful. I mean, it was great that he didn't think I was crazy. But it always feels so real! Yet no one else feels it! So it seems like it's more than what he was talking about.

As I wait for it to stop, I grip my desk tightly and squeeze my eyes shut. To other people, it looks like I'm having a migraine or something, but I never care. My mom says when the shaking starts, try to get a good grip on something and close my eyes. She also suggested trying to count to ten over and over until it goes away. It never hurts. It just feels like someone gently but firmly rattling my head, except it's more in my mind and body than my actual head. Plus, my head doesn't actually shake, so all people see is me tensing up.

I take a couple deep breaths and count. *One . . . two . . . three.* Suddenly the bell rings. Papers flutter as all the last-minute quiz takers crowd around Mr. Nelson, handing him their papers. *Four . . . five . . . six.* People begin to flood out of the classroom. *Seven . . . eight . . . nine.*

Mr. Nelson raises a perfectly arched eyebrow at me. "Miss Mason, I believe class is over," he says sternly.

I nod. "I know," I say, the rumbling ringing in my ears. *Ten.* It hasn't stopped yet. What's going on? I begin to silently count again. My chest feels tight and my throat is incredibly dry. "I'm sorry, Mr. Nelson. I just have a headache," I say smoothly. It isn't a total lie. The shaking is troubling me some this time. Romi and Phoenix are still in the room. They both now know about what's going on. Phoenix begins to pack up my things, and Romi strokes my arm and helps me stand up. Man! It's usually not this terrible. I feel like the floor is cracking beneath me even though it's not. Well, I peek to be sure. Nope. It's still there.

But the shaking sensation that's inside my head and inside my body still hasn't stopped. Mr. Nelson looks a little weirded out. I feel slightly awkward. He clears his throat. "Miss Mason, do you need me to send you to the office to call your mother?"

I nod, my eyes still closed because that helps a little. "Yes, please. Thank you, Mr. Nelson," I say. He tells Romi and Phoenix to escort me, which I know they would have anyway, and the three of us head out the door.

Usually my rumbling only lasts about ten seconds, and it's really faint—but right now, it's lasted much longer and is ringing in my ears! It's even getting worse, and the world is spinning. I grab a hold of my pen from my pocket. Strange. It's still vibrating and sizzling. Phoenix and Romi lead me through the crowd of shuffling students and to the principal's office.

"You guys don't have to do this," I say, my head really starting to form a headache now.

"Don't you worry about it, Eva! But, wow, you never told me it's this bad—that you can't even carry your stuff," Romi says, adjusting my book bag on her shoulder. I shake my head rapidly. "It never *is* this bad," I say.

"Hello?" my mom says in a muffled telephone voice on the other end of the phone. "Mom? My rumbling has started and it's really bad. Plus, it's not going away."

"I'll be right there," she says quickly.

I lay on my bed at home with my earbuds in. I watch my pen make a whirring noise as it continues to vibrate on my desk. For some reason, I want nothing to do with that pen at the moment. I think it's finally busted. The rumbling still isn't going away, no matter where I am. Even on my bed, I still feel like the bed is shaking. I close my eyes and stuff my pillow onto my head. But no matter what I do, the shuddering feeling doesn't stop.

My mom gave me medicine, took my temperature, put oils on my forehead, and even gave me a liquid that makes you sleep for a couple hours. But even after taking a three-hour nap, which was really refreshing, it's still here. There's a knock at my door, and I force myself to lift the pillow from my head and open my eyes.

"Room Service," my older brother Marty says, cracking the door.

"You may enter," I say, slowly sitting up.

Marty walks over with a plate in his hand. "Mom says you don't have to come eat dinner if you don't want to, so I made you your favorite: strawberry cream cheese sandwiches."

"Aw, Marty," I say, wrapping my arms around his neck. I take the plate from him and prop up my pillow as an eating tray. "These are my favorite. Thank you!"

Marty brushes his dyed-blue hair from his eyes and bumps me with his arm. "No problem, baby sis. Hope you feel better." Marty strolls out of my room, closing the door behind him.

"Me too," I say to myself. I sigh. When will this ever end? I bite into one of the sandwiches. Gooey, strawberry cream fills my mouth, and oh, how it tastes so good. I reach over and grab my phone. Three phone calls from

Romi, and one text from Phoenix saying, "Hope you feel better, Sporky!"

I call Romi and she answers almost immediately. "Hey, girl! How ya doing?"

"Okay, I guess," I answer honestly.

"Aw," Romi pouts.

"I know. It's just not going away for some reason, and I don't know why! It never lasts this long. It only lasts about ten seconds, but today it's lasted about four hours!" I fume and take a bite into another strawberry cream cheese sandwich.

"I know, hon. Well, at least you're not actually sick, right?" she pipes up. Romi loves calling me hon. Like she's a mom or my aunt or something. She's hilarious.

"Yeah, I guess you're right. It's just a little frustrating. Is it okay to be frustrated about this?" I ask.

"Of course! Of course it is. You're good, Eva," Romi cries. "You're perfectly normal for feeling frustrated."

"Thanks," I say.

"Alrighty, well, I gotta go eat dinner now so . . . hopefully I'll see you on Monday at school," she says.

"Hopefully," I say back.

"Okay, bye," she says.

"Bye," I sigh and put my plate of sandwiches onto my nightstand. I glance back over to my desk. I groan. It's still vibrating. And my brain is still rumbling.

CHAPTER FIVE

Grammy

I lie in my bed, eyes wide. I glance at my clock. It says 1:45 in the morning. I had a strange dream, and I can't go back to sleep. I dreamt that a boy about the age of seventeen fell into a hole. I couldn't see his face, but I had a very strong connection to him. And then, Phoenix, Romi, and I were standing in front of a coffee shop with a shimmery sign that said *Mrs. Creamer's Coffee*. It looked completely new and shiny with off-white banners. And then, we were riding a dragon! A gigantic, purple, scaly dragon with sharp claws and beautiful eyes! All of a sudden, I saw Captain Seaweed himself pop up out of nowhere! It was an amazing moment until the part where he scowled at me and kicked me off of his ship. Literally, kicking my bottom with his dirty shoes so I stumbled off the ship and into the water. I tried to swim, but I couldn't. At that moment, I woke up in the middle of the night, gasping for air, beads of sweat dripping down my forehead, my heart beating fast.

And now I can't shake it. I wipe my brow and get up to turn my fan on. But as I do, two things happen. The rumbling hits me like a wave. My legs begin to feel shaky and unsteady like jelly, and the world starts to whirl like a spinning roller coaster. It's hard to explain exactly what my rumbling is, but it's like when your feet begin to vibrate on something and you can feel it in your body and in your head. Only, for some reason, it's super intense right now! Finally my legs can't even hold me, and I collapse.

I groggily glance over at my desk. The pen is *still vibrating*. Yep, it's definitely broken. I push myself off of the ground and stumble toward the light switch by my door. But then, I hear voices. My parents' voices. And one more voice. It's high and shaky, unlike Marty's voice. I open my door a crack and peer down the hall. My room opens up to the living room, and the voices sound like they're in the kitchen. I cup my ears to try and hear, and then it hits me—the third voice is Grammy's!

Quietly, I close the door. Grammy's voice? Why would Grammy be here at our house at one in the morning? What's going on? Reopening the door, I tiptoe out of my room. I creep to the edge of the wall and cup my ears again. It sounds like my mom's crying. My head throbs along with the rumbling. There's a table at the edge of the wall with a lamp on it, and I lean on it to hear better.

Grammy's talking, "Papa B used to get these too, right after we got married. And you say she gets them often?"

What? What does *she* get? Who is *she*? I lean farther to hear better.

"Is it curable?" my dad asks. "We feel so useless when she has these rumbling sensations. Karen and I don't have a clue what to do!"

Oh! Me! They're talking about me and the shaking feeling. I lean farther still.

I hear Grammy sigh. "There isn't really a cure for it. It has to do with her pen," Grammy explains.

My pen? My *pen*?

"Her pen?" Mom and Dad copy.

"Yes, her pen," Grammy says. "I'm assuming her pen is vibrating as well?"

There's silence. My legs still feel weak, and I put a little more weight on the table, but it's too quick. The lamp wobbles, and I quickly grab it to keep from falling. Phew.

"Well . . . yes, it was, now that you mention it. On her desk. The pen was vibrating," Mom says finally.

"But what does her pen have to do with anything?" Dad asks.

I hear Grammy sigh again. "It's because of the portal Papa B drew with that pen," she says.

My eyes go wide. My brain fills up with questions like a cup fills with water. Pen? Portal? Papa B? *What?!* I grow even weaker with all the rumbling and thinking and questioning. The table gives in and the lamp wobbles. I find my legs up in the air as the lamp and table topple to the ground, right in front of the kitchen. The lightbulb shatters, and I cringe as noise after noise appears: the table slamming to the ground. The glass of the lamp. The lightbulb. A shriek from someone. Oh, wait. That someone is me! All eyes turn toward me. Silence drowns the room until everyone comes to their senses.

"Good heavens!" Grammy says.

"My lamp!" Mom gasps.

"Eva!" Dad says. "What are you doing up?"

CHAPTER SIX

Georgia Honeycutt

Several years passed. Almost a decade in total. Billie fled the town that owned the coffee shop, never wanting to see that dreaded portal ever again. For some reason, the weight of knowing a portal that he had created was out there with his brewing world of stories inside it made it hard to breathe completely. So he decided not to think about it.

"Maybe *this* world isn't so bad; it's the only world I live in," Billie chuckled to himself. How foolish he had been.

Billie decided to leave home and his old life behind him. He had no idea where he was going, or where he wanted to go, but Billie kept going. He stole away on a train to Ohio and then rode with a nice family in a fancy, sky blue Corvette to Montana who had volunteered to give him a ride. That's where Billie met Georgia Honeycutt, the love of his life, the daughter of the couple who gave him a ride. Georgia loved Billie and Billie loved Georgia. And after sharing cotton candy and their first kiss on the top of the Ferris wheel at a county fair, the rest was history.

A little while after, Billie Mason and Georgia Honeycutt were married in the fall of 1977. They settled down in a little, pink, two-story cottage in a large pine forest in Colorado. The house was just the right size: the downstairs had the kitchen, Billie's study and writing room, and the living room, while the upstairs contained two bedrooms and one quaint bathroom. The perfect home to live in.

Georgia was very aware of Billie's love for writing fictional stories. She was also aware that Billie's brain was a little different—in that, people told her that his brain caused imaginary rumbling sensations. But Billie knew that was a lie. He knew the real cause of the rumbling and shaking was his pen. He knew that when he wrote stories, they came to life in his story world on the other side of his portal.

Sitting in his study, Billie tapped his pen against his chin. With how good his life was now, he'd started to forget about that portal tucked away under blankets and a desk in the attic of Mrs. Creamer's Coffee in Wyoming. Billie sighed. He knew he should tell Georgia his secret.

He had to. She was his wife! And besides, she was pregnant as well. But would she believe him?

"Georgia, dear?" Billie asked one night. He was lying in their bed, fumbling with his pen. The little keychains on the hooks of the pen clinked against the Turquoise Wood.

"Yes, dear, what is it?" Georgia said, grunting as she bent down over her large belly to grab a roll of toilet paper from under the sink.

Billie shifted in the bed and adjusted his pillow before saying, "We need to talk."

Georgia smiled warmly. "And what is it you want to talk about?" she asked, tightening the knot on her fuzzy pink robe. She shuffled over to the bed, her dark curls hanging over her shoulders, and climbed in with a grunt.

Billie sighed again. This was going to be very difficult. "We need to talk about my rumbling sensations."

"Oh, I see," Georgia nodded, patting his knee.

"Well, see, the rumbling is, well, it's from my pen. You see . . . "

"Wait, what? Your pen?" Georgia asked.

"Yes, the pen. You see, when I was a young man, I found the last Turquoise chip of wood that was the only proof of magic in this world," Billie explained.

"Oh, you mean those mythical pieces of magical wood? But they don't really exist. Honey, I . . . "

Billie took Georgia's hand. "I'm not making this up!" Billie protested.

Georgia gave a very deep and aggravated sigh. "I'm listening," she muttered.

Billie went on, "See, when I found the chip of wood, it was magical. You know, in the books, it says that the last chip of wood will pick your most desired wish. Mine at the time was to create a real, living world of my own stories that actually lived and breathed and existed. And it was granted for me. So, there actually is a living, breathing world of stories out there of my own. Isn't that amazing?"

The more Billie thought about it, the more he longed to go back to Mrs. Creamer's Coffee and discover the depths of that world and go into the portal. Georgia's eyes were wide with fear. She let go of Billie's trembling fingers and began to climb out of bed. "Georgia, wh-where are you going?" Billie asked, his hopes plummeting.

Georgia began to pick up the house telephone. "I'm going to call the town doctor and make you an appointment, Billie!" Georgia spit out his name.

Billie's eyes filled with tears. "No, Georgia, I'm not crazy! Please! You're my wife. Can you please let me finish?" Billie grabbed her wrist in an attempt to make her stop. His eyes were sad and pleading.

She put down the phone. "Continue," she sighed.

"Anyways, there's another world out there, Georgia. It's real. And I created the portal to it using my magic pen. That portal is the door to that world. You see, every time I write a story, my pen vibrates and I feel the rumbling. No one else can feel it because I'm the one that created the pen and story. I decided to name it the Portal Pen."

Billie's eyes twinkled at Georgia as he continued. "The rumbling is like a reminder that a real-life version of my story has been created in that world. It's very fascinating. Don't you agree?"

Georgia stared into Billie's longing eyes. At that moment, he was a child again, innocent, sincere, and hopeful. Georgia leaned over and gave Billie a long, perfect kiss. "I suppose so, Billie," she smiled.

Stroking her curls, Billie suddenly realized—maybe, deep down inside, he really did want to see the world that he, himself, had created. Did he? *Yes*, Billie thought. *I think I oughta.*

"Come on," Billie said, getting up out of bed. "We might as well go see it for ourselves, don't you think?" Billie's hand was outstretched toward his wife.

Georgia darted back, startled. Her smile faded, "Billie, you and me? Go see the portal? What about our lives? What about this house? What about the future baby? What about … ?"

Billie walked up to Georgia and took her hands. As he looked her right in the eyes, Georgia could see the great longing and determination inside her husband. "What if we lived in that magical world together? What if we raised our future son in that world? Creatures so magnificent that our little baby boy can't even imagine," Billie whispered.

Georgia let out a little gasp. Live in a world full of magical stories? Raise their son there? "Billie," Georgia said sharply. "What is all this really about? Running away from the terrible troubles of this world? Well, guess what, Billie? That's life! Sometimes it's hard. But sometimes it's wonderful too!"

Billie frowned. Georgia threw her hands up and began to walk around their small bedroom. "Georgia . . . "

"If we raise him there, he'll never know what true life is! He'll never make real friends or go to a real school and . . . and what about us, Billie?" Georgia was practically sobbing now. "What will we do? Live in a treehouse and collect magical fairy dust and play pretend? Billie, shame on you! You can't just run from every problem. And we've got to think about our family."

Georgia sat down on the bed and covered her face. Billie was astonished. How could she refuse this? It was an amazing offer! But still, he knew Georgia was right about it all. "I'm sorry, Georgia," Billie said. "I really am. And you're so right. I am a coward—hiding in the shadows to avoid the real world."

Georgia sniffed and peeked out from between her fingers. Billie threw his hands up in the air, "Why, I'm ridiculous! We can't raise a family in a different world full of magical creatures! What am I thinking?" Billie sat down next to Georgia and sighed. He really was a fool for thinking Georgia would actually agree to something like that. "But, Georgia?" Billie suddenly stood up, spun around, and looked at her right in the eyes. "Can we at least go and see the portal? Just for a moment?"

The journey was not too long, but it was stressful. Their sky blue Corvette complained about the trip, it's tires bouncing on the road. And the trek was tiring, driving from Colorado and up to Billie's hometown in-Wyoming where the coffee shop was. The night sky was a pool of black with twinkling stars above them. Georgia lay asleep in the passenger seat next to him, snoring gently. Billie gripped the steering wheel while taking deep and slow breaths. He knew he probably sounded like the craziest man ever, and he knew that Georgia Honeycutt was probably having second thoughts about their marriage—but he also knew in his heart that she would understand.

As the Masons drove past the green "Welcome To Wyoming" sign, Billie felt his heart skip a beat. It was a mixture of anticipation, anxiety, excitement, and nervousness. The more he thought about it, the more he ached to see what the very world that he created looked like.

About an hour later, he anxiously turned on to an old road, the gravel cracking and popping under the pressure of the car. The road led to an old town square, where most of the buildings were torn down or showed the remains of the life that was once there. In the center was a fountain, spurting out shimmering water. Georgia was now awake, eyeing the eery buildings and nibbling at her thumbnail.

Billie drove straight through a row of buildings until they stopped at a two-story at the very end. After Billie killed the engine, the two climbed out of the car. In the middle of the night, the place was even creepier. The old, white paint of the building was cracked and chipped, and a family of vines climbed up the old brick chimney attached to it. All the windows were bolted shut and covered with wood. The curtains on the sides of the windows flapped and fluttered eerily. Everything was rusty, especially the poor Mrs. Creamer's Coffee sign, barely visible over the layer of rust.

"This is where the portal is?" Georgia whispered nervously.

"Yes, dear," Billie answered.

Together, they held hands as they neared the old building. Billie clearly remembered that day many years ago when he had stolen away to this place. As they walked closer, Billie noticed a sign on bright yellow paper flapping in the wind. He squinted his eyes and read it. Then he gasped.

"What? What's the matter?" Georgia cried.

Billie's heart was plummeting, "The owners are going to allow this place to be torn down!" He showed her the sign. "It says if no one buys it by this date, they'll demolish it. That's like—tomorrow!"

"But they can't do that . . . the portal's inside," Georgia mumbled.

"But the workers don't know that. And we have to keep it that way," Billie said. He was suddenly filled with the determination that he must go into that portal before they tear it down. Billie slipped his hand into Georgia's. He tried to open the door, but the floorboards of the porch jutted upwards, blocking the door from opening. Billie tried to push it. He pushed and pushed until, finally, the door gave in and the couple stumbled inside. Billie's hands trembled. He was so excited and nervous at the same time that he had to keep moving around—he was so jittery.

The inside was in a bit better condition than the outside. There was the coffee counter and tables and chairs. Everything's color was faded. Georgia spotted the old coffee pots, blanketed in dust, sitting on the counter. "This place must not have had very good business," Georgia said.

There was a small patio in the back of the shop where people could eat outside. The glass windows showing off the patio were covered in a thick blanket of dust. Billie motioned Georgia to follow him. They walked down a hallway that had a faded "EMPLOYEES ONLY" sign. There were two rooms in the hallway, with a staircase at the end. A light switch hung from the ceiling in the middle of the hall, and Billie pulled it. The lightbulb sputtered and flickered until an eerie, yellow glow illuminated the room. Billie's heart pounded. This was truly it.

Slowly, Billie and Georgia climbed the rickety brown staircase up to the second level. One step moaned loudly as Georgia stepped on it. They got to the top of the stairs and entered the storage room. Billie's fingers trembled, and his heartbeat rang in his ears.

"We're here," he whispered. Boxes were stacked everywhere, and papers littered the floor. An open window let in the moonlight, making floating dust flurries visible. There was a short bookshelf leaning crooked against a broken black piano. Old, rotting wooden shelves lined one of the walls, and ancient coffee mugs rested on some of the shelves. License plates lined the wall with the window for decoration, the majority of them from Wyoming. Billie gasped when he turned and saw an upright desk with two blankets pinned to both sides. His heart knew exactly what the desk and blankets were hiding. Shakily, he wrapped his fingers around

Georgia's fingers and gingerly pulled her with him as he approached the desk.

"What? What is it?" Georgia asked. She still couldn't believe that in this room, some form or other of a portal lay somewhere. Billie ignored her, dropping her hand and rushing over to the desk.

"Quick! Georgia! Help me lift this desk to the side!" Billie began to lift it, and Georgia rushed over to help him. Together, they moved the dusty desk. Georgia brushed the dust from her hands. Underneath the desk lay a faded blanket covering a patch of the floor. Billie let out short breaths as he stooped down. His fingers wrapped around the blanket edges until finally he yanked the blanket off the ground to reveal a deep black hole with stars and rainbow shadows inside. Georgia couldn't help but gasp. The portal itself was right there in front of her!

"Billie?" she gasped and grabbed at her husband in fear, her eyes still transfixed on that magnificent hole.

Billie couldn't contain his smile. "This is it, love!" he breathed. "The portal that I created."

Georgia's eyes were huge, and she dropped to her knees as she cautiously peered into the hole. Billie peered in with her, his body lost in happiness and excitement. That world was waiting for him! He just knew it! This was his chance to explore his very own stories! He would go dodging the venomous snake bites of the jungle with Dakota the hunter, or fight with a gleaming sword alongside Captain Seaweed, or taste the exotic foods of the Spoon Kingdom. Billie couldn't contain his joy. He chuckled to himself. He felt like a boy again! But then Billie turned and saw Georgia. Her eyes were frozen and sad. She was slumped in a chair with her hands on her belly, and there were trails of tears streaming down her cheeks.

"Georgia?" Billie stood up.

"I know how much you want this, Billie," Georgia said, choking back on her tears, her lip quivering. Billie glanced down the hole. He became excited just by staring down it. But he sadly looked back at his wife. "I see it in your eyes," Georgia laughed as hot tears poured down her cheeks like waterfalls.

"Oh, Georgia," Billie sighed.

Georgia let out a sob, "I've watched from the day I met you—the way you loved writing your stories. I can see it, Billie. I know what you want. You want to go. And . . . you can go if you want to, but I . . . I just . . . I can't go with you." Georgia continued to cry quietly.

Billie's heart ached. He was so torn. "You go. I want you to, Billie. I love you. But I love you too much to let you drag your family into this with you." Georgia wiped her face, but it was simply a motion, for the tears didn't cease at all.

Billie slowly got up and walked over to his wife. "You're right," Billie said, choking back tears himself. But then his eyes went wide, and he smiled hopefully at his wife. "But please don't worry! I'll come back real soon. I promise. I just need to go in there. I just need to see it all." Billie took a step back.

Georgia smiled and said, "I already miss you."

Billie thought for a moment and then handed her the pen. "I won't need it while I'm in there. You keep it. And it will help you know I'm coming back!" Choking on a sob and trembling, she took the pen from him. Billie knew his time was now.

"I love you so much, Georgia," he said and kissed and hugged her tightly. Then Billie leaned down to Georgia's large stomach and rubbed it, "And goodbye for now, my little future son. I'll be back to watch you grow up." Georgia's face was red and blotchy as hot tears stung her eyes. Billie stared at his wife, then pulled her close and kissed her until she pulled away.

"Now go," she said, wiping her cheeks. "Go before I regret not coming with you."

Billie nodded. Then he turned, and with one final wave, he ran and jumped into the hole. Georgia stood there for a couple moments, now alone in the old, dusty building. Then, she slowly walked over to the desk and shuddered as she pulled the blanket back over the hole and shoved the desk where it once had been. It took her a while since Billie wasn't there to help her lift it as they did together before, but she was able to push until it covered the hole.

Her tears stained the blankets that she pinned to the sides of the desk. Then she got up and took a step back all alone. This seemed like just a dream, except that it wasn't. And now she had to face life alone—having this baby alone, wondering if she would ever see her husband again. But suddenly, Georgia realized something dreadfully awful and crumbled to the ground in giant sobs. She reached into her jacket pocket and pulled out the Portal Pen. She had no idea how it worked or how to use it. She was terrified to use it because of its power. On top of it all, she began to worry that maybe he needed the pen to get back to her.

The young woman sobbed, "How will he get out now?" She had to let herself cry it out before she picked herself up slowly, her vision wobbly. Stumbling down the stairs and outside into the fresh air, she ripped the yellow sign off the building and crumpled it up into a little ball, her hot tears staining the paper. Georgia walked to her car, but didn't drive away. She thought she'd finished with her tears upstairs, but it just wasn't true. So she sat and cried for another hour—until she couldn't cry anymore.

Tired from her emotions, she fell asleep to her shaking breaths and woke up to the loud churning of the cranes and tractors. Startled, she looked out the window of her car to see the machines piling up dirt and the building being poked at, ready to collapse with one blow. Georgia scrambled out of her car and ran up to a worker.

"Stop right now!" she screamed at a bulldozer charging at the building. Everyone looked at her.

A man in a black suit got out of a black car sitting by the road. He walked over to Georgia. "Ma'am, I'm afraid this is private property only," he explained.

Georgia stopped and brushed her skirt off awkwardly. She touched her swollen belly gently. Then she gazed into the man's eyes and said, "I'd like to buy this place, please."

CHAPTER SEVEN

Daisy's Donuts

I freeze. All eyes are on me. Ugh, I'm so busted. But suddenly, I feel my eyes begin to fill with tears. Then, I feel tears escape my eyes and slide down my cheeks like raindrops. I sniffle as I untangle myself from the lamp and table mess. Then suddenly, I'm sobbing. Grammy rushes over to me and scoops me up in a hug. My parents slowly form a group hug.

"Sweetie pie," Grammy murmurs, her breath tickling my wet cheek. She strokes her old hands over my hair. I don't know why I'm crying. The four of us slowly go to the living room couch and sit down.

"Eva, why are you up this late?" Dad asks me, but Grammy shushes him.

"Gavin, that doesn't matter right now," Grammy whispers.

I slowly unwrap myself from our hug. "I'm sorry," I sniffle. "I just . . . I don't know what's wrong with me . . . I mean, this strange uncontrollable feeling I get and the pen and . . ."

"Shhh, honey," Mom says. "Don't apologize."

I wipe my tears and say, "I was going to turn my bedroom fan on, and I heard Grammy's voice, and then you guys talking about me and my pen, and well, I wanted to hear what you were saying."

Grammy nods. "Sugar, you were right to listen. We should've let you be a part of this." Grammy clears her throat. "Now, shall I continue?" she asks, winking at me.

"Uh, I guess so," Mom says.

"Alrighty then," Grammy says, clearing her throat. "I suppose I should start over since Miss Eva is joining us now. So, Eva darling, you're going to be so happy when I tell you this—as for your rumbling sensations . . . there is nothing wrong with you. Your brain isn't messed up. In fact, your Papa B—he had the same thing."

I gasp. My heart soars, "Really?"

Grammy nods.

"But how?" I ask.

"Well," Grammy continues, "You have such a creative mind, Eva. And your pen, well, it's a magic one called The Portal Pen."

My eyes grow wide. What? My pen? Magic? "Grammy, are you sure you . . . "

But I stop when I see my mom and dad shuffling into the kitchen. Dad begins to zip up Grammy's purple bag, and Mom's dialing a number on her phone.

Grammy stands up and huffs. "What in the name of . . . Gavin Henry Mason! Karen Rose Mason! Just what do you two think you're doing?!" Grammy snaps with such authority. I've never seen Grammy this way. She's always so gentle and kind and sweet and just—Grammy. But now, I see a strong, humble woman. And what *are* my parents doing?

My dad walks over to Grammy and puts his hands on her shoulders. "Mom, listen, you . . . "

But Grammy interrupts and pushes dad's hands away. "No, Gavin, *you* listen!" Grammy's eyes fill with tears. She grabs my hand and squeezes it tightly. My heart starts to pound. What is going on?

"Grammy?" I whisper.

"Mom, please!" Dad's eyebrows scrunch together in concern.

Grammy wipes her eyes with her free hand. "Gavin, Karen, I'm not making this up! This is serious! I wish

67

you would believe me. My mind is just fine." Grammy cries.

My dad's jaw clenches. My palms become sweaty. Grammy's still gripping my hand, and I'm getting uncomfortable. I don't want to be here. I don't want to be anywhere. I let go of Grammy's hand and run down the hall. I run past my room, Marty's room, my parents' room. I throw open the front door and let the cool fall breeze hit me like a wave. Letting the front door slam behind me, I run. I don't know where I'm running—I'm just running. I run into the woods beside my neighborhood. I run, tears streaming down my face, leaves swooshing upwards behind me.

I'm so confused and angry. I don't know what's going on between my parents and Grammy—all I know is that it doesn't feel right. I don't want to be near my parents. I don't want to be near Grammy. They'll find me if I go to Marty. I want to be free. I find a tree that I can climb easily and scramble up its branches. I hear my name being called faintly.

"Eva! Eva, where are you?!" I hear my parents call. I bury myself behind the leaves of the tree and I cry. Hard. My tears spill onto my shirt, but I don't care. I don't know what Grammy's talking about or why my parents are disagreeing with her. But even though I'm thirteen, doesn't mean I can't get scared or I can't cry. The night sky looks like a pool of darkness. Only the house lights of my condo are the source of light. From what I know, my parents think Grammy's crazy. I don't think she's crazy. I believe her with my whole heart. What she said just makes sense. My eyelids become heavy, and I lean back against the trunk of the tree. Eventually, sleep finds its way to me.

The next thing I know, I'm sleeping next to Marty in his bed. Marty's snoring. The house is quiet and peaceful. I rub my eyes and yawn. I throw off the covers and shuffle over to Marty's window. Grammy's car is still parked in the road. I glance back at the clock. Ten thirty in the morning! Wow, I slept kind of late. I carefully crack open Marty's door and trudge into the living room. Dad's asleep on the couch. I turn around and walk into my room. Grammy's sleeping in my bed. Mom's probably still in my parents' bed. I go into the bathroom and sleepily stare at myself in the mirror. My hair's a mess with leaves and twigs stuck to it. I'm still in yesterday's clothes, and the tear stains are visible on my shirt. My nose is red, and there are large droopy bags under my eyes. Oh, I'm so glad it's Saturday. I shuffle back to Marty's room, climb back into bed next to him, and let sleep take over once more.

I let my eyes flutter open. I stare at the ceiling. I'm so tired. Lifting my head to look at the clock, I see it's now eleven thirty. I sit up. I hear the crunching noises of the coffee beans in my dad's coffee grinder, and I hear the muffled voices of the TV. I also hear the shuffling of feet and talking.

Marty's not in bed.

Throwing off the covers, I walk out of the room. Sure enough, everyone's up. Grammy's watching TV with mom while they eat scrambled eggs, dad's making coffee, and Marty's digging through the fridge, looking for who knows what.

It's like nothing happened at all last night.

"Good morning, sunshine!" Mom says as I enter the living room. "Well. Very late morning." I wave as I rub my eyes groggily.

"Hey ya, sport! Did you sleep well?" Dad asks as he's about to take a sip of coffee.

"Yep, I did," I say, plopping down on the couch next to Grammy. "Morning, Grammy!" I say.

"Aw, good morning, baby," Grammy says, patting my head. She pokes around at her scrambled eggs then puts the plate onto the table in front of the couch. Grammy sits up and stretches when the commercials come on. "What do ya say me and you go get some donuts together?" Grammy says, nudging me.

I sit up too. "But, well, what about the pen and last night . . ."

Grammy puts a finger to my lips and shushes me. Then, she brings her plate of scrambled eggs to the trash can and begins scraping out the remains into the trash. She puts the dish in the sink and walks over to me, her honey-yellow top swishing as she moves.

"Grammy, what . . . " My question hangs in the air as Grammy pushes me toward my bedroom.

"Go on now, and go get changed. We'll talk over donuts."

I choose a dark turquoise, short-sleeved top with black-and-white trims, and a white jean skirt paired with my favorite polka-dot high-tops. I quickly comb my hair and put it into a high, sloppy bun, brush my teeth, and grab my phone. Together, Grammy and I jump into her car and drive.

"Which donut shop are we going to?" I ask as we drive downtown.

"Let's go to Daisy's Donuts, okay? And we'll get it to go. Then, we can just drive," Grammy says.

"Okay," I say as my fingers find a loose string on my skirt that I decide to play with. It's silent as we pass shops and the town square. I open my mouth to say something, but I don't know what to say. So I close my mouth and stay silent.

A little bit later, Grammy pulls into a parking spot at Daisy's Donuts, and the old car shudders as she turns it off. Together, we go in. Daisy's Donuts is a quaint little shop with bricks painted pink and decorated with small, white tables outside. It reminds me of a little doll house.

We end up ordering four donuts in total—two for me and two for Grammy. I order a donut filled with lemon jelly and drizzled with honey-lemon glaze and a simple glazed donut with chocolate frosting and rainbow sprinkles. Grammy orders a donut caked in cinnamon and brown sugar called a Pinecone and a glazed donut with a hill of shredded coconut covering the top.

A little while later, Grammy's old blue Corvette sails down an old dirt road that cuts through a corn field. I have no clue where we're going, but that's the reason I love it so much. Just being able to drive and not have a goal or a place that you have to go. To ride somewhere and see the world freely and explore wherever you want to explore—it's a great feeling.

"Eva," Grammy says as I munch on my lemon-jelly donut. "I'm so sorry about last night. I just—do you believe me, Eva?"

I stop chewing. "Of course I believe you, Grammy! I know you're not crazy! I never believed you were." I lick my lips and focus my eyes on the bumpy, dirt road ahead of us. The lemon leaves a slightly sour taste in my mouth.

"Good," Grammy sighs. "It's just that, well ... " Grammy sighs again, and her eyes flicker from sadness to curiosity. "Eva, let's start over from the beginning, okay? I know you probably have tons of unanswered questions, so let's just get this whole thing over with."

I nod. I like where this is going even though I have no idea where it *is* going. Grammy rolls down her window and lets the cool air hit her face.

"A long, long time ago, before I had your dad, your grandpa Billie sat me down and told me that he'd found the last remaining chip of this very rare and special Turquoise Wood."

My eyes light up. "You mean the wood from the history books? The last chip of wood that was the last piece of evidence that magic had existed in the early ages?" I ask. We learned about it in class once from my history teacher, but she had taught us that it was only a myth. I guess she was wrong.

"Yes, that one," Grammy says. "Anyways, Billie said he found it when he and his family had gone on a family vacation to Mount Everest when he was young. He said that he found it in a small cave, so he took it to his home and told no one about it."

"But wait," I say, interrupting. "I read that the chip of Turquoise Wood can also grant your most desirable wish. Is that, er, *was* that true Grammy?"

"Oh, yes!" she exclaims. "And Billie knew this too. In fact, as soon as they got home from the trip, he took it and turned it into a pen. It granted him his most desired wish: to create a real, living world full of all the stories he had written with that pen."

Whoa. That's a big wish. But, this actually happened. This was real!

"And sure enough, the piece of wood made that happen. And so, somewhere out there is a world full of stories that Papa B made. But that's not all. One day, Billie was severely bullied by Sparrow McFully."

Oof, Sparrow McFully. Grammy has told me stories of that rotten jerk—how he called Billie horrible things, cheated off of him, taunted him, even hit him.

"Sparrow McFully and his sister, Alice, bullied him once again that day, and Billie said that he ran off to an old, abandoned coffee shop, and with his magic pen, wrote that there was a boy who wished to live in another world full of magical creatures. And that happened! Billie's world full of his written stories was created into an actual living and breathing world of stories!" Grammy explains with a faint twinkle in her eyes.

"Grammy, was Sparrow the whole reason he wanted to create the portal? I mean, obviously he had some tough situations with Sparrow, but was he really the only reason Papa B ran away and created the portal?" I ask. I mean, there are bullies in every school, but there must have been something more.

Grammy sighs. "Mostly that, but also, his parents abandoned him when he was older. It was around that time when they gave him up. His mom was living off of pennies and couldn't afford to pay for Billie, and his dad . . . well, let's just say that his dad wasn't around much."

Um, whoa. Why hadn't anyone told me this before? "Is the portal real, Grammy? Is it true that Papa B made his pen out of Turquoise Wood, and then that pen made the portal?" I ask carefully.

Grammy's car jerks slightly as she scoffs at my words, "Eva Mason, of course it's true! I wouldn't be telling you lies, now would I? And besides, I saw the portal with my own two eyes."

"You did?" I ask. I unwrap my second donut and nibble on it. This is crazy stuff! Now I can see why my parents thought Grammy was insane. But I know that she's telling the truth. It's a lot to take in, but I still believe her.

"Yes, I sure did. In fact, my husband even tried to persuade me to move into that world with him and raise your father there." Grammy chuckles, but there's a sadness in her eyes. "But I couldn't do that."

I stare at the colored sprinkles on my donut. Then, it hits me. "Grammy, in Papa B's story about the boy traveling into the portal, was that story about himself?" I ask. Grammy nods. I let out a small gasp. Whoa! My brain begins to fill up with more questions. "Did he end up going into the portal?" I ask.

"Yes, he did," Grammy says softly.

"Then, how come you told us that Papa B ran off and went missing? When, really, he just went into a portal of his own stories?" I ask quietly.

"Well, because . . . because I wanted to protect our secret." Grammy's eyes are frozen on the road.

"But why?" I ask. There's a silence that drowns the rumbling of the car engine.

"Eva," Grammy says finally. "Remember last night? When I tried to explain all of this to your parents? Remember?"

"Yes," I say slowly. Then it hits me. *Oh.*

"It's because of that, baby. Your parents tried to pack up my things and call a doctor because they thought I was crazy!" Grammy's voice is sharp and her eyes fill with tears. She parks the car out in a clear area right in the middle of nowhere at the edge of the woods. "That right there is the very reason. It happened to Billie too when he tried to explain it to me. I tried to call a doctor because I thought his mind had gone mad."

Grammy sobs quietly. I guess I never realized that. If it were me, I probably would've kept it a secret for fear of being called crazy, or someone trying to call the doctor, or knowing that people would think of me as insane.

"Yeah," is all I can say.

Grammy takes a shuddering breath. "I came last night because your parents called and told me about your rumbling, and they knew that Papa B had had that too. So they thought I knew what it was. That's when I knew I should tell them the truth, but I knew deep down that they'd never believe me."

I stare at the road. Then, I realize something. I reach into my skirt pocket and take out my lucky pen, which I always take everywhere. I hold it up and stare at the Turquoise Wood of the pen.

"Grammy . . ." I start, but Grammy interrupts me.

"I realized that my family would probably think I was crazy, just like I'd done to your Papa B. You see, it was supposed to be a quick trip that day, the day he took me to take a look at the portal. I'd already told him we wouldn't live there together, but he'd talked me into seeing the portal at least. But then Billie saw a sign on the building where the portal was. It said the city would be tearing it down if the building didn't sell by a certain date. He realized that date was the very next day, Eva, and so he insisted on going in and seeing this world for himself. As soon as he went into the portal, I realized I had the magic pen. I was worried the pen would be his only way out. And I was right! That's why he's never come back."

Grammy sniffles, "But, you know what? They never ended up tearing down the building." Grammy grips the wheel tighter. She takes a shaky breath and continues. "Anyway, I pretended it was just a regular pen, passed down from your papa, but I knew, deep down, the rumbling would appear someday. You see, your father wasn't creative in that way. He liked math better. He never used that pen once. But you, Eva. Oh, you have your Papa B's creativity in you."

Turning the pen around in my hand, I think about all she's said. "So this is the . . . the magic pen that Papa B made and used?" I ask, my breathing uneven and my heart beginning to beat wildly. Grammy nods.

I dry heave on the spot, and Grammy holds out the Daisy's Donuts bag in front of my mouth. I breathe in and out heavily. It hits me like a giant wave. *This cannot be happening! This cannot be real!*

When I recover, I ask shakily, "So, then, what *is* the rumbling exactly from?"

Grammy strokes my hair. "Every time you write a story with that pen, the rumbling is to tell you that your story has magically appeared in the world of stories. Whenever you use this pen, it magically forms your story in that world that Papa B created. But when you revisited your grandfather's portal, and reopened it because you were writing about it, the rumbling lasted longer. That's what happened, right?" Grammy asks.

I nod. It was what had happened! "So, you're telling me that whenever my brain rumbles, and I feel the earth shaking underneath me when no one else does, it's actually my stories forming into living, breathing creatures in Papa B's world of stories?" I ask.

Grammy nods, her smile wide. "Yes," she whispers.

I can't take this. I believe Grammy, but it's too much to handle. I feel like the weight of the world—or should I say *worlds*—are on my shoulders. I glance at my pen, my stomach doing flip-flops.

"Grammy?"

But I feel my stomach jolt. I scramble out of the car and barely make it to the woods before puking all over my polka-dotted shoes. Grammy scrambles out of the car and rushes up to me, her arms loaded with the napkins from Daisy's Donuts. My body trembles, and I slowly sit down away from my sickness. I clutch my stomach as my eyes dart around wildly. There's another world out there, full of Papa B's stories and . . . and *my* stories! This is so crazy! Grammy sits next to me. She wipes my mouth and strokes my hair.

"Now I understand everything," I whisper quietly.

"It's a lot, isn't it?" Grammy smiles a little.

I nod furiously. "I believe you, Grammy," I whisper, shuddering. Everything is suddenly very cold. I turn around and feel my stomach lurch and prepare for another sickness attack. Ugh. It's just too much for me.

Once I'm all cleaned up and Grammy's sprayed Lavender Mist perfume all over me to keep me from smelling of puke, we get back into the car.

"Eva, I'm sorry if this was all too much," Grammy says.

I wave her off and rest my head against the window. Taking long, slow, deep breaths, I close my eyes. "It's fine, Grammy. I'm glad you told me," I say. I decide not to eat the rest of my donut and wrap it up in a napkin.

Grammy nudges me, "What do ya say, we drive up to Wyoming where the actual portal is?"

"Wait, it's still out there?" I ask.

Grammy throws up her hands and says, "Of *course* it's still out there! The pen wouldn't vibrate, and you wouldn't rumble if it wasn't still out there!"

I shrink a little in my seat. "Oops, sorry," I say sheepishly.

Grammy nudges me again. "Well?" she asks.

I don't know what to say. This is all so new and fresh to me. "Um . . . I, well, I guess so," I sputter.

"Good choice," Grammy says, starting up the car. The blue Corvette spurts and sputters, and the passenger seat vibrates as the ancient car roars to life. With one final sputter and groan, we're off. "We'll be back home by this afternoon," Grammy says. "It's not too far away."

We race down the dirt road, and Grammy makes a few turns until we're on some highway. "Billie and his family had gone to Mount Everest when Billie was about fourteen years old. His family wasn't broken then. But he was still severely bullied. Billie was a small boy and a very easy target. He would escape into the stories he wrote. It made up for all the holes, doubts, and pain in his life. It was his safe place; his distraction from reality."

Though Grammy's eyes are on the road, they look so far away. I let the moment of silence last until Grammy continues, "It was actually Sparrow McFully who had taught Billie how to make homemade pens."

"Papa B had been friends with Sparrow McFully?" I ask.

"Yep, he sure had—all through elementary and middle school. In high school, well, bitterness got a firm hold on poor Sparrow. Unfortunately, that can happen to some kids who forget who they are. But anyways, Sparrow taught Billie how to create pens. Soon, Billie was making his own. Then, the family vacation to Mount Everest came, and Billie created a pen—but it was the magic pen that you now own. Billie named it the Portal Pen. Funny, Billie created that pen his junior year of high school, but Billie and Sparrow were good friends pretty much most of their lives before that. Thinking of timing, it seems like Sparrow became a bully after Billie made that pen," Grammy says.

Huh. "Maybe Sparrow knew Billie's secret and wanted the pen for himself or something like that," I say. "That's usually what happens in my books or comics. The bad guy is always wanting more or is power-hungry."

Grammy shrugs, "Maybe."

"Grammy, what if Papa B is still alive? I mean, he still could be in there doing who-knows-what," I say.

"I don't know Eva," Grammy says, her eyes flickering with sadness. "It's been so many years . . . "

"Grammy, this is *his* world full of stories and *mine* now too. Would you go back to that world if you had the choice? Would you go into the portal?" I ask.

Grammy grips the skinny steering wheel tighter. I can see her jaw clenching. "Eva," she sighs. "That's a very tough question for me to answer."

I wait. Grammy continues. "I don't know, honestly. I couldn't do it when Billie first left. It was my fault that he's trapped in there. I don't know if I could bring myself to go now. I mean, what if he's not alive? I'd be all alone there. I don't know . . . "

Grammy's face is full of sadness. "I don't think I'd want to go all that way and search for him, and then what if he's . . . " her voice drifts off. She doesn't need to finish.

"But what if he's not?" I whisper.

She slowly begins to shake her head. "No," she whispers. "I can't."

I turn to stare out the window. Trees pass quickly in brown and green blurs.

"It'd just be too much for me. And for your parents. I just . . . I can't, Eva. I'm getting older. Life goes on. This was Billie's choice. And what if . . . what if he doesn't even want to see me? Or . . . or . . ." Grammy's eyes go wide and fill with tears. "Or what if he doesn't remember me?"

The car is silent. Sadness covers it like a thick blanket. I have to slice through tension. "Then I'll go," I find myself saying.

Grammy turns toward me but remembers to keep her eyes on the road. "No, sweetie cakes, you can't go," Grammy's voice curls up into a whine as she clicks on the turn signal in the middle of the highway and we pull over.

"Grammy, what are you doing?" I ask anxiously.

Cars zoom past us in a blur. "Maybe we should just go back home," Grammy says slowly. Her body language is slumped, and sadness falls over her face.

I think it all just hit her. Her husband went into a portal and didn't come back, and now it's come up in conversation again—and I mention going it that portal . . . and Grammy doesn't want to drag her or her family into it all again. Grammy reaches for the steering wheel, but I stop her.

"No, Grammy. We have to go see it. There's the Wyoming sign up ahead!" I bounce a little in my seat to lift the somber mood in the car. Grammy doesn't budge.

"Grammy," I whisper. "We can't run from the past. It is what it is. You can't avoid this forever. *We* decide what the future is." I put my hand on her leg. Grammy lets out a slow, shuddering breath.

"You're right," she says. She suddenly straightens herself up and hits the gas. We're off once again.

About thirty minutes later, we pull into an old, run-down town square. There's a fountain in the center of the square, mold clinging to the sides and vines creeping their way up the fountain, which looks like it hasn't had water come out of it in a very long time.

We drive down the square, the ground cracking underneath the weight of the car. "It's been almost forty years since I came here," Grammy breathes. Everything looks *so* old. It reminds me of a ghost town.

We drive through this little square for a moment until Grammy turns down a street that was most likely once full of shops and a busy town life, but is now just some old buildings and many empty spaces where buildings should be. The road is covered in dirt and the car groans as we drive over it. Finally, at the end of the street is a little, white building almost completely covered in vines. A tin sign wobbles lifelessly in the breeze, but it's too rusty to read. Overgrown weeds cover an entire window on the first floor of the building, and the roof is slightly slanted.

"Why didn't they tear this one down?" I ask.

"The owner is very particular about this place," Grammy says, winking at me.

"Do you know the owner?" I ask.

"Well, yes. It's me," Grammy explains.

"What?" I gasp.

Grammy nods, "I never use the place—I only bought it so that no one would ever tear it down or harm it. Yes, it's a little misshapen and covered in vines and all, but it would kill me to see this place ripped to pieces with the portal and my husband in there." Oh. I get it now.

Grammy wipes her eyes for the millionth time. We park the car next to a dirt pile and climb out. It's a little two-story building, or at least, I think it is. It's really hard to see through all of the vines.

"Come on," Grammy takes my hand, and we hurry up to the building. The old porch moans as we put weight on it. We walk inside. Everything is covered in layers upon layers of dust. Cobwebs make themselves at home, all sprawled out on tables, chairs, lamps, and pretty much everything. The coffee counter is rusty, and there's an old coffee pot that looks like it was there since the beginning of time. The curtains by the windows are ripped and floppy.

Grammy leads me down a little hallway with a super dirty sign that I can barely read, but then I see it says "EMPLOYEES ONLY." Grammy finds a string dangling from the ceiling and pulls it. Nothing happens at first, but then a faint light spurts and flickers, illuminating Grammy's face. We keep walking down the hall until we get to a staircase. Each step is caked in dust, and each one creaks as we step on it.

The upstairs is even worse. There's a hole in the ceiling, letting in daylight. The windows are shattered, and curtains lay torn on the floor. Boxes are piled high to the ceiling, and papers lay limp all over the dusty floor. I cough as dust flies everywhere. Grammy's eyes are full of so many emotions. She spots a rotting wooden desk and jogs over.

"Quick! Eva, help me move this desk!"

I rush over, and together, the two of us move the stubborn desk to the side. My hands are covered in dust. Grammy's hands are shaking. There's an old blanket lying where the desk was, and slowly, Grammy reaches down and lifts the blanket, revealing the floor underneath. Only . . . wait a sec. That's not a floor underneath! It's a giant, sparkling hole that looks like rippling, black water and the night sky at the same time!

"The portal!" we both cry together. I can't help but gasp. Oh. My. Gosh. That's really it! I cautiously approach the portal and peer down. I can't see anything down there. It's so deep and so black that it feels like it goes on forever. But at the same time, something is drawing me toward it . . .

I hear Grammy's shuddering breaths beside me and look over. Grammy's looking away, shiny tears shimmering in her eyes. She's shaking her head back and forth rapidly. I can imagine a million things running through her head right now. I peer down into the magnificent portal once more. All of Papa B's and my stories are actually living and breathing and crawling down there—and maybe Papa B himself is living down there too. But we'll never know unless we go. Grammy stands up from the creaky chair she's sitting in and trudges over to me. She rubs my back and sniffs several times.

"I'll go down there," I find myself saying. "Maybe I can find Papa B."

Grammy shakes her head even more rapidly and murmurs, "Oh, Eva, no." Over and over.

I gently inch away from Grammy's touch. "Why not?" I can't help but ask.

Grammy squeezes her eyes shut, "Well, because . . . I don't want you finding nothing. Papa B might be dead, Eva. I don't want you getting hurt either."

I huff, "But, Grammy, I don't want to live in fear, and I'll always wonder what happened. Papa B might be gone, yes, but at least I'll have tried. Plus, I know our stories like the back of my hand—his and mine. It's unlikely that I'll get hurt."

My words seem to sink into Grammy, and I see her eyes flicker with consideration. "Eva, I don't want you to go," she says firmly. My urge is strong, but she continues, "If I'm not going, then you're not going."

"But, Grammy! Why can't you go?" I ask. Grammy can be very hard-headed sometimes.

She stands up. "Eva, do you know what I had to go through to come back here? To this place?" Grammy's eyes are angry. I scoot back a little. "My husband willingly risked his own life to go into a different world! He left us behind for that place. My child grew up without a father, and I lost my husband! Gavin, your father, asked every day if his father was coming back, and I was forced with the enormous weight of not knowing how to answer him—and I also carried the weight of not knowing if the love of my life is alive or dead to this day!" Grammy's breathing hard.

Wow. That *is* tough. I try to put myself in her shoes here. I don't think I'd want to go either. I'm thinking about all she's said so far, but Grammy has more to share. "And now you want me to go down there and search for him? No!" Grammy wipes her eyes. "My husband made me so angry with his choice! That he chose his stories over his family. I wanted him to follow his dream, but ultimately, I wish he would've have used his heart and stayed! And now, I have to face my granddaughter who wants to do the same thing and risk everything! I already lost my husband. I can't bear to lose my granddaughter!"

Grammy's words hit me hard. I blink. Tears sting my eyes. "Grammy, I would never abandon you. I want

to help you," I say softly. "Maybe Papa B is still alive."
Grammy looks so angry and sad at the same time.

"And besides, maybe I don't have to be the only one
who goes—maybe I don't have to go alone," I say.

Grammy peers at me. "Who would go with you?" she
asks.

I grin. "My friends Romi and Phoenix love stories
and adventures. I'm sure they'd totally want to come.
We're an awesome team together," I say confidently.

Grammy stares at me, then slowly begins to nod.
"Maybe, but I just don't think I can risk anyone else's life
with this portal," she says.

"I know, but you can trust me." I say. We both grin at
each other. The room is quiet. The air is quiet. Then suddenly, I hear a siren. I jump and my body jolts, sending
the pen straight out of my hand.

"No!" I scream. Everything seems to happen in slow
motion. The pen is sailing through the air, my hand
outstretched, my fingers barely touching the Portal Pen.
Then, it begins to descend. Down, down, down. I wait
for it to hit the ground, but I see it sailing straight into
the portal. I shriek and run to the edge. But it's too late.
The pen falls into the rippling darkness, and the portal
gives a low satisfying groan. My magical pen—the pen
that creates portals and other worlds and stories and
power—is gone.

CHAPTER EIGHT

Betrayal

The two sat on Billie's bed. Sparrow's fingers twisted around the pen while his eyes lit up with wonder. "How do I know you're telling the truth?" Sparrow asked playfully.

"I'll show you," Billie said.

Sparrow McFully and Billie Mason were best friends. They did everything together.

Until they didn't.

Billie snatched a piece of paper from his desk, and the two plopped down onto the floor. "I need a story," Billie said.

"What?" Sparrow asked.

"You know, a story. We need to think of a story idea so I can write it down."

The two thought about it. "Hmm, what kind of story?" Sparrow asked.

Billie shrugged, "A fantasy maybe? With fierce pirates?"

Sparrow snickered, "Eh, that's for little kids. How about a betrayal story? It'll have a good, thick twist to it! Best friends—then one turns on the other!"

Sparrow rubbed his hands together. Billie scratched his head. Sparrow was Billie's best friend, but he was also bigger and larger, more broad and more intense. Sparrow preferred evil, revenge plotlines while Billie preferred adventurous, heroic stories.

"Well. I suppose," Billie said. It couldn't do too much harm, could it? Billie shrugged it off. At least it wouldn't be their friendship, Billie told himself.

"Okay, um . . . " Billie concentrated on the paper. Revenge and betrayal stories weren't really his style of writing. *Once upon a time,* Billie wrote.

"Bah!" Sparrow crumbled up the paper and took the pen from Billie. "You don't start revenge stories with that cheesy sentence!" Sparrow grabbed a new sheet. "Let me show you how it's done," he said.

The year was 1967, Sparrow playfully wrote. *There were two friends who were inseparable. They did everything together. Until one day, one grew envious of the other. A rage of jealousy and desire entered his heart, for his friend had something so rare and magical that only he possessed.*

Billie began to shift uncomfortably. He didn't like where this was heading. He knew the full power of his Portal Pen, and he was scared of the outcome of Sparrow's savage story.

So darkness and jealousy entered the friend's heart as he plotted to steal this priceless possession. He betrayed their friendship. The two became enemies, and their families became enemies for generations to come . . .

Sparrow cackled and rubbed his hands together. Suddenly, Sparrow had a rumbling sensation, and Billie did too. "What's going on?" Sparrow demanded.

"The pen is magic like I told you. But it's magic is creating real-life stories out of the ones it writes. This story is forming," Billie said sheepishly.

Sparrow pumped a fist in the air. "That's so neat!" he cheered.

"Yeah . . . neat," Billie said, wanting to hide. Soon the rumbling stopped, and Billie and Sparrow amused themselves for the rest of the afternoon. They ate pizza, played board games, and threw a football outside until Sparrow had to go home. Billie nervously read the story over and over again. He then crumbled it up and threw it into the trash hoping that this story would never become a reality.

The next day at school, something had changed in Sparrow. The story had changed his heart, and he truly was jealous and greedy. It was like a switch that had been turned on in his brain and heart. His eyes seemed a little darker, a little colder. Sparrow watched from afar as Billie sat with a bunch of boys and showed them a book about planets. One of the boys laughed out loud as Billie sprawled out his hands, waving them in the air with big gestures. Sparrow noticed the Turquoise pen dangling from a hook on Billie's belt. Sparrow's eyes narrowed. *I want that pen,* he said to himself. *I have to get it.*

The sound of a ruler slapping a desk woke Sparrow with a startle. He had fallen asleep in history class. Billie sat in front of him, and Sparrow heard the sound of the Portal Pen writing across the paper. His history teacher talked rapidly, making Sparrow's head hurt. Then, Sparrow's mind began to kick in, and he found himself angry at his own best friend.

Little helpless dork, Billie, Sparrow thought with a sneer. *Wait, but aren't you still his friend?* Sparrow found himself questioning and struggling with this idea. He stared at the back of Billie's head guiltily. *Yes, I am,* he thought. *Billie IS my friend.* Still, as he watched the Portal Pen move rapidly while Billie wrote, Sparrow wanted it desperately.

I can write whatever I want with that thing, and it would come true, Sparrow thought. *Whatever I want.* Sparrow was incredibly preoccupied with the pen, but he did notice the teacher step out of class for a minute. This was Sparrow's chance to grab that pen.

Suddenly, Billie shifted and his pen fell to the floor, the metal noise ringing louder in Sparrow's ears— louder than ever. Billie stood up to grab it. This was Sparrow's chance! He wanted that pen. His eyes became darker, and instantly, Sparrow's foot was shooting outward in front of Billie. The poor boy tripped and fell to his knees. He grabbed at his chair on the way down, yanking his backpack with him. His backpack hit the floor and papers fluttered everywhere, all containing Billie's treasured stories. Billie struggled to pick up his papers. Sweat poured down his forehead.

Sparrow stood up. The eyes of everyone in the class were on him. Billie tried to stand, but Sparrow swiped his legs out from under his once-friend, causing the frail boy to topple back down onto the floor.

"Poor Billie," Sparrow sneered as Billie scrambled for his papers and his balance.

Billie finally regained himself and pulled himself upward. Sparrow wanted that pen badly. This was his chance to take it! Sparrow grabbed Billie's wrist. But instead of helping him, he pushed him back down.

"You're so weak," Sparrow spat, the words pouring from his mouth. "You're so frail. You're nothing. Alice will never like you." Sparrow's face was stone cold.

Billie sniffled like a little child. The words would hurt from anyone, but this was his friend.

Sparrow picked up some of Billie's papers. "You think you're so smart. You think your stories are so special. Well, guess what? It's a lie! It's time you worry about other things besides your stupid stories with that stupid pen of yours."

Sparrow tore a piece of paper in half. Billie gasped. His face went pale. He wanted to leave. His hand went to his pen. Billie stared at Sparrow with his eyes full of such confusion and sadness—his heart was breaking.

"We've all grown up. And you should too. No one likes your stories. No one likes your little pen. No one likes you. You'll never be enough," Sparrow sneered as Billie shuffle to his desk, feeling like he would collapse.

"Sparrow, what?" Billie sputtered. Suddenly, Sparrow noticed the paper on Billie's desk. He gasped. There, on his desk was a letter that read, "Dear Alice, Can you give me another chance? I love you, and I want you to know that. I hope you feel the same for me. Love, B . . . " But Billie hadn't finished his sentence; therefore, the love note was never completed—and the power of the pen never caused Billie to truly fall in love with Alice, all thanks to Sparrow.

Sparrow's eyes filled with rage. Billie was writing a love note to his sister with the Portal Pen? Sparrow punched Billie in the gut just as the teacher came in.

Billie, defending himself, flung himself upon Sparrow, and the two rolled around in a heap, swinging punches and slaps.

"What in the world?" the teacher cried.

"Billie! I'll get you back!" Sparrow roared.

"What did I ever do to . . . ." But Billie couldn't finish his sentence because the bell rang, and Sparrow sprang up and dashed out of the classroom. Billie's eyes filled with tears. He packed up his things and headed for the door. All around him, his classmates pointed and laughed.

"That kid is so strange," Billie overheard a classmate say to another friend. Billie cringed. He dashed out of the room and ran down the hall. Sparrow saw him and the two locked eyes. Billie looked so sad and disappointed that Sparrow's gaze wavered. But Billie's gaze didn't. Sparrow felt Billie's eyes on the back of his head as he turned around to grab his bag from his locker. Then it hit Sparrow and Billie at the same time. Sparrow turned around. Crowds of students pushed and shoved around them, but the two didn't flinch. Sparrow had created this story—and it was coming true. Sparrow was becoming the jealous friend who betrayed the other.

Billie's eyes filled with tears. He never should have let Sparrow write that story. Disappearing behind a clump of students so Sparrow couldn't see him, Billie ran and ran.

Sparrow turned around in shame. *What have I done?* he wondered. But then, he thought about the pen, and he suddenly walked off with his head held high.

Chapter Nine

Into the Void

I gasp and clutch my stomach. This can't be happening!

"The Portal Pen . . . it's gone!" Grammy cries. I choke on a sob as I can't believe the horrible turn of events. The sirens that had startled me turn off, and then we hear the creaky door open from downstairs.

"Grammy?" I ask.

Grammy slaps her forehead. "Ugh, I forgot. I purchased this place privately. The policeman probably doesn't know I own this place. He just thinks we're trespassers."

"Hello?" A deep voice calls from downstairs.

"Quick! Put the blanket over the portal, and we'll move the desk over it together!" Grammy says. She clips blankets to the sides of the desk while I lay the blanket over the hole. Then we drag the old desk over the hole together.

"Hello? I know you're in here! This is private property, and you're trespassing," the voice barks again.

"We're coming!" Grammy yells to him. "Come on," she whispers to me. My stomach twists into a knot. Even though Grammy owns this place, I still get nervous around policemen, especially one who's yelling for me to show myself.

Grammy and I climb down the stairs until we're facing a tall police officer with a long, black beard and a tough, jaw-clenched face. "What are you two doing here?" he barks.

"Sorry, officer, my granddaughter and I were visiting the old coffee shop that I own. This place has been around for such a long time. So many memories . . . " Grammy pretends to get a dreamy, faraway look in her eyes.

"Uh, I see," the officer says.

Grammy's attention snaps back to the officer. "Sir, I'm really sorry if we caused a commotion about all of this. We mean no harm. You see, I'm the owner, so I was just coming to check in on the place."

The officer glares at Grammy. Obviously he's not convinced. Oh boy. "Where do you live?" he asks.

Grammy starts to laugh. I elbow her slightly. Now is not the time to laugh. It's not like we're lying. Grammy just isn't really doing a good job of acting natural. "Uh, sir, well, you see, we live in Colorado," I stammer.

He raises his eyebrows all over again and asks, "Miss, are you aware that this is Wyoming?"

"Yes, I am aware," she says, getting serious again. "But this is my shop," Grammy repeats.

The officer still ushers us out the door. My heart is thumping in my ears like a drum. He points to our blue Corvette. "Is that your car?" he asks.

Grammy nods. "Yes, sir," she says.

"Listen," he tells us. "Whether you own this place or not, it's not a good idea to be wandering around these old buildings. How about you make your way back to . . . Colorado?"

Grammy seems annoyed but doesn't want to bother with it, so she just turns and walks to our car while he climbs into his own car and shuts the door, but doesn't drive away. He waits until we've pulled out of the little parking spot and are driving away before he pulls out and leaves in the opposite direction. Hm, that's smart. Grammy starts to drive off, but I stop her and the car lurches.

"Grammy! What about my pen?! We have to get it back! Who knows who'll find it down there!" I begin to panic. This is really terrible. My mind races with thoughts of what could happen to that world, to Papa B, to the portal, and maybe even to all of us if the pen gets in the wrong hands.

"Then I suppose you'll have to go," she says quietly.

"Wait, what? Really?" I ask. My brain begins filling up with thoughts and questions.

Grammy slowly nods. It's like the slowest nod ever. "But you can't go alone," she says.

"Will you go with me?" I ask, but Grammy is already shaking her head.

"I'll stay back and explain everything to your parents," Grammy says. "They'd have a horrible time if they just thought we disappeared." She starts to drive. Her eyes are overflowing with a faraway sadness.

"But, Grammy, you know what they'll do," I say. I have flashbacks to Mom dialing a doctor's number on her phone and dad packing her bags.

Grammy nods. "I know, but I want you to go."

"Okay, Grammy. But Phoenix and Romi are coming too. I trust them," I say.

Grammy nods. "Tomorrow's Sunday right? Call your friends and tell them everything, please. Maybe you can invite them over?"

I nod. I absolutely know Phoenix will want to go. Plus, curfew isn't big in either of their families. Phoenix lives with only his mom who works all the time, and Romi's parents are in Alaska at the moment so her older brother is watching her. And I know Phoenix will believe me. Romi will too.

"Okay," I say. "Who will get us back here?"

Grammy points a thumb to herself. "Me. I'll drive you while your parents are out tomorrow."

"Okay," I say. My thoughts race: *Am I really going to do this? Yes. I am. It'll be an adventure!* I bite my lip. I pinch myself. *Wake up, Eva! These are your stories—and your Papa B's too! You know them inside and out! What could really go wrong?* A little pink bump forms in the spot that I pinched. I breathe in and out and turn to stare out the window. The sky is turning a pretty orange with a hint of pink, and the sun shimmers on cars. *Am I really, truly doing this? What if all of it's fake?* I press my forehead against the window and bite my lip harder. I taste a little blood from biting it so hard. I quietly slap myself.

What are you talking about, Eva? This is actually happening! Of course you're going! Besides, I say to myself, *You're not going to be alone. You'll have Romi and Phoenix with you.*

When we get home, my mom is sprawled out on the couch, tapping on her phone, and dad and Marty are playing football outside. Mom sits up when she hears the door slam.

"Wow, you guys were out for a while," she shoots Grammy a suspicious glance, but Grammy has turned her back and is reaching for one of the grilled cheese sandwiches that mom has ready on the table. "Where did you go?" Mom asks. I untie my shoes.

"Um, well, we got donuts, and then . . . we found a . . . a town square thingy and went into shops and stuff," I fumble.

I glance at Grammy, but she's grabbing the jug of strawberry lemonade from the fridge. Argh, where's Grammy when I need her help?

Mom nods and says, "Sounds fun! Wish I could've gone!" She resumes typing on her phone.

"Yeah . . . " I laugh nervously.

I kick my shoes off and dash down the hall. I run into my room and close the door behind me. Leaning against my door, I let myself sink to the floor. For some reason, it feels so empty without my pen resting on the table. Not having that pen makes me nervous. It's a magic pen that creates portals and stories! And now it's lost in a foreign world that I've never been to! Well, not physically. Only in my imagination.

This is really it. I'm going to do this. It's now or—no, it needs to be now. After standing up, I grab my phone. I dial Romi's number and wait until she picks up. Then I grab my tablet and dial Phoenix's number.

"Hi, Sporky!" Phoenix teases.

"Girl, what's up?" Romi asks.

"Listen guys," I say. "We need to talk."

Chapter Ten

Entering

I glance at the clock the next day after lunch at home. It's 1:50 in the afternoon. Phoenix and Romi will be arriving in ten minutes. I have no idea what I should pack. It's not gonna be like a vacation. It's going to be dangerous and magical and crazy! I'm not bringing a suitcase. Hm.

I scan my closet until I see my large white leather backpack and yank it down. I stuff in three pairs of jean shorts and five shirts. I can always re-wear the jean shorts. After I'm done, I look around. Hm. Now what? I pack a bag of goldfish, peanut butter crackers, and a bottle of water. I'm sure I'll be able to refill it. I also pack a hat, sunglasses, Marty's pocket knife, a lighter, and my notebook.

Then I roll up my sleeping bag and stuff it under the carrier my dad put on the bag one summer we went camping. I bring a small but fluffy pillow too. I also bring my phone and charger. You know . . . just in case. All the while, I forcibly ignore the permanent shaking in my hands.

Okay. I think I'm all set. My heart is pounding, and my palms are sweaty. I really don't want to puke again. Oh no! I think I am! I dash to the toilet in the hall bathroom just as the doorbell rings. Great. Romi and Phoenix are gonna walk in on me. Just lovely. Sitting up, I turn the bathroom fan on. Phew, that was a close one. I almost puked, but I didn't. After I wash my hands, I calmly walk out of the bathroom. Plastering on a smile, I run to the door just as Grammy opens it. I ignore my crazily beating heart.

"Come on in!" she says cheerfully. A little too cheerfully in my opinion. Grammy hasn't been herself since yesterday—all quiet and protective of me. I think she's super nervous for us.

"Hi, guys," I say.

Phoenix waves and Romi smiles. They both have on backpacks. Phoenix's is huge.

"Let's go to my room," I say. Grammy winks at me as we head down the hall, but her eyes look nervous and sad.

"Man," Phoenix says as we enter my room. "I can't believe it's true! We're really doing this!" He sits down on my bed.

"Me neither," Romi says.

"I feel you," I sigh.

My head feels like it could topple over from all the thoughts racing through my brain. I sit down next to Phoenix on the bed, and Romi sits down next to me.

"Guys, this is legit," I say. "It's not a fairy tale."

Phoenix and Romi nod. "We know," Romi says.

Then it hits me. "Phoenix, the story you wrote with my pen about the Quartz Prince? You used the Portal Pen, so, that story will be in the magical world too!" I cry.

Phoenix sits up. "What?! Yes!" he shouts. He runs up to me and hugs me. I tense up. No boy's ever hugged me before. Then Phoenix backs up. His face is flushed. "I'm sorry," he whispers.

"It's okay," I say awkwardly. I feel all weird and fluttery inside.

Grammy pokes her head in the room. "Everybody ready?" she asks.

Romi stands up and brushes herself off. "I think so," she says.

Phoenix and I nod. I gotta admit, he looks really cute wearing that big backpack. Wait, what? Phoenix? No way, he's my best friend. *Just* my best friend.

"Alrighty then," Grammy says. We all head out into the kitchen. I push down the lump in my throat. Grammy's made a trail mix out of M&Ms, nuts, white chocolate chips, cheese triangles, pretzels, raisins, and cheerios. She has the mix separated in three big bags along with three bottles of strawberry lemonade. "Save this for when you arrive in the story world," Grammy says.

I gulp. "Okay," I croak. I'm so nervous. I feel like I do when I'm about to take off on a roller coaster. We all grab our baggies and bottles and climb into Grammy's car. The bag is vibrating in my hand because I'm shaking so badly. The car groans under our weight as Grammy backs up and we drive out of my neighborhood. I stare longingly at my house. Oh, my little red brick, one-story house with its little white roof and the pillow on the porch that says, "Hey, Good Lookin'." I don't know when I'm going to see it again. My eyes fill with tears as Grammy drives down our steep driveway into my neighborhood, and pretty soon we're whizzing past cars on the highway. I feel the old car rattling under my feet. I sigh.

Romi turns to look at me. "Hey," she says, squeezing my hand. "You okay?"

"Yeah, I'm fine," I say, swallowing hard. "Just . . . nervous, that's all." I stare out the window.

Romi squeezes my hand. "Me too," she whispers.

About an hour and a half later, we pull into the old town square, and the car creaks as we make our way toward the end of one of the roads. I've seen it all before, but Phoenix and Romi's eyes dart around at the old buildings, their mouths gaping. Grammy pulls in front of the coffee shop. Grammy and I get out, but Phoenix and Romi are glued to their seats.

"Come on," I gesture. Romi shakes her head slightly in awe as she and Phoenix quickly scramble out of the car. We walk into the little building. Phoenix and Romi glance around nervously. I silently pray that we don't get caught by a police officer again. This is the real deal this time, and we can't afford anything getting in the way.

We go down the hallway and Grammy switches on the little, flickering light. Then we slowly take the creaky stairs. Everything looks the same as when Grammy and I came—except it all looks even dustier somehow. Phoenix and Romi cough and sputter.

"Ugh! It's so dirty and old in here!" Phoenix wheezes.

"Over here everyone," Grammy gestures. We all walk over to the desk. "Help me lift this," Grammy says. All three of us move the desk to the side. Romi and Phoenix look super confused. "Ah, here it is," Grammy says toward the blanket covering the portal.

Romi scrunches up her nose. "What's so special about a blanket?" she asks, because she has no idea what's coming.

I squeeze her hand. "You'll see," I say.

Excitement slowly takes over my body. Together, we throw off the blanket, exposing the portal. Romi and Phoenix gasp.

"Oh my goodness!" Romi cries. Phoenix dashes up to the edge of the portal and peers in.

"Perfectly round, maybe two hundred feet deep . . ." Phoenix murmurs to himself. Boy, he sure is dorky. Me and Romi share a glance and chuckle.

"This is really it?" Romi asks, standing next to Phoenix.

"Yep," I say. My heart is pounding. I can hear it in my ears. While Phoenix and Romi peer in, Grammy and I share a sad stare before Grammy wraps me up in a hug.

"Please, please, *please* be careful," she whispers into my ear. I feel one of her tears wet my cheek.

"I absolutely promise, Grammy," I whisper back.

We let go of each other and face Romi and Phoenix. "Okay, guys," I say. "This is it."

Phoenix and Romi nod. This is really, truly, finally *it*. Grammy gives the two of them big hugs and then wishes us farewell.

"Please save your snacks for when you arrive," she says. "I don't want you going hungry." Grammy busies herself by making sure bags are zipped and everything is perfect. Grammy tries to zip up my backpack even though it's already zipped. I hold up my hand and smile at Grammy, "We're good. I packed more, too."

Grammy steps back and gives a little nod. "Okay then. Good luck," she says, her voice cracking.

"Thanks, Grammy," I say.

"Well, let's get this show on the road then!" Phoenix cries. He takes a step back, runs, and jumps. "Geronimo!" he cries as he jumps into the portal.

Romi and I gasp together, then we start giggling. "Bye, Eva's grandma," Romi says kindly. "Thanks for everything." And with that, Romi slides her feet, then legs, then waist into the portal until she lets go of the rim and her whole body disappears.

Grammy turns to me and kisses my forehead. "I love you so much, Eva," she says.

"I love you too," I say. I wave at Grammy and then jump into the portal, squeezing my eyes shut. Eeeeeeeeeeek!

The air is freezing cold, and everything is flashy, neon, and multicolored. I feel like I'm falling through what space might be like. I hear my own screams, yet they sound hollow, like I'm in an empty room. My body feels like sand. And I'm falling, falling, falling.

It's like I've been falling for hours when the blackness all around me begins to wiggle in waves. Then slowly, the black begins to get lighter and lighter until all around me are bursts of neon lime, pink, blue, and red. The colors are so blinding I have to squeeze my eyes shut again. The air suddenly feels hot and cold at the same time.

Before I know it, I'm falling through a starry indigo sky. I feel a warm, tingly breeze as the wind gently tickles my ears. This is kind of nice, actually. Until I glance down and see I'm headed right for a patch of trees. Aaaaaaaaah! I tumble into a tree headfirst, my arms and legs flailing around like a bird trying to fly. Ouch! Ouch! Ouch! Branches smack my limbs and leaves get tangled in my hair. Then, a large, gnarly limb is heading toward me before everything goes black.

CHAPTER ELEVEN

Lovely Valley

I let my eyes open at will and try to look around me. Everything is hazy with a purple glow. "Wha . . . what's going on?" I sputter. Oh man, my mouth hurts. I try to move. Oof. My legs hurt. I try to sit up. Yikes! My everything hurts. I feel trapped. I let out a loud groan. Suddenly, there's a buttery substance being slathered all over my forehead.

"Shhh, it's okay," I hear a voice whisper. It's high and fluttery and sounds hollow.

I begin to sweat. My senses kick in, and I begin to panic. *Where am I? What's going on? Who is this person talking? What's that stuff on my forehead?* I let my eyes open more and my sight begins to clear up. I'm in a tiny room. Everything is a light pink. My aching fingers grab next to me, and I feel the soft cushion of pillows. I must be in a bed. I see swishing, fluttery curtains and bright pink shelves. Bottles of all different shapes and sizes sit on the shelves, full of strange-looking liquids. A large mirror is hanging on the wall to my right, and I catch a glimpse of myself. My hair is a mess and there are bruises all over my face. My lip looks swollen, and I have a deep, red cut over by my left ear. I also see that the stuff on my forehead is like a Mountain-Dew-green color.

I can't help but moan. I wish I could move around. Wait, where's Romi? Where's Phoenix? "Romi?! Phoenix?!" I call but my mouth is suddenly closed shut by a warm hand.

"Please don't try to struggle, honey flower. It won't make anything any better," the light voice says.

I groan again. "Is it bad?" I ask.

"It can be fixed, no doubt," the voice says.

"Where are my friends?" I say a little louder. My voice cracks and croaks, and my throat hurts.

"Don't worry about them. They're being cured too. Now let me give you some special treatment to help with your sores," the voice says.

A tall figure looms over me. It's a teenage girl with super pale skin, basically paper white, with shiny black hair styled into a bun. There's a pink flower in her hair, and her face is covered in so much makeup. She has blush, fake eyelashes, eyeliner, and her lips are covered in a shimmering pink lip gloss. She's wearing a pink-and-purple dress that seems to move—wait, her dress is made of fluttering, purple and pink butterflies! I let the girl slide her soft hand behind my head and sit me upright. Ouch. My head throbs.

"There," she says. "Sit here for a moment. I need to get your treatment." The girl practically glides over to one of the shelves and searches it.

"Where am I?" I ask.

The girl's shoulders gently bounce as she giggles. Her laugh is gentle like the ringing of bells. "Why, you're in Lovely Valley, of course," she says like it's the silliest question ever.

Omg. Lovely Valley!

"Wait, Lovely Valley? As in, the place where you took the Banshee's hair and cured her disease?" I ask.

The girl laughs again. "Yes, this is the place. I didn't work here at that time, but that story is well known around here."

Oh. My. Gosh! I knew all of my stories were going to be in the portal, but it's really happening! My stories are actually, like, living and talking and breathing!

"Wow," I can't help but say. I sigh. This is so amazing.

The girl looks at me skeptically. "Is your head feeling okay? Maybe I need to reapply the Dragonfly Gel ... " The girl rushes over to me and rubs my head.

"I'm fine!" I cry happily. "I'm just ... very happy, that's all."

"Well, okay," the girl says. "Oh! I forgot to introduce myself. I'm Majesty, by the way."

Whoa! Majesty is a fancy name. "Nice to meet you. I'm Eva," I say.

Majesty bows. "Nice to meet you, Eva. I need to go get a special ointment for you. I'll be right back. Just holler if you need anything." Majesty picks up her fluttering butterfly dress and hurries out of the room. I take deep breaths. My cheeks hurt from smiling. This is really happening! I glance out of the round window next to me. I see a pond with purple water and a bunch of purple trees surrounding it. Oh, man. This is so amazing.

Majesty rushes back in the room with a teeny vial of sloshing, purple liquid. She sits down on the edge of my bed and pops off the lid. "This is Dawn Blossom Tea," Majesty says. Dawn Blossom Tea! I feel like I could faint! "It should take away all of the major bruises. But you still may have some minor scars," Majesty says.

I nod. She lifts the vial to my lips, and I feel the purple liquid rush down my throat. It tastes like cinnamon, vanilla, and coconut but also feels like super hot, sticky fudge at the same time. Immediately, the big marks and bumps on my body begin to fade, leaving little scars in their place.

"All better," Majesty says. She takes a washcloth from the nightstand next to me and begins to rub off the green stuff from my forehead.

"Do you think I could maybe see my friends?" I ask Majesty.

"Oh! Of course, Eva. But be careful, some of your bruises are still pretty bad."

Majesty slowly lifts up my covers. Wow. Even after the tea, I'm still fairly black and blue. I must have bruised myself very badly falling through that tree.

"How did you find me?" I ask.

Majesty chuckles. "One of our maids was out collecting tree trunk chips when she noticed three unconscious figures lying on the ground, bleeding and bruised. So she quickly gathered two other maids and brought you to one of the treatment houses. And now you're here," Majesty says.

Whoa. Poor maids. I clutch Majesty's pale arm, and she helps me get out of bed. She leads me outside, and the warm air feels like a warm washcloth on my face. We walk behind the little pink house I was in, only to discover even more tiny pink houses, scattered over the purple ground. Majesty leads me to one that's a little slanted on a purple hill. Following her in, I see a room identical to the one I just woke in, except there are two beds, one containing Romi and the other Phoenix.

Two women who look a little younger than Majesty are rushing around, wiping foreheads, filling vials. They both have butterfly dresses too, except the butterflies are orange and yellow.

"Romi! Phoenix!" I cry.

"Eva!" They both shout back. Majesty and I walk in, and I gently hug each of them. They too have the green jelly stuff slathered across their foreheads, and one of the women is feeding Romi a glass of shimmery stuff that looks like a green smoothie.

"Are you okay?" Phoenix asks me.

"Yes! But what about you guys?" I ask.

"We're okay now. Mmm, this stuff tastes like pineapple!" Romi cries.

Oh, good. I'm so glad they're okay. Suddenly I remember. The Portal Pen! "The pen! Have you guys seen it?" I cry.

Romi and Phoenix shake their heads. "We even asked Silver and Lila, and they haven't seen it either," Phoenix says, gesturing toward the two bustling ladies.

"I'm afraid I don't understand what you're talking about," Majesty says.

"We lost this super special pen of ours. It's why we came, and we were wondering if you've seen it," I say.

Majesty taps her perfectly curved chin. "Hmm, no, I haven't seen one." Then her face seems to get even paler. "But you know who might have it?" she whispers like she doesn't want anyone to hear, even though we all can.

"Who?" all three of us whisper back.

"The Adventure Man," Majesty whispers.

"Who's the Adventure Man?" Romi asks.

Majesty winks at us. "He's a strange man, you see. No one really sees him that much, but there are stories that we've heard about how he's stolen things that are sometimes impossible to get—or other stories about how he's killed large beasts, or he's made tricky trades with stubborn kings and queens. The Adventure Man lives in an old tree called the Curly Tree. It's located in the heart of of the Spirit Forest where the Spirit Animals live," Majesty says.

"He sounds cool!" Phoenix says.

Majesty nods. "Yes, he is very," she snickers when she says the next word, "cool."

One of the women begins to rub what looks like soap on the sides of Phoenix's face. When they wash it away, his cheeks are shiny, clear of any injuries.

Majesty continues, "The Adventure Man collects exotic things too. He once stole the eye of a sea monster and the wand from a fairy. If this pen is really so special, the Adventure Man is bound to have it."

"Where can we find him?" Romi asks as one of the women wipes away the gel on her forehead.

Majesty clucks her tongue and strolls over to the dresser in the corner. She pulls out a dusty-looking map and unrolls it. Then, she walks over to Phoenix's bed and lays it out, "If you're here in Lovely Valley, the journey to Spirit Forest would take at least four days by foot."

Phoenix, Romi, and I groan. Four days! I seriously didn't expect it to take so long to travel around here. And we don't even know our surroundings—so it could take longer!

"But," Majesty says. "The closest place to Lovely Valley is The Dragon Gate. Maybe if you're lucky, you can get a dragon to take you to Spirit Forest," Majesty explains.

Hmm. Hopefully. Except that seems both exciting and scary. How will we know how to use a dragon to travel?

"Then we need to get to The Dragon Gate!" Romi cries.

One of the women shushes her and lets her sip a large bottle of yellow liquid. "Yes, you sure do. But you need to get well first. We can't have you going on a large journey with bleeds and bruises." Majesty shakes her head in disapproval.

Suddenly, a little bell jingles, and the women sit up. A woman in a blue-and-purple butterfly dress peeks her head in the doorway. "Remember, we have a schedule, ladies. Two more guests have arrived. A tiny lizard and a fairy. The lizard has a terrible cold, and the fairy seems to have broken all of her fingers!"

The woman rushes out, and the door swoops back and forth. The women quickly clean up Romi and Phoenix, then pick up the bottoms of their dresses and hurry out of the door as well. Majesty sits up too and brushes herself off.

"I'm afraid we must part ways," Majesty says.

"What do we do?" I ask.

Majesty pats my head. "Your things are back at the very first house to the left. There's a large purple house over the hill. There, you can find things to eat and places to rest. And here." Majesty hands me the map. "You'll need this," she says.

"Thanks for helping us, Majesty," I say. I hug her tightly. I feel the butterflies on her dress flutter happily. Then I remember—they don't do anything for free here. I need to give her something! I look at my wrist and see a scrunchie. I hand it to her, wondering if it's enough. "Here. For the medicine."

"Oh! I love it! And, you're very welcome." Majesty puts the scrunchie on her own wrist, smiles at me, and then picks up her dress and strolls out the door. Romi and Phoenix climb out of their beds and grab their things.

"Alright," Romi says, clasping her hands together. "Let's go eat some food!"

I munch hungrily on a bowl of little, blue pebbles that taste like vanilla ice cream. Romi and Phoenix eat across from me. Tons of women in butterfly dresses hurry around us, some leaving, some eating, some getting their food.

"I don't know what this is, but it's yummy," Phoenix says, holding up his fork to show us a heap of red, globby stuff that looks a lot like slime.

"I can't believe we're actually in your world of stories," Romi breathes, grabbing her jug of water.

"I know, right?" I say. "Plus, there are also my Papa B's stories here too. So, some of them, I'm not too familiar with." I slurp on some green soup that tastes like lemonade. "Like the Dragon Gate. My Papa B wrote that one."

We all pick at our food for a moment. None of this food looks like real food back home, but all of it tastes sweet and fresh.

"I really hope the Adventure Man has the Portal Pen," Romi says.

"Me too," I sigh. "My Papa B and I are the only ones who really know its powers and how to use them. Who knows what someone like the Adventure Man could do with that pen." I push aside my blue pebble things.

"So, explain—how does the pen work?" Romi asks.

"Well, I mean, whenever I write stories with that pen, I feel rumbling inside me. Now, I know that feeling is like the pen telling me that the story is forming into an actual living and breathing place here in this world," I explain.

Romi picks at a heap of what I hope are mashed potatoes as I go on, "My Grammy told me that on the day when my rumbling wouldn't stop, it was because I had written about the portal, and that was like me revisiting the portal my Papa B made, which made it open up once again."

Romi nods. "Can you write anything you want?" she asks. She peers at me curiously.

"Um, yeah, I guess," I say. "But I basically only write fun, adventurous, and magical stuff." I take a sip of my water. Romi nods again.

"I really hope we come across Spindle's Chase," Phoenix squeals, his fork clanking against his plate as he bounces. When Romi raises her eyebrows, Phoenix laughs. "It's the setting of the story that I wrote with Eva's pen. It's about this kingdom made of only gold and jewels and a prince made of quartz who gives his life to a homeless family so they can use his body to buy a farm and food and things." Phoenix's cheeks go red when I grin at him.

"They use his body? That's a little creepy," Romi snickers.

"His body's made out of quartz!" Phoenix says, his cheeks reddening even more. "It's worth something, and they use it like money basically, Romi."

Suddenly, a tiny voice that sounds like trickling water echoes the room. "All Lovely Valley Treatment women, please report to your treatment houses at this time." At that, all the women in the building drop their things and begin to pile out of the double doors.

"Maybe we should get going too," I say. "Obviously, we don't want to stay here too long."

"Majesty told us to rest and get better," Romi reminds me.

"I know, but I've noticed we all look way better already," I say.

"Yeah. And we don't want to wait forever to get out there and find my story!" Phoenix says. We both look at him. "I mean, yeah . . . and the Portal Pen, of course."

Romi smiles. "You're right. We gotta get to that Portal Pen."

After we clear our meals, we head for the door, following behind all the women until we're out in the pink glow of the sunshine.

Romi opens up the map. "Next stop: The Dragon Gate."

CHAPTER TWELVE

Figures in Black

Phoenix studies the map intently. "There's a small area in between Lovely Valley and The Dragon's Gate," he says. "Mostly just houses and a market and stuff called Goggle Village."

I tug on one of the straps on my backpack. It's the middle of the day, and the sun is beginning to set. I can see the pink houses in the distance behind me, and up ahead looks like a forest with super tall and skinny trees. I'm secretly trying to look out for someone who would resemble Papa B. After all, finding Papa B and the Portal Pen are the main goals of being here in the first place. So far, the only "people" I've seen are the pale women with long, black hair and butterfly dresses.

Technically, we can stay here as long as we want. But I do want to go home soon. I mean, I definitely know my parents will be freaking out when Grammy explains that their daughter and her two friends jumped into a portal that leads to another world full of magic to find a pen and her long-lost grandpa. But I'm still so grateful that Grammy is willing to face my parents and tell them the truth.

Trees begin to tower over us, their leaves dancing in the wind. The air is growing a little chilly. I zip up my sweatshirt.

"Where are we, Phoenix?" Romi asks. She seems super happy for some reason. Maybe she's trying to lighten the spirit. Meanwhile, I'm kind of getting a little frustrated and confused because we have no idea where we are.

"We're in a random forest, Romi," I say.

"How am I supposed to know?" Phoenix grumbles.

Romi stops and puts her hands on her hips. "Uh, because you have the map, Pebbles," she snaps.

Phoenix huffs. "Well, maybe I don't know every-thing, okay?"

Romi smirks. "Yeah, that's for sure."

Phoenix begins to stomp toward Romi, but I hold him back. "Guys!" I cry. "This is no time to argue."

My heart is beating fast. I can't have my friends mad at each other; we have to stick together. I glare at the both of them and start to walk. Phoenix rushes to catch up to me and resumes reading the map. Romi finally huffs behind us. The sky begins to turn into an ugly gray, and suddenly, large, plump raindrops splash onto my face.

"Argh! Seriously?" I cry.

Romi throws her hands up. Phoenix stops suddenly, causing me to run into him.

"Hold up! The map . . . it just changed!" Phoenix cries.

"What?" I ask. Me and Romi peer over his shoulders. A black squiggle covers the trees. I see black squiggles all over the page.

"I could've sworn that wasn't there before!" Phoenix tries to rub it off with his thumb, but it doesn't budge. "What in the world?" he shouts, but suddenly, we hear rustling all around us.

The rain begins to pour. One particular bush beside us begins to rattle, and I jump back. Out of nowhere, a figure in black summersaults out of the bush. I glance beside me. Romi is scurrying up a tree. Phoenix is stuffing the map into his backpack and taking out his pocket knife.

"You don't scare us!" Phoenix cries, waving his knife in the air.

"Uh, I wouldn't do that," I whisper. I rack my brain. I don't remember writing any stories with people dressed in all black. And my Papa B didn't write any either. Maybe I'm just forgetting. Suddenly, the figure in black draws a large sword and flips it around his fingers. Okay, I definitely don't remember writing that. I hear a rustle from my left and turn to see another black figure perched in a tree, two nunchucks in his hands. Another emerges from the right, backflipping and karate-chopping the air. Soon, we're surrounded.

"Um, Eva, what's going on? And what are these creatures?" Romi whispers from her perch in the tree.

"I'm not sure. I honestly can't remember writing about them," I whisper back, terrified as I think about what might happen.

"Oh, no, this is *not* good!" Phoenix whispers. "We can't fight them all off."

My heart is beating so fast I feel like it might burst. Without warning, a nunchuck is flying toward my face, and I duck in the knick of time.

"Run!" someone screams. Oh, wait. I'm the one screaming. Romi quickly climbs down the tree, and we bolt. Trees whiz by us. My throat hurts from yelling so intensely. Phoenix throws his pocket knife to the figures behind us, but misses entirely. A giant sword flies by my head and stabs a tree. I yelp, "HELP! Someone help us!"

Suddenly, more black figures swoop down from trees like spiders, trying to grab us from above. We duck, but Phoenix accidentally trips. Without warning, a hand with a black glove grabs his arm, and soon he's flying up, up, up into the air.

"Phoenix!" I scream. I try to climb a tree, but there are tons of black figures crawling in it. Romi's already in a tree. She's out in the open and is fighting a figure with her pocket knife. She's doing really well, actually. The figure slips and falls from the tree. Go, Romi!

"Romi!" I yell, hiding behind a tree. I point to Phoenix. The figure that caught him is throwing him up in the air, each time higher. Romi nods and hurries higher up the tree. She expertly jumps from one tree to another, until she's on the same one as Phoenix and the black figure. Carefully, she jumps onto a branch and grabs the figure just as Phoenix flies through the air. But Romi and the figure are too busy wrestling to notice Phoenix. I scream in terror. He's falling toward the ground!

A black figure throws a javelin, and it barely misses my head, though I feel the wind of it as it zooms by. I hurry out into the open. Phoenix screams as he falls. I hold my hands out, hoping my weight will be enough to carry his. Romi hops down from tree to tree. The figure she fought rubs his head, crumpled into a ball on the ground. Phoenix tears through the trees and I grab him, but he takes me with him too. We fall to the ground in a heap. Romi stands up and pulls out a small, orange ball.

"Get up," she says, a knife flying in between her legs.

"Huh?" Phoenix says.

"Get up!" Romi cries with more authority.

We scramble up and Romi throws the orange ball onto the ground. It explodes into an orange spray, fogging the air around us. Romi grabs our hands and we run. We run through the woods and away from the black figures. Sweat is dripping down my forehead. I glance back and see the black figures waving their hands around in confusion, as if they're hoping to clear the air of the orange fog.

We run and run and run. There are trees and trees and more trees. The rain runs down my back and drenches my shirt. Honestly, it feels so refreshing. Finally, we stop to catch our breath. I'm so happy we made it out alive. I hug Phoenix, and he hugs me back. Romi wipes her forehead.

"I had no idea you had smoke bombs," I say to her.

"I like to stay prepared," Romi smiles.

I lean back against a tree. "Where do you think think those guys came from?" I ask.

"If *you* don't know, Eva, then I definitely have no idea," Phoenix says.

Romi opens her bag and takes out a water bottle. She pops the lid off and gulps it down.

"Man, Romi, you were so awesome back there," I say.

Romi wipes her mouth and grins. "Yeah, thanks. I knew those guys would like the smoke bombs," she chuckles.

I chuckle with her. Then I stare at her. Was she joking? How did she know that?

Phoenix sits up and takes the map out of his backpack. "Good news!" he says. "We're super close to Goggle Village. Maybe someone can help us get more info about the pen or something there." Phoenix folds up the map.

I stand up. "We need to get going," I say. I just have a feeling that if we stay here too long, those figures will find us. Romi sticks her water bottle back into her bag. Together, we cautiously continue walking through the forest.

After what seems forever, there's a clearing in the woods, and we can see several houses tucked into the trees. It's Goggle Village! The more we look, the more houses we see—some are literally hanging from the limbs, while some sit inside trees, and others are perched on top. I see an open window with flower pots on the window sill and a clothing line dangling from another. Oh! And is that a mini-cafe on the top of that tree? This is super cool! There's even a bridge that stretches across the clearing up in the sky from across the trees. There's spray paint on the ground that points to different houses. Must be directions or something.

Abruptly, a sword swoops by my face and gets lodged in a nearby tree trunk. I look behind me. Two black figures are walking toward us.

"Climb!" The three of us quickly climb into one of the trees and behind a blue house where we peer out. The two figures have their swords drawn as they enter the center of the clearing. They walk onto a purple circle in the middle of the red spray paint we'd seen on the ground. Immediately, a giant net flies off the ground and traps the two figures. They squirm like worms. People peer out of their homes, clapping and cheering. Then, the net goes flying over the tops of trees and into the distance. I'm so glad we didn't step there!

The three of us come out of hiding and scurry onto the bridge to look around. The sky is now dark, and people stop cheering so they can light torches to hang up on their houses. Everyone's dressed in scraps. One man with red-and-black striped pants has a large bandana tied around his neck that drapes over his bare chest. He lights a large torch and sets it in a little holder in the bridge.

"Who are you?" he asks. He has what sounds like a British accent.

"Oh, um, I'm Eva, and this is . . ."

The man yawns. "Enough," he says and walks off.

Okay then.

I remember writing the story of the Goggle Village. It was called "The Fortune Teller of Goggle Village." I did write that the people were like intellectual barbarians and didn't have time for small talk. Wait! The Fortune Teller!

"Guys!" I clutch Romi's arm. "I wrote the story of this village. There's a fortune teller who lives here. She knows everything. Maybe while we rest for the night, we can go to her and get some more answers about my grandpa and the pen."

"Good thinking," Romi says. We head off the bridge, which wobbles under our weight.

"People aren't too nice here, so it might be a teensy bit hard to find her," I say. I knock on the door of the blue house, and a short man—shorter than me—with blue sleeves on his arms (but no shirt) answers the door. His belly jiggles as he moves.

"Hi, um," I begin.

"Yes, I haven't got all day," the man grumbles.

I huff, "We're looking for the fortune teller?" I somehow manage to make the statement sound like a question.

The man rolls his eyes and points. Then, he slams the door in our face. We turn around to where he pointed. Sitting on a super skinny tree is a large house—well, it's literally three small houses piled on top of each other, except the middle house is on the edge and the top house looks like it's about to topple over.

We all grin at each other and then run over the bridge. Phoenix knocks on the door of the bottom house. There's a silence and then the sound of footsteps. We hear several locks being unlocked, and the door opens a crack. A plump woman with tiny eyes peeps out.

"Hello?" she says.

"Um, hi, we're looking for the fortune teller," I say.

The woman swallows. "Do you have an appointment?" she asks.

Huh?

"Er . . . no," I say.

The woman shrugs. "Okay then. Miss Amelia's schedule is clear anyways."

The plump woman opens the door to let us in. She gestures her fat hand into the house. We walk into a small hallway with ill-hanging, crooked pictures on the wall.

"It smells like cat pee in here," Romi whispers to me.

I nod. It really does. There's a fan on the ceiling, but it dangles super low. The woman ducks under it, so we do the same. We walk into a small kitchen with clay counters and broken cupboards. A hamster is sleeping in the sink. Why? I made the story, but some of the details seem to have made themselves. There's a pot bubbling on the stove. I feel my stomach growl.

"Ya hungry?" the woman asks.

We all nod. She opens the pot and grabs a spoon from the counter, dipping it into the pot and dumping white rice into three teeny bowls. She hands us those bowls and some clay spoons. The pot continues to gurgle.

"Enjoy," she says blankly. Hmm. I'm not too sure about this rice, but my stomach growls for it. "Follow me, please," the woman says. She shuffles up a set of skinny stairs, and we follow as we eat. We've just entered the second house. The lights are dim, and there are two green couches in front of a stack of books. This carpet is super scratchy.

Our guide doesn't stop there, though; she leads us into the third house. Clothes hang everywhere, and there are shelves covered in jewelry. She leads us to a door that's bright pink. It clashes with all the bland stuff in here.

"Put your rice bowls away," the woman says. "Miss Amelia does not allow food in her study room."

We set our bowls on a shelf, and the woman opens the door to what looks like former kitchen turned into a study. Lights hang over the ceiling and are draped across the door. There are crooked bookshelves everywhere, and the kitchen counters are being used as one big desk. A round, white ball sits in the center of one of the counters, illuminating the room. An older woman with incredibly pale skin and frizzy, golden hair that falls down her shoulders sits in the chair. Her bangs fall into her eyes, and she has on bright green eyeshadow and bright red lipstick. Big, golden hoop earrings dangle from her ears. She's wearing a white bandana tied into a bow on her head, a floppy indigo jacket with a white tank top, and a red dress skirt. Bracelets jingle as she moves her hands. She has tight, skinny cheekbones and a beauty mark. Her eyes seem to be in a trance as she stares at the ball, her hands slowly moving around it.

"Servant girl, who are these peasants?" the fortune teller asks with a thick Italian-sounding accent. Oh my gosh! It's really the fortune teller that I created! The plump woman bows.

"Miss Amelia, they wanted to see you," the woman stutters.

"Ah, yes . . . " she murmurs.

CHAPTER THIRTEEN

Miss Amelia

The fortune teller still doesn't look up. Or speak.

Finally, Phoenix says something. "Ma'am, we have some questions for you. We've heard you're a fortune teller, so we were hoping you can answer them," he says politely.

"Yes, I can answer them!" Miss Amelia cries. She finally lifts her gaze from the ball and looks right into my eyes. Her eyes seem to shoot through me and pierce my soul. "Eva Mason, how can I be at your service?" she asks.

Omg. She knows my name. So—she's really a fortune teller! Her eyes are yellow. She's very . . . intimidating. I immediately feel a shiver go down my spine.

"Well . . . " I start, but Miss Amelia puts her hand up.

"Wait! Don't tell me!" She lets her eyes drift to her ball and licks her lips. "You want to find more about who the Adventure Man is, and you want to find your long-lost grandfather, and you also want to find your precious pen," Miss Amelia says almost immediately. I can't help but smile.

"Well . . . yes, that's exactly what I want to know about," I say. She's good. "I just basically want to know if the Adventure Man really does have our pen so we don't travel all the way there for nothing."

"Mmm," Miss Amelia says. Her long eyelashes flutter before she closes her eyes. Humming, her hands wave around the ball. The ball turns green, and Miss Amelia opens her eyes. "The Adventure Man does indeed have your pen," she tells us. Yes! Phoenix, Romi, and I high-five. "It shouldn't be too hard to get there," Miss Amelia continues.

We stop cheering and focus on the fortune teller once more. She waves her hands around the ball again, and this time the ball turns completely gray. Miss Amelia clucks her tongue and shakes her head. "I am sorry, Eva Mason, but I do not know for certain about your grandfather," she says.

My spirits plummet. I slump down in a chair and put my head in my hands. Grammy was so right. I guess he's not here anymore. I feel a tear slide down my cheek.

"No, no, please don't cry, darling," Miss Amelia places her hand on my shoulder. I rub my eyes. I never should have come to see the portal in the first place. That way, I wouldn't have lost the pen. And then I wouldn't have had to drag my friends down here to a place that's been more dangerous than I thought it would be. And I wouldn't have had to face the tragedy of knowing that my Papa B is dead.

Miss Amelia gets up and sits back down in her chair. "Darling, the next place from Goggle Village is The Dragon Gate. You have to go through there completely, because it would take three extra days to go around The Dragon Gate. And maybe a dragon can give you a ride to save more time," Miss Amelia explains.

Romi rubs my back. I sniff. We can still get my pen at least. "Okay," I say.

Miss Amelia frowns at her magic ball. "There's more," she says quietly.

"Good news?" Phoenix asks.

Miss Amelia cocks her head. "Bad news," she says. Her ball turns black. Oh, great. "Stay on your toes, children. There is an evil coming in the future. It is ... " She squints at the ball. When it turns a light gray, she waves her arms around it more aggressively. When nothing happens, she frowns, "It is unclear what it is, but I see a glimpse of armies of men and women dressed in black clothes and black gloves." Miss Amelia nervously looks each of us in the eyes. She stares very intently at Romi. Then, she glances back down.

"It is coming," she says again. She stares at me. "I know the pen's power, Eva Mason. I know it will be in great hands once you get it back. Stay here in Goggle Village for the night to get your rest and gain your strength, but be sure to get going first thing in the morning. This evil force I see seems to be moving quickly." Miss Amelia stands up and opens the door for us. "Be brave and best of luck to you," she says.

The plump woman leads us out of the room and through the houses until we get into the first house. Walls have been built so it's really just one big room. There's a hammock hanging from the ceiling and two couches with pale blue pillows.

"I'm sorry, but I'm not allowed to feed you in the morning due to a sudden food shortage in Goggle Village, so I hope you brought food," the woman frowns.

"Oh, don't worry, we have food," I say.

"Okay then. Remember what Miss Amelia said—so you need to get going first thing in the morning." The plump woman shuffles out of the room, and I hear her footsteps as she goes upstairs into the second house. Romi and I take the couches, and Phoenix takes the hammock. This couch is really itchy, and the pillows are flat, but hey, at least we have somewhere to sleep.

"Now we really have to hurry," Phoenix says.

"Yeah," I say, letting out a sigh. Grammy was right for not coming. She would've been super disappointed as well.

"Hey, I'm really sorry about your grandpa," Romi says.

"It's okay," I say. That's all I can say. There's nothing I can do. I close my eyes for a moment before staring out the window. All I see are the tops of trees for miles and the dark sky. Shadows dance on the walls as the flickering candle melts the wax. I hear Phoenix snoring as I fall asleep to the glow of the candle and the sadness of my heart.

I wake up with a jolt. That was a terrifying dream. My heart is beating hard, and my forehead is damp with sweat. Glancing out the window, I see the sun is just beginning to rise. The hammock and the other couch are empty. I wipe my brow.

In my dream, there was a black dragon with deep red scales, but we weren't riding the dragon as it flew. We were stuck in a net that the dragon was holding on to with its sharp teeth. It brought us down to the ground where thousands of people in black surrounded us and then . . . everything went black. I shiver as I remember.

I hear talking and see the shadows of Phoenix and Romi on the front porch. I throw off my covers, grab my backpack, and open the door. Phoenix and Romi are eating their snack mix and drinking water.

"Morning, Sporky," Phoenix says.

"Morning," I say.

"We're just taking in the view," Romi says.

Wow. The view. Miss Amelia's house is up in the highest tree, and we can see the whole town of Goggle Village—all the tree houses and bridges. There are even three trees put together for tents and booths that are loaded with silks, fruits, vegetables, breads, paintings, and more for trades and things. People shuffle around houses and walk across bridges. No one really talks to one another. That's basically how I wrote the story.

"We should get going," I say. "We need to get a move on so we can get to The Dragon's Gate as quickly as possible." We pack up our things and head off the porch and onto the crowded bridge where people are waiting to see Miss Amelia. They eye us and glare at us as if to say: "How come you got a turn?"

We wiggle our way through all the people and hop onto a nearby tree with a house that has a rusty sign that says "Laundry" on it. We slide down the tree and avoid the purple circle in the middle of the clearing.

"What's the map say, Pebbles?" Romi asks.

Phoenix glares at her but opens up the map anyway. "Well, if Goggle Village is here, and The Dragon's Gate is there," Phoenix slides his finger around the map. "The

Dragon's Gate is only about two hours away if we're walking," Phoenix says.

"Two hours? We can't walk for *two hours*!" Romi pouts and plops down onto the ground.

"Maybe we can hitch a ride," I say, pointing to a man with a yellow straw hat hooking up the reins to his horse. A wooden wagon loaded with cabbages is attached to the horse's saddle.

"Yes!" Romi sits up and claps.

"Hey, but remember, the people of Goggle Village aren't exactly the nicest of people," I say.

We walk over to the man. He's yelling at the poor horse.

"Excuse me," Romi says to him.

The man whips around. "I ain't got time for dumb, little children," he grumbles.

Well, excuse me. I'm thirteen. I am most certainly not a dumb child.

"Excuse me?" Romi says.

The man scratches his straw hat. "What do ya want, ya little fleas?" he asks.

"Just who do you think you are?" Romi asks. "You are so rude, mister. We didn't even ask our question!"

Yes, Romi!

The man laughs a wheezy laugh. "Ask away, then. I ain't got all day," he says.

"We want you to take us to The Dragon's Gate!" Romi demands.

The man laughs even harder. He slaps his knee. "The Dragon's Gate? The Dragon's Gate! Such fools you are!" He pats his horse, who neighs and seems to laugh at us too. Romi huffs but flinches slightly. "No poor villager can go into The Dragon's Gate without some sort of trade. Goggle Village has nothing. And you children look like you have even less than nothing. You'll be roasted like a turkey within seconds!" The man collapses in laughter.

Romi steps up to the man. "You will take us!" she cries.

"Not without trading something with *me* first!" the man snaps.

Wow. I never intended for Goggle Village to be this cruel. Romi glances back at us. I have nothing. Phoenix shrugs his shoulders. Romi digs through her bag and pulls out a yellow smoke bomb. The straw hat man looks intrigued.

"What is that?" he laughs.

"It's a special concoction. I filled it with colored dye and baking soda . . . " Romi scrunches up her eyebrows. "Anyway, you throw it onto the ground, and it explodes in color. It helps you get away from enemies and things," Romi explains. The man looks super interested.

"I think he likes it," I whisper to Phoenix.

"Deal!" the man exclaims. "A trip to The Dragon's Gate for a brilliant yellow smoke bomb!" We climb into the cart. "I suppose I can make one stop before delivering these cabbages," the man says. He slaps the horse with the reins and cries, "Yah!" The horse whines and begins to trot, and soon we're cruising through the woods.

"Sorry, I didn't introduce myself. I'm Danny. So, where are y'all from? You don't look like you're from Goggle Village," the man says.

"Well, we're uh . . . we live very far away," I say.

"Aye, a traveler!" Danny cries.

"I guess so," I say.

The cart sways and bounces as the horse trots along. Suddenly, the horse shrieks and rears up.

"Whoa! What is it, pal?" Danny cries, clutching his straw hat to keep it from falling off.

The horse's eyes bulge. I have a bad feeling about this. A knife flies by my head and stabs the tree next to us.

"Giddyup!" I scream.

"YAH!" Danny cries, and the horse takes off into a wide gallop. The cabbages bob up and down. I let myself be buried underneath the cabbages. Not these guys again! I hear the hollering from Danny and the pounding of the hooves. I peer out from under the cabbages and see six people in black chasing us. One pulls out a sphere with spikes and chucks it at us. Whoa! That's a new one! I scream as it slices a cabbage just above me to bits.

Danny yells in fear as he yanks the reins rapidly. The horse runs faster. "Come on, girly! Giddyup! Faster! *Faster!*" Danny screams, his muscles bulging as he whips the horse.

I get an idea. "Danny! Now's your chance to use your lucky trade!" I shout.

"Good idea! It's in my satchel in the cart!"

I quickly crawl over to Danny's satchel and dig out the yellow smoke bomb. I aim and then chuck the smoke bomb onto the ground. It explodes into a yellow mist, and the men stop in confusion. Some try to run after us, but the smoke bomb has already slowed them down so much and the horse is already galloping so fast. All of us cheer and high-five, but deep down, I'm still really worried. When will they strike again? What if we get hurt?

"That was crazy!" Danny cries. The horse doesn't slow down, and I'm glad because we need to keep moving. "The truth is, we've been attacked by those guys before. They stole some of our food and hurt some of our villagers. That's why we set up traps—to catch them," Danny sighs. Huh. He must be talking about the trap we saw when we entered Goggle Village.

"How long ago were you attacked?" I ask.

"About three months ago," Danny says. "We've had news that they've attacked other places too. I heard that they even tried to steal a dragon from The Dragon's Gate!"

My mind flashes back to my dream. The black figures and the black dragon . . . .

"But," Danny continues, "We get reports that other kingdoms and villages have secret weapons and traps just in case the figures in black come back." Danny shakes the reigns and the horse slows down a little. The horse gallops over a root, and the wagon bounces. I hug my knees tightly. I can feel myself shaking. I hope we get there soon.

CHAPTER FOURTEEN

Climbing Over the Fence

After about thirty minutes of trees, trees, and more trees, all of a sudden the dirty ground melts into golden tiles.

"Good news, children! We're nearing The Dragon's Gate!" Danny calls. There are no more trees, but loopy, red glass structures take their place. This place is cool. The ride is much smoother now that there are no roots and rocks and things. The horse slows to a polite trot until gigantic, red double doors block our path. Danny yanks on the reins, and the horse slows to a stop. Danny helps us out of his wagon.

"Thank you so much, Danny," I say.

"Yes, thank you," Romi and Phoenix say.

"Of course. Now be on your way. I have a schedule to keep." Danny jumps onto his horse. "Oh, and one more thing: remember what I said earlier—you must have something valuable to trade in order to get in."

Oof. We don't have anything valuable. When Danny sees our worried faces, he gets off his horse and unhooks the reins. In the center of the reins is a ruby. "Here," he says, handing the ruby to me. Oh my gosh! It gleams in the sunlight with a deep shade of red. "Trade this. I have a feeling your mission is important," Danny says.

"Thank you so much!" I cry. I give Danny a big hug. Danny blushes and tips his straw hat. Then, he hops onto his horse, hooks the reins, and takes off with his cabbage cart bobbing behind him.

"Okay then," Romi says. She walks up to the doors and knocks. Nothing happens. She knocks again. Still nothing. "Hello? Anyone home?!" she cries, banging on the door. She turns toward me. "Why can't we just go around The Dragon's Gate?" she asks.

"Um, because!" I say. "You heard what the fortune teller said! It'll take days to go around! It'll save us so much more time if we go through. And besides, maybe we can get a dragon to give us a ride the rest of the way!" I brush off my jacket.

Romi scoffs. "I doubt it," she says.

What's up with Romi? I go up to her. "Hey," I say. "Don't be so negative." She shrugs and knocks again.

"How can we help you?" two voices say.

We turn around. Two large, muscular men with red scales and golden suits of armor stare at us. They're voices are like thunder. I gulp.

"We, uh, we, well . . . um, er, see . . . " I stammer.

"We're trying to get to Spirit Forest, and it'll save us a lot of time if we go through The Dragon Gates," Phoenix says smoothly. Go, Phoenix!

The men stand there, as still as stone, until one holds out a scaly, red hand with sharp claws. "Fine. But you must trade a valuable item in order to get in," he says.

"Eva?" Phoenix says, motioning to me. I gulp again and hand him the ruby. "Will this do?" Phoenix asks. The men stand still until they both nod, and Phoenix puts the jewel into the scaly soldier's hand.

"Follow us," they say.

I secretly thank Danny. They bring us to the doors and push them open with their own hands! They must be super strong. The doors open and gongs ring in our ears. The men slam the doors shut behind us and stare coldly at us.

"No funny business," one says.

"Don't stay long," the other says.

The two open the doors once more and return to their guarding stands outside, the doors slamming shut behind them. We turn to face The Dragon Gate. The ground is still golden tiles, but there are clouds everywhere. And they're super close to the ground too. I reach up and touch a green cloud. Fluffy.

We look around. I think we walked into a stadium or something. There are bleachers all around with scaly people clapping and cheering. We walk through crowds of people jumping wildly. As we walk, we catch glimpses of one orange and one turquoise dragon wrestling and hurling fire balls at each other. The noises are super loud.

"Let's keep moving," I say.

We walk behind the net and past probably some of the workers. They're just like people, only covered in scales. We go through a pair of rusty doors that say EXIT, and soon we're out in the open. A river of lava runs down a little canal in the street. There are fountains that are spewing out lava into the canal, and dragons swarm the sky. Posters are everywhere. They're all advertising for Dragon Fighting which is what I guess we were just watching.

I don't really know this story well, but I remember my Papa B wrote about Dragon Fighting being a sport and about people who got along with dragons and things. But his story was called "Misty of The Dragon

Gate." Misty was a dragon who made the bond between dragons and people, according to Papa B's story.

"Whoa!" Romi says, taking in all the sights around us.

We keep walking. Not only are the dragons flying, but the people are flying too.

"Let's try and maybe find a dragon who can take us to Spirit Forest," Romi says.

"Where do we look first?" I ask.

Honestly, we just need to get through The Dragon's Gate and find a dragon, so we don't really need to rush. As we keep walking, we see little white houses shaped like eggs with wooden spiral stairs going up to them. Bronze signs are labeled on all of them and they all say BABY DRAGON CENTER.

"Baby dragons! Let's go see!" Phoenix jumps up and down.

We make our way up to one of the white egg houses and go through. I guess you can just walk in because there's no door. Inside, women with all different colored scales rush around. Straw nests are layed out everywhere, and each one has at least five eggs in them. The eggs are perfectly round, and all of them are mint-colored with red specks.

"Can I help you?" one of the scaly women asks. She seems very annoyed.

"Uh, no, we're just looking," I say.

We head out of the egg house and keep walking. The sky is blue, but smoke fills the air. We look up. Dragons are blowing fire all through the sky and swooping around, their giant wings making wind storms.

"Whoa!" Romi says again as her dark curly hair swoops around.

"This place is so awesome!" Phoenix cries over the wind.

"Yeah! Let's see what else there is!" I holler.

We hurry past the egg houses down the golden tile road. A dark purple dragon swoops down in front of us and blows blue fire at a huge wooden basket of kernels. The kernels light up with blue fire, and popcorn sprays everywhere. Scaly people clap and cheer. Huh. I guess that's how they heat up food around here.

We walk farther. The golden tiled floor gets thinner until there's another teeny gate that we pass through. On the other side of the gate is a market with tents. Scaly people yell and advertise their items to people.

"Get your s'mores! The crispiest in town!" a man cries. There's a dragon behind his tent who scorches a paper white marshmallow into a toasty marshmallow the color of charcoal.

"How are we going to find a dragon?" Romi whispers to me. "This place is enormous!"

I put my hand on her shoulder as we keep walking. "Don't worry," I say. "We'll find one eventually." But even I know it might take a while. And we don't exactly have the time and supplies for a *while*.

"Scale clothing! The best and finest in town! Dried apples! The sour ones are half off!" People holler and wave to get our attention. A scorched carrot-looking thing flies by my head.

"Whoa," I cry, ducking. "Let's get out of here before they literally grab us!"

The three of us speed walk our way through the narrow street that's lined in tents, careful not to look like we are trying to flee.

"Hey, kids! Looking for a pet dragon? Visit the Dragon Center today!" a man with green scales cries, waving a poster of scaly people riding dragons.

Wait, what? "Hold up!" I say, backing up in front of the man. "What did you say?" I ask him.

The man shares his toothy grin. "I said the Dragon Center. People of all ages come here to get dragons for pets. Here's a poster if you want," he says, handing me a poster.

"Guys," I whisper to Phoenix and Romi. "This could really be it!"

"Sweet!" Phoenix cries.

"Where is the Dragon Center?" I ask the man.

He points to a large, completely square, silver building in the distance. "There," he says. "But be careful. You don't choose your dragon. Your dragon chooses you," the man says.

We all nod. Great. A dragon has to choose us.

"Thanks," I say as we walk on.

"Great!" Romi cries. "Hopefully, this won't be too hard."

For about an hour, we walk through the winding golden tiled street, passing tons of tents and buildings. My feet seem to scream every time I place one on the ground. We sit down against the back of a building and let our bodies rest.

"Make way! Make way! Dragon Center Arrivals coming through!" a man shouts. A pathway is formed for a chubby scaly man holding a leash. A gigantic dragon with magenta scales and smoking nostrils stomps through the market.

"Whoa!" Phoenix cries.

"Hey! It's going to the Dragon Center! Maybe we can follow it," Romi says.

We get up and casually walk near the stomping dragon and chubby man. The beast is enormous. It's taller than two story buildings. The tip of its tail has a licking flame still clinging on to it.

"Dragons are so cool," Phoenix sighs.

We follow the man and the magenta dragon through the city and out of the market, and the golden tiles of the ground disappear. Eventually we approach yet another gate. It must be the back entrance to the Dragon Center, because we see a little ways away, a long line of scaly people waiting to be chosen by dragons. The chubby man punches in a code on a little golden box attached to the gate, and the doors open. Carefully, we try to quietly slip inside with him. But, the man hears us anyway and whips around, his fat scaly belly jiggling.

"What do you think you're doing?" he snarls.

Oh great! "Um, we're sorry, sir, but, well, that line sure looks long, and it's kind of an emergency and we really need to find a dragon," Romi stammers.

The man squints at us. His eyes are tiny, like little black beads.

"I don't think so," he says. The magenta dragon flares its nostrils and gently shoves us back outside of the gate.

"Aw, come *on*!" Phoenix cries, throwing his hands up.

The man grips the dragon's leash tighter. "Those who want a dragon, must wait for a dragon!" And with that he turns on his heel and walks off, the giant dragon trudging behind.

"Ugh!" Romi cries. "We were so close!"

We really were. "Well, the line's not *too* long," I say and glance over at it. That's not exactly true. It trails out the doors and zig-zags down a set of stairs and snakes around stalls and tents. I see a woman buying sliced apples while she waits.

"Uh, nevermind," I mutter. "Wait! Can either of you remember the code?" Phoenix is a math whiz. He also has a good memory. "Phoenix?" I ask hopefully. He scrunches up his face.

"All I remember is the man punched in a two," he says. "Other than that, I've got nothing."

I throw my hands up and plop down on the ground. "There's no other way!" I cry.

Romi squeezes my shoulders. "Or maybe there is," she says, pointing to a stall down the road with a ladder leaning along the side.

Lightbulb! "Yes!" I cry.

We all hop up and dash up to the stall. A scaly, gray man who looks just about as old as time itself, practically, is counting coins but keeps having to start over. His impatient customer is tapping his foot anxiously.

"Excuse me, sir?" Phoenix asks the man.

"Huh?" The man mutters. He bumps the table with his sharp elbow, causing several coins to fall to the floor. The customer glares at the old man and stomps off. Poor guy.

"We were wondering if maybe we could use your ladder?" Phoenix asks.

"What ladder?" the man asks.

Oh, brother.

"Er . . . there's one on the side of your tent," Phoenix says.

"No there's not!" the man spits. I can see that he has no teeth, only gums. Yuck. He hobbles over to the side of his tent. "See? No ladder!" he says, waving his arms around. But there's clearly a ladder. His sight must really be bad.

"But, sir . . . "

"No LADDER!" the man screeches and hobbles back to his desk.

We trudge away from the tent. "If the man says there's no ladder, why not just take it anyway? Then there really will be no ladder!" Romi says.

I mean, we tried to be polite, and he doesn't know he has a ladder anyway, so we run over to the tent, scoop up the ladder, and hurry off back to the gate. When no one's looking, we prop up the ladder and climb up. The gate's pretty high, but the ladder's just the right height, lifting us up and over the gate. I land on the other side, and soon Romi is next to me. Phoenix kicks the ladder as he pushes off, and we hear it clatters to the ground.

This side of the gate is so pretty. The ground is made of shiny red tiles, and there are giant rock hills with glistening blue waterfalls spewing from their cracks and crevices. Little ponds litter the landscape, each full of glistening turquoise water, and trees with pink blossoms tower over the ground. In the middle is a stony staircase leading up to the silver building. There are dragons all around us, drinking from ponds, chewing on flowers, blowing wisps of fire. Scaly people stand nearby to dragons, clutching their leashes.

"Let's go before anyone sees us!" I hiss. We hide behind a tree, and when no one's looking, we make a run for it up the stone steps and to the doors of the building. The back doors to the building are super large. Phoenix tries to push one, his face turning bright red. Romi goes up and pulls on the door. It swings open easily.

"I think you're supposed to pull," Romi says flatly.

Phoenix's face goes red again as his fists ball and un-ball. "Yeah, I think I noticed, genius," he mutters.

Ugh, not this again. "Guys!" I say in a warning tone. Why are my friends fighting? We need to all get along because we are all in this together. It makes no sense. "We can't be fighting right now!" I say. "Let's just go inside and find our dragon."

But just as I am about to open the door, I feel a sharp pebble hit the back of my neck. I spin around to see five figures in black, sling shots loaded in their hands. A scaly person opens the door.

"Welcome to the Dragon Center. May I help you?" he asks.

"RUN!" all three of us shout.

Chapter Fifteen

Misty of the Dragon Gate

We quickly push past the scaly man and open up the doors. I hear him say, "What in the world is going on here?!" But we're already surging down the hall. The building is huge, except that it's designed to look just like outside. Fake grass has been put into the floor, and flower trees bloom in the corners. People walk around, holding leashes with dragons trailing behind them.

"Where do we go?" I ask.

"Uh, um, how about, upstairs?" Phoenix cries.

There's a large white spiraling staircase to the left, so we turn and climb up it. Suddenly, an alarm goes off. "Figures In Black Attack. Figures In Black Attack," a computer voice repeats. A sign on the wall upstairs says: DRAGON ROOMS. There's no ceiling, so the blue sky and clouds seep in. All around us are large stalls, each containing an indoor pond, a tree with flowers, and a huge den made of coal. Dragons of all colors and sizes sit in each stall. There are names engraved on the stall doors. As the alarm goes off, people quickly secure the locks on the stalls and set up glass walls so no one can get in. I feel another rock hit my neck and turn around to see one figure in black chasing us.

Aaaah! We scramble down the hall. All the dragons are going crazy! Fire and smoke fogs up the glass walls as roars echo throughout the halls. We find a stall door slightly ajar and without thinking scramble into it just as a scaly person secures it up. Two guards run up the stairs and chase the figure in black until their thudding footsteps get fainter and fainter. I wonder how they got into The Dragon Gate?

Whew. I wipe my brow. It's slick with sweat. We all heave and huff, our chests rising and falling rapidly.

"They keep appearing," Romi says breathlessly. "And each attack is more and more dangerous."

All we hear is our own hard breathing. Except, wait. There's one more breath from someone other than the three of us. And it's much lower and more dangerous sounding. We turn around to see a dragon with lavender scales flaring its nostrils at us. It has long black eyelashes accenting its dark brown eyes. I read the name on its door. MISTY, it says. Oh my goodness! It's Misty from Papa B's story! *The* Misty! I feel a grin spread on my face.

"Hi, Misty," I say nervously.

The dragon inches over, each step making her look more and more deadly. She towers over us. I can feel her flaming hot breath against my face. All of us cringe. Misty leans down and snorts, puffs of smoke escaping from her large nostrils and covering our faces. We all wheeze and cough. Then something weird happens. Misty opens her mouth and gives me a friendly lick on my face. Ew! It's slobbery! But hey, at least she didn't eat me! She must like me! Misty gives a little groan—it sounds like a happy groan—and curls up next to me. She could easily crush me under one of her gigantic lavender feet, but she coos and closes her eyes.

"Uh, I think you might've found your dragon," Romi says, grinning at me.

"Yeah, I think so," I laugh, letting my hand stroke her scales.

They're slick with a buttery kind of feel, but smooth and hard like metal at the same time. My heart beats fast.

"Okay, now, how do we get out of here, and get Misty to take us all the way to Spirit Forest?" I ask nervously.

Misty might be sweet now, but I don't want to see how she gets if I force her to do something she doesn't want to do. "How about we . . . feed her some trail mix?" Phoenix suggests, taking out what's left of the trail mix that Grammy gave him at our house.

Grammy.

Suddenly, my heart aches. I wish Grammy was here right now. She's always so good with animals as well. She once cared for a nest of baby birds when the mother left, and it was the sweetest. I feel sadness creep into me. No! We have a mission! Now is not the time for sadness. But, I still do miss her.

"Good idea," I murmur. I carefully pet the resting dragon. Misty opens one brown eye, then another. Her eyelashes flap like slick black butterflies. "Okay, Misty," I say, reaching for the locks. They're keyholes. Great. It's not like we have the right keys with us. I throw my head back. Now we'll have to bust through this door, and I bet Misty will get into some serious trouble—and we'll be in even worse trouble. The sirens are still wailing throughout the building, and it's causing the walls to glow red.

"We kinda need you to break through your stall doors," I say, stroking her lavender scales. Misty stares at me. Then she snorts. "We have trail mix," I say, waving the baggie in the air. It makes a shaking sound like a child's rattle. Misty seems to like the idea. Slowly, she stands up on all four legs and bends her head low. Then she rears up, and charges toward the doors. They don't budge. Misty rears up again and crashes into the doors once more. The doors give in and shatter to the ground. Luckily, the sirens and chaos are too loud to notice or hear the noise of the doors.

"Good girl!" I coo, letting Misty munch on some of the bag contents. "Okay, girl, now we just need you to take us to Spirit Forest."

Misty gazes at me. It almost feels like she understands me perfectly. Misty smacks her lips together, then, slowly bends down. Wow. I guess she really does understand me. I can't help but grin. My pen is magical, I jumped into a portal, I escaped knives and nunchucks, and now, I can control a dragon! How much more awesome can this get?

Slowly, Phoenix, Romi, and I slide onto Misty's slick back. Her scales are slightly cold, but her purple spikes are like little places to rest our backs. Misty still has a leash around her neck, so I grab hold of it.

"Um . . . okay, Misty. I don't know how to fly dragons, so you have to help me out here," I say, adjusting my legs.

Phoenix rolls out the map. "According to the map, it looks like it'll take about thirty minutes to get out of of The Dragon Gate, and then there's a bay called Blue Bay and . . . oh my goodness! We're going to pass the Jewel Kingdom!" Phoenix squeals.

Romi snaps her fingers in his face. "Focus please," she says.

"Right." The paper flutters as he moves around. Misty huffs impatiently. Suddenly, we hear faint footsteps thundering up the stairs. Uh oh.

"Come on, Phoenix!" Romi hisses.

"Okay, uh, but Spirit Forest is only about four hours away from here. It would take us days to get there without Misty," he says. "Oh! And the leaves of the Spirit Forest trees are multicolored and made of glass, so if you see that, you'll know we're there. Okay! Let's go!" Phoenix cries.

The footsteps get louder until three guards are dashing towards us. "Hey! What do you think you're doing with that dragon?" a guard cries. But Misty is already spreading her wings and flapping. Great gusts of wind shoot from her wings, knocking the guard backwards.

"We're really sorry," I yell as Misty hovers above the air. "But, well, er . . . Misty is my rightful dragon," I say. Okay, that's a lie. A big lie. But . . . technically she was my Papa B's since he, well, he *created* her. Plus, she picked me, so technically she's mine.

The guards stand up. "She belongs to you?" the guards ask.

"Yes!" I shout back.

The guards smile and skip around. "We've finally found Misty's long lost owner! Misty never lets anyone ride her, so that girl must be telling the truth!" they cry.

Wow. Okay. "You hear that, Misty? You belong to me now," I whisper into her ear. Misty snorts and bellows a happy bellow. With that, she flaps her gigantic wings and huffs and puffs until we go through the top of the ceiling-less building. And with one great heave of her wings, Misty is slicing through the air like a plane.

Oh my goodness! This is the best feeling ever! I laugh as the warm air hits my face. Below us is the landscape of The Dragon Gate. It looks super cool from up here. We see several people look up and point.

"Look, it's Misty! She has an owner!" some of them holler.

Soon, people are whooping and cheering and clapping and waving at us. I wave back. Then I let my hands let go of the leash and put them up to the sky. I can feel the dampness of the clouds! It's like touching moist cotton candy. I look behind me. Phoenix is looking around in wonder and blowing kisses to the people, and Romi looks super happy. This is probably the best moment ever, right here. Misty flaps her wings, sending us shooting through the sky, and soon we're soaring over the tops of trees. The sky's the brightest blue I have ever seen, and the clouds are super fluffy looking.

"You are such a good dragon, Misty," I whisper. Misty groans happily. I feel her body vibrate as she does so. Her giant breaths are so huge compared to mine. I feel her stomach heave in and out and it feels almost relaxing.

I suddenly feel a little droopy and I let my eyes close.

I open my eyes with a start. How long was I asleep for? I look around. No one's holding the leash, but Misty seems to know exactly where we're going. We're flying over some sort of land with blue sand and trees with silver trunks and bronze leaves. Below us is a huge bay with splashing navy water and dark rocks jutting from the ground. There's a huge rock pile surrounding the bay, and the bay itself is huge. There are trees in the water, and rocks. I see a person on a rock. She has yellow hair the color of straw. She must be a person. But then, she shifts and I get a glimpse of . . . a tail? My heart starts to ring in my ears.

"A mermaid," I whisper to myself. "Guys, look at this . . . " But Romi is all the way in the back, and seems lost in thought, and Phoenix is asleep on my shoulder with his arms slightly around my waist. I feel my body tense up. A boys never put his arms around my waist or leaned his head on my shoulder. I feel myself blush even though Phoenix is asleep. I turn my attention back to the mermaid, but she's already a ways behind us. That must've been Blue Bay! Blue Bay must have mermaids in it.

I sigh. I know it's been, like, two days since we've entered this place, but it's still so amazing and crazy to me at the same time. I mean, I'm actually seeing people and stories that Papa B and I wrote into actual living, breathing worlds! It's so crazy! And everyone here has no idea that they were either talking to their creator, or their creator's granddaughter! Phoenix lets out a little snore. And I think about how I get to experience this with my friends too.

The wind is now soft and cool as it tickles my face. Misty glides up into the clouds. The air gets thinner, but strangely I'm not affected by it. It must be because we're in a magical world. The world around us is now blanketed in fluffy clouds. The sky is a royal blue and deepening into navy, and the clouds cast purple shadows. Stars twinkle faintly above, and I almost feel as if I could just reach out and touch them. Maybe I can. I reach my fingertips up, up, up into the sky. Oh my goodness! I feel one! I look up and see that I'm actually touching a star! A star! I yank my hand away. The star is piercingly cold, yet boiling hot at the same time. Like a dry ice cube.

Misty dips down a little, her wings slicing through the clouds. She dips down more and suddenly, we're flying over a large rocky valley with a crater in the middle. The crater is huge and inside I see a huge castle and buildings. It looks like a little kingdom! Except—wait. I grab Phoenix and shake him. He yawns.

"Huh?" he mutters.

"Phoenix! It's Spindle's Chase! And the Jewel Kingdom!" I whisper.

His sleepy eyes go wide. "Where?!" he practically shouts. I point and he gasps. His eyes roll back into his head, and he goes floppy. I shake him again. Wow. He was so excited that he fainted!

"Phoenix! Look," I say. We peer down at The Jewel Kingdom. Everything is literally made either from gold or jewels. The castle itself looks like a giant golden cake, littered with rubies and emeralds and amethysts. The little towns beside it look like they're made from crystal and bronze and things. I can see tiny people made out of silver and gold. Phoenix keeps gasping.

"Breathe!" I tell at him.

He clutches my arm, and I feel my face flush. "How do I breathe again?" he gasps. I giggle.

Soon we're above clouds again, and the sky is now a deep black littered with stars. "Guess what?" I say.

"What?" Phoenix asks.

"I touched a real star while you were sleeping," I say.

Phoenix gasps again. He and I both laugh together.

CHAPTER SIXTEEN

The Recipe

Billie rubbed the large bruise on his head. He'd fallen into a tree and now had a soft purple lump on his forehead that was giving him a headache. Billie kept walking. He was in a giant forest. Yet, it wasn't any regular forest. It was almost like a glass forest. The trunks of trees were made of gray glass tubes, and the leaves were diamond and circle shaped and made of glass. The leaves were blue and magenta and chartreuse colored, and the ground was made of a thick, dry mud, almost clay. He walked for what felt like hours, the clay of the ground squishing between his bare toes. His shoes had flown off in his fall, and his clothing had ripped to shreds from the branches of the tree. Now he wore flamingo khaki shorts and a gray T-shirt. Over the shirt was a neon yellow jacket. It was a . . . different clothing combination that Billie had scraped together from his backpack, random travelers, and trades. But at least he had clothes.

Billie thought he saw a snake slide down a tree, but when he turned, it disappeared in a mist of bright green smoke. A crow swooped past his head, but when he looked up, only a spray of dark gray smoke remained. A fox brushed his leg, but when Billie looked down, he only saw a faint red mist. But Billie was not fazed. He knew this forest well. It was the Spirit Forest, holding Spirit Animals. It was a quiet and peaceful forest, and all Spirit Animals were kind. But, every person who enters the Spirit Forest has a Spirit Animal who can grant one wish.

A giraffe nibbled at Billie's hair, but when he looked up, a long thin string of thick, yellow mist remained. He shrugged and kept walking. He knew Spirit Animals liked to pick at travelers, but he knew that if he ignored them and minded his own business, they would go away. Unless it was his Spirit Animal.

Billie's pebble hit the edge of a large tree with a thump. Billie looked up and saw the thickest tree ever. It's trunk was made of gray glass and was as thick as three logs standing next to each other. The tree was as tall as three logs standing on top of each other. Blue, magenta, gray, and chartreuse diamond and circle leaves clinked and chimed as they clunked into each other in the breeze. "This will be my home," Billie found himself saying.

Over the years, Billie turned that tree into his home. He built a balcony on the top of the tree and set traps around his tree, just in case. He built a pulley system to collect water from the stream a little ways behind his tree, and he made clever tools for picking berries or collecting fish. There was also a market just outside Spirit Forest, and every Saturday, he would travel to the market and stock up on food. He dug a tunnel under his tree for a fireplace and built stairs going up to the balcony. He made a couch and a bed for himself. He draped his trunk in colored clothes of all different patterns and hung wind chimes and dream catchers from the branches of his tree. As Billie got older, he became more well-known and grew a love of collecting odd and unique things. He owned a scale from a mermaid, a jar of Spider Jam from a strange foreign market, a clam shell filled with hair gel. If it was weird and unique, Billie wanted it.

One day, when Billie was about thirty, he was sitting on his balcony, sipping from a coconut, when something took a bite from his coconut. Billie whipped around, but only a yellow mist remained. He sighed and threw the coconut over his shoulder. Spirit Animals—always so annoying and picky. Billie put his feet up on the ledge and closed his eyes, his arms supporting his head. He was quite comfortable. Something kicked his chair, and he toppled over. Billie shrieked in alarm and scrambled to his feet.

"What is going on?" he shouted to no one in particular. The yellow mist drifted away. Billie huffed and stomped on the ground once. He stomped into his house, slamming his wooden door behind him.

Another time Billie was examining some sort of eyeglasses when the eyeglasses were shot up out of his hand.

"Stop it this instant!" Billie cried, but the yellow mist drifted off. As soon as Billie turned around, something poked his head. When Billie spun around cursing, a large yellow giraffe with brown speckles towered over him, the eyeglasses sticking out of his mouth. Billie stared, astonished. *This must be my Spirit Animal*, he thought. The giraffe bent it's long neck down to Billie, and Billie took the eyeglasses from him. The giraffe licked his cheek.

"Well, hello there," Billie said.

"And hello to you," the giraffe replied. Billie jumped back, bumping his work table. He knew the Spirit Animals were smart and could grant wishes, but he didn't realize that they could talk.

"You . . . you're talking!" Billie cried.

"Why, I suppose I am. Don't you find it splendid?" The giraffe had a deep, masculine voice with a British edge to it.

"I do, I guess," Billie said.

The giraffe trotted around in a circle and lay down. "I hope you don't mind that I'll be making myself cozy in your little ... tree house," the giraffe said.

Billie's eyebrows furrowed. "Actually, yes, I do mind. Don't you have a home of your own?" Billie asked.

The giraffe guffawed like that was the funniest thing ever, "I'm a Spirit Animal! Spirit Animals don't have their own homes!" The giraffe winked at Billie.

"Oh, uh, well, I mean, if you're my Spirit Animal, then I guess you could stay. But, are you my Spirit Animal?" Billie asked.

The giraffe snorted. "Of course I am! What a ridiculous question! Spirit Animals only show themselves when they find their person. I am visible, aren't I?" The giraffe asks.

"Er ... yes," Billie said.

"Right, then! Let's start with a little introducing! Name me!" the giraffe cried.

"Excuse me?" Billie asks.

"Name me! You get to name me!" the giraffe hooted.

Billie scratched his forehead. "Well ... I'm Billie, so you'll be ... Noah," Billie decided.

The giraffe smacked his lips together. "NO-AAH. I do rather like that name. Right, then. Let's go grant your wish!"

Noah clomped out the door and into the sunshine. Billie stumbled after him. He knew how this worked. But now that it was actually happening to him, his mind was spinning and flickering to blank, and his words fumbled.

"So, how does it work? I'll just say one wish?" Billie asks. That was a stupid question, but in the moment it had flown from his lips.

Noah laughed. "Duh!" Noah clomped around in a circle. That Spirit Animal was crazy.

Billie put his hands up, "Okay, fine." He thought about it. He was already so content and wouldn't want anything more. But then, he had an ambitious thought. "Noah, I want you to give me the directions on how to make Turquoise Wood, but only let me remember how when I truly need to," Billie said.

It was a weird and crazy request, but Billie felt deep down this was what he needed to wish for.

Noah raised an eyebrow. "But why do you only want to remember it when you need to?" he asked. "I mean, it's . . . "

"Noah, because I just need to," Billie said. He didn't ever want to have to use a Portal Pen again, but if he truly ever needed to, he would remember how to make the Turquoise Wood so that he *could* make another pen.

"Okey Dokey then."

Noah heaved in a large breath and then blew a large bubble at Billie. Billie popped it and instantly, a recipe for Turquoise Wood came to his head. But just as quick as it came, the recipe disappeared, leaving Billie confused.

"Welp, that wasn't too hard," Noah breathed.

"What wasn't too hard?" Billie asked. "Did you grant my wish?"

Noah nodded. Billie shrugged. The two went back into Billie's tree house, leaving Billie wondering what he'd wished for.

CHAPTER SEVENTEEN

The Adventure Man

It's now morning. Misty soars over a pine tree forest. I get a whiff of the pine scent. Ah, I love the smell of the forest. Suddenly, there are two tall mountains coming in view. Misty swoops upwards to avoid their peaks, and soon I see that one of the mountains is covered in snow and the other is littered with cacti. Down in between the two mountains is a large cottage made from bamboo. I see little animal-looking things scurrying around. Then suddenly a thought hits me—Yeti Foots!

"Oh my gosh, it's the Yeti and BigFoot and their Yeti Foots from my story!" I cry. My breath catches in my throat.

"Oh my goodness!" Romi cries. Misty roars at the Yeti and the BigFoot, and they politely wave back. I almost faint. My Yeti and my BigFoot and my Yeti Foots just waved at me!

Soon the mountains disappear from view, and suddenly, we're soaring over trees with glass leaves. No joke! The leaves are either magenta, chartreuse, or blue. They're shaped like triangles and circles, and they're made of glass!

"Spirit Forest," Romi says.

Misty's wings flutter and her tail swishes. After she dips down into the forest, her great body lands, making the trees closest to her tremble, the glass leaves clinking and clunking against each other. Now I can see that the trunks of the trees are made from a foggy gray glass. And the ground feels like clay, kind of like mud.

"Now we just have to find the Curly Tree," I say. "Which way, Phoenix?"

Phoenix unrolls the map. "Uh, looks like we just keep going straight until we get to the Curly Tree?"

"But, how will we know if it's the Curly Tree?" Romi asks.

Good point. I rack my brain. "Um, because it'll be ... curly?" I say. Duh.

We all walk through the strange forest, with Misty thumping behind us. Misty snatches a blue circular glass leaf and chomps on it.

"Misty, no!" I scold.

Suddenly, Misty arches down and growls, her nostrils flaring and heaving out puffs of smoke. I feel a cool breeze brush against me and the faint feel of fur, but when I turn, there's only a faint purple mist clinging to the air. That was trippy.

"Oookay, um, let's just keep going," I try to sound brave, but I'm a little frightened. I feel a sharp peck on my head and look up to see a mango-colored mist drifting away.

"Hey!" Phoenix cries, grabbing his bottom. A blue mist lingers behind Phoenix.

"Watch it!" Romi karate-chops the air, but a white mist is all that's there.

"What's going on?" Phoenix whispers, but Romi and I just shrug.

Suddenly, something rams into me, flinging me into the ground. My bottom hits the ground hard and I cringe. Standing over me is a wolf the color of grass. Its teeth are bared and, let me tell you, those are some sharp teeth! I feel the wolf's hot breath.

"Nice, wolf," I say, squeezing my eyes shut and preparing for the worst.

"Oh yes, I am quite nice I suppose. I'm sorry if I scared you," a light female voice says.

I open my eyes. Wait. "Did you just talk?" I ask the wolf.

The wolf giggles and prances around in a circle, "Of course I can talk! What a ridiculous question to ask!" The wolf nuzzles me.

I gasp. "You must be my Spirit Animal!" I breathe.

Oh, this is so cool. Romi and Phoenix look around them, but no animals have appeared for them yet.

"Why isn't it working for us?" Romi asks.

Hm. I think about the pen. "Oh! Maybe it only works for the people who wrote this story? I mean, I know Papa B wrote this one, but I actually added to it some once, because I thought it was so cool," I suggest.

"Ohhh!" Phoenix and Romi nod.

"That makes sense," Phoenix says.

As he comes to pet the wolf, it looks like Romi is fuming.

"It's okay, Romi," I say. Romi's attention snaps back to me.

"What? Oh, yeah, I uh, I know that." Romi plasters on a smile. Poor Romi.

"So what's your name?" I ask the wolf.

"You're my spirit owner, so you get to name me," the wolf says.

I gasp. "Really?" I whisper. The wolf nods. "Okay . . . how about Emmie?" I say. The wolf scrunches up her nose. "Nevermind. How about . . . Ginger?" I ask.

The wolf yaps and nods. "Perfect!" she cries.

I bend down. "Okay, Ginger. Now aren't Spirit Animals supposed to grant a wish for their owner?" I ask. I recall back to when I read Papa B's story. Yeah, that seems right. Papa B sure is clever.

"That's right, Eva! Now, what will your one wish be? Choose wisely!" Ginger chirps.

I think. What do I really want? I suddenly think about Grammy. Lonely Grammy. Then I think about Papa B. I never got to meet him and neither have my parents. And it would probably be nice to know if he's alive or not.

"Okay, Ginger, I wish for you to tell me if my grandfather, Billie Mason, is still alive and living in this world!" I declare.

Ginger cocks her head at me and shrugs. She heaves in a big breath, then blows out a bubble. I have this urge to reach up and pop the bubble, and when I do, a very clear sentence forms in my head: YOUR GRANDPA IS HERE. Oh my goodness! I shriek with joy and hug Ginger's furry neck.

"Thank you, Ginger!" I cry.

"Don't thank me. It was your wish," Ginger says.

"I hate to break up the fun fest, but we have a schedule to keep," Romi says.

"Right," I say. "And now we can go find my Papa B too!"

"No," Romi winces.

"What?" I say.

"No! We came here to find your pen. No detours. We have lives of our own too, you know," Romi says, hands on her hips.

Wait, what? Ow, that stung. "What? But guys!" I say.

"Phoenix? What about you?" I ask.

Phoenix slowly shakes his head. "I don't know, Eva. We have no idea how to find him, and it could take a really long time. We can't stay here forever. Our families might start to really freak out!" he says. I slump and sit down.

But we're so close! And now that we're here, and we know he's here, we might as well go and find him! But, nooo my friends don't understand. I stand up.

"Fine," I say. "Let's just go get my pen. Ginger, do you know how to get to the Curly Tree?"

Ginger nods, "Yep!" She begins to trot but stops. "Wait, that's where the Adventure Man lives. You want to see the Adventure Man? He's practically on the very edge of sanity!" Ginger shivers. "He once asked if he could keep the eyes of the king of another kingdom. He barely escaped getting thrown in prison." Ginger shivers again.

I'm having slight regrets about going to see the Adventure Man. If he's crazy, I don't want to persuade him into giving me the Portal Pen! "Maybe we should just go . . ."

But Romi grabs my arm. "What?! We can't stop now! We're so close! Don't you dare turn around!" Romi gazes at me. Her eyes seem slightly crazed. I shake off her grip.

"Okay then," I say slowly. "Ginger, lead the way."

"If you say so," Ginger says and begins to trot deeper into the glass forest.

"We're here!" Ginger cries about thirty minutes later.

Standing in front of us is a huge, thick tree house with a wooden balcony and dream catchers dangling from the glass leaves. There are ripped pieces of colorful cloth covering all different parts of the tree and a windmill sticking crookedly out of the top of the tree, spinning rapidly in the wind. We step forward, but a net swooshes up from underneath us and pulls us into the air, curving around us until we're stuck.

"It's a trap!" Romi cries, sweat dampening her forehead.

A yellow haze fills the air around us, transforming into a tall giraffe. We all scream as his tall head peaks through the net to stare at us.

"We caught some!" The giraffe screeches in a deep, male voice that's slightly British. A couple moments later, a man with a red beard that's streaked with white soars through the tree on a zip line, screaming at the top of his lungs and holding a gnarly stick in his hand. The man is wearing a sky blue-colored pair of khaki shorts with flamingos on them, a ripped gray T-shirt, and a blindingly yellow jacket with zippers all over it. He has a belt across his chest with pins lining it and a feather earring in one ear. We all scream as he crashes into our net, crawling around it like a spider.

"We finally caught some!" he cries, a crazed look in his eye. His eyes are green with little specks of hazel. I feel like I've seen those eyes before. I feel like I know them. The man has several rings on all of his fingers and a dead snake is draped around his neck. Ginger was definitely right. The Adventure Man sure does look crazy.

The man squints. "Wait. How did little children and a dragon wind up in my trap for the figures in black?" he asks.

Misty whines and blows a puff of smoke in the man's face. The man coughs and sputters, waving his hand around to clear the smoke.

"Well, er, we didn't mean to get tangled in your trap. We're looking for the Adventure Man," Romi says.

The man hoots, his holler echoing through the forest. "That's me!" he cries, sliding down the giraffe's back and pulling a knife out of his pocket.

I feel like a man like him really shouldn't have a knife in his possession. But maybe I'm wrong. The man expertly cuts through the net, trimming knots and ties with perfection. He climbs up to the top of the net, and with a couple quick slices from the knife, the net falls apart, and we fall to the ground.

"There," the man says, dusting his hands off. He puts the knife back in his pocket. "So, children, what can I help you with?" he asks.

Now that I get a better look at him, he doesn't seem too crazy. More . . . adventurous looking. I guess that's why he's called The Adventure Man.

"Well, we think that you might have something in your possession that's very valuable, but, well, it actually belongs to me," I say.

The man guffaws and scratches his streaked beard. "Is that so?" he chuckles. "Then why was it lying out in the middle of the beach of Lovely Valley without you?"

"Well . . . it's a long story, but we fell from the sky, and it fell before we did," I say. I don't exactly want to tell The Adventure Man about a portal in the sky or exactly where we came from, but he keeps asking questions.

The man strokes his beard. "How did you fall from the sky?" Oh boy. But before I can answer, the Adventure Man hops up. "You know what? Let's go inside for some milk and cookies. Then we'll talk." Walking briskly toward his tree, he soon disappears inside his house.

The Adventure Man gives me a strange feeling. Maybe it's because he looks and acts a little odd, but it almost feels like deja vu. Like maybe I've met him before. But no way! I've never met the Adventure Man in my life. How could I have known him before?

Misty decides to take a nap and curls up in a ball outside. We walk into his house. There's a small wooden cave for the living room, and a tiny nook for the kitchen. Over in the corner is a little wall. His bedroom must be behind that wall, giving him some privacy. A nest of sticks and leaves sits in the corner by a large bamboo fireplace where the giraffe sits.

The Adventure Man leads us into the living room, where there's a lopsided bookshelf bursting at the seams with books and little objects and trinkets. A larger bookshelf sits by it, full of all different kinds of strange items. There's a wooden couch and two fluffy stools with knots and ties dangling from them. The Adventure Man plops down on one of the stools, and the three of us take the couch. Oof. For a couch made of wood, well, it's not very pleasant. It makes my body very stiff, actually.

But at least we're not sitting on the cold dirty ground. The giraffe gets up and goes into the kitchen to make milk and cookies.

"So," the Adventure Man says. "Where did we leave off?" He snaps his fingers as he remembers "Ah!" he cries. "The item of *mine* that you think is *yours*." He lets out a wheezy chuckle. I think we left off at us falling out of the sky, but I'm glad he's changed the subject. Now I don't have to explain the whole portal thing.

"What is this very special item that you've come to retrieve?" he asks. *But*, I think, *doesn't he know?* He was already talking one moment ago about finding it in the Lovely Valley. Maybe he was messing with us. He sure is strange.

"A pen," the three of us say.

The Adventure Man raises both eyebrows. He jumps up from his stool and skips over to the shelf. "Pens! I have tons of pens! Shiny pens, fat pens, skinny pens, colorful pens, broken pens . . . " He shuffles through all the hodgepodge on the shelf.

"It has wood the color of turquoise on it," I say.

The Adventure Man nods and keeps searching. Then he turns around. "Not here," he says. My heart falls. Great.

"But," the Adventure Man says, reaching one by one into his many pockets. Finally, he takes out the Portal

Pen from a pocket on his flamingo khaki shorts. My heart soars.

"Is this what you're looking for?" he says, examining it. "This was one of my recent finds. Half buried in the sand when I stumbled upon it." He takes a closer look. The keychains hanging from the top dangle and shift. Phoenix reaches out to take it, but the Adventure Man pushes his hand away.

"Too easy," he says. "I want a decent trade. This pen is so unique and beautiful. Something just as much should be traded." The Adventure Man fumbles with a keychain of a cloud. I smack my head and turn to Romi and Phoenix.

"There's always a trade, isn't there?" Phoenix grits his teeth.

"And we're so close!" I cry. We really are! After I get the Portal Pen, then, maybe we can go search for my Papa B, and then go home! Then my parents won't think that Grammy is crazy, and everything will be back to normal again.

"What do we have?" I gesture with my hand out.

"Ticktock," the Adventure Man whispers.

"We're figuring it out," Romi says. She's clearly very annoyed and aggravated. The Adventure Man is not the easiest person to deal with.

"We have . . . peanut butter crackers," Phoenix offers.

"Or . . . I brought a flashlight," Romi offers.

"I have a . . . water bottle," I sigh. Ugh. This is hopeless. Wait. "Romi! Smoke bombs! Do you have any left?" I hiss.

Romi brightens and digs around until she pulls out a pink smoke bomb. "This is my last one," she says.

"Do you think he'll like it?" Phoenix asks.

I nod. When you throw it on the ground, it explodes into a beautiful pink explosion of mist. I think he'll like it a lot. I take the smoke bomb from Romi and tap the Adventure Man on the shoulder.

"We have our trade," I say. The Adventure Man eyes the little round sack of pink in my hand.

"Oh?" he asks. "What is it? A wobbly pink blob?"

"Nope. When you throw it onto the ground, it explodes into a fog of pink. Helps confuse your enemies," I say.

The Adventure Man looks fascinated. What is it with these people and smoke bombs? He straightens up. "We have a trade," he says, handing me the Portal Pen.

I have it! In my hands! Yes! All three of us embrace and cheer in a group hug. "Thank you so much!" Romi cries. She practically hugs the Adventure Man.

"I think we'll be going now," I say happily. My cheeks hurt from grinning. Just then, the giraffe stumbles in, cups of creamy milk wobbling on his back and a plate of chocolate chip cookies swaying on his head.

"A snack?" the giraffe offers.

"Uh, no thanks, we should get going now," I say.

The Adventure Man stands up. "No, please," he says, gently but sharply. "We haven't really gotten to talk. You seem like a nice group of kids. And your wolf is very pretty," the Adventure Man says, winking at Ginger, who blushes. Her cheeks become a deeper green.

I glance at Romi and Phoenix. "How about just ten or fifteen more minutes?" I ask.

Phoenix shrugs. "Couldn't hurt. There's also cookies," he says.

Romi huffs impatiently. "Eva, there's no time. We need to . . ." I cock my head.

"No time? We're not exactly in a hurry, Romi. And we got what we came for! Come on, let's relax and eat," I say.

Romi throws her head back and sighs. "Fine," she grumbles. We sit down and take a cup of milk and a cookie. Mmm, the milk is thick and creamy, and the cookie is nice and crunchy. Just how I like them.

"So," the Adventure Man says, wiping his milk mustache. "I believe we truly haven't been formally introduced."

The Adventure Man smiles at us. His smile is super warm. I expect there to be some sort of trick or catch with a guy like him. I mean, at the first sight of him, I wanted to run for the hills. But now, I don't think he's so bad. He's just a little quirky and awkward, but hey, he *did* invite us into his home, and he *did* give us milk and cookies. No catch. Just sweetness.

And his eyes. They remind me so much of so many things, yet I can't put a finger on any one of them. It's like trying to remember a line from a movie, but you just can't remember what movie it's from. I feel like that. But why? I've never met this man before. It makes no sense. I take a sip of my milk.

"Well, outside is Misty the Dragon," I say.

The Adventure Man gasps, "From the Dragon Gate? Oh, good ol' Misty. She's such a good dragon." The Adventure Man sighs.

"And this is my Spirit Animal, Ginger," I say.

"Oh, yes! Hello, Ginger! This is my Spirit Animal, Noah. He's very kind," the Adventure Man says.

"And I'm Eva, this is Romi, and that's Phoenix," I say, pointing.

The Adventure Man nods. "Very good," he says. He puts down his cup and cookies. "Now, you do know that, the Adventure Man isn't my real name, right? Over the years, the nickname just formed. So, allow me to introduce myself with my rightful name: I'm Billie Mason."

CHAPTER EIGHTEEN

Family Reunion

My heart stops. My breath catches in my throat. Everything around me seems to pause. I feel like I'm floating. The Adventure Man and I lock eyes. Those green eyes with the hazel specks. Those are my father's eyes too. And . . . my eyes.

I see all of my family rush through the man in front of me. Especially Grammy. Oh, Grammy. I can only imagine how she would react right now. The man and I stare at each other until my heart starts beating again, and I take a deep breath.

"Papa B," I say. I feel like my words echo through the whole world. Then, everything goes to normal. My eyes fill with tears, and I rush up and squeeze the Adventure

Man tight. Romi and Phoenix gasp. I let my tears fall onto his back. The Adventure Man pulls away.

"What is going on?" he says, a confused smile pressed on his face.

My grin goes wider. "Billie Mason, I'm your grand-daughter, Eva Mason. You're my long-lost grandfather everyone thought was dead, but really, you came to your world of stories and have lived here ever since," I say.

Papa B's breath catches. He gazes at me for what seems like forever, until his eyes fill with so many tears that some escape and stream down his cheeks.

"I . . . I remember now," he whispers. I smile and laugh faintly. "I remember my best friend-but-also-ene-my, Sparrow McFully, and our pink house, and my pen, and the portal, and . . . " Papa B looks up at me. His eyes grow sad.

"Oh, how many years it's been. I just got so used to this life that I forgot," Papa B says. "And Georgia! My sweet Georgia! Your grandma. How is she?" Papa B asks.

I nod, tears filling my eyes too. "She's perfect," I whisper.

"Oh, Eva," Papa B says, embracing me in another hug. "Oh, Eva," he keeps saying. His fingers run through my hair. My grandpa. I always wanted a grandpa. And now, here he is. He and I together, creating this world.

Papa B pulls away. He taps on the Portal Pen that I'm holding. His eyes stare off. "That's the very Portal Pen that I made when I was just sixteen years old. Oh, how long it's been. I got so wrapped up in this world I didn't even recognize what it was! Does it still work?" he asks. I nod frantically.

"Yes!" I cry. "All of these other stories here that you didn't create, those are my stories." My eyes well up again. I finally get to tell my Papa B this. I feel like I'm soaring.

"So, please tell me, what is life like, you know, up there?" Papa B says.

I laugh. This all feels amazing. "Well, my Grammy, Georgia, lives in a house about an hour's drive away from our house in Colorado. My dad, your son, Gavin Mason, is married to Karen Mason and they have me and my older brother, Marty," I say.

Papa B's eyes stare off into space. "When I went into the portal, your Grammy was about to have a baby. Was Gavin Mason, your father, the baby in her belly at the time?" Papa B asks. It feels so weird, him asking these questions because usually the grandfathers are there. But he's asking his own granddaughter who his own son is. Crazy stuff.

"Yes," I say. "He was." I grin wide. This is so cool and so crazy at the same time.

"And your father. Does he have any siblings? Did Georgia ever get . . . remarried?" he asks slowly.

"No. It's just my dad. Grammy's still . . . she never married again," I say. Papa B stares at me for a long time.

"Well, if you guys need to get going soon, I'll help pack up your things."

I'm a little surprised. I want to tell Papa B that he should come with us, but he starts getting our things together. It's like he's rushing us out. I can't find the words and feel like he should offer to come, but he doesn't, so we grab our bags and Noah the giraffe takes the empty cups and the plate with crumbs on it back to the kitchen. We head out the door. Misty has a pile of triangular, glass leaves between her claws and is munching contentedly. We all wave goodbye and Romi, Phoenix, Misty, and I take off.

"I'll miss you, Eva," Ginger says. I stroke her soft, green fur.

"I'll miss you too, Ginger."

"Say my name twice if you need me," Ginger says. She licks my hands then scurries off into the glass woods, disappearing in a green mist.

I can feel Papa B's eyes on me as we walk away, until I hear his footsteps dashing up to us.

"Maybe I could come too?" he asks.

I spin around. "Wait, what?" I say.

Papa B fumbles with his words. "I mean, I've been here for such a long time, and, well, Noah is fine with it.

But I just think I need to see my family again and that I'm glad I lived here, but maybe it's time to go home. My real home," Papa B says.

I feel a smile creep onto my face and soon me and Papa B are hugging. "Of course!" I cry. "Of course you can come with us!" He's doing it! He's going to come home!

So Papa B rushes back into his house. We hear all kinds of strange noises, clanking, clattering, crashing, until he stumbles out with a giant backpack on. "All ready!" he cries.

As we walk, Phoenix asks, "What could you possibly need that big of a backpack for?"

Papa B shrugs. "Clothes, food, weapons, and some littered trinkets and collectibles. Maybe I'll even find some collectibles along the way," Papa B says excitedly. We walk farther away from the Curly Tree until it's out of sight.

"Okay, so Lovely Valley is about a two day's journey from here if we ride on Misty," Phoenix says, his finger tracing places on the map. "But once we get there, we can just write a story that will open up the portal for us and let us through. Easy peasy," Phoenix explains.

"Let's hope it's that easy," I say.

"I know a shortcut to Lovely Valley," Papa B says. "It's not on the map, but it's about a day's journey quicker."

Yay!

"Where do we go for the shortcut?" Romi asks.

"We have to go through the Spoon Kingdom. We can sleep there and finish our journey in the morning," he says, and we all climb onto Misty's scaly back. "But be careful. The people of the Spoon Kingdom love giving away food. You're fine to take a couple things, but you'll get sucked into the chaos if you stay too long."

I nod and take Misty's leash. "To the Spoon Kingdom!" I cry.

Misty flaps her great wings, making the glass trees shiver and shake. Gusts of wind whip our hair around, and Misty flaps up into the sky. Then, we take off. My stomach lurches as Misty dips and soars through the sky. We slice through wispy clouds and fly over the tops of trees. I'll never forget this feeling.

I open my eyes to see that we're flying over a large kingdom with little yellow-and-white cottages and homes scattered all around. I must have fallen asleep. Misty's back is very comfy. The sun is just beginning to set. There's no way Misty will be able to stay in this kingdom with us. She would just trample over everything.

A giant fence painted lime green surrounds the whole kingdom, which sits on the edge of a cliff dropping off to the churning sea. Luckily, the green fence blocks off the cliff too. In the center of the kingdom is a gigantic, pink cake smothered with white icing. Wait, or it is a palace? It's a palace! There's a balcony on the second layer of the cake and two large, golden doors down at the bottom. A cherry rests on top, and I can barely make out a little window in the cherry. A cake palace! Clever!

Misty begins to dip, and I grip the leash tightly. Misty swoops down and swerves. We sail over a little corn field. People with hats and tractors and wheelbarrows pluck corn stalks from the fields. Misty touches down in a patch of weeds, and we all climb off.

"Okay, Misty. Be a good girl. Come back and get us tomorrow morning, okay?" Misty nods and snorts, then turns and takes off, soaring through the air like a giant, lavender bird.

The four of us walk through the corn fields. People stop to wave hello. They especially get up and shout and wave when they see my grandpa.

"Why, if it isn't the Adventure Man himself," a man in a straw hat says. I swear, he could literally be Danny's brother. "What brings you here on this fine day?"

"We're on an adventure," Papa B says, winking at the man.

"Ah, I see. Well, the Spoon Kingdom is more than happy to offer our service and food to you," the man says.

Papa B pats him on the back, "Thank you, my friend. We appreciate it."

As we walk on, the man tips his hat and continues working. We push open a skinny, brown gate, the entrance to the kingdom. Through a narrow alleyway we walk, coming out in the middle of the town. Everything is so colorful. Most of it has tons of different shades of green, yellow, and white.

And oh, the smells! I close my eyes and let the scents fill my nostrils. I smell mushrooms, breads, soups, pastas, sauces—it's all so delicious! We've entered the market area. Every building in this part is a tiny, square-shaped room with an opening to order food. Dishes are laid out on the front of the square room, and people peek out from them, waving and smiling. Posters hang everywhere, advertising tons of different things. Food Festivals! The Ravioli Games! Make-Your-Own Macaron Class. Ooh, I would love to do that one.

"Oh boy, I've been here so many times. Everything the Spoon Kingdom cooks or bakes is so delicious. Especially the wild mushroom flatbread. You can find that anywhere, and everywhere it's spot on!" Papa B rambles.

Past the market, we walk through a part of town that's all colors of pinks, reds, yellows, and oranges. A giant statue of a strawberry rests in the center of this part of town.

"I know a place where we can stay for the night," Papa B says.

The sky is now purple, fading into dark blue. The stars begin to show their faces. We weave all through the town. Then, we enter a little, tiny town square. Everything is either white or light pink. I see a house shaped like a cupcake. Oh my goodness! There's a person watering her garden, only she's watering little caramel candies! We go up to a large, dark pink building, and Papa B knocks on the door.

A man with a super curly, black mustache and teeny, tiny glasses answers, "Welcome to the Creampuff Inn. Have you already registered?" He opens the door, and we go inside.

"Uh, no, we haven't," Papa B says.

This place is huge! A giant waterfall of what looks like fruit punch spews out of a rock wall behind the man's pink desk, and there's a cafe in the corner with white chairs and wooden tables.

"Well, then, what kind of room would you like?" the man asks. He's holding a tablet and his fingers tap the moving screen.

Papa B glances at us. "Uh, we might need two rooms," he says.

The man smiles. His teeth are perfectly straight and perfectly white. "Splendid! And if you're a traveler, which I think you are," the man winks at Papa B. "The Creampuff Inn is free for one night. So make yourselves at home!"

Romi and I sleep in one room with two large beds, and my Papa B and Phoenix sleep in the room next to us with two large beds as well. I flop down on my bed and kick my shoes off. Ah, freedom. My feet hurt so bad.

I look around to take in the room and sights. Ooh, we have a balcony! I see a paper on the nightstand next to me and pick it up. Ooh, and we get to have dinner in here! Plus, we have unlimited room service! Sweet!

After I order the Potato Marmalade Soup (which sounds gross but is actually super-duper delicious), and Romi gets the Wild Mushroom Flatbread, she and I go outside to sit on our balcony. There's a huge view of the marketplace below us. I sigh. Romi sighs.

"By this time tomorrow, we'll be home," I say.

Romi nods. "Let's hope so," she says. She takes a slice of her flatbread and takes a bite out of it.

"What do you mean? Of course, we'll be home. My grandpa said that this was a shortcut, so we're already more than halfway there." I take a sip of my soup.

Romi sighs. "I miss my family," she says.

I nod, "Me too."

After dinner, we crawl into our beds. The pillows are fluffy, the sheets are silky, and the comforter keeps me warm but not too warm. The bed is perfect.

"Good night, Romi," I say. I turn over and let my body sink into the bed.

"Good night, Eva," Romi says back.

I hear Romi turn the lamp off, and the room goes dark. Only the slight hum of the fan can be heard. It's so peaceful here. I close my eyes and instantly fall asleep.

I open my eyes and rub them. I had that scary dream again last night—with the dragon and the figures in black. I look around. The clock says it's 2:30 in the morning. But Romi's not in her bed. I throw off the covers and shuffle around. I notice a shadow outside. Romi's sitting out on the balcony with her head bent low. I see that she has a sheet of paper, and she's scribbling something down furiously. A letter to her parents maybe? Romi never writes letters to her parents. Then, I notice something that makes me gasp. She's writing with my pen. The Portal Pen! I slide open the door, my brows furrowed.

"Romi?" I ask.

Romi jumps with a jolt and immediately hides the pen. She's acting so strange. I feel a slight burst of anger. *What's she doing with my pen? Why is she hiding it from me? Why is she writing at 2:30 in the morning?*

"Oh, uh . . . hi, Eva," Romi says, smiling.

I don't smile back or return her hi. I just jump right in. "What are you doing with my pen?" I demand.

Romi laughs nervously. "I, uh . . . well, you see . . . " Romi never spits it out.

I hold out my hand. "Romi, you know my pen is magical, so why are you writing with it?" Something isn't right. What *is* she writing? I try to see, but she slams the notebook shut.

"I, uh, my pen—it ran out, so I thought maybe . . . " Romi plays with a lock of her hair. She's never gonna tell me.

"Just give me the pen and get some sleep," I say, holding out my hand. Romi stands up. She doesn't give the pen to me. She gets out of her pajamas and puts on a T-shirt and shorts. Then, she packs up her backpack and puts it on her back. Romi is being super stubborn and weird.

"Romi, give me my pen!" I demand.

My hands begin to get clammy. Something is really not right. Romi glares at me. I shiver slightly. Romi never glares at me.

"I don't think so," she says, and she runs to the balcony and jumps off the edge.

I scream, "Romi!" and run to the edge to peer over. But she isn't hurt. In fact, she's running off down the street with five figures in black by her side. *What the . . . ?* I begin to panic. Was she forced into being kidnapped? Has she gone mad? What's going on? Maybe I'm just dreaming! I rub my eyes and pinch myself. Ouch! Nope, not dreaming. I anxiously throw open my room door, sweat forming on my face. I go to the room next to me and bang on the door as hard and loud as I can. I don't care if people wake up. My friend just jumped off her hotel room balcony and ran off with a bunch of murderous people in black jumpsuits!

When no one answers the door, I bang harder. When no one answers again, I try the doorknob. It's unlocked. Those boys. I peek in the doorway. Papa B is curled up in a ball on one bed, and Phoenix is sprawled out in an odd position on the other bed. I hurry over and turn on the lamp. It illuminates the room with an orange glow, and I squint at the light.

Papa B rubs his eyes, "Eva? What's going . . . "

I freak out and start speaking way too quickly. "Romi jumped off the balcony of our hotel room and ran away with the figures in black!" I sob.

Phoenix wakes up too, rubbing his eyes.

Papa B's now sitting up straight, his eyes wide. "This isn't good," he says.

"Wait, I'll try calling her."

I pull out my phone. I haven't used it at all on this trip! Yay! There's internet connection. I dial her number and wait anxiously, biting my nails. Phoenix and Papa B quickly change into traveling clothes when I'm not looking. Romi ends the call almost immediately.

"Romi doesn't want to talk! Or did they take her phone? What's going on?" I cry.

"Does she have the Portal Pen?" Papa B asks.

I nod, still biting my nails. "I woke up in the middle of the night, and she was writing something down on the porch with my pen—and she wouldn't give it back," I say, pacing the room. "She's been acting so strange lately. It feels like she's envious of me and the pen, and she's been kind of quiet and mysterious." I bite my lip. What happened to the sweet and supportive Romi that I used to know?

Papa B goes pale. Like, ghost pale.

"Papa B, are you okay?" I ask.

He sits down on the bed and pulls out an old photograph from his backpack that's yellowed and bent at the edges. Papa B stares at the picture, and looks up at me. "Eva, what's Romi's last name?" he asks firmly.

"Smith, why?" I say. What does that matter?

Papa B furrows his eyebrows together. "What about her mom's maiden name?"

"I have no idea, Papa B."

"It starts with an M," Phoenix offers. I stare at him like it's weird he knows. "I've seen her mom's name on permission slips. She always signs the full thing. I can't think of what it is, but it starts with an M."

Papa B continues with his questions, "Eva, do you know about her grandfather?"

What? "Er . . . yes. Romi loves him a lot, but she said that he's in jail," I say and shift uncomfortably.

Papa B's eyes go wide. He stares at me. "I knew it all along," he whispers.

"Knew what?" Phoenix asks. "What does Romi's grandfather have to do with this?"

Papa B mumbles something.

"What did you say?" I ask. My stomach is twisted into a tight knot.

Papa B looks up at me. "I'd recognize her eyes anywhere," he says.

"I don't understand," I say.

"Her mom's maiden name is McFully. Isn't it, Phoenix?" he asks.

Phoenix remembers now. "Yeah! Yeah . . . that's it!"

I can't believe it. And then Papa B looks away and says, "Romi's from the McFully family."

CHAPTER NINETEEN

Trapped

I gasp. Phoenix gasps. Papa B just nods.

"But . . . but, that can't be true!" I fight the urge of letting the truth get the best of me, but I know that Papa B's right.

"I had a feeling from the moment I met Romi," Papa B says sadly. "The McFullys were cursed into being a family of bullies and tricks and betrayal—by Sparrow McFully himself, using the Portal Pen," Papa B explains.

I slump down.

"So Romi was lying to us all along?" Phoenix asks.

"Well, if she was hiding the pen from you and wouldn't give back and ran off with the people who tried to attack us, then I suppose she was lying to us all this whole time," Papa B says.

I feel tears rush to my eyes and stream down my cheeks like waterfalls. Then a sad thought hits me. "Papa B," I say. "Those figures in black. Neither of us wrote stories about figures in black, and if Romi ran off with them, and they didn't attack her, then . . . " My voice trails off.

"Romi created those figures," Phoenix finishes.

I choke on a sob. Papa B covers his mouth.

"I'm afraid you're probably right," he says.

"But . . . we've been told the figures in black have been here for a long time, so how did she create them a couple months ago?" Phoenix asks.

Suddenly, memories flash through my mind. She slept over at my house once, and I caught her snooping around in my closet where I keep my pen. Then, we got ice cream after my performance—how she fumbled with her purse in the car and changed the subject. And she wanted to get the pen instead of saving my Papa B.

"She's been stealing it from me," I whisper.

"What?" Phoenix asks.

"She's been using it for months without me knowing. Pretending to be my friend. And then, ever since we got here, she's been using us this whole time to track down the pen, acting like she's here to get it with us. But once we found it, that was her chance to take it, and we totally fell for it," I cry and tears roll down my cheeks as I talk.

Papa B nods. "Sparrow McFully himself did the same thing many years ago. I caught him trying to break into my locker several times after I told him my secret about the pen," Papa B says.

The room is suddenly thick with disappointment. "This is so my fault," I say. "I should've known. I always had a strange feeling when she was around, and it's been even worse since we've been here, but I always pushed it away. Ugh, I should've known!" I stomp the ground angrily, my face red and blotchy from crying. I probably look like a complete mess.

Papa B tries to offer some kind words, "Oh, Eva. You really couldn't have known. The McFullys are very clever, and . . . you never suspect a friend." He looks out the window like he's lost in his own memories.

"So, I'm not trying to cause more problems, but how will we get home now?" Phoenix asks.

I begin to cry again. "We can't," I whisper. "Because Romi has the Portal Pen, and the only way to get out is to use the pen." I rub my eyes.

"And if Romi's a McFully, who knows what she'll do with that power," Phoenix says.

Papa B rubs his face. "Oh no, you're right. Depending on what she writes, this world of stories could become something utterly evil," Papa B says.

I hate that word. *Evil*. It reminds me of an old hag with gnarly fingers who cackles. It also reminds me of darkness and red eyes and lots of scary things.

I stand up. "We can't let that happen!" I cry.

Phoenix stands up too, "But Eva, what can we do? She's probably writing stories to make armies of figures in black or other deadly creatures. We can't just go up and take it from her."

He and I plop down on the bed.

"This is hopeless," I mutter.

Phoenix rubs my back to comfort me. Usually I would blush or tense up, but now, I don't care anymore. He's a real friend and always there for me—and I love that about him.

Papa B stands up. "Guys?" he says.

"Yes?" I ask.

"I think," he says.

I sigh. "Papa B, it's hopeless. There's nothing we can do!" I say.

"I think that we need to make another Portal Pen," he says.

My eyes go wide. "What? We can't make another one! Isn't that impossible?" I ask.

Papa B shakes his head. "I have tons of pens at home. I just need the recipe to make Turquoise Wood and once I attach it to the pen, we have a Portal Pen," Papa B says.

"But aren't there just pieces all around, and you just have to find one?" Phoenix asks.

Papa B shakes his head again. "In the human world, there used to be pieces scattered all around because a long time ago, magic collided with our world. But the magical world separated from our world, and pieces of magic were left here in the shape of Turquoise Wood. When I was sixteen, we went on a family vacation to Mount Everest. I found the very last piece of Turquoise Wood on Mount Everest, so I used it to turn it into the Portal Pen. But in this magical world, since magic is so common, you have to do it the hard way and find the ingredients to make Turquoise Wood," Papa B explains.

"If I can just remember the recipe . . . " Papa B squeezes his eyes shut, then he opens them with a start. "I remember now!" he cries. "I remember the recipe!"

Huh? I guess he forgot it or something. Papa B claps his hands together and dances around the room.

"Quick! I need a piece of paper and a pen or pencil!" he cries.

I take out my notebook and flip to an empty page. Phoenix hands him a pencil.

"Okay, I'll write it down, and we'll go over it," Papa B says. He quickly scribbles down the ingredients. I cringe as he writes. These are going to be some tough things to get.

Ingredients for Turquoise Wood

• *All seven colors of the rainbow mane of the unicorn in Pixie Grove*

   • *A strip of leather from Captain Seaweed's jacket*

   • *Venom from Dakota the Hunter's pet, King Cobra*

   • *A turquoise Sea Flower from the mermaids of Blue Bay*

   • *A piece of wood from Tiki in the Talking Tree Trove*

   • *A bag of clouds from the Cloud King on Cloud Kingdom*

We all stare at the list.

"This is going to be a bit tricky," I say.

"Hey, if we stick together, we'll be safer," Phoenix says.

"Maybe our Spirit Animals should come too," I say. "Then we'll really be protected."

"Good idea," Papa B says. "You know what to do."

And I do. I remember what Ginger told me before I told her goodbye.

"Ginger! Ginger!" I call.

"Noah! Noah!" Papa B calls.

Within fifteen seconds, the giraffe and the wolf appear.

"Yay! You actually need our help!" Ginger howls happily. "I was worried I might not see you again!"

"Yes, now, Noah, Ginger, this is very important. We need to retrieve all six of these ingredients, and we don't exactly have a ton of time to do so—so we need you to help as much as you can, okay?" Papa B instructs.

"Aye, aye, captain!" both Spirit Animals say.

I like Papa B when he's in his commanding mode. Well, this is the only time I've seen him in his commanding mode, but I like it.

"Plus, we have Misty too," I say.

Phoenix stands up and clasps his hands together. "Alrighty then! Let's get this show on the road!"

After we pack up, we pile out of our hotel rooms and thunder down the stairs. A few people open their doors sleepily to see what the commotion is, and some of them scream when they see a green wolf and a cheddar-yellow giraffe thumping down the stairs behind us. We dash out the front doors and into the dark night. I adjust my backpack on my shoulder before we run through the sleeping kingdom, down the curvy streets, through the markets, down the alleyway.

I open the gate to the corn fields, and we pour into it. We dash through the tall corn stalks to the end where a giant, purple blob is sleeping. Yay! Misty's back! I gently wake up the enormous beast until one huge, brown eye the size of my face opens up. Her long eyelashes bat at me.

"Time to get up, sleepy head!" I sing-song. "Today is going to be one crazy day!"

Misty slowly sits up and yawns, a fireball shooting out of her mouth and barely missing our heads. She cooes at me and snorts, smoke seeping from her nostrils.

"Bend down, big girl," I say. She bends down, and we climb onto her scaly back.

"Phoenix, the map?" I ask.

Phoenix unrolls the map. "Uh, well, Dakota the Hunter lives in the Rainy Fog Forest, right?" he asks Papa B.

"Correct," he says.

"And where does Captain Seaweed sail?" Phoenix studies the map intensely, his brows furrowed.

"Usually on the west coast of the Tsunami Ocean," Papa B says.

"Okay . . . then . . . we're closest to the Blue Bay where the turquoise flower will be," Phoenix says.

I pat one of Misty's scales. "Ya hear that? Take us to Blue Bay, Misty," I say.

Misty snorts and flaps her wings. Soon, we're up in the air, sailing away from the Spoon Kingdom. The stars twinkle right above us.

"Touch a star," I say to Phoenix.

"What? Are you crazy?" he asks.

"No, I told you I touched one, remember? Now it's your turn."

Slowly, Phoenix reaches his hand up and wraps his fingers around a star. Phoenix yanks his hand back down. "Yeow! It's super cold but super hot at the same time!" he yelps.

I giggle, "Yep."

Phoenix nudges me with his elbow, and we both start laughing. Noah reaches his tall neck up and licks a star. He screams and brings his head down, his tongue hanging limply from his mouth. Ginger, Phoenix, Papa B, and I all burst out laughing. Even Misty gives a happy dragon chortle.

Soon, we're flying over the treetops. The trees whiz past us in brown and green blurs. Ginger perks her ears up.

"Shhh! I hear something!" she hisses.

We all get quiet. Misty moans, and I feel her shifting nervously. Noah stretches his long neck over the side of Misty to look down at the ground.

"Whoa! What are those?" he cries. Suddenly, a wooden arrow with a black tip barely misses Noah's neck. Noah yelps and jumps back. Ginger growls and barks while Misty screeches and flaps her wings anxiously. Another arrow shoots past Papa B, skimming his beard.

"It's the figures in black!" I scream.

Over the foggy haze of night, we can see people in all black clothing aiming arrows at us from the treetops. One aims and lets go, and I see the arrow zoom just inches away from my nose.

"Misty! You need to fly higher!" I demand. Misty wails and flaps harder. We propel up into the sky, disappearing above the clouds. I relax a little. But all of a sudden, a figure in black jumps into the air and goes above the clouds. He shoots an arrow straight at Phoenix, but Phoenix ducks. The figure in black falls back down, disappearing under the clouds. All of our eyes dart around, waiting. Misty begins to spit balls of fire down below the clouds. She peeks her head below the clouds. Then she brings her head back up and flaps her huge wings harder. We soar through the sky. Misty's flying very fast, and the cold wind from her flapping stings my face and whips around my hair. An arrow barely misses Misty's right wing.

"Come on, Misty," I whisper into her ear. "You can do this."

Misty wails and presses herself forward. She dips a little so we can see the treetops way below us. The clouds must have been super low back there. The figures in black run from treetop to treetop, but Misty zips through the sky. Phoenix clutches his map to his chest. He nervously takes a peek at it.

"Blue Bay is coming up to the left," he says. Misty snorts and tilts a little to the left. We see a huge bay surrounded by a rock wall with churning, navy water on the inside. We don't see any mermaids; they must be asleep or underwater. There's a beach that slopes upwards on the edge of the cliff, and little caves litter the side of the cliff. As we get closer, we see pearl necklaces, rings, bracelets, and all kinds of sparkly jewelry wrapped around the jagged rocks of the rock wall. It looks like a bay with jagged rocks on the top, but I wonder what lies underneath the water.

Misty swoops down into a cave just above the sand and lands. The cave is tiny, but we all fit. I feel my eyes drooping. I hadn't realized how tired I am. It makes sense. I woke up super early. Misty curls up in front of the entrance of the cave, and we all bundle up under her giant wings. I lean against Ginger, her belly slowly rising and falling. Her fur is prickly, but soft, like grass. I let my eyes close, and sleep eventually finds its way to me.

I feel something poke my cheek. Then something lifts up my foot. I squint and open my eyes. There are three teenage girls with curly locks of brightly colored hair and wide, gorgeous eyes staring at me. I jump up and scoot back. One of the girls gasps. Her bright pink locks swish as she scooches closer to me. She has on shimmering, white seashells and a starfish tucked in her hair. Her lips are green. She takes one of my fingers and locks her pinkie around mine.

"Such a weird creature . . . " she murmurs.

"Hey! Watch it!" I swat away another girl with royal blue hair, purple seashells, and red lips who tries to stick her finger in my ear. I stand up and look around. Where is everybody? When I stand , I notice the girls don't have legs. Instead, flopping tails with shimmery scales lay behind them. Mermaids!

As I walk out of the cave, the three mermaids scooch after me. The Blue Bay is so pretty during the day. The water is clear and sparkly, and the sand is nice and squishy. I see Misty staring down a turtle, Ginger trying to climb the jagged rocks, and Noah arching his long neck so he can lap up water. But I don't see Phoenix and Papa B anywhere.

"Where are my friends?" I ask.

"The other strange-leg creatures? They're relaxing in the Sea Spa," the third mermaid with yellow hair, pink lips, and gray seashells says.

"The Sea Spa? Where is it?" I ask.

"Underwater," the three of them reply.

My mouth drops open. "Underwater? How do they breathe?" I ask.

"We gave them water bubbles of course!" the blue-haired mermaid says.

"Can I have one please?" I say, wading into the water. A little fish swims around my foot, leaving a trail of tiny bubbles.

The yellow-haired mermaid opens up the shell on her necklace and pulls out a bubble. She hands it to me. I gingerly reach out and let the slippery bubble roll into my palm. "Now eat it," the yellow-haired mermaid instructs.

Eat it? I slowly open my mouth and pop the bubble inside. Then I swallow.

"Come on! We'll show you where the Sea Spa is," the pink-haired mermaid says. The three mermaids scoot up to the water and dive in, their tails flopping and slapping the water. I walk deeper into the water until it's up to my stomach. I really hope this works. I close my eyes, plug my nose, and stumble into the water. As I feel the water cover my head, I very slowly open one eye. It's blurry at first, but then my vision clears. I open the other eye and carefully unplug my nose. I take a slow, deep breath. I can breathe underwater!

Kicking my legs, I swim toward the waiting mermaids. Their tails swish repeatedly, sparkling in the sunlight. We swim deeper into the water. The rock walls go all the way down to the bottom of the sea floor. Mermaids and mermen swim around, and there's coral and kelp everywhere. We swim under a little stone bridge and down to the bottom of the floor where a little room made of coral sits.

The mermaids enter, so I swim after them. Papa B and Phoenix sit in chairs made of seaweed, sipping drinks with purple liquid in them. They both have sunglasses on, or should I say, seaglasses on. A mermaid with red hair and green seashells swims up to the two.

"More clam cakes?" she offers.

"Sure!" Phoenix pulls down his seaglasses to grab two more clam cakes. He spots me and waves, "Hey, look, Billie! It's Eva!"

Papa B pulls down his sunglasses too. "Eva!" he exclaims. "Welcome! Care to join us?"

I feel a pang of anger and impatience. We didn't come here to lie in seaweed chairs and feast on clam cakes! We came here to make another Portal Pen before Romi destroys everything!

"Actually, I do care," I say. "We didn't come here to eat clam cakes, remember?"

Phoenix takes off his seaglasses. "I know, but you were sleeping so we decided to relax for a bit," he says.

I roll my eyes. "Okay, fine," I say. Papa B and Phoenix both swim toward me. "Papa B, we need the turquoise sea flower. Do you know where it is?" I whisper.

Papa B shakes his head. "I've never come to the Blue Bay before," he says sheepishly.

I swim up to a random merman with frizzy, green hair. "Excuse me," I say. "Do you know where the turquoise sea flower is located?" I ask.

He looks at me strangely. "The turquoise sea flower? That belongs to the queen! Don't go to the palace!" he cries and swims off.

That was weird. I go up to the three teenage mermaids who have started a braid train. "Can you guys take us to the queen's palace? We need the turquoise sea flower," I say.

The mermaids gasp, "No! You can't go see the queen!" They put their hands out to stop us.

"Uh, why?" Papa B asks.

The pink-haired mermaid glances around, then whispers, "She's gone mad."

We all gasp. "What do you mean she's gone mad?" Phoenix asks.

"Yeah," I say.

"Just last night, the queen was in her chambers, charging her magic sea scepter, when all of a sudden, she just went mad! Destroyed her palace to bits with her scepter, swam up the walls, tore her *crown in half*!" the blue-haired mermaid sobbed.

"She swam out of her palace in a mad furry, and no one knows where she went. Her son, Prince Isaac, has taken over for now, but he's telling everyone to stay in their coves until all the stingrays and sharks clear the bits of the broken palace away. They've got other sea creatures searching the Blue Bay for the queen," the yellow-haired mermaid says, biting her lip.

Whoa. That's crazy. But then I get a sad feeling in my stomach. "I bet it was Romi," I say.

"Huh?" the mermaids ask.

"My friend, well, she's more of my enemy I guess now—she has a pen that has super strong powers, and she can change people and stories if she sets her mind to it. I bet she wrote a story about the queen going mad, and it came true," I say.

The mermaids gasp. "She sounds awful!" they cry.

I shrug. "Yeah, I guess so," I say. I feel so weird. Like a rock's just sitting in the pit of my stomach. I feel guilty for some reason. How come I didn't recognize that she was a McFully, and that she truly *was* trying to steal my pen? I sigh. At least I've still got Phoenix.

"Anyways, do you think she took the turquoise sea flower with her?" I ask.

The mermaids glance at one another. "The officers said she just fled, leaving everything behind. She most likely left the turquoise sea flower behind too," the pink-haired mermaid says.

"Can you take us to the palace ruins?" Phoenix asks.

The mermaids nod and swim off. We try our best to keep up with them. They swim around a field of kelp and a drop-off where the sand plummets like an underwater cliff. "Down there, at the bottom," the yellow-haired mermaid says. We all swim down. Half of the palace is still standing. It's gigantic. But the other half looks like someone threw bombs at it. The mermaids glance around nervously.

"Come on," they say. We swim into the castle. The floors are made of white marble and plants full of coral sit everywhere. There's a winding, gold staircase. The mermaids lead us up to the staircase.

"She keeps the turquoise sea flower in her chambers. The sea flower is tucked away in a little music box. Let's hope our queen didn't destroy it," the blue-haired mermaid says.

We swim to the top of the stairs, and the mermaids lead us to the left. We swim along the hall until it stops. There's no chamber, only open ocean. This was probably where the queen went mad. We see painting shattered on the floor, a coral plant tipped over, it's soil littering the floor. The roof has giant holes in it and the ground is full of cracks. We swim to the edge and look down. There's pieces of the palace swept up into a pile on the sand. We swim down.

"What do you need the flower for?" the pink-haired mermaid asks.

"To stop the girl, Romi, we were telling you about," I say.

"Ohhh," all the mermaids say in unison.

We throw bits and pieces of the palace, this way and that. I don't feel or see anything like a music box. A little while later, after going through the whole pile, my hands and arms ache.

"Anything?" I ask.

They all shake their heads. I groan. We all slump in disappointment. I hear a faint noise. It's a little muffled because of the water, but it sounds like delicate music.

"Wait, what's that?" I say.

"What's that?" everyone asks.

"The music. Don't you hear it?"

Everyone goes quiet to listen, and slowly everyone nods.

"It's the queen's music box! That's where she stores the flowers!" the yellow-haired mermaid cries.

We all remain quiet to try to locate the sound. There's a little closet with a crooked door that remains. The sound seems to be coming from inside. We all carefully swim toward the closet door, and Phoenix throws it open. Stacks of clothes topple out, and we swim out of the way. There are boxes stuffed into the closet, and

I notice the glimmer of a tiny purple box in the corner. The music is very clear now.

"That's her music box!" the pink-haired mermaid points.

I reach up and take the purple box down from the shelf at the top of the closet. Carefully, I open the lid. The music rings in my ears now. Yep. This is definitely it. Inside is a perfect little flower with turquoise petals.

"The turquoise sea flower," I grin.

We all crowd around. It's the prettiest little flower I've ever seen.

"Yay! We found it!" the three mermaids cry, swimming around in happy circles.

I turn to the them. "Thank you so much, ladies," I say.

The mermaids giggle. "We're so happy to help. Good luck!" they say.

We swim to the surface and put our heads above the water. The sunlight immediately hits us, and it's blazing hot. After crawling out of the sloshing water, we wipe the sand from our knees. My clothes are all soaking wet. But hey, we got the turquoise sea flower!

Ginger and Noah are using a knot of leaves to play ball with their noses, and Misty is cooing and snorting at a tiny crab peering up at her. We wade out of the water, dripping wet. The three mermaids appear above the water, their hair flowing around them.

"Thank you for visiting the Blue Bay!" they sing. Man, they're really good at harmonizing.

I call Ginger and Noah over, and we all climb onto Misty's back, who looks sad now because the crab grew bored and crawled off.

"Okay, Phoenix, where to next?" I ask.

Phoenix studies the map as Misty takes off. "Well, we're already near the ocean, so we might as well find Tsunami Ocean and track down Mr. Seaweed or whatever his name is," Phoenix says.

"Captain Seaweed," Papa B corrects.

Phoenix nods, "Right."

Misty cooes at us and flares her nostrils.

"We did it, Misty," I say, stroking her lavender scales. I sit the music box down in the bottom of my backpack. Misty begins to fly higher over the trees. "Next stop: Tsunami . . . " But I can't finish because an arrow with a black tip comes shooting through the sky like a rocket, slicing the clouds and stabbing Misty's left wing.

"NO!" I cry. Misty lets out a heartbreaking wail, and we plummet toward the ground. Trickles of blood leak out from where Misty was hit. We all scream as the ground gets closer to us. Despite her pain, Misty covers us with her wings before we hit the ground. Dust from the ground flies everywhere. I tremble. That was terrifying. We crawl out from under Misty's wings to see that we're surrounded by a circle of figures in black. One holds up a tiny gun and aims it at Misty.

"Don't you *dare!*" I holler, but the figure in black ignores me and pulls the trigger. A little needle with a puff of fuzz on the end hurls itself at Misty and hits her in the neck. Misty lets out a terrifying roar, causing the trees to tremble, their leaves fluttering. Then Misty goes limp, her eyes numbly open.

"No," I whisper.

I see a pair of red sneakers come up to me. "Hi, Eva," a sickening voice says.

I sob, "What happened to you? Where's Romi?" What happened to my best friend?

Romi grins down at me. "What happened to me? Well, the best thing in the world! I finally got your precious Portal Pen. Three generations of trying and failing—and finally succeeding. And it wasn't even hard! Would ya look at that!" Romi smirks at me. "Now I'll be taking the prize for myself. And no, it's not a trophy for tricking you. It's your whole entire world of stories that I want. Take them away!" Romi demands.

She spins on her heel and walks off, her dark curls bouncing on her shoulders. The figures in black surround us with a giant blanket and drape it over us. They tighten the blanket, and all of us are squeezed together. Then, we're being lifted up into the air. Ginger and Noah cling to each other. I put my head in my hands. What do we do now?

CHAPTER TWENTY

Centipede Spray

We hang out in the blanket net thing for about
two hours. Or at least I think two hours. Could be two
minutes. Or two days. All I know is that we're sitting in
the blanket net thing. Misty's still limp beside me, her
breathing very slow and very faint. I tear up. I guess I
just don't understand how someone as nice as Romi
once was can just . . . turn. Or maybe she wasn't nice in
the first place. Maybe it was just an act or something.
A facade. I sigh. It's not like it matters anymore. We're
stuck in a net, and Romi's keeping us here.

I lean against Misty's head. It's nice and cool.
Phoenix is trying to study the map while munching
on his snack mix, and Papa B is resting his head on his
knees. Ginger's curled up in the bottom and is trying to

nap, and poor Noah is trying to count to one thousand. They all look nervous. Honestly, I'm not nervous about anything right now. I don't really care about much right now. All I know is this: I'm never gonna see my family again, and I was a total klutz for thinking Romi was actually my best friend.

At some point, I feel the ground flatten out underneath us. A knife cuts through the blanket, and we quickly scoot back to avoid being sliced. The blanket falls into two halves. A figure in black silently gestures for us to come out. We slowly crawl out of the blanket. Twenty figures in black hurry over to Misty and lift her gigantic body out of the blanket net. We're in the middle of a forest, but the trees have been cut so that a giant, cylinder-shaped building can rest in the middle. The building is gray and dull. There's a giant, outdoor courtyard with huge doors. Except it's not really outdoors because there's a thick net hovering over courtyard. Probably so no creatures can fly away.

I've never seen this building before. It looks so dull and . . . sad. Romi probably made it with the Portal Pen.

The twenty figures in black heave Misty through the doors and lay her down in the courtyard. Then, they hurry out and lock the doors. More figures in black stream out from the building and grab our hands. Their grip is super strong, and I feel my circulation being cut off. They march us into the building. It's basically just a giant factory, except that there are rows upon rows of small, glass rooms.

The figures in black yank off our backpacks and hand them to other figures in black. I'm marched into a glass room, and the door is quickly shut and locked. Phoenix is put in the one beside me, and Papa B is on the other side. There's a little hole in the ceiling so we can breathe. Two figures in black grab Ginger and Noah and hold them down. I hear Ginger's yelps and barks and Noah's desperate British pleas. Banging on the doors, I kick and scream. I try everything to open those doors, but they won't budge.

I see a figure in a white lab coat hurry over to the Spirit Animals with a sharp, needle-like thing. I ram into the door, but it still doesn't budge. Hot tears roll down my cheeks. I wipe them away and try as hard as I can to get those glass doors open, but the stupid doors won't move. I look to see Phoenix kicking the doors and punching them. It's not working for him either. I turn just in time to see the figure in the white coat poke Ginger with the needle. She instantly turns into a hazy, green mist.

"NO!" I scream.

There's got to be another way. There's *got to*! The man stands up and pokes Noah's tall neck with the needle. He becomes a yellow mist within seconds. I bang on the doors, but it does nothing. There's no use and no hope. I slowly let myself slide down to the cold, hard ground and collapse in tears. I can feel Phoenix staring at me from his glass room. And of course, I had to drag my best friend into this too! And my own grandpa! And my favorite Spirit Animal friends and my favorite dragon!

I stand up. Ugh, I'm so angry! I punch the doors. I punch the walls. I yank my shoes off and throw them at the wall. I know I probably look like I'm savage or something, but do I care? Nope. I will kick and I will scream and I will throw my sneakers at the wall and I will do whatever it takes to get us out of here.

A figure in black marches up to my glass door and puts a finger to his lips. I punch the door and stick my tongue out him. I hear a banging sound and look to see Papa B banging on my door on the other side. He seems excited. He makes wide gestures with his hands and tries to mouth words to me, but I raise an eyebrow and shrug. He sighs and breathes on the glass, fogging it up. When it's foggy, he uses his finger to write, IF WE CAN JUST GET MY BAG, but the fog disappears.

He smacks his head and tries to fog it up again. I can't help but laugh. He fogs up the glass again and writes, I HAVE CENTIPEDE SPRAY IN THERE ... the fog disappears again, and he quickly re-fogs it. CENTIPEDE SPRAY CAN BREAK THROUGH ANYTHING. Then Papa B points.

In the far corner of the building is all our stuff. A figure in black sits by them, sharpening a knife. I shiver.

Would not want to be stabbed by that thing! I turn and fog up my glass wall.

I write, HOW WILL WE GET THE BAG?

Papa B slumps and writes, GOOD POINT.

We both slump. Then I hear a banging noise to my left. I turn to see Phoenix fogging up some of his glass wall. He writes, WE'LL USE TRAIL MIX.

Papa B cocks his head in confusion, but I just grin. One thing that I've learned is that Misty can sniff out trail mix from miles away. Maybe even if she's unconscious. From the large pocket of his shorts, Phoenix takes out a bag of what's left of his trail mix and starts waving it around in the air so it makes a shaking sound. He opens the bag so the smell will come out of the top.

I sit down on the floor and wait for our escape to come. But first, I write a quick, encouraging note to Phoenix: KEEP IT UP!

Someone—if it isn't the Queen of Horrible herself—waltzes over. She decides she wants to be a part of our fog-writing. Romi fogs up my glass door. HI, she writes. Oh, no way. I just glare at her. WHAT'S PEBBLES DOING? she writes.

Okay. She wants to play this game. I guess I'll play too. DOES IT REALLY MATTER TO YOU? I write.

Romi laughs. NO, IT REALLY DOESN'T. I huff and write, WHAT DO YOU WANT, MCFULLY?

Romi pauses. Or does she actually flinch? DON'T CALL ME THAT, she writes furiously.

WHY NOT? I write back.

Romi rolls her eyes. NEVERMIND, IT DOESN'T MATTER, she writes.

I swear that girl flinched when I called her McFully. I re-fog up my glass. HOW LONG HAVE YOU WANTED MY PEN FOR? I decide to write.

Romi smirks. EVER SINCE THE VERY FIRST DAY YOU SHOWED IT TO ME.

AFTER MY CREATIVE WRITING PERFORMANCE? I write.

Romi shakes her head, then writes, NO, IT WAS THE VERY FIRST TIME YOU SAW IT TOO.

The fog fades and Romi stamps her foot, then quickly fogs it up again to write: YOUR GRANDMA WAS OVER AND TOOK IT OUT TO SHOW . . .

Romi re-fogs up the glass, then writes, SHE SAID IT WAS JUST A PEN, BUT I KNEW RIGHT WHEN SHE SHOWED US THAT IT WAS THE PORTAL PEN.

Romi seems a little sad. But then she notices that I notice her sadness because she snaps out of it and smirks, BUT GUESS WHAT? NOW I HAVE THE PORTAL PEN, AND YOU'RE IN A CAGE, AND THERE'S NOTHING YOU CAN DO. She rubs off her words from the glass and walks off.

The only word left is NOTHING. It sits alone on the glass wall, surrounded by fog. Then slowly it begins to fade. *Nothing.* What a horrible word. *You're nothing; that's nothing.* Maybe the reason Sparrow tried to steal the pen wasn't just because of the curse, but because he *had* nothing. And he wanted everything. Same with Romi. But I have everything, no matter what, because I have a family who loves me and a best friend who loves me—and I love myself.

I watch the word fade away until all that's left is just the glass door again. I go up to my door and fog it up. Then I write the word EVERYTHING on it. And every time it fades, I rewrite it. Romi cocks her head at me but I ignore her. EVERYTHING, EVERYTHING, EVERYTHING.

Phoenix is now moving his hand around inside the bag of trail mix, trying to get the scent to waft out of it. The smell is not strong enough. I take out the bag of trail mix from my pocket too, opening it up to help out. Phoenix and I lock eyes. He smiles at me, and I smile back.

Everything. Everything may look like Nothing on the outside, or Nothing may look like Everything on the outside. I think Romi has Nothing on the inside, but it looks like she has Everything.

Suddenly, three frantic figures in black hurry up to Romi. Their mouths move rapidly. Romi scowls and glances my way. I keep gently shaking my bag of trail mix hoping the sound and smell will do something.

Suddenly, the ground begins to shake. Oh, *yes*. I see another figure in black hurry out of the doors, a broken leash in his hands. Oh, yes! The rumbling gets stronger and stronger. The doors burst open, shattering—and there, in all her amazing, lavender-scaled glory, stands Misty, sniffing the air. Phoenix and I grin at each other and shake the bags of trail mix around more anxiously.

Misty spots us holding the bags and licks her lips. Then she thunders toward us. She bangs into my glass room. I waggle a finger up and point to Papa B's bag. Misty tramples over to his bag, nearly squashing figures in black. I see Romi watching from afar. She looks ... sad? She watches as Misty slips the bag through my peep hole and I reach up and feed her the trail mix.

Misty climbs over to Phoenix's peep hole and eats his trail mix too.

And still, Romi seems sad and ... is that a jealous look on her face? Oh boy. Romi catches my gaze and quickly turns around and runs off.

I look questioningly at Papa B, and he writes on the glass, SHOULD BE A BROWN SPRAY BOTTLE WITH A CENTIPEDE ON IT.

I nod and quickly dig around in the bag until I find the bottle. I spray it on the glass door, and the door slowly melts. I climb over the puddle of what used to be a glass door and quickly spray Phoenix's and Papa B's door. The doors melt, and I hand the spray and his bag to Papa B. All the figures in black have fled, and Romi is nowhere to be seen. We quickly climb onto Misty.

"Wait, what about Ginger and Noah?" I ask.

Phoenix looks around. "Ginger! Ginger! Noah! Noah!" he calls. We wait. Giant puffs of green and yellow smoke appear and Ginger and Noah start to take shape. They wobble around and shake their heads.

"Whoa! That was weird!" Noah cries, his long, scrawny legs swaying back and forth. Just then, two figures in black run in, swords drawn.

"Come on!" I cry. Ginger and Noah scamper over, and we help them on. "Go, Misty!" I cry.

Misty flaps her wings, causing a gust of wind that sends the two figures in black to go tumbling backwards. She takes off and bursts through the building, metal and glass flying everywhere. I feel like we're like on a big, superhero team. You've got two thirteen-year-olds, one man who creates magical pens, a green wolf, a yellow giraffe, and a giant, lavender dragon. We're the perfect team! We all breathe happy sighs of relief.

"Still got the turquoise sea flower?" Papa B asks.

Reaching into my backpack, I open the music box and take out the little flower. I tuck it back in the music box, put the music box pack in my backpack, and zip it up.

"Yep, still got it," I say. Suddenly, a thought hits me. I turn toward Papa B and Phoenix. "You know how if you write a story with the Portal Pen, that that story comes true?" I ask. The boys nod. "Well, Romi could've easily written a story that banishes us or hurts us or things like that, but she hasn't." An idea plants in my head like a seed. "Maybe deep down, she secretly still wants to be our friend."

Phoenix stares at me. "You're right," he says.

I nod. We smile at each other before I turn around to face the land ahead of me. I rub Misty's scales. What if it is true? What if Romi really still does love us deep down?

"Okay, Phoenix, you have the map," Noah says.

"Oh! Right! Okay, so Blue Bay. Check! Now like I was saying earlier, since we're near the ocean, it would probably be best to get a piece of leather from Captain Seaweed next," Phoenix says.

"Captain Seaweed! We'll actually get to meet him!" I cry.

Papa B nods, "Yes, but we'll need to be super careful. Captain Seaweed and I are distant friends, and let me tell you, he is the most annoying and stubborn person ever. He especially loves his jacket. And his ship! Oh golly, don't get me started on his ship! He likes it clean and shiny, and if it's not, he barks at you and smacks you on the head if you don't do it right." Papa B shakes his head.

"We'll need to be super tricky with him. And please, let me do the talking," Papa B says. We nod.

Misty soars up and over a giant cliff that drops into the ocean. We sail over the sea for a while. Ginger curls up and takes a nap. I bet I have bags under my eyes. I haven't slept much or well these past few nights.

For a while, we sail over the sea. But the waves start getting bigger, more rapid, and then darker colored before large masses of soggy moss start floating around in the water and giant, black rocks begin shooting up out of it. They look like sharp, black teeth.

"There it is! The Tsunami Cruiser!" Papa B shouts. He points out to the water, and there, bobbing on the waves, is a gigantic pirate ship. It's sails are lime green with a black outline of a wave on them. It's huge. It's made of a maple-syrup-colored wood, and I can see windows down towards the bottom. There're also little holes peeking out just above the windows where they probably fire their cannons.

"Here's the thing with Captain Seaweed. He can smell fear. If you show any signs of being nervous, he'll call you out on it and sometimes will make you walk the plank," Papa B explains.

Misty circles around the ship. Some pirates look up and point.

"So, I've just learned, you have to act like you own the place, no matter what. Then, if you're intimidating, Captain Seaweed will be nicer to you," Papa B says.

Huh. That's kind of cool. "Okay," I say.

Phoenix and I glance at each other. I can only imagine how this will go. Misty swoops down and lands on a flat rock next to the ship. As soon as we climb off, Misty curls up and takes a nap. All of the crew crowds around us. Their clothing is rugged. Most of them are wearing stripes and bandanas. Every single one of them has an eye patch. Must be like a symbol or something.

"Remember: Act like you own the place," Papa B says.

So, Phoenix and I stand tall and act like we're bored. Phoenix is taller than me, and I'm pretty average, so Phoenix is the same height as some of the men. Some men are shorter than me. Then, the pirates make way for the one and only: Captain Seaweed himself. He hobbles through the crowd. He's shirtless, and a tattoo covers the left side of his chest and stomach. He has a wooden leg and a gray leather jacket. His hair is scraggly and chartreuse colored. The front of his beard is pulled into a low ponytail, and a black bandana is wrapped around the top of his head. He looks about in his late fifties. A thick black eye patch covers his right eye. His good eye is bright blue and icy. His cheekbones are very thick.

Captain Seaweed walks up to us. He's exactly my height. I stand as tall as I can. He's actually pretty short, for the leader of a bunch of pirates.

Captain Seaweed goes up to Phoenix. "You have food stuck in your teeth," he says.

Phoenix gasps and looks at me. He smiles. "Do I?" he whispers to me.

I shake my head. "I think he's joking," I whisper back.

Captain Seaweed goes up to Papa B and sucks in his breath. "My, how you've grown. Didn't you have a birthday recently? How old did you turn? One hundred?"

Captain Seaweed laughs at his own joke. His voice is thick and raspy. It makes me want him to clear his throat. Ugh, Papa B was right. He's pretty nasty.

But Papa B just laughs and shoots back with, "Says the man who turned ninety, fifty years ago."

Captain Seaweed guffaws and smacks Papa B's back. "Now, Billie, don't be bitter."

Papa B rolls his eyes.

Captain Seaweed hobbles over to me and clucks his tongue. "My, what a darling you are," he says. I feel my cheeks reddening. Captain Seaweed cocks his head. "Except . . . your hair color. It reminds me of a rotten strawberry and a rotten carrot," he says.

Ouch.

"Well, yours reminds me of dead grass that's been sitting out in the hot sun!" I blurt out. Yeesh. I need to work on my comebacks.

Captain Seaweed spins around. "Not bad!" He grins. He has a golden tooth. "But you need lots of practice."

Captain Seaweed snaps his fingers and his crew gets back to work. Some dust the steering wheel, others mop the floor, and some bring in dripping nets full of fish. The pirate grins down at Ginger, who snarls.

"What a cute puppy!" he coos. He stares up at Noah. "And . . . what is this? A yellow stick?"

Noah frowns and Captain Seaweed chuckles. He spins around and walks off. Captain Seaweed leads us into his study room. There are maps everywhere. Especially of oceans. Captain Seaweed plops down in his desk chair and pulls out a lighter and a pipe from his desk drawer.

"So!" he says, popping the edge of the pipe in his mouth and flipping on the lighter. "What can I help you with?"

Oh, boy. This is going to be tricky. Captain Seaweed takes off his jacket and lays it on the chair. He's got some serious muscles for an old guy!

"Well, it's difficult to explain, but you know the figures in black?" Papa B explains.

Captain Seaweed stands up and smacks the table, making us all jump. "Those little thieves! Stole five of my men! Tried to steal my ship! The rats! I'll catch one and I'll take my sword and I'll..."

Papa B puts his hands up. "Okay! We get it! Well, long story short, we know the person who's controlling the figures in black, and so we're making a special... concoction to stop them, and, well, one of the ingredients is a piece of leather from your jacket," Papa B explains gingerly.

Captain Seaweed sucks in a big breath and takes his cigarette out, "Oh! You want to steal my prized possession, eh?" Smoke spews from his mouth in big whisps.

Phoenix and I cough. "We're not stealing! We're trying to stop the figures in black," Papa B says.

Captain Seaweed stands up and hobbles over to Papa B. He grins at Papa B for a long time. He draws in a big breath and blows the smoke at Papa B. Papa B ducks and coughs.

"Well? What'll it be?" Papa B wheezes. Phoenix glares at Captain Seaweed. Captain Seaweed waits for Papa B to stand up. Then, he hobbles over to his jacket and takes out his sword. He slices the end of a sleeve off and rips it in half. He hobbles over to us and hands Phoenix the piece of leather. Whoa! Phoenix and I grin and high-five. That was easy! But maybe it was too easy.

"Wow, well, thanks, Captain! We best get going now," I mumble.

Captain Seaweed puts his sword out in front of us. We stop quickly to avoid being stabbed by it. "Not so fast, little mice," he growls. We spin around. I knew it was too easy. Captain Seaweed snatches back his piece of leather and sucks in his cheeks. Then, he says something that makes me gasp.

"You'll have to give me the girl if you want the leather."

Chapter Twenty-one

Dakota and Dagger

My heart pounds. I can't live with this guy! I can't become a pirate who scrubs the deck with a dirty mop and eats fish and mussels! I have a life, and a home, and a family.

"No," I hear myself say. Ginger growls at Captain Seaweed. He stuffs the leather into his pocket.

"Fine. No girl, no leather." He takes a long draw from his cigarette and blows out smoke. I feel my palms begin to collect sweat.

"I can't!" I whisper to Papa B and Phoenix.

"And we won't let you," Phoenix says. I smile.

Then, suddenly, Phoenix has his arms wrapped around me, and mine around him, and ... he's hugging me! Phoenix is hugging me. I feel his face go red and mine goes red too. We both pull away and blush.

"Aw, so cute. Now give me the girl!" Captain Seaweed barks.

Ginger leaps in front of me. "Take me instead!" she cries.

Captain Seaweed raises an eyebrow. "Maybe ... but no. Not enough," he says, spinning around in his chair.

Oh my gosh! It takes everything in me not to grab him by his scraggly chartreuse beard and smack him.

Noah steps forward. "Take me as well," he says.

Captain Seaweed's face lights up. "Okay, then!"

Papa B gasps. "No! Guys, we need you!" he cries.

"Hey, a deal's a deal," Captain Seaweed growls.

"Well, your deals are unfair!" I shoot back.

Captain Seaweed grins. "That's me!" he says. I groan.

Ginger nods at me. "We'll be okay, Eva. We promise." I look at Ginger and wrap her in a hug.

"Okay," I say. Ginger and Noah walk toward Captain Seaweed.

"Hurrah!" he cries. He hands Papa B the piece of leather and strokes Ginger's fur. I feel a large lump in my throat. "Now get off my ship! I have some animals to feed," Captain Seaweed says.

We turn and trudge off the ship. Misty's gnawing on her tail. I tuck the piece of leather into my backpack, and we slip onto Misty. We got the leather! Yay! But I don't feel as happy as I want to. We had to trade in two of our good friends for a piece of leather? That's a very unfair trade, in my opinion.

Misty soars through the sky, a nice, cool breeze tickling my face. I have this feeling like a lump of coal sitting at the bottom of my stomach. Why did I ever become friends with Romi in the first place? If I hadn't, just Phoenix and I would have been on this trip, and we would have been home already. And right now, we would be at our houses, and Phoenix would be playing Mario Kart or something, and I would be eating strawberry cream cheese sandwiches and reading my fashion magazine, and my parents would be downstairs making dinner, and Marty would be solving a Rubix cube. Everything would just be normal again. And we wouldn't be on the long haul of a trip, searching for bags of clouds and turquoise flowers and pieces of leather and things. And we wouldn't be constantly on the run from mean and silent figures in black throwing knives and metal balls with spikes and nunchucks at us!

I sigh and let myself lean against Phoenix's shoulder. Maybe I do like him. Maybe he likes me. All I know is that we are in this together, and Phoenix still sticks by my side and I stick by his like glue. I guess Romi's glue just wasn't sticky enough.

Phoenix unrolls the map. His voice sounds tired. I think we're all pretty tired. "Okay, we have the turquoise sea flower and the leather. Now what?"

There's silence. We all shrug. No one really has the energy to say anything. But Misty snorts in frustration as if to say, "Come on, guys! We gotta do this!" She soars higher and higher into the sky. After reaching the clouds, Misty keeps going higher. The air gets thinner and thinner, but it doesn't seem to affect me. There are clouds all around us. I can't see the sky at all—just big, puffy, white clouds. Misty keeps going higher and higher. How much longer of going higher?

Suddenly, a giant castle comes into view. Well, it's more of a cloud castle, so it looks all fluffy and full of clouds—so not too much of a castle. Whoa!

"I guess Misty decided to take us to get the bag of clouds next!" Papa B says.

Misty snorts happily in reply. There's literally no ground, nor sky. Everything is clouds. Misty lands on a thick-looking cloud, and we all slide off. I very carefully step onto a cloud. It jiggles slightly, but it almost feels like walking on gelatin. We all gingerly walk over to the castle. As I raise my fist up to knock, the puffy doors disappear. They just disappear!

"Um, okay," I laugh. That was weird. We cautiously step inside. Clouds, clouds, clouds galore. I don't know any other way to say it. And look! There's actually cloud servants and cloud butlers and cloud maids! We walk up to a cloud servant girl using a cloud mop to scrub the cloud floor.

"Excuse me," I say.

The servant girl looks up. She looks a little like a snowman, and what I think is her hair floats around her like a puddle of foam. "Yes?" she asks. Her voice is scratchy and hollow.

"Uh, hi, we're looking for the Cloud King?" I say.

The servant girl frowns. "You mean Cloud Council?" she asks.

Huh? "Er, who's the authority here?" I ask.

The servant girl huffs. "The Cloud King stepped down from his throne after we kept getting attacked daily by figures in black. He summoned a group of five wise cloud men to help him run the district. Now they're the Cloud Council," the girl says. Her voice sounds very dry, and I almost want to offer her a glass of water. I bet it'll probably cause her to dissolve or something, though.

"Okay, then, where can we find the Cloud Council?" I ask.

The girl gives me an icy glare. Sheesh! Talk about attitude. If looks could kill I'd be a goner by now. The girl's got some major attitude problems! "They're in the Skyward Institution Hall," she rasps.

I look around curiously. "If this is a castle, and the Cloud King isn't the Cloud King anymore, why is the castle still here? Why are you keeping it up?" I ask.

The servant rolls her eyes and throws her mop on the ground, which literally evaporates into the cloud floor underneath her. "After the figures in black attacked the castle, we figured the Cloud Council should find a hiding spot. The castle holds all of our traps for the figures in black, but it's mainly our entrance to the Cloud Kingdom, but other than that, it's just for looks." The girl grabs a clump of cloud from the floor and suddenly the mop is in her hands again. "Now go away! This floor won't clean itself," she grumbles.

"Talk about a cranky pants," Phoenix mutters. I nod. Yes! Except, wait. I spin around.

"If we just need a bag of clouds, can't we just go and take them? We don't need the *Cloud Council* to grant our permission! A few clumps of stolen clouds can't hurt," I say. Phoenix and Papa B nod.

"Sure! Why not?" Papa B says.

"Okay, quick! Open up my backpack and start scooping up some clouds from the floor!" Phoenix and

Papa B bend over. A cloud servant boy sees and scurries over.

"Wait! You can't ... "

But it's too late. Papa B has already shoved pieces of cloud in my backpack. Suddenly, the ground begins to shake. Everyone pauses from working and stares at us. Bits of clouds fall from the walls and dissolve into the ground. Bits of the ground begin to fall too. Cloud servants scream as they fall through. Six cloud men in flowing, blue robes that look like rippling waterfalls rush into the room and stare at us in horror.

"What have you *done*?" one cries.

"We're sorry! We didn't mean to cause any ... " I say.

But the floor evaporates under the Cloud Council, and they plummet into the sky. The servant boy is clinging to a pillar.

"What's going on? I thought these clouds were sturdy!" I cry to the boy.

"They were until we were cursed!" he yells back.

The roof starts to collapse. I scream, but it just bumps off of me like balloons since it's made of clouds.

"What do you mean, *cursed*?" I cry.

"If anyone tries to steal any clouds, our whole kingdom collapses!" the servant answers.

I feel my stomach do a flip-flop. "It's Romi," I whisper to myself. "She knows what we're doing. She's turning the whole world on us and is using the Portal Pen to curse everyone we visit!" But my words are heard by no one and disappear into my screams as the floor underneath me disappears and I drop. My stomach lurches, and I scream as my limbs flail through the air. Phoenix and Papa B are falling beside me. All around us, clouds and cloud objects sail through the air. One thought is running through my head this whole time: *How could she? How could she?*

The world of clouds disappears, and I can now see that we're falling toward the ground. We're also plummeting toward very sharp mountain peaks. I scream harder. Phoenix screams. Papa B screams. Every cloud person around us screams. Screams echo through the thin air, bouncing across the sky. Of course, no one but ourselves can hear. The mountain peaks are getting closer now. They look pretty sharp. I cringe, close my eyes, and wait for the worst.

Suddenly, I hear a swooping noise. Then, a giant, lavender dragon bursts through the clouds and swoops down. We land on her back, and I clutch her tightly, never daring to let go. Papa B clutches me, and Phoenix clutches Papa B. All around us, the poor people of the Cloud Kingdom are falling through the sky. Some hit the mountain peaks and dissolve. We manage to save quite a few, but we can't save all of them. We save six servant boys and four servant girls, a cloud dog, a cloud janitor, three little cloud babies, and two butlers. We save three out of six of the Cloud Council, not including the king. It's literally raining cloud people. They all hit the mountain peaks, which stab them like knives before they dissolve. I have to look away—we're part of what caused this to happen. Romi set up the curse, but we put it in action. We made the giant kingdom collapse. I feel all the emotions except happiness. Anger. Fear. Sadness. Fury. Disappointment. All of the above.

"Come on, Misty," I say, patting the dragon's back. "Let's get out of here." Misty glides over the mountain peaks and down to the ground. We land in a jungle with thick leaves. Mangoes and berries lie nestled behind the leaves. There are little bamboo houses over in the distance out in a patch of sand. We help all the cloud passengers we'd gathered off Misty's back.

"We're disappointed in you, but thank you for trying to save us. You didn't know the effects of your actions," one of the Cloud Council members says.

We aren't sure what to say. "You're welcome" feels awkward. Together, all the cloud people bustle into the jungle in a tight group, walking toward the bamboo houses. I feel so bad. My stomach feels like I've swallowed rocks that are building up inside me. Guilt after guilt. I keep trying to tell myself: *This is Romi's destruction. This is Romi's destruction.* But I was the one who triggered it. Man. One little mistake here can perish an entire kingdom, can't it?

I feel like my lungs are full of cold water. I slump down on the ground and pick at a weed that's sticking out of the ground. *Poor little weed, you have yet to face the evil and shame of this dreaded world,* I think.

"Hey, at least we got three out of six items," Papa B says, holding out a piece of cloud. It looks like white cotton candy. Cotton candy. Grammy and my parents used to buy me cotton candy all the time at the fair, and we'd sit on a bench and share it together. All of us. I quickly burst into tears. Papa B and Phoenix rush over and wrap me in hugs. I'm so tired. And I'm so depressed. I want Romi to be a normal friend. I want my Grammy. I want my sweet brother, Marty. I want my loving parents. I want to go home. I want to smash the Portal Pen into a million pieces and then dump them in the trash and dump the trash into the fire.

I wipe my eyes, but it doesn't stop the flow of tears. "I just want all of this to be over!" I sob.

"Me too," Papa B whispers.

"Me too," Phoenix says as he rubs my back.

"But, hey, once we get back, we can make new memories, and you can show me everything," Papa B says.

"But what if we don't get home? What if Romi takes over, and we fail!" I cry. My emotions are bubbling inside me like a rapidly boiling pot of water. And they're all exploding. I stomp the ground.

"No, Eva, don't say that," Papa B says. I kick a tree trunk.

"What if we're failures?" I screech. I snatch a fat leaf from the tree and rip it in half. "No, wait! We *are* failures! We're total failures!" I sob. My tears are big and fat, dripping down my neck and dampening my shirt.

"Eva, don't," Papa B says. But I don't listen.

"We stole a dragon! We stole from mermaids! We lost our Spirit Animals to get a stupid piece of leather. We caused an entire kingdom to collapse!" I cry. "And Romi's still winning. Look at us! We're failures!" I kick the poor tree again. Little perfect pink berries fall to the ground. I stomp on the berries. Papa B grabs my shoulders, spins me around, and shakes me until my head hurts.

"Eva Mason! You shut your angry mouth right now!" Papa B cries. His eyes are watery too.

I go quiet. My angry, bubbling thoughts calm. Phoenix hands me a water bottle, and I dump the water onto my face. It drips over my arms and down my shirt. I feel my temperature cool off a bit. "I don't wanna hear those nasty words come out of your mouth again! Understand?!" Papa B cries, shaking my shoulders again.

I shrug. "But we just destroyed that innocent kingdom," I say.

Papa B stares into my eyes. His eyes make my heart tighten. "For a good cause that's fighting the evil! We're not failures! We're saving this world, Eva! Don't you understand that? Romi McFully caused all this. Evil wants you to fail. Evil wants you to be angry. But I won't have it. Not on my watch." Papa B lets go of my shoulders.

"It was a horrible thing, but we didn't mean it to happen. And we can't give up now. We're gonna get back on that dragon, and we're gonna go get those last three items!" Papa B cries.

I look up. "Okay," I sniff. "I'm sorry."

Papa B leans down and puts his hand on my cheek. "Oh, Eva, don't ever be sorry for doing the right thing," he whispers back. He stands up. "Things look bad now, but we're stopping a bigger evil. And we *are* gonna go make the second Portal Pen, and we *are* gonna stop Romi! Now who's with me?" Papa B cries.

"I am!" Phoenix shouts.

"Me too," I say. I wipe my tears away and rub my face. I still have rocks sitting at the bottom of my stomach, but we have a mission that we're on, and I won't let the rocks—and my fears—get in the way.

I look up into the sky. There are still falling cloud people. Maybe we can save a couple more. "Misty! Go up there and save as many cloud people as you can!" I instruct. Misty snorts and flies off.

"Okay, Phoenix, where to now?" Papa B asks, taking off his backpack and stretching his back.

Phoenix stares at the map. "Well . . . whoa! The map is almost completely covered in black scribbles!" Phoenix cries. We get up and crowd around the map. Then, a thought hits me.

"Guys. The black scribbles are probably Romi's armies expanding all over this world!" I say.

"You're probably right," Phoenix says.

"This is no good," Papa B exclaims, pacing. "They're crawling over this world like bugs! Two thirteen-year-olds and an old man won't be able to move as fast as thousands of trained figures in black with swords!" Papa B wipes his brow.

"Well, then we need to get a move on!" I say.

"Phoenix, where to next?" I ask.

Phoenix's finger moves around the map, his brows furrowing as he concentrates. "Well, if we're here . . . and that's here too . . . then we're closest to Rainy Fog Jungle!" Phoenix says, pointing to the jungle right in front of us. Perfect! "Come on, let's go," Phoenix says, stuffing the map into his backpack.

We walk through the giant jungle. Tall trees with vines crawling up their dark trunks are scattered all around us. The ground is mushy, but soft like moss, and the sky is barely visible because the treetops are so large and so close together. There are weird-looking plants growing about. One plant in particular is pink with spiky leaves that seem to have an electric pulse. I watch as a fly darts into the plant and is immediately electrocuted. We walk faster.

"Okay guys," Papa B says as we notice a set of swirly-looking, blue vines curl around a bug and choke it. Ick! This place is freaky! "Now, I've been to this jungle many times, and I basically know it like the back of my hand."

Papa B steps over a particular patch of moss on the ground. We decide to follow his gesture. Phoenix bumps the patch of moss before he steps over, and the moss opens up into what looks like a large, gaping mouth with hundreds of layers of teeth. I scream and put a hand to my heart to steady it. I stay very close to Phoenix and Papa B.

"In my story, this jungle is the most dangerous jungle in the world. Trees can stomp on you, plants can devour you, or like you just saw, the ground can even swallow you whole." A purple plant with polka dots hisses at us, it's blue tongue slurping the air. I gulp.

"Yeah, no kidding," I mutter.

Papa B turns around. "But if you know where to put your feet, and you know what not to touch and what not to eat, you'll be fine. But anyway, the Rainy Fog Jungle is home to the fierce warrior woman, Dakota the Hunter. She lives nowhere and everywhere at the same time. She'll pop up at any time that she likes. But Dakota is very competitive and intense. She always carries around tiny daggers."

I feel my body shiver. My eyes nervously dart around. She could be anywhere. Anything could be anywhere.

"But," Papa B says, kicking a plant shaped like a sphere that tries to chomp into his leg, "That's not even the worst part." Oh, great! What could be worse? "Dakota is accompanied by Dagger himself, the largest and most poisonous snake in the world. Plus, he's also immune to his own poison and other creatures' poisons. He has two razor-sharp fangs that are so sharp—filled with venom so dangerous—that if he were to tap you with one of his fangs, you would die almost immediately."

I clutch Phoenix's arm and don't let go. I'm suddenly very light-headed. My knees are super wobbly, and my eyes can't stop darting around. My heart's beating so fast I feel like it might explode. Fear fills up my body as fast as water filling up a cup. I try to take deep breaths. My stomach begins to grumble. And it's not a hungry grumble. Oh, boy! I let go of Phoenix's poor arm and stumble over to a tree. I let it out into a bush behind the tree so no one can see me. Papa B gasps and poor Phoenix is trying to be sympathetic and supportive but look away at the same time. Ugh, I feel horrible. I throw up all over the poor plant. I quickly grab a leaf that looks completely normal, and wipe my mouth off. Oh, man.

I take a water bottle and pour some into my mouth. I swish it around and spit it out. I shakily straighten up and wobble over to Papa B and Phoenix.

"Eva!" they cry in horror.

"Sorry," I croak, still clutching my stomach. "I have a thing where I puke when I'm nervous, scared, over-whelmed, or under pressure," I say. "And all the things you were describing sound utterly terrible." I wipe my overheated forehead and grab a water bottle from my bag and dump it all over me. Ah, it feels so good.

Papa B comes over to hug me. "Oh, Eva, I'm so sor-ry," he says. He pulls away. "I had no idea."

I shake my head. "It's fine. I'm okay now," I say, taking a swig of the rest of the water in the water bottle.

"But please, you don't need to worry. I've been through this place practically a hundred times. I know every deadly plant, every trap, every step, every turn, and every single one of Dakota's battle moves," Papa B says proudly. I nod and wipe my forehead again.

"Let's keep going," I whisper. Phoenix gentle grabs a hold of my arm for balance and we keep on walking.

"So, if we need the venom from Dagger—without dying and all—how do we get it?" Phoenix asks.

"That's the part I don't know," Papa B says.

"Oh my gosh!" I cry, throwing my hands up. "I thought you knew everything about this place?"

Papa B spins around. "I do! Just not how to get venom from the most dangerous snake in the world!" he cries.

I smack my forehead. Gee, I feel really safe now. "Where exactly are we going?" I ask.

"I don't know! We're going to find Dakota and Dagger!" Papa B cries.

I huff.

"Maybe we should be a little bit more prepared," Phoenix says gently.

"What do you mean, son?" Papa B cries.

"Well, I don't think we should find Dakota and Dagger yet. Since they're both deadly and dangerous, I think we need to be ready and prepared. Not walk through the forest, exposed and vulnerable," Phoenix explains.

I nod. "Yeah, we need to be battle-ready," I say.

Papa B nods. "You're right," he says. "But where should we go? And what weapons should we use?"

Phoenix taps his chin. "I took a quiz online about living in the wild and making weapons out of your sur-roundings, and I got all the questions right. Maybe I can use that now . . . "

He begins to pace. A mosquito flutters onto my arm, and I smack it, leaving a splatter of blood. Gross.

"I think we need to build a place at the tops of trees. That way we can see everything below us and aim downwards," Phoenix says.

"Perfect!" Papa B claps his hands together.

"We'll also need bamboo to create shields. Just in case," Phoenix says, pointing to a patch of bamboo.

I like Phoenix in action. I'm glad *someone* knows what they're doing.

"And for weapons, we'll need poisonous berries, sharp rocks and sticks, and does anyone have any string?" Phoenix asks.

Papa B raises his hand. "I have spider silk. It's very thick and doesn't snap," he says.

Phoenix points at him. "Perfect!" he cries.

"Eva, you and me will collect bamboo and sharp sticks and rocks, and Billie, you'll climb a tree and make sure to find a flat treetop that's easy to see the ground from," Phoenix instructs. "Then we'll go from there."

The three of us scatter. Papa begins to climb a tree and expertly swoops onto the top. Phoenix and I hurry over to the bamboo patch where Phoenix begins cutting bamboo with his knife.

"Are you okay, Eva?" Phoenix asks suddenly. Phoenix begins making a pile of chopped bamboo, so I unzip my backpack and begin to put the bamboo into it.

"What do you mean?" I ask.

Phoenix cuts another bamboo stalk. "I mean that you just seem very tired and nervous and frazzled, and not to mention, that incident back there," Phoenix says, his cheeks going red.

My cheeks burn red too, and I look away. "Yeah," I say. "It's just a lot to take in and I've just been really ... scared," I say. "Because we barely survive every time those figures in black attack us, and with Papa B explaining the dangers of this jungle and everything ... "

I sigh and dump more bamboo into my backpack. And suddenly, Phoenix is hugging me. He's nice and gentle, but it's a firm hug too. I feel myself hugging him back. I close my eyes and smile. Phoenix pulls away. I blush.

"I've been super nervous too, but I'm not nervous anymore because I've got my best friend by my side," he says.

I feel my eyes tear up. "Aw, Phoenix," I say.

He smiles at me. Then he helps me put the rest of the chopped bamboo into my backpack, and we get up and start walking. I feel like Phoenix has gotten braver and more mature ever since Romi turned. He's always been kind of goofy. But now, he's making a battle plan and he's taking the lead—he's really starting to show his true self.

We hear shouting and look up to see Papa B waving at us from a tall treetop. "Throw me the backpack and climb up!" he shouts. Phoenix swings the backpack up to Papa B, and he snatches it out of the air. "Be careful of the tree next to this one. There's poisonous poison ivy on it!" he yells.

Good to know. We begin to climb up the tree. The bark is rough, and my knees rub against it, giving me burns. I quickly scramble up the tree, and Papa B helps me onto the soft leaves of the treetop. Phoenix climbs up behind us.

"This tree is perfect," Phoenix says. It really is. We can see the whole jungle from here—lots of colorful plants and weird-looking animals. And there's a swamp with . . . eyes? I shiver.

"Okay, Billie, you help Eva with the bamboo shields. I'll make the weapons," Phoenix says.

Papa B hands Phoenix the spider silk, and Phoenix begins cutting the silk with his knife. He then sharpens sticks until they have pointy edges.

"Oh! Does anyone have any type of glue so we can glue the bamboo together?" I ask.

Papa B reaches into his backpack and pulls out a pink gel. "Starfish gel. The stickiest gel I've ever used," Papa B says.

"Wow, Papa B, you have everything," I say, unscrewing the lid and dipping my fingers into the goopy substance.

"Hey, I like to come prepared," he says. "And I've just been collecting different things for so many years." I smear the goop on the side of a bamboo stick and squish another bamboo stick to the other side. I try to pull them apart. "It's like cement!" I say. Papa B nods eagerly. Meanwhile, Phoenix has finished sharpening a rock so that the end is nice and sharp. He takes a stick and slathers some starfish gel onto the rock, then mushes the rock onto the stick. He then takes a piece of spider silk and begins to tie a knot onto the rock and stick.

"That's really clever, Phoenix," Papa B says.

Phoenix grins. "Thanks," he says.

After twenty minutes of slathering starfish gel, sharpening, tying, cutting, and pasting, Papa B and I have finished making three thick, stiff bamboo shields, and Phoenix has made six spears using rocks and sticks.

"Look at this teamwork!" Papa B cries. We all high-five together.

"Okay, next step. We need to be able to see them coming. Billie, do you have any binoculars?" Phoenix asks. Papa B nods and reaches into his backpack.

"Here you go," he says, handing them to Phoenix.

"Thanks!"

Phoenix puts them up to his eyes and peers into them. I sit back against the soft cushion of leaves from the tree and put my hands behind my back. The sky is blue and the sun is shining bright. It's really hot up here with the sun beating down on us, but I like this view. It's nice. And it's safe.

"Wanna look?" Phoenix asks, handing the binoculars to me. I scan the jungle. There's a cheetah crouching in the leaves and staring at a little frog-creature thing. I take my eyes off them just as the cheetah pounces. Poor little frog-creature thing. I hand the binoculars to Papa B, and he takes a look too.

"So, how exactly are we going to get poison from one of Dagger's fangs?" I ask Phoenix. He seemed very determined on the weapons, so I assume he must have some sort of plan.

"Well," Phoenix sighs. "If he's immune to poison, we might have to throw spears at him," Phoenix says. Papa B puts down the binoculars and turns to look at Phoenix. "Dagger is a tricky snake. But you're right. Poison doesn't do anything since he's full of it, but stabbing him with sharp edges might just work," Papa B says.

"Then, once he's unconscious, we'll get the poison and go," I finish off.

"But we need a bottle to hold it," I say.

Papa B takes out a teeny glass vial. "We have to be very careful though. We can fill the vial all the way up, but the recipe only calls for four drops of venom. However, Dagger never dies," Papa B says. My mouth drops open.

"What?" I cry.

"His poison refills itself so he never dies. His poison's what keeps him alive. Even though Dagger is gigantic and dangerous, he's still a beloved character to me, and I would never want him to go away," Papa B says. Holy cow. That's crazy. "So, as soon as we get the venom, we have to bolt. He'll wake up within thirty seconds," Papa B says.

I gulp. Oh, boy. "But wait. What about Dakota?" I ask.

Papa B taps his chin. "She's tricky too. But she's vulnerable when she's distracted. I've learned that Dakota is fierce, but she can get carried away very fast," Papa B explains, digging out a ball that's magenta and covered in glitter. "But this bad boy should keep her occupied for a little while. It'll be just enough time to get the venom." Papa B rubs his hands together. "If we tug our strings just right, this should be easy. But nothing's ever easy when it comes to venom and knives."

We all gulp at the same time. "Oh! And also, Dagger can *shoot* his venom at you," Papa B says matter-of-factly.

"What?!" Phoenix and I cry.

Papa B puts his hands up. "Children, I'm just going to warn you—if one of you gets hit by poison, help the other out. I have a medicine that cures it. The ladies of Lovely Valley gave it to me. It's called Sucker Juice.

It can suck out all the poison from your body within seconds. But if I don't get it to you in time, well . . . "

I choke on a sob. "Don't finish the sentence, Papa B," I say, hating the thought of that happening to one of us. I turn to face the jungle. I don't want them seeing my tears. I've cried too much already.

As I stare over at the landscape, something catches my eye. Something big. A huge, thick substance curls around trees, knocking them down. It has spots on it, and animals peep in fear and scurry off as it comes closer. I hear an awful rattling noise. And suddenly, there's a giant head, slithering through the forest. It's mouth is open, and I can clearly see two, stunningly sharp fangs with liquid the color of cranberry juice dripping from the tips. Its eyes look like shiny, black beads. I want to faint.

"There . . . there . . . there's D-Dagger," I stammer, feeling as light as a balloon.

I'd rather just jump into his snake mouth and die than face or fight this enormous poisonous snake. His large body bends trees and snaps sticks as he slides through the jungle. Suddenly, I see a woman about late thirties maybe, swooping through the trees. Her skin has been baked by the sun and is a deep sandy-tan color like bronze, and her hair is short and curly with a deep red color. She wears a dress made from zebra fur that goes down to her knees. She wears brown boots that are tearing at the seams, and her dress looks ripped at the bottom. Her face is covered in dirt and her eyes are wild like a lion's.

Dakota the Hunter.

She swings onto the giant snake's back and crouches down on all fours like an animal. Then, she scans the sky and growls. Wow. She really is a wild human.

We quickly duck. Technically, we're supposed to be trying to get her attention, but . . . well . . . it's just that she's a wild, crazy jungle woman riding a snake bigger than three skyscrapers! My heart pounds. I bet Phoenix's and Papa B's hearts are pounding too.

"When do we attack?" Phoenix whispers.

He's already clutching a spear in his hand and waiting to throw it. We glance at each other and look back at the snake. But Dakota's gone. We scan the jungle for the wild woman, but all we see is the snake. Then, our tree is suddenly rattling. I get a terrifying feeling in me. The rustling gets closer. Then it stops.

Phew.

Until Dakota pops through the leaves and grins at us. We scream and scoot back.

"Ah, think you can run from me, eh?" Her voice is dripping with an Italian-sounding accent, and it's very deep. Her eyes are bright hazel. She lifts a leg up onto the tree, then another, until she's upside down. She swings her arms until she swings up onto our tree. She crouches down low and takes out a dagger. Oh, my gosh.

Oh my gosh. She crawls toward us like a spider. Her eyes have a savage look on them.

"You know, you would make a fine dinner for my pet," she says. Her voice seems to tickle my ears. It's very creepy but deep and intriguing as well.

"Hello, Dakota. Uh, how pretty you are today," Papa B says. I see out of the corner of my eye, his hand slowly reaching into his backpack. Dakota cocks her head and growls.

"Am I not pretty every day?" She brings the dagger up to Papa B's neck, it's sharp point poking into his skin. "Or am I only pretty today?" she asks. Her voice is almost like what animals' voices would sound like in human form. When she talks, it sounds like a tiger, viciously purring to lure you into their deadly trap. I stop breathing. I want to strangle her, but I know how it'll end if I do.

"Uh, no! Of course not!" Papa B cries. "You *are* pretty every day!"

Dakota smiles and takes the dagger away from his neck. "I am very pretty, aren't I?" She purrs, fluffing her dirty hair. All of us nod and gulp. Dakota shrugs. "But, you'll still make a delicious dinner for my pet," she snarls, her grin widening. She grabs Phoenix by the collar and begins to drag him to the edge of the tree.

"Don't you dare!" I scream. I immediately cover my mouth.

Dakota's head turns to me, and she cocks her head like an owl. "Why not?" she coos.

"Because! He's my best friend! Just like Dagger is your best friend!" I cry.

Dakota giggles. "Dagger is not my best friend. He is my pet. And now my pet is hungry. So I will feed *your* best friend to *my pet*."

Dakota's fingers begin to let go of Phoenix, one by one. Dagger is below, his giant mouth wide open, saliva dripping from it and his tongue eagerly licking the air.

"Please!" I scream. But just as Dakota completely lets go of Phoenix, a ball with sparkles flies through the air. Dakota looks up, and her tongue hangs out like a dog. She cocks her head to the side and leaps after the ball. I turn just in time to see Phoenix plummeting toward the ground, his face ghost white. I immediately scramble to the edge and grab Phoenix's hand. He dangles from the edge of the tree. Tears stream down my face. But they're happy tears. That was a close one.

"Help me!" I call to Papa B. Together, we lift Phoenix up onto the tree, and he hugs both of us.

"You saved my life!" he cries, happy tears rolling down his cheeks too.

Papa B claps his hands. "Come on! There's no time to lose!" He grabs a spear and chucks it at the giant snake. It sails into Dagger's side and Dagger hisses wildly, writhing around in pain. Dakota, meanwhile, is leaping from tree to tree, chasing the ball and running off farther and farther away from us. Score!

"Hustle! Hustle!" Papa B cries.

He's already sliding down the tree. We slide down after him. Dagger squirms like a worm on a hook, the spear dangling from his side. Ew!

"Quick! Throw another at him!" Papa B cries.

Phoenix throws another at him, and it stabs Dagger in the neck. Dagger screams and tries to grab the spear with his teeth. Deep red blood oozes from his cuts like red waterfalls. Then suddenly, Dagger's choking, and cranberry juice-colored liquid comes squirting from his throat.

"Venom!" I scream.

We quickly scatter away from the squirming snake. I hide behind a tree. The venom splatters onto the tree. I peer out from behind it. Papa B's perched on a tree-top, flinging spears at Dagger. Dagger screams in pain. Spears stick out of him all over. I almost feel sorry for him. Almost.

Papa B throws a spear straight into Dagger's mouth. It bounces off his tooth, and wedges itself between both sides of his mouth. Dagger shakes his head, his mouth stuck open. He shakes his head more furiously.

"Bullseye!" Papa B shouts, pumping a fist in the air. He climbs down from the tree and pops open the mini vial in his hand and runs toward the writhing snake.

"He's not unconscious!" I yell. He could still hurt one of us.

Papa B brings a spear up to the snake and gently pokes it between his eyes to make Dagger pass out. The snake goes limp, his beady, black eyes blindly staring at me. I shiver. That is a sight I will never be able to clear from my mind.

"Now's our chance!" Phoenix cries. Papa B brings the vial up to one of Dagger's teeth. Phoenix kicks the tooth, and the slippery venom drips from it. The smell is very strong, like a rotten Sour Patch Kid. Papa B pops the top of the vial on and stuffs it into his bag. He gently takes out the spear between his eyes and removes the spear stuck in his mouth.

"Run!" Papa B cries.

We turn and bolt. But Dagger wakes up almost immediately. At the same time, Dakota comes bounding back with the sparkly ball in her mouth. She drops the ball when she sees us fleeing and takes in her damaged snake.

"Get back here, rats!" she calls out. Dagger begins to hiss and slither our way, shooting venom at us. I scream as the deadly liquid splatters on the ground, instantly killing the moss it lands on. We run out into the clearing where Misty is now sleeping. Papa B wakes her up, and he and Phoenix climb onto her back. I'm still running.

Suddenly, something very hot splatters onto my arm. I turn to look. My face goes pale. *There's venom on my arm.* Phoenix is reaching his hand out to me. All at once, my vision goes blurry. Everything and everyone turns to colorful blobs. My eyes feel like bouncy balls. My body feels like pudding. Then, I can't feel much of anything. I can't hear Phoenix's and Papa B's screams. I feel myself slow down, and the ground is rising up to my face. Or am I falling? I hit the ground, and everything goes black.

I don't feel when Phoenix scoops me up and puts me onto Misty. I don't hear the deadly hissing of Dagger. I can't see the jungle getting farther and farther away as Misty flies off in a fury. I don't feel when the venom is rubbed off my skin and a liquid is dumped into my mouth. I don't feel anything.

I just feel darkness.

Chapter Twenty-two

Two Against One

I wake up with a start. I feel air pour into my lungs. And I gasp for more. My heart beats fast. I'm suddenly very, very, very tired. Then, I feel something cold on my face. I lift my aching arm up to my face. It's a cool washcloth. I slowly sit up and look around.

We're in a little room with baby blue walls. I'm laying on a fluffy bed with a flower comforter. There are two large windows across from me. It's nighttime. The stars twinkle. I smell something delicious. I look over beside me to see a neat tray of pizza and a Coke. Yum. My favorite. I reach for a pizza slice and bite into it. A sour taste fills my mouth. Yuck! Yucky pizza! I set it back down. Ew.

I feel a hand stroke my cheek. I look up to see a man with a red beard with silver streaks gazing down at me. I also see a handsome young man with dimples and brown hair gazing at me with a concerned look on his face. He smiles with relief when I look his way. I slowly sit up.

"What happened?" I ask.

"You were struck by Dagger's venom, and we saved you before you . . . " the man's voice trails off.

Suddenly, everything comes back to me. My heart swells and soars at the same time. Tears fill my eyes.

"You saved me," I whisper. Papa B and Phoenix both hug me tight. I smile. "Where are we?" I ask.

"I gave you a healing medicine, and Misty took us to a little town tucked into a mountain where we booked two hotel rooms. I made the chefs downstairs make a pizza especially for you," Papa B says.

"But the pizza tastes sour," I say.

Papa B nods. "That's because of the medicine I gave you. It'll go away once you drink something sweet," Papa says, handing me the Coke.

I take a long sip. The fizzy, sweet liquid flies down my throat. Yum. I take my tray of pizza and munch into it. Yum! I've never tasted pizza better than this.

"We were super worried," Phoenix says. "You weren't doing well. Your skin was turning the same color as the venom. Billie quickly gave you the medicine just as your whole body turned that color. Then, your normal color came back, and now you're alive," Phoenix explains with a smile.

Wow. I can't believe it. I'm so grateful for Papa B. I'm so grateful for Phoenix. I reach my arms out and Phoenix leans down to give me a hug, but I kiss him on the cheek instead. He pulls away and blushes like crazy.

I slowly get up from under my covers and sit on the edge of the bed. I offer Phoenix a slice of pizza, and he takes it gratefully. Papa B opens my backpack and starts taking out the items.

"Okay, guys. We have the turquoise sea flower from the Blue Bay, the piece of leather from Captain Seaweed, the bag of clouds from the Cloud Kingdom, and now, the vial of venom from Dakota the Hunter's snake, Dagger." I shiver. I never want to see those two again. "So, that's four down, two more to go," Papa B says.

We cheer. I didn't think we would get this far. But we did!

"So, now what?" I ask.

"Well, I think we all need a good night's sleep and a filling dinner first. But tomorrow, we're getting up bright and early, eating breakfast, getting ready, and going to Pixie Grove to get those rainbow hairs from the Unicorn's mane!"

Papa B gives me a hug and kisses my forehead before he says. "Now, you take time for yourself, young lady, okay? Finish your pizza, maybe watch some TV, and get some rest. We have a tight schedule to keep!"

Papa B and Phoenix leave the room, closing the door behind them. I grab the remote. Huh. They actually have TVs here. I flip it to a random channel and sit back, munching on my pizza. A fairy with her green hair pulled up into a tight bun is clutching a microphone and talking to the screen. Up in the corner it says Pixie News 4 U! That's a cool name. The fairy's speaking rapidly. I turn up the volume.

"Yes, hi, I'm Petunia, your trusty news reporter, and today we have some terrible news coming in from all different parts of the world. As you know, mysterious figures in black have been attacking towns and villages with their deadly weapons. But now, more attacks have been happening—almost daily sometimes. We're trying to discover who the leader of this is, and what they are up to. But, today, the most terrible news has come in. Last night, exactly twenty figures in black broke into The Dragon Gate at 1:00 in the morning and stole The Dragon Gate's deadliest dragon, Midnight."

A picture appears on the screen of a dragon as black as night with glowing, red eyes. The fairy continues. My mind is racing. This is not good at all.

"Midnight was born with deadly fire in his veins, and he's very hard to control. He was locked up in a dungeon down in the basement of The Dragon Center, but last night, somehow, twenty figures in black stole the dragon and have him under their command. Midnight seems to be obeying everything they order him to do. Today, Midnight attacked a town called Lovely Valley, destroying everything." I gasp. NO! I quickly change the channel.

Another reporter with a beak is speaking: "Lately, strange things have been happening. Curses have been put on different lands. Just today, travelers were stealing clouds, and the whole Cloud Kingdom collapsed! We're trying to get to the bottom of who is causing these curses and why."

I anxiously keep flipping channels.

"Causing many mysterious disasters . . . "

" . . . who is behind all these deadly scenes?"

"Figures in black terrorizing the town . . . "

" . . . where will they strike next?"

I shut the TV off and bury myself under my covers. I know the answer to almost every question. And it all points to Romi. I set my pizza on the nightstand and turn off the light. I close the blinds on the windows and drape the curtains over them. I jump onto my bed and hide under the covers. I squeeze my eyes shut. Sleep finds its way to me—only bearing a nightmare.

I wake up screaming. Venom and Romi and swords and yelling and Midnight and . . . Phoenix and Papa B burst into the room.

"What's wrong?!" Papa B cries, his hair all crazy and his eyes dark and droopy.

"I had a nightmare," I sigh.

I rub my eyes. That was the worst sleep I've ever had. I was half asleep the whole night, tossing and turning and moaning and groaning. I paced the room a couple times in the middle of the night. I stared at the ceiling for an hour. I went back to sleep to the same nightmare. And then I woke up screaming. It was oh, so lovely. Not! I wipe my forehead.

"Okay, well, knock on our door if you need anything okay, Eva? Otherwise, we'll meet you downstairs in a few minutes for breakfast?" Papa B says. I nod. I quickly get up and style my hair in two Dutch braids. I wash my face, put on mascara, and brush my teeth. I slip on a T-shirt with tours from my favorite band on it and a pair of light-blue jeans. Then I zip up my backpack. Everything normal that I'd do at home. Only, we're not at home! I pull on socks and tie my shoes and march downstairs for breakfast.

"You okay, Eva?" Phoenix asks me at the breakfast buffet.

"Yep. I'm just, like you said, a little frazzled," I say, spooning a pile of scrambled eggs on my plate. I put two sausages on my plate as well and reach for a cup of yogurt.

"I want to go home as much as you do, Eva," Phoenix says. He sighs. "Who am I kidding? I want to go home right now!" His fork bangs against his plate. I grab a bowl and fill it with colorful cereal. I press the button on the milk machine and the creamy, white liquid pours into my bowl. It's funny how some of the places in this world are so fantasy-like, and some are so normal. But that's because that's how Papa B and I wrote: sometimes about these fantastical places and sometimes just about normal stuff.

I'm tired. "Yeah" is all I say. I snatch a bagel and a cup of cream cheese. I take a cup and pour apple juice in it. I'm so hungry. Phoenix snatches a waffle, and we walk over to our table. I plop down in the booth and spoon some of the colorful cereal into my mouth. Yeesh! It's very fruity and sugary!

Papa B sits down beside us. "Today's a big day. I want to get the last two items, and then we'll go back to Spirit Forest to make the Portal Pen," he says eagerly. I nod. "Eva, are you okay?" Papa B asks.

I slam down my spoon. "I'm *fine!*" I yell. Phoenix and Papa B jump back. I stand up. "I'm tired of this! I'm tired of all this running and collecting and stopping and did I say running?"

Phoenix and Papa B nod. I sigh and plop down. I pull open the cup of cream cheese and grab my knife.

"I wish I was at home, in Colorado, eating breakfast with my family. I wish Romi wasn't a stupid McFully and was actually my friend still. I wish I didn't have to drag my best friend and my grandfather into this mess!" I say as I spread the cream cheese over one side of my bagel.

"Yeah, me too," Phoenix says, staring at his untouched plate. It's silent except for the sound of silverware clanking and chatter and the annoying buzz of the lights around us.

"I wish for a lot of things," I mutter.

"Well, Eva, all those things can happen if we just put more time and energy into this," Papa B says.

"I know, I just wish it wasn't this hard."

I bite into my bagel. All of us nod. Our heads bobble as we nod. There's a lot of nodding. We all stare at our plates.

Suddenly, we hear a loud clatter. Then another and another. People begin to run around in fear. The doors to the cafe shatter into a million pieces, and a giant, black dragon stomps in, surrounded by an army of figures in black.

"Midnight," I mutter.

"That's the dragon we saw on the news last night!" Phoenix exclaims.

"You guys watched the news too?" I ask. They both nod.

People scatter out of the doors and flee. Midnight opens his mouth and red fire spurts from it. A ball of fire hits a table, and it erupts into flames. We scramble up out of our seats, abandoning our breakfast.

Riding the dragon is none other than Romi. She looks completely different. She has dark makeup around her eyes and and a purple crown on her head. She's wearing a shimmering, black dress with blue swirls and stripes. Attached to her dress are dragon wings that sit on her brown shoulders. Her hair tumbles down her back in bright pink curls with blue tips at the end, and she holds a notebook in one hand and the Portal Pen in her other hand.

Romi spots us and points the pen our direction. "Oh, look! My *friends*!"

Romi's voice is dripping with meanness. Figures in black begin to creep toward us with their hands outstretched.

"Run," Papa B whispers.

We turn and bolt into the kitchen, and the doors swing behind us. Outside the doors, I hear the thumping footsteps of the figures in black running toward us. We run through the tiny kitchen and burst through the doors leading outside. We scramble out to where Misty is chewing on a pile of waffles. We glance at Papa B.

"What? She was hungry," Papa B says sheepishly.

We quickly jump onto Misty, and she begins to flap her wings. Rapidly, Misty soars higher and higher into the air. Suddenly, the giant, black dragon bursts through the roof of the hotel, shattering the glass. Midnight roars as his beady red eyes glare at Misty, who snarls back.

Romi is riding on Midnight's back, smiling at us. Her eyes look icy and electric, surging with magical power. Romi laughs as Midnight sends a red ball of fire at us. Misty flaps her wings and quickly dodges the flaming ball. Romi writes something down with the Portal Pen, and suddenly Midnight's lunging toward Misty.

"No!" I scream. We grip her scales tightly. Midnight kicks Misty in the stomach, and Misty summersaults through the air. I don't dare let go. I squeeze my eyes shut. Misty roars in rage and races toward Midnight. She kicks Midnight back and blows fire balls at him. Romi scribbles something down, and suddenly, Midnight's eyes are glowing green. Electric waves leap and bound over his black scales as his claws get larger and wider.

"He's too powerful," I whisper. "Misty will never be able to defeat him."

Midnight opens his mouth, and green lava shoots from his throat. I can see the rising steam. Misty barely misses getting hit by lava. Misty flaps her wings, but I can tell she's getting tired. Romi writes more things down and raises her hand. Then, she slowly begins to put her hand down. I can feel Misty begin to get more tired. Misty begins to drop down to the ground slowly, her eyes struggling to stay open.

No! No! No!

Misty flaps her wings, but her mood and thoughts seem far away. Gently, she hits the ground and great snores fill her body. Romi laughs while Midnight roars.

"You can't run now!" she cries. She writes something down and the three of us are lifted into the air. Oh no! Oh no! Romi grins. We flail our arms around like confused birds. Romi writes something else down, and a net appears. It slowly begins to lift upwards on both sides, slowly trapping us. No! We're so close! Not here, not now!

All of a sudden, something is slithering through the jungle. It races out and over the sleeping Misty. It's Dagger! The giant snake slowly reaches up, up, up and into the sky, his mouth open and his sharp teeth exposed. We scream even harder. Venom drips from his teeth. Dakota's riding on his back, crouched like an animal ready to pounce. Dagger reaches up, up, up and the net snaps, and then, we're falling through the sky. Romi writes something, and Midnight's lunging after us. But Dagger gets to us first. Dakota grabs me and helps me from slipping.

"But, why? After what we did to you," I ask.

Dakota shakes her head. "No, my friend. The enemy of your enemy is your friend," she says. I hug Dakota. She smiles and hugs me back. "And I hate that evil dragon and that evil dragon queen," she says. I grin. Dakota helps us slide down Dagger's back to the ground. We immediately rush toward Misty.

"I have a little bit of the medicine left that I used for you, Eva!" Papa B exclaims. "There is darkness running through Misty's poor body. We need to get it out."

I unzip Papa B's backpack and he feels around. Then, he pulls out a plastic bag full of sloshy blue liquid. He tilts the bag into Misty's mouth. Misty swallows in her sleep, and suddenly, her eyes pop open. She coos and nuzzles her giant head against us. I turn around to see Dagger and Midnight fighting in the sky. Dagger is so much bigger than Midnight. Dagger opens his mouth and spits out venom which covers Midnight, and the dark dragon begins to fall in a daze, but Romi writes something, and Midnight's back up again, his eyes a flaming green and his body shivering with power. He opens his mouth and big blasts of green lava pour out, drenching Dagger. Dagger shakes it off, unfazed. This is going to be a long battle if Dagger can't die and Romi's controlling Midnight.

Midnight kicks the giant snake and he falls back. Midnight swoops down and chomps into poor Dagger's neck. Dagger screams and venom shoots from his mouth. It splatters over Midnight. Midnight shakes it off.

"Come on, Dagger!" I shout.

I see Dakota whispering into his ear. Romi laughs. Dakota gives her the absolute deadliest glare I have ever seen. If looks could kill, Romi McFully would be dead meat.

Dagger shakes his head and snarls at Midnight. Midnight snarls back. Dagger lunges at the dragon, and his deadly fangs stab Midnight's side. Midnight roars and chomps down on Dagger's neck. Midnight kicks Dagger, and Dagger lets go. Poor Dakota's hanging on for dear life. Dagger tries to bite Midnight but misses. He knocks into the dragon with his giant head, and Midnight begins to tumble to the ground. Meanwhile, Misty wakes up and decides to get in on the action. She flies up into the air and begins to repeatedly kick Midnight in the face. This is the scariest—but also most amazing—battle I've ever seen!

Romi screams and quickly jots something down. Midnight shakes his head, and once again, his eyes sizzle green. His scales also turn green as he shoots fireballs at Dagger and Misty. Misty flies up and blows fire right back. Dagger slides up and starts shooting venom at Midnight. I'm super happy that Misty and Dagger are on the same side.

But the Portal Pen is too strong. Midnight is unfazed by the fire or venom and lunges at Dagger. He spits lava into his eyes, blinding the poor snake. Then, he scratches Dagger over and over. I look away and my eyes fill with tears. I don't know what happens next, but I hear a giant kick and a snarl from Midnight and a swoop of wings, and then a blood-curdling scream from Dagger floods the air.

I turn to see Misty flying toward us in fear. Dagger's sailing toward the ground, blood seeping from deep gashes in his sides. Poor Dagger. He's had to go through so much today. Dakota cries out in fury and strokes her pet snake. Dagger goes limp, but I know he'll be back. Misty roars at the evil dragon.

"Go away!" Dakota screams.

"Yeah, get out of here!" Phoenix shouts, shaking an angry fist in the air.

Romi just laughs, but I can see the worry and hesitance in her eyes. She and Midnight turn and fly off. We rush over to Dagger and Dakota.

"Oh my gosh! We are so sorry!" I cry.

Dakota sniffs. "It's okay. He'll heal. That little rat! She will pay!" Dakota yells to the empty sky.

"She'll be sorry in the end," I say. "And she'll probably regret it."

"Oh, she'll regret it," Papa B assures us. He strokes Misty, who has a gash on her tail. "But once she regrets it, she'll never be able to erase it." His words linger in the air.

Suddenly, Dagger's head snaps up and he opens his mouth toward the sky. Seeing that they're gone, he lets his head drop to the ground. Dagger gently purrs. Dakota strokes him.

"We need to get going now," Papa B says.

Dakota nods. "Okay. And I know Dagger's mean and scary sometimes, but thank you for taking our side," Dakota says.

We all nod. "Of course. You two came to our rescue today," I say.

Dakota leads a frazzled Dagger back into the hidden depths of the Rainy Fog Jungle, and we hop onto Misty, who whimpers.

"It's okay, girl," I assure her. "The mean people are gone now." I sigh.

"Next stop: Pixie Grove," Phoenix says. "That's luckily not terribly far from here." Misty nods and begins to flap her wings. She soars through the sky. I lay down on Misty's smooth back and let myself think. I think back to the glass rooms. *Everything.* Romi used a magical power to get everything, but I have people who stand by my side—just like Dagger and Dakota did. Romi only has a magical pen and an evil dragon.

We sail over fields and towns and kingdoms. We sail over prairies and valleys and rivers. All of it is so beautiful. But everything has much more color than just greens and browns and yellows. We pass the Spoon Kingdom and the Blue Bay. It feels like forever ago when we went there. So much has happened since then. We got the turquoise sea flower, we had a mission . . . Romi betrayed us. I feel myself slump a little. If she ever gets out of this world, and so do I, and everything goes back to normal, things will change between us. Nothing will ever be the same.

Chapter Twenty-three

The Curse of Pixie Grove

Pixie Grove is much larger than other places we've traveled to. Everything is also blindingly sparkly.

Misty touches down in a field of wildflowers, dancing joyfully in the breeze. Pixie Grove is not really like a kingdom. It's more like a bunch of different places inside a kingdom. We can see colorful, rolling hills with homes nestled under them. There are also huge trees bursting with fruit and a giant, glistening river with clear water. We can see the castle—except it looks nothing like a castle. There's a bottom layer made of gold with a bunch of miniature looking houses on top. On top of those are even smaller houses, but the crazy part is that a giant, golden house with tons of windows is balanced *on top* of those tiny houses.

We walk through Pixie Grove. There are clear tubes circling around the castle, and creatures without wings go zooming through them. That's such a cool way to get from place to place! I wish I could travel like that.

There are also things floating in the air. Shops! I notice a pink blob floating in the air with a fairy peeping out of it and handing another fairy a strawberry smoothie. Yum! A smoothie stand. Speaking of smoothies, my stomach has been growling for the past hour. It sounds like a lion growling at me to give it food.

The inside of Pixie Grove is like a utopia for fairies and creatures. There are tall and short buildings. Some buildings even weave around other buildings. Creatures in flying pods whiz around us, glitter sputtering from the engine. There's a part of the land that has a giant, pink building stuffed smack-dab in between other buildings. The pink building has a huge front yard and the ground is rainbow-colored. A floating sign above it reads, "Rainbow-colored gummies for your floors! Walk fast and enjoy a snack!" Ew. If that were me, I don't think I would want sticky, multicolored gummies for my floors. But lots of people disagree with me, because a long line of fairies and unicorns and other mythical creatures snake out the door and around the block.

"Alright, this place is crazy and can get a little too glittery and chaotic sometimes. Prepare to be bribed, and whatever you do . . . " Papa B spins around and looks at us. "Do *not* take any food."

"But why?" I hear myself whine like a child.

Papa B peers into my eyes. "Not too long ago, I was in Pixie Grove, looking for things to collect when a curse was put on this place."

A curse? Ugh! Romi must have stolen my pen and put a stupid curse on this place.

"But how did you know it was a curse?" Phoenix asks.

Papa B looks around. "Because we could all feel it. In the wind, in the air, in the buildings, even in the ground. A sickening feeling that hung in the air. Then, suddenly, people began offering things to me. I took a biscuit, and then I was lured into this trance and couldn't stop taking food."

"What happens?" I ask.

"Well, the curse is supposed to lure you into eating sickening but delicious food. Each piece of food makes you more and more tired until you fall asleep and . . . " Papa B has tears in his eyes. "And you never wake up."

Phoenix and I gasp.

"But the people of Pixie Grove only eat food from the castle because that was the only place that wasn't cursed. There was a force field over it at the time, so the curse bounced off. Anyway, the people of Pixie Grove know never to eat in the city. It's only clueless travelers who get sucked in."

We glance around. I notice that people ignore sellers completely. "Are we clueless travelers?" I ask nervously.

Papa B stands tall. "We are travelers, but we certainly are *not* clueless. Now, follow my lead. Do *not* take anything!" Papa B's voice is gentle, but firm. We nod. Oh, boy.

We walk in a straight line through the city. I try to avoid as much eye contact as possible, only keeping my eyes straight ahead. But it's really hard when people are waving and beckoning with plates of apples drizzled in caramel, and pretzels caked in white chocolate and sprinkles, and steaming pots of rice pudding. It's like Spoon Kingdom, only if you eat something here, you'll sleep forever. And I don't want to sleep forever.

"So, Pixie Grove doesn't have one ruler in particular. In fact, it's just like the Cloud Kingdom." Papa B shoos away a man shoving apples coated in cinnamon in our face. I hold my breath so I don't breathe in what I bet smells amazing.

"There are four members that run Pixie Grove." Papa B continues. "Alyssa, who is a water fairy; William, who is a troll; April, who is made of flowers and soil; and Silvie, the unicorn with the rainbow mane."

We slip around a crowd of gazing travelers. I cringe and turn away. Please don't take anything; please don't take anything. I turn around to see a traveler with a beak nip at a biscuit covered in honey. He immediately drops to the ground, his furry stomach heaving with giant snores. I gasp.

"Keep walking," I say. Our feet move faster.

"How do we get all seven colors of her mane?" Phoenix asks. He turns and his hand slowly reaches out to a woman holding a bowl of dumplings. Just as he touches one of the dumplings, I quickly slap his wrist and give the confused woman a warm smile.

"Don't you dare," I warn.

"Silvie sheds seven hairs almost every day. She keeps her hair in a box. I've tried searching for it, but the palace is gigantic. It's designed to appear as a giant maze, so only the four council members and guards know where to go."

I smack my forehead. There's always a catch, isn't there?

"Luckily, I know what room the box is kept in. It's in the Scroll Room. The only problem is, I haven't had time to memorize the layout and direction of the maze." Papa B says as he strokes his beard.

I see a tall giraffe with brown spots pluck a green cabbage off a plate and take a bite out of it. I whip around and face ahead of me, but behind, I hear gasps and loud snoring. Sweat begins to cling to my forehead. Oh, boy. We really need to fix this. We've got to end all these curses.

The palace looms over us. Its golden walls gleam and brag in the sunshine. Two broad male fairies stomp in front of the door in the rotation of an eight.

"Let me handle this," Papa B says. The fairies point their silver spears at Papa B. "Good morning, gentlemen. Me and my friends here would like to get into the Scroll Room," Papa B says.

My mouth drops open. He's just gonna tell them what we're doing? I would think Papa B has gotten used to sneaking into places, not actually doing it the regular way.

The fairies scowl. "No one, except the council goes into the Scroll Room!" one of the fairies barks.

Papa B scratches his head. "Well . . . you see, it's important," Papa B says.

"It's only important to the council!" the other hollers.

Yeesh. We're right here in front of you. No need to yell. Just then a man walks by, holding a tray of steaming croissants dripping with creamy butter. Lightbulb! I snatch four croissants from the tray and hold them out to the guards.

"We're, uh, exchange bakers for the royal . . . er, bakery," I lie. Wow! Very smooth, Eva!

The fairies aren't convinced. "We have no exchange bakers," one growls.

Suddenly, more guards are behind us. What do we do? What do we do? Suddenly, a strange thought hits me that I regret thinking: *What would Romi do?* I grin and stand up taller.

"Excuse me?" I sass.

The soldiers stay where they are, but confusion and hesitance flickers across their face. "There are no exchange bakers," one says again, his voice a tad bit softer.

I put a free hand on my hip. "Excuse me?" I repeat. "Just who do you think you are?"

Phoenix and Papa B raise an eyebrow at me. "We're . . . uh, the palace guards," one says.

"Well, humph. Because I've been recruited by Silvie the Unicorn herself," I say.

The guards gasp. "What?" one cries.

"Silvie? But she's locked up!" the soldiers cry.

"Wh-what?" I say, surprised.

One of the soldiers steps forward. "Haven't you heard? Silvie's gone crazy! All of her beautiful rainbow hair fell out, and her white mane turned black. Her eyes glow with fire. We have her over there."

The soldiers point to a tower in the distance. My heart pounds. This happened to the mermaid queen too! It's Romi. All Romi.

"Silvie is not allowed to request anything anymore and has been banned from the council."

The three of us gasp. Ugh!

"So, there's no way Silvie requested you," the soldiers say, surrounding us and pointing their spears at us.

"Well, uh, the rest of the council sent us, and . . . they uh, did it in Silvie's honor. In the memory of the leader she once was." I hold out the croissants and hold my breath.

The soldiers back away. "Very well then. In you go," one soldier says.

They hit the door with their spears, and the heavy golden doors creak open. We show off fake smiles as we walk into the palace. The soldiers slam the door shut behind us. I quickly throw the croissants aside.

The interior looks nothing like I would picture a castle. There are paintings on the walls and over to the right is a little reading corner with bookshelves and beanbag chairs and a fluffy carpet. Easels line the walls, and creatures and fairies color on them. There's a huge furnace on the other side of the big room, and under the staircase is a large kitchen with a fridge and an oven. There's also a pool in the middle of the floor and an ice cream dispenser leaning against a bookshelf in the middle of the huge room. Awesome! We walk over to a super skinny maid with hair that looks like it's made of straw who's scooping up bugs with a net in the pool.

"Hi. We're looking for the Scroll Room?" Papa B asks.

The maid looks up. Her eyes sag with tiredness, and her cheekbones get tighter as she sucks in her cheeks in bitter disgust, "The Scroll Room is hidden in the maze of this castle. Maids get to go through tubes to get places. Travelers don't." The maid leans her skinny body over the pool and continues her work. Attitude!

A chubby maid bounces over to the stick maid. "Rosalind, be nice!" the chubby maid cries. The stick maid scowls.

"Hi! I'm Patty!" the chubby maid waves. "Anything I can do to help?" she giggles.

Yay! Now we're getting somewhere. "Yes, we're looking for the Scroll Room," I say.

Patty frowns. "Oh. The Scroll Room?"

"Yes! Can you show us where that is?" Phoenix asks.

Patty shakes her head. "Sorry, but like Rosalind said, this palace was designed as a giant maze for a theme park. But after more and more people began to move here and they needed leaders, we built a castle on top of it. Luckily, there are signs." Patty fluffs her hair. "And, we do have tiny, indoor mobiles that drive around for travelers to get to rooms faster. Those should help a lot!" Patty skips off. "Good luck doing whatever your doing!" she cries.

We shrug and go over to the giant furnace where a small parking lot packed with mini-cars are stationed. I hop in a yellow one, Phoenix hops in a red, and Papa B, a blue.

"Get ready to be searching for three hours," Papa B says. He backs up his car and speeds off.

I back up and slam the gas. Whoo! We speed through the main room and down a hallway. There are signs everywhere. I don't know where to look. I see BAKERY, PING-PONG ROOM, TV ROOM, MOVIE ROOM, ROYAL DRESSING ROOM, BALCONY ROOM, MEDITATION ROOM, SELF-HELP ROOM. Goodness! They have a self-help room here! We whiz past random staircases and zoom through halls and pass cranky maids. There are little stop signs so other travelers in mini-cars can pass. There's even a yellow sign that has a picture of a vacuum on it. It reads: DANGER! MAID CROSSING! Oh my gosh!

After a while of thousands of signs, halls, rooms, and maids, we tiredly whiz through another hall. I've seen every room I can imagine, and more! A smoothie room! A yoga room! A snorkeling room! A magic enchantments room! A room just for making coffee! Crazy stuff! We pause at a stop sign, and I rest my elbows on the steering wheel. I'm so tired and hungry. After more cars pass, I press the gas and we're off again. LIBRARY, INSTRUMENT ROOM, PILLOW-MAKING ROOM, SCROLL ROOM, WAX CANDLE ROOM—wait, what?

"Stop!" I cry. I press the brakes and back my car up. Phoenix and Papa B do the same. I point to the sign. "Scroll Room!" I cry. An arrow points to a hallway to the right under a staircase.

"Let's go!" Papa B cries.

We press the gas, and our cars zoom down the hallway. The good news is, we're on the right track. The bad news is, there are still thousands of more confusing signs for more confusing rooms. Arrows on each sign point this way and that. LAUNDRY ROOM! LAVA LAMP ROOM! JEWELRY ROOM! FAIRY WING IMPLANT ROOM! Ew! Fairy wing implants? Gross. Luckily, Scroll Room signs keep popping up and leading the way.

We speed down a hall and screech to the left. Then to the right again, then to the left. After thirty more minutes of signs and screeching and right and left, we finally get to our destination. A large sign reads, WELCOME TO THE SCROLL ROOM. There are large, wooden doors painted green. We park our cars in a little parking lot next to the doors and go in.

The doors open, and an explosion of lights and noise hits us. Laser lights fly through the air, and I hear peppy music and bass. I look around. It's an arcade! Creatures put in coins and spin levers and drive fake cars and press buttons. I stomp my foot.

"This is not the Scroll Room!" I cry.

Papa B scratches his head, "I remember the doors were green. They must have upgraded it!" Papa B runs off and Phoenix races after. Papa B takes out a couple coins and inserts them into a game. He and Phoenix tap buttons and spin around levers, their eyes determined.

"Guys? Guys!" I cry out.

But my voice is drowned out by the noise and music and voices. I cover my ears. I stumble through the arcade, searching for Phoenix and Papa B, but they've vanished. I spot Papa B driving a fake race car, and Phoenix is shooting hoops into a basketball net. Ugh!

"This is not what we came here for!" I scream, but they can't hear me.

I sink down against an arcade game and squeeze my eyes shut. So much noise, so much chaos. I open my eyes to see an arcade game diagonal from me. It's edges are golden, and there's a unicorn in the top right corner. She has a rainbow mane, and she's arching her hoof as if to wave. A bubble lettered sign on it reads, "RAINBOW MANE GAME. INSERT TWENTY NICKELS TO PLAY AND SEE WHAT YOU CAN WIN TODAY!"

I sit up straight and scramble up. I run over to the arcade game and take a closer look. Inside the game are prize—there's a claw that you control to grab one of those prizes. There are mostly cheesy unicorn stuffed animals and bracelets and junk like that, but I spot a cardboard slit with seven slim hairs hanging from it. As soon as I spot it, I know that these are real hairs from Silvie. I can practically see magic sizzling from them.

I reach into my backpack. I find two pennies, lint . . . hmmm. No nickels. I dig around some more. Aha! I manage to find ten nickels. Now where can I find ten more? I turn to hear shouting. An old man with tentacles is waving around coins.

"Anybody need any coins? I'm going home for the day so take them if you need them!" What? No way! I run up to the tentacle dude.

"Hey! You got exactly ten nickels?" I ask.

The tentacle man reaches into his pocket and hands me ten slimy nickels. "Got anything to eat? I'm starving! Been working this room all day and haven't eaten since yesterday!" The tentacle man cries.

I grin. "I have . . . snack mix?" I offer.

The man licks his blue lips and smiles. "Thanks!" he says as he grins and shuffles off.

I quickly run over to the arcade game and insert all twenty coins. Ker-plunk! Ker-plunk! The game shudders to life and a cheesy male voice cries out, "Turn the lever to control the claw!" I turn the lever, and the claw jerks and wobbles. Okay. It's game time now. I faintly hear someone shouting my name. "Eva! Eva, help!" Eh, just my crazy thoughts I guess. Someone bumps into me, and the claw jerks.

"Hey! Watch where you're going, please," I say, my eyes focused on the arcade game.

The person spins around. I pay no attention. But they don't go away. Almost there! I reach the claw out to the hair and press a button. The claws open up as it grabs the hair. But suddenly, it lets go as the person grabs me. Then I notice that he's covered in all-black clothing. Oh no. Within seconds, my hands are tied and everything goes dark.

CHAPTER TWENTY-FOUR

New Girl in Town

Romi's pink curls bounce against her chocolate-brown arms as she paces the floor. Figures in black surround her, and Midnight is standing almost in a daze behind her.

"I curse one kingdom, but it doesn't stop them. I curse another, but still they don't stop! I kidnap them, but they escape!" she says, stomping her heeled shoe.

Romi wraps her fingers around the pen, shivering with power as waves of magic scurry through her bones and tumble through her body. Romi turns around and faces her figures in black. Then, she gets an idea and starts writing something down on her notepad. *Once, Romi tracked down her friends Phoenix and Eva and kept an eye on their every move.* Romi had decided, once she got the pen in her hands for good, to just embrace her grandfather's last name as her own. As soon as the words are on the page, a screen appears in front of Romi. Phoenix and Eva and Eva's grandfather are gazing up at a pair of green doors that say, WELCOME TO THE SCROLL ROOM.

Romi smiles and says, "I can't have my friends getting away!" Then she writes more, *Once, Romi's figures in black found Phoenix and Eva at lightning speed.*

Suddenly, several figures in black disappear into thin air. Romi turns around and marches up to what used to be the King's throne of the Spoon Kingdom. The kingdom is deserted, but Romi still gets all the food she wants with the Portal Pen. Romi scribbles something down, and instantly, a fruity drink appears in her hand, a shiny strawberry bobbing around in the punch. Romi takes a sip.

"Ah," she says, leaning her elbow on one of the arms of her throne and gazing at Phoenix and Eva on the large screen. A tiny pinch of sadness begins to grab at the edges of her heart.

"I could be helping them right now," she whispers to herself. "I could be helping Eva find the hairs of the rainbow mane." Romi stares at the Portal Pen. The pen that Eva's grandfather created and used to form this magical world of stories, and later on, Eva as well. The pen she was now using to take over this world and make it her own. Romi's heart is torn in two.

The night when Romi jumped from the balcony, she knew she was finally getting what her family wanted. For three generations, her family tried to snag that pen. And now, it was in her fingers, the cool Turquoise Wood cooling her fingertips. But now, with her cursing this world, taking over kingdoms, watching her friends go through pain to stop her, Romi's heart aches with pressure. Is this what she truly wants? *Yes!* she thinks. *Of course it is!* But still, her heart beats with loneliness.

The truth is, Romi truly didn't want to hurt Eva and Phoenix. Especially Eva. She was the one who had stayed by her side through tough times, who told Romi embarrassing secrets that she trusted her to keep, who let Romi pick out the movies at their sleepovers, who wanted Romi to be the one to come with her on this journey.

Romi rubs her forehead. And now, look what she's done. *What* have *I done*? Romi thinks. But Romi really did want this. Even though Eva was her best friend, or *had been* her best friend, Romi had secretly watched Eva easily make friends in school and bravely stand up to bullies. Romi watched the way Eva's family was all together and happy when she was over their house. There was love all through that family, as sure as the solid ground underneath her feet.

Romi had watched the way Eva's eyes would light up when she'd talk about her stories. Even on the Writer's Circle, that story app, Eva always had a ton of positive compliments and tons of followers who loved her amazing stories. And through all of that, it's like there was always a cracked pipe that would drip out the sour liquid of jealousy into Romi's heart. Because Romi had nights when her parents yelled at each other, where her mom left and didn't come back until two days later, where Romi was completely ignored in the family and at school, and where even her older brother and his girlfriend pretended like she didn't exist. For so many years, little Romi had gotten used to it, and the feelings stayed bottled up until more resentment and more anger and more jealousy built and built and built up . . . until suddenly—when Eva was sleeping in the hotel and the Portal Pen was lying there on the nightstand, its Turquoise Wood shining in the pale moonlight—Romi's heart began to pound, ringing in her ears, and her fingers had trembled, and her lip had quivered. Voices rattled her brain: "Take it! Just take it! And everyone will know your name! And people will pay attention! Just take it!" And then, it was in Romi's fingers, and before she knew what was happening, she began to continue writing her stories of thousands of armies with figures in black, creeping around like spiders with swords and spears and weapons in their clever hands.

A few months before all of this was the night when Romi slept over at Eva's house. Because of stories her grandfather had told her, Romi knew about the Portal Pen, and she ached to touch it. To feel it's cool wood, to feel the magic in it that Eva had no idea about at the time. After three movies, pillow fights, popcorn with caramel M&Ms, and lots and lots of talking, it was about 2:00 in the morning and Eva was conked out. She looked like an innocent little child, all curled up in her blankets and pillows, her stringy red hair scattered over her peaceful face. Romi turned and saw it. The Portal Pen, resting in all it's magical glory, on Eva's desk. And that's when Romi realized that she needed that pen desperately. She wanted it more than anything—more than anything in the world.

So Romi felt herself scrambling up and stumbling over to the desk. Grabbing the pen, she sighed. She had it in her hands! Romi sat down in her sleeping bag with the pen and a notebook and began to write. She knew this magical world was out there. She knew this way before Eva ever did. Romi began to write stories about armies of figures in black swooping around like ninjas. How they jumped in trees and threw swords and . . .

"What are you doing?" Eva said groggily. She stretched.

Romi put down the pen and grinned. "What? Oh, I was just looking around," Romi had stuttered.

Eva rubbed her eyes and yawned. Her long dark eyelashes fluttered sleepily. "At 2:00 in the morning?" she asked.

"I . . . uh," Romi fumbled with a lock of her curly, dark brown hair.

"Romi, let's just get some sleep, okay?" Eva had gotten up and grabbed the pen, laying back down and falling asleep with the Portal Pen pressed to her chest. Romi hadn't slept at all that night. She'd been so close. So, so close . . .

Romi snaps back to reality. The reality is, she's sitting on a throne with the Portal Pen in her hands and a crown on her head. Thousands of figures in black bow to her every command, and an evil dragon is in her possession, able to knock out anyone if Romi just writes it down. She has the whole world in her hands. This is what Romi has wanted for such a long time. All of this can replace all of the cracks and holes in her life. Now she can feel whole.

Midnight interrupts Romi's thoughts as he storms in, his teeth bared and his eyes fire. Romi writes something down, and suddenly, she's floating in the air, her giant, blue cloak billowing around her, and her pink-and-blue hair floating around her shoulders.

"Now, now, Midnight," Romi whispers.

The Portal Pen is very, very, very powerful. It can bend both good and evil, depending on whose hands it is in. It makes the most amazing stories come to life, but it can also create the deadliest evil. And in creating evil, it can suck its owner in with it. And that's what Romi is trapped in. Romi is drowning in all of her guilt and jealousy and loss. Though she wants the magic pen to right all of those wrongs, she's actually using it to create more evil. And that's no way to fix a wounded heart.

The pen begins to glow, filling Romi's eyes with an entrancing green light. Romi shivers as the power fills up her body.

"Come, Midnight. Let's make trouble."

Romi flies onto her dragon, and they burst out of the palace. Romi's eyes still glow green, entranced by the magic Portal Pen. Once giving in to its powers, there's no way you can get out. Unless someone stops you.

Romi scribbles down something on her pad, her green eyes illuminating the paper with an eerie green glow. *Once, Romi created a great storm. Big, dark clouds filled the sky and rain poured. The storm never stopped.*

Immediately, the blue sky begins to fade into a misty gray, and the fluffy, white clouds turn dark and threatening. Great booms of thunder echo, and lightning flashes through the sky, illuminating the town in bursts. Romi laughs, the colored rings around her pupils a fierce green. The Portal Pen's beautiful Turquoise Wood turns green, and the keychains shine more brightly. The Portal Pen begins to sizzle and rumble with destructive power. Romi laughs. She laughs because all the power is in her hands. She laughs because no one can stop her. She laughs because she can still remember Eva's horrified face staring at her when she jumped off the balcony.

"There's a new girl in town now, and she's taking over!" Romi yells.

Her voice leaps and echoes through the sky, harmonizing with the thunder. People and creatures look up and scream and point at the girl with a crown and a magic, evil pen riding an evil dragon. Romi's words echo in people's ears. Then, the rain comes. It hits the world below like a wave while people cringe and cover their heads, leaping and bounding under roofs and shelters. Romi's eyes glow brighter with bad magic. She writes something down and lets her face get soaked by the rain. She writes, *Once, Romi created an evil army of giant dragons.*

Suddenly, the ground begins to rumble and shake. Cracks race each other through the ground as people jump back in terror. Out of nowhere, hundreds of dragons burst through the clouds. All of them have gleaming black scales and glowing red eyes. All have sharp, shiny teeth and huge wings. All have claws like daggers and tails that can cause a fierce blow. All are under Romi's evil command.

People gasp and scream and run. Romi licks her lips and scribbles something down. *Once, all of Romi's evil dragons scattered about to all the kingdoms and villages and towns and gathered up all the people and brought them to Romi's fortress in the Evergreen Woods. Then, they locked all the people up in glass cages.* Once the words were written, the dragons begin to fly off in tons of different directions. Some swoop down into the Spoon Kingdom. They snarl and drop giant nets around the people. The dragons grab the nets, now filled with people, and hover in the sky for a moment.

Midnight roars and Romi laughs as the two swoop toward the other dragons. Romi writes something down and she lifts her hands up. A magic force generates through her fingers, and a purple mist seeps into the nets. Everyone immediately falls asleep. But it's a deeper sleep. More like a coma.

"When you wake, you will all bow before me," Romi says. Her voice is light and hollow and electric. She points to the sky and the dragons take off with the nets of people in their teeth. Romi writes more down: *Once, the mermaid queen and Captain Seaweed and the council and Tiki the Talking Tree, and all of the other kings and queens, and the Spirit Animals of Spirit Forest gave up their kingdoms to Romi and bowed before her.*

Romi can feel the kingdoms bowing before her. The kings, queens, and creatures appear in front of her, holding out their riches in terror. Romi throws back her head and laughs. Her blue cloak billows around her like a giant blanket as she scribbles down even more. In response to the pen, the terrified kings, queens, and creatures are whisked away in nets by dragons.

Romi and Midnight fly over to Lovely Valley and land on the sand of the beach. Romi begins to walk toward Lovely Valley. It's still pink and purple, but now it's in chaos. Nets and dragons swoop down, and moments later, swoop back up—the nets bursting with horrified people.

Romi barely looks like herself anymore. Sparkles, trails of blue and pink, and green wisps of magic follow behind her as she walks. With each step she takes, the flowers under her feet shiver and wilt. Romi's colorful hair whips around, brushing her face. Midnight walks beside her, his back arched and his teeth bared. Romi stops at a tree. She goes up to the tree and feels herself gasp. Her stomach tightens and a lump forms in her throat.

"This was where we fell from," she whispers, stroking the trunk with her fingertips. At that, the tree begins to darken, and the leaves fall off. Romi watches, feeling her eyes fill with tears. Without warning, she feels like she's taken a step back into her old life.

"Look who I've become," Romi says out loud to herself. "This isn't who I am. This isn't me." Romi feels her hair and looks down at her clothing. Instead of her dirty red sneakers, she's wearing high-heeled boots that are blue fading into black.

"What am I wearing? This isn't me!" Romi's head begins to spin. "Who have I become? What kind of friend am I?"

Questions fill her mind. But then she sees the glow of the Portal Pen.

"Who am I?" But Romi's eyes turn green again. "I am the queen of the world!" she bellows, her voice roaring like thunder. Romi cackles. All the hesitation and questions that she had a second ago are gone. Now, there's only Romi and the Portal Pen. Her Portal Pen. Romi writes something down, and she and Midnight disappear in a puff of blue smoke, her laugh sending shivers through people's bodies.

Chapter Twenty-five

The Second Portal Pen

I wake to a white wall. It's blindingly white. I try to move, but there's a thick rope around my hands. I'm stuck. I glance around. I can tell that we're in one of the rooms in the castle. A sign says, SCIENCE LAB ROOM. There are tables all around with weird bottles containing colorful liquids. There's a bulletin board with notes and pictures of planets, stars, animals, plants, and so on tacked up on the wall. Figures in black surround us, and Romi stands in the corner, watching a figure in black search through Papa B's backpack.

I can see her more closely now. She looks so different than the old Romi. The old Romi had frizzy, dark hair and chocolate-brown eyes and dimples and red sneakers and loved fashion and always wore hoop earrings. Now, her hair is pink with blue tips, her lips have been painted a shiny pink, and there's eyeliner lining her eyes, along with dark eyeshadow. Her hair is much longer too, trailing down to her waist. She twirls the pen in her hand and frowns as one of the figures in black rummages around in Papa B's bag.

"What are you doing?" I cry.

Romi looks up. "Hi! You finally woke up! It's nice to see you," Romi says warmly. Sarcasm and attitude drip from her words.

"It's *not* nice to see you too," I snarl, glaring at Romi. I hear shifting and groaning beside me and turn to see Phoenix. He's fidgeting. "Don't struggle. It'll only make it worse!" I tell him.

Phoenix stops and stares at me. His eyes are sad and empty. The hope has drained out of them like water drains from a sink. It's crazy how long it takes for hope to be built up—and how quickly it can plummet and die. The figure in black digging through Papa B's backpack finds the Centipede Spray.

"Is this what you used to escape my glass prisons before?" she asks.

Papa B shifts. "I'll never tell!" he cries.

The figure takes out his sword. Papa B flinches. Romi walks up to Papa B, her heels clicking against the floor. She raises her head slightly.

"You *will* tell me or you will pay," she says softly. She grips the pen tighter and her eyes suddenly glow green. "Understood?" she says.

Papa B gulps and nods. I notice that the pen's wood is now green, and my keychains are brighter. What happened?

"Now, please tell me: Did you use the Centipede Spray to escape?" Romi asks. She slowly writes something down on a notepad and Papa B's eyes glow green.

"Yes, I did," he says robotically, his now glowing-green eyes glazed over.

"Stop it right now!" I cry. "You better stop or I'll . . . "

Romi cocks her head at me. "Or you'll what? Yell at them?" Romi giggles and flips her hair. "I don't think so. Let *me* do the orders and let me handle the consequences." Romi spins around and the figure in black continues searching through the bag. Phoenix is wiggling around. I turn toward him.

"Eva," he whispers.

"What?" I whisper back.

"There's a pocket knife in my pocket. If I can just get it . . . "

Romi strolls over. "Whatcha talking about, Pebbles?" she asks.

"How you were such a horrible friend to us and betrayed us and stole and lied," Phoenix lies back. Whoa.

Romi's eyes flicker to hurt. She grabs her stomach a little and steps back like she's been stabbed. Her eyes are hurt and confused. "Wh-what? But I'm your friend," she stutters.

Like magic, her green eyes disappear and the old Romi is back. I can see it. Romi glances at me, horrified. Tears well up in my eyes.

"I wish I could say that you're still my friend, but you're not," I say.

Romi's eyes begin to spill with tears. Then, fire flickers in her eyes once more. "You wanna play the friend game now? Let's play," she scowls. Her hurt turns to anger, and she scribbles something down. Romi storms off and figures in black begin to surround us.

"The knife!" Phoenix whispers again.

I scooch toward him. I can see the shimmer of the knife sticking out from his back pocket. I inch toward his pocket and grab it with my tied hands. I get a grip on the knife and press it under the ropes of Phoenix's tied hands, cutting him free. Phoenix springs up and grabs the knife. He stabs the air with his knife. Then he lunges toward me and cuts the ropes on my hands. I get up and shake my hands free. The figures in black get in closer.

Phoenix scurries over to Papa B and bends down to cut the ropes just as Romi strides in. She shrieks when she sees what's going on. She quickly writes something down, and Papa B suddenly falls through the ground.

But as he falls, he shouts something to me. "Get a metal bowl, three triangular-square leaves, my Marmalade Chowder Glue mix, and blend with the rest! Mix for one hour until hardened!" he cries.

What? I don't even know what that means! I cry out. Romi grins. Phoenix and I back up in horror. Tears stream down my cheeks. I give Romi the nastiest glare I can muster. Romi glares back, only her eyes are pure ice.

"Lock them up," Romi growls.

Figures in black run toward us, but Phoenix runs toward them.

"Phoenix! What . . . ?"

But he's grabbed my hand and is pulling me through the figures. The figures race after us but collide into each other until there's a heap of figures in black. Everything is blurry from my tears. Phoenix guides me out of the room, and we race down the hall. We're actually not that far from the Scroll Room. We burst open the green doors to get hit, once again, by upbeat music and colorful lights. Now it's my turn to grab Phoenix's hand, and we race through the room toward the unicorn arcade game. A little girl with a beak and wings is trying to play. She puts in twenty nickels but fails to grab anything. The peppy male voice cries, "Try again!" But she's already walking off.

I gasp, "Now's our chance!" I concentrate. *This is it, Eva. You have to get this.* Tears sting my eyes. This is for Papa B.

I press the button to start the claw, and it creaks and lurches to life. I slowly inch the lever forward, and the claw copies the move. Toys and prizes have been shifted a little, but the rainbow hair is still there. It's sitting directly on top of the pile. I inch the lever forward a little more until it's hovering directly over the rainbow hair. I take a deep breath and press the button. The claw slowly sinks down, it's metal fingers eagerly outstretched. I hold my breath. The metal fingers get a grip on the cardboard holding the hair and then the claw begins to lift—with the packet of hair in its claw! It drops the packet into the slot, and I pull it out eagerly. I can feel the magic from the rainbow hair surging through me. I squeal and hug Phoenix.

We scurry out of the Scroll Room, which is now jam-packed because a whole family of what looks like blue hippos pound in. We open the doors and look around. We quickly jump into our mini-cars, which are still parked right outside, and zoom off. As we zoom through the halls, I notice that all the maids and servants are slumped in corners, sleeping. Argh, that darn Romi! We drive until we see signs pointing to the entrance of the palace. I feel a lump in my throat.

"Phoenix, what about my grandpa?" I ask, even though I know the answer already.

"Eva, we need to make the second Portal Pen first. Then, we'll write a story that gets him back," Phoenix says.

"But what if we . . . don't?" I say slowly and nervously.

"We can't give up yet, Eva," Phoenix says. "We're so close."

We park our mini-cars by the giant golden doors and climb out. The doors open very slowly, like at snail's speed, and we squeeze through and dash out. We're hit by a huge thunderstorm.

"Remember, no touching or eating the food," I warn Phoenix. I see a heaving, purple blob with thin wings in the wildflower patch in the distance. Phoenix and I quickly walk through town. Romi's sleeping spell has fallen on some of the people, but not everyone. There are hundreds of people and creatures lying sprawled out in the grass or in the streets, all curled in balls and trapped in a deep sleep. But there are still tons of people walking around buying and selling.

I shake my head and push away a plate of strawberry-flavored, hardened pudding in the shape of a flower and sugar-coated with at least a bucket of sugar. Oh, it looks so delicious! Maybe just one bite . . . my hand seems apart from my body, reaching out to touch the scrumptious treat. I can feel the curse in my fingertips as I touch it, but I don't care. It's food!

"Eva!" Phoenix cries. He slaps my wrist and I draw back. "I guess I have to warn you too," he says. I grin sheepishly.

We hurry through the soaking-wet market, our shoes squishing with water. Thunder booms across the sky, and I can see the flicker of lightning in the distance. We rush over to the wildflower patch. Misty is frowning at the rain and shaking her wings off.

"Come on, girl. We have to go now," I say.

"Wait!" Phoenix cries, jogging up to a stand that surprisingly isn't selling food. The stand is full of house antiques and gardening supplies and things that I would hate shopping for, but my mom would love. I can picture her beaming over that paper-white mug that says *Coffee Break* on it. My heart aches at the thought of mom and my family. Tears fill my eyes. I miss them so much.

There's a stash of umbrellas in the corner of the stand, and Phoenix quickly grabs two and rushes back to us, puddles splashing under his feet. We climb onto Misty, and he hands me an umbrella.

"Thanks," I say, popping it open. I lift it above my head. "Okay, Misty, take us to . . . " But my voice trails off. "Where does Misty take us to?" I ask.

Phoenix opens the map. "Our last stop: TalkingTree Trove."

Misty bellows in reply and flaps her wings. The rain makes soft tapping noises against my umbrella. It makes me super nervous sitting on Misty's slippery scales in the rain, up in the air where the dark clouds and thunder and lightning are. Misty flies off. The giant kingdom of Pixie Grove seems to be covered in a thick blanket of fog. Everything is misty and murky. My wet hair clings to my face and shoulders. I'm so grateful that Misty can fly through rain.

We fly for hours. In rain. And thunder. And lightning. It does not stop. We can't see anything around us or below us or above us, but somehow Misty seems to know exactly where we're going. Her wings flap tiredly, and she grunts. Her tail flicks back and forth impatiently.

"It's okay, girl," I whisper into her ear. "We're almost there." I honestly have no idea if we're almost there or not, but I really hope we are.

We keep flying for hours and hours and hours in the sky, but good ol' Misty never stops. Suddenly, a blinding bolt of lightning lights up the sky in front of us and Misty shrieks. I scream and Phoenix screams. I try to grip one of her scales, but they're slick and slippery from the rain, and I almost fall off. My heart is beating fast and I shiver.

"Come on, girl," I say. "You got this. We're almost there."

About ten "almost there" encouragements later, the rain seems to lighten up slightly, and the lightning ceases for a little while. Misty tiredly dips down into a forest. She grunts, and after we climb off, she flops down onto the ground and lets her wings drape over her body, her stomach heaving with deep, dragon snores.

"Welcome to TalkingTree Trove," Phoenix says.

We look around. The ground is completely covered in tree roots and bumps. There's a dirt path that forks in a bunch of different directions, jumping over hills. The trees are bursting with multicolored leaves, and the trunks look thick and heavy. Everything is still. The earth is still. The noises are still. We start following the dirt path.

"Okay, so we just need to find a talking tree named Tiki and get a snippet of his tree bark, and then we can go and make the Portal Pen," I say.

Out of nowhere, I hear a symphony of cracking noises and then a loud thump. I turn around. There's a tree with pink and bronze leaves on it. And there's also a wooden face that appears to be carved in the wood. Whoa! It's a female face with a wooden button nose and wooden almond-shaped eyes. I cautiously go up to the tree. Her wooden lips are curved into a peaceful-looking frown, but she doesn't seem to be angry or mad. I gently knock on her trunk. It makes a deep, full knock that seems to echo through the whole tree.

The female tree's wooden eyes flutter open. She looks around. Then, she begins to move around. Roots spring up from the ground as she shifts, and her trunk bobs around unsteadily as she tries to get comfortable. As soon as she spots us, she leaps back, causing a huge thump and the ground to shake for a second. Her frowning mouth is moving rapidly, but her wooden lips are sealed shut.

"I think she's trying to say something," Phoenix says to me.

The tree nods, or I think she nods. Then, she lifts her eyes up to her leaves and shakes them, causing a bronze leaf to fall from one of the branches and flutter down to the ground. The tree moves her closed lips again. I feel bad for her. She can't talk. Her eyes dart down to the leaf, and she moves her lips more rapidly than ever. I pick up the leaf. It looks like a leaf, but it's bronze and hard like metal. I examine it as the tree moves her lips like crazy.

"Wait. Give that to me," Phoenix says and takes the leaf from my hand. He steps up to the anxious tree and brings the leaf up to her lips. The tree tries to curl her wooden mouth up into a grin, but it doesn't seem to be working very well. Phoenix carefully slides the leaf into the tiny sliver between her lips and the tree manages to curl her lips forward, sucking in the leaf and swallowing it. Suddenly, she gasps and her branches flutter obnoxiously.

"Oh, thank goodness! I haven't been able to speak or breathe very well for days!" the tree cries. She is indeed a female and her voice is super high, reminding me of the shrillness of a flute.

"What was that all about?" I ask, still alarmed that there's a talking tree in front of me.

The tree gasps again, her pink and bronze leaves shaking. "A couple of days ago, maybe a week or so, me and my tree friends were out braiding each others roots when suddenly, a strange girl about thirteen appeared. Then she disappeared, but our lips were sealed and we couldn't talk! But we trees have secrets, and we knew that our bronze leaves have slivers of magic in them," the tree says.

I grumble under my breath: *Romi, Romi, Romi!*

The tree huffs and blows a pink leaf out of her wooden face, "Oh! Apologies, I forgot to introduce myself! My, there's so much to say and such little time when you haven't talked for days!" The tree shifts.

"I'm Gloria," the tree says.

I smile. "I'm Eva and this is my friend Phoenix," I say.

"Eva and Phoenix! What unique and pleasant names!"

Gloria smiles, her wooden lips widening into a wooden smile with perfectly straight teeth. "So, what brings you here to this place?"

"Well, we're looking for Tiki. It's really important," Phoenix says. Gloria's wooden cheeks suddenly seem to glow with a rosy wooden color for a moment. Is Gloria . . . blushing? Can a tree blush?

"Tiki? Of course, of course, of course! I would be more than happy to take you to him," Gloria says.

"Great!" I say.

Gloria smiles at us. "What do you need Tiki for? He's a very popular tree around here. Though he's not royalty, all the trees think he should be," she says as her cheeks turn rosy again. "Especially me."

Phoenix and I look at each other and snicker slightly.

"Well, we kinda have to get a slip wood from his trunk. It's super important," I say.

Gloria gasps. "What? You can't do that! It's against the law for someone to steal someone else's wood from their trunks! Our trunks are what store our magic, what hold up our roots and souls. And you most certainly cannot take wood from a trunk like Tiki's!" Gloria huffs.

Phoenix and I look at each other. "This might be a little tricky," I whisper to him.

Phoenix nods. "Can you at least bring us to him?" he asks.

Gloria fluffs her leaves and straightens her roots and says, "Certainly, certainly! He lives at the edge of the forest near all of his popular friends." Gloria seems to grow a little sad. "If only I could be a popular tree. Then maybe Tiki would like me," she frowns. "I'm not pretty enough or smart enough. All I have are leaves and a trunk."

She kicks at a rock with one of her roots. I feel myself gasp. Gloria is the most beautiful tree I have ever seen!

"Gloria, no!" I demand. "Don't say those things. You're gorgeous. Look at you! Someone could easily mistake you for a queen!"

Gloria looks up. "You really think so?" she asks.

I nod. "Yep," I say.

Gloria beams. "Follow me," she squeals. She shifts and begins to move slowly, but because she's using her long roots to walk, every step is a giant one. We have to run and stumble to keep up. We walk past tons of other trees. They all have bronze leaves tucked behind their colored leaves, and they all, sadly, have sealed lips. Some trees point at us with their branches. Trees walk around everywhere. It's like one giant, moving forest. And everything is quiet.

"So, what's your important mission or whatever?" Gloria asks as we march along.

"Well, it's kinda complicated, but long story short, we're trying to get the wood from this forest to make a magic pen so we can stop the girl who cursed you," I say.

Gloria beams. "Really?" she cries. "That would be so amazing if you got rid of this curse. I miss talking to my friends. Every day, all the trees wake up, and we have to face the brutal punishment of silently waving or silently talking, or not being able to go shopping for Silverberries together and chat, or ignoring your friendly neighbors because you simply can't open your mouth! It's dreadful! Simply dreadful." Gloria sadly waves at another chic tree with curvy eyes and a chill expression.

"That's my friend Maybelle," Gloria says. She points to another tree with purple and bronze leaves who's staring longingly at two trees trying to silently mingle. "That's my other best friend Evelyn," Gloria says. Evelyn waves at Gloria, and Gloria waves back. Gloria points to one more tree with blue and bronze leaves who's braiding her own roots. "And that's Faith. We're all a group. Me, Maybelle, Evelyn, and Faith. But lately, we haven't been able to talk."

That must be awful. Not ever being able to talk to your friends. "Can't you just feed everyone bronze leaves?" I ask.

Gloria shakes her head, the leaves ruffling, "It doesn't work like that. Technically, talking trees can only eat so many bronze leaves before their roots begin to shrivel up. It's called Root Fever. You can be stuck with it your whole life." We walk along the dirt path into a clearing. "And besides, bronze leaves only let you talk for at least fifteen minutes."

"How old can talking trees get anyway?" Phoenix asks.

Gloria giggles. "I turned 712 two days ago," she says. Whoa!

"That's crazy!" Phoenix laughs.

"Tiki is 801," Gloria sighs. "Everybody says the 800s are the good ages." Phoenix and I look at each other and snicker.

We enter a thick part of the forest where we have to squeeze through gaps because there're so many trees. And worse, all of them are pushing and shoving each other, trying desperately to move around. Gloria spreads out her branches to make way, and everybody stumbles back. We keep walking until Gloria throws one of her branches out in front of us so that we can't go any further.

"Stop," she says.

We look ahead. There's a beautiful view of the sunset piling itself on to the waves of the black ocean. Sea gulls scream overhead. We're on the drop-off of a cliff. A waterfall spills from the rocks at the edge of the cliff and tumbles over the rocks, seeping into the ocean. The forest forms a U-shape, so we can go around to the cliff on the other side. A waterfall plummets from that cliff too, and the rays of the sun catch water droplets, forming a misty rainbow that shivers through the waterfall.

"So pretty," I breathe.

"Isn't it?" Gloria sighs. "Ah, I wish I could live here."

On the cliff across from us is a patch of trees. The trees aren't moving. There's one particular tree in the middle of the clump with bright green and golden leaves. Like pure gold. The trunk is a hazel color with wisps of silver curling around its roots. I can see pure sparks of magic leaping and bounding over the tree's roots and under rocks, but still staying close to the roots.

"What tree is that?" I ask. It's the most gorgeous tree I've ever seen.

"That's Tiki," Gloria says. I nudge Gloria's rough trunk, and she gives me a playful look.

"Come on, slow pokes! Let's go!" Phoenix cries, already turning and running through the trees. Gloria and I turn and follow him, Gloria making the ground rumble every time she moves.

We go through the forest and around the U-shape until we arrive at the other cliff. Gloria gulps.

"What's wrong?" I ask.

"I've . . . I've never been to Tiki's house before," she says.

I pat her rough back. "Come on," I encourage. "You said he's nice, right?"

Gloria nods furiously. There's a little slope, and we carefully scooch down it. The trees still aren't moving.

"Knock, knock," Gloria says. "Tiki, you have some visitors."

Silence. Gloria cocks her head. Or, at least, tries.

"Tiki? You awake? It's not even Talking Tree Table Time, so you don't need to sleep yet," Gloria says.

"What's Talking Tree Table Time?" Phoenix whispers.

"You humans call it dinner or supper," Gloria says.

Oh! That makes sense. Gloria thumps closer to what appears to be Tiki. We walk around him to the front. His face looks quiet and peaceful. He has a sort of long nose, but not too long. His wooden mouth is curved into a frown, and his eyes are closed.

"Tiki?" Gloria whispers. She gently lifts a branch to his face and strokes his wooden cheek but suddenly jumps back. "Ouch! His face is burning hot!" she cries.

I lift my pointer finger up to Tiki, and I can feel the heat even before I touch him. "Oof, he's burning up," I say.

I examine him closely. His wooden brows are curved into concern. This isn't right. I glance down and notice red sparks of magic crackling and popping as they dance between his numb roots.

"It's Romi's evil magic," I say.

We glance around. All of his friends are sleeping too. Red magic licks their trunks and leaps around. "She's put them to sleep," I gasp.

Gloria's eyes suddenly look shiny. "Oh, goodness," she whispers.

Phoenix turns toward us, "We'll fix this, Gloria. But right now, the only way to fix this is if we get a piece of wood from Tiki's trunk."

Gloria swallows and nods. Her leaves shake and rattle. "Okay," she says after a moment.

Phoenix slips off his backpack and rummages around. He pulls out a pocket knife. He brings the knife up to Tiki, and Gloria lets out a tiny shriek.

"Please be careful!" she blurts out, then covers her mouth in shame.

"Don't worry. I've got this," Phoenix says as he brings the knife up to the side of Tiki and curves the knife to a cutting position. Carefully, he presses the edge of the knife up to Tiki's side and gently scrapes off a piece of wood. Perfectly jagged, perfectly hazel-colored.

"We got it!" Phoenix cries. He runs up to Gloria and gently gives her a hug.

"Good job, guys. Hopefully Tiki will understand," Gloria says sadly and glances at Tiki. "When he wakes up."

Phoenix hands me the piece of wood, and I slip it into my backpack. We turn and begin to climb up the slope. That was easy. But . . . too easy. Romi wouldn't let us get away so easily. But she wouldn't stop us either. I know that for a fact.

Suddenly, we hear a cracking sound. We pause and slowly turn around. Oh my gosh. All of the trees are facing us with Tiki in the front. Their wooden eyes are now glowing red.

"I have a feeling we should run," Phoenix says.

The trees lift their roots from the ground, red sparkles climbing all over their wooden bodies. All the trees charge at us and begin to climb the slope.

"I think you're right!" I cry.

Phoenix and I bolt and run as fast as we can, but Gloria's having trouble keeping up.

"I can't . . . I can't do it!" she cries. All of a sudden, her face curls into a furious expression as her eyes fill up with a red glow.

"Not Gloria too!" I cry.

Phoenix grabs my hand, and we dash through the forest, weaving and darting around trees. Every time we pass a tree, its eyes turn red and it slowly faces us. The stampede of spelled trees behind us begins to increase as more trees turn on us and begin chasing us. The ground rumbles. I feel like we're running on top of a giant earthquake. We run through the forest and past the clearing. I can see Misty in the distance, chasing a butterfly.

"Misty!" I gasp. "Misty! Over here!"

Misty's adorable, innocent eyes look over at us, and when she sees the angry trees behind us, she turns her whole body and faces us completely, growling in concern and protection. Then, Misty flaps her wings and leaps into the air. She dives down over the trees in front of us and rams into the trees chasing us. She's like a bowling ball crashing into bowling pins. I cheer. That slows down the trees a bit, but not completely. They're still chasing us. Misty soars into the sky and flies down to us. She crouches low, and we rapidly scramble onto her back.

"Fly!" I practically scream.

Misty flaps her wings and soars off. I clutch her giant, lavender body with relief. My heart is beating so fast. I let out a big breath and close my eyes. I kiss Misty's scales.

"I don't know what we would have done without you," I whisper.

Misty coos in response. I glance back. All the trees are climbing over each other at the clearing of the forest. They're thrashing and clawing, but all the while, still gazing at us with red eyes. I shiver. Creepy.

Phoenix nudges me and I turn to face him.

"Guess what?" he says.

"What?" I say, heaving.

"Eva, don't you see? We have all the items!" Phoenix whispers.

I gasp. Duh! "Yes!" I cry.

We both laugh. I pump the air. Misty coos happily. Suddenly, Phoenix turns toward me and leans in. Then, he kisses me on my lips. It's a quick little peck, but it's still a kiss! My heart flutters. He pulls away and grins his dorky Phoenix grin. I smile back. He's the most amazing friend anyone could ever have. My eyes well up with tears, and I throw my arms around his neck. I let myself bury my face into his shoulder and rest there.

"I don't know what I would've done without you, Phoenix," I say.

"You're an awesome friend, Eva," he says. I squeeze my eyes shut and grin.

A few hours later, we're soaring through the night sky. The breeze is bitter and cold, and I shiver. The rain is also heavy once again, and thunder rumbles mysteriously behind the thick clouds. The raindrops are fat and cold. One drops from the sky and slithers down my back.

"Question," I say.

"Ask away," Phoenix says back, letting the rain hit his face.

"Where exactly are we going?" I ask.

Phoenix sits up. "Uh, good question," he says.

My eyes go wide. "You mean Misty's just flying around without any direction?" I ask.

Phoenix clasps his hands together. "Well, er . . . "

We think. Then, it hits me. A memory flashes back to when we were trapped in the science lab. As Papa B was falling through the floor, he cried, "Get a metal bowl, three triangular-square leaves, my Marmalade Chowder Glue mix, and blend with the rest! Mix for one hour until hardened!"

I gasp, "Phoenix! We need to go to Spirit Forest!"

Phoenix scratches his head. "What? Why?" he asks.

"Remember when my grandpa shouted out that sentence right before he fell through the floor at the palace in Pixie Grove?" I ask.

Phoenix slowly nods, "Yes, I think so. Something about a metal pot?"

"Yes! He was giving us the recipe on how to make the Portal Pen!" I cry.

Phoenix gasps. "You're right!" he cries.

I face the front. "Misty, take us to Spirit Forest," I say. Misty bobs her head up and down and tilts her body. We slowly turn around, and Misty zooms through the sky once again. A raindrop plops into my eyes, and I squeak and rub them furiously.

"You okay?" Phoenix asks.

"Yeah, I'm fine," I say. Still, I get a weird tingly sensation. I keep glancing back behind us, but all I see is the fog and clouds.

"Relax, Eva, you're stressed," Phoenix says.

"No! No, I'm not." I glance behind me again. I see a dark shadow flash in the light of the lightning. "I think we're being followed," I whisper. "Misty, go lower."

Misty does as she's told, and soon we're under the clouds. I look up. Yep. Sure enough, I can just barely see the outline of a black dragon. It's claws are slicing through the clouds. Misty whimpers and flaps her wings harder. But the dragon above always seems to keep up with her, no matter how fast she goes.

"Well, well, well," a voice thunders across the sky. *Romi.* Lightning crashes and illuminates Romi and her dragon. I can only see her shadow, but from far away, I can immediately see her glowing green eyes. They stare back at me. Her eyes are piercing, and I feel like she's staring into my soul.

"Hi, Eva. Can we join you for dinner? No, never mind it would be much more fun to ruin it," Romi growls. Her voice is slow and she's not yelling, but her voice echoes across the sky.

"No thanks!" I shout back. Ew. My voice sounds awful.

Midnight roars and dips down so that they're right behind us. His beady eyes glare at us. Misty flaps anxiously. She tries to swerve, but Midnight copies her exact movements. Great. Just great.

"What do you want now, Romi? We've got nothing," I call.

"You have exactly what I want." Midnight flies faster and pulls up beside Misty. Romi's eyes are bright green. "Give me your backpack," she growls.

"Never," I say sharply.

Romi frowns and says, "I don't want to make this difficult, Eva. I'm your friend."

"My friend?!" I yell back. "You think you're my *friend*?" Tears burn my eyes.

"Yes," Romi says simply.

I laugh. I clutch my stomach and laugh. Romi peers at me, confused. Tears roll down my cheeks. "My friend?" I scream. "You have never been my friend, and you never will be."

I see Romi flinch. Her green eyes flicker until they're replaced by her regular brown ones. I throw my hands out, gesturing at the stormy sky around me. "All of this, is because of you! You think you're my friend? Well . . . " I let out a sob. Romi's lip quivers slightly. "Well . . . think again," I choke out. I pat Misty's back, and she surges forward, leaving Romi and Midnight in the clouds.

My friend. Romi thinks she's my friend. Hilarious.

Soon, we touch down into the clearing of glass trees of the Spirit Forest. We climb off of Misty, and I wipe my eyes. All of a sudden, a yellow-and-green mist curls around us, and then, Noah and Ginger are in front of us.

"Oh, thank goodness!" Noah cries.

"What?" I say and my tears turn to laughter at the sight of them. "How did you . . . ?"

Ginger chuckles. "We annoyed that dumb pirate till he couldn't take us anymore. He kicked us off his ship," Ginger says.

"*And* he said some very foul words that I refuse to repeat," Noah scoffs, pointing his nose to the sky.

I grin. "I'm so glad you're here," I say, stroking Ginger's green fur.

Ginger barks. "How did you do?" she cries.

I beam. "We collected all of the items," I say.

Ginger jumps around and kicks her hind legs up in the air with joy. "Whoo! Yes!" she cries.

"Now we just have to go to Papa B's house to make the second Portal Pen," I say.

Ginger frowns and cocks her head. "But where is Billie?" she asks.

I swallow the lump in my throat, "He, uh, he got taken. We couldn't save him in time."

I sniff. Ginger whimpers.

"But as soon as we make this pen, we'll be able to set him free," Phoenix says.

I nod. Ginger yaps and her tongue dangles from her mouth happily.

Noah trots toward us. "Well, come on then, chaps! This way to his tree house!"

The Spirit Animals sprint off, and we scramble to keep up. They lead us through the woods. Out of no-where, all around us, colorful mists drift into our path and form into animals, who whoop and cheer for us. I wave as we run. Animals hoot and holler and chirp and bark. It's amazing. And they're all cheering for us.

"Oh, yeah, and we might have told all of our friends about your bravery and heroism while you were gone," Noah says. I grin.

Soon, we make it back to the tree house. It looks sad and lifeless without Papa B clambering and jumping around in it. We burst through the doors and I quickly unzip my backpack. I lay the contents on the table. There's the turquoise sea flower. It flutters in the breeze and little water droplets lie nestled on the petals. Then, the dry piece of black leather from Captain Seaweed's jacket. Next, there's the tiny vial of purple venom from Dagger, the clouds from the Cloud Kingdom, and the rainbow hairs from Silvie the Unicorn. And lastly, the rough piece of hazel bark from Tiki.

"Yep, all of them are here," I smile.

Phoenix claps his hands together, "Okay. Metal pot." He dashes into the kitchen, and I hear drawers opening, cabinets slamming, plates clattering, and pots and pans banging. Finally, Phoenix stumbles out with a metal pot. "Found it," he says breathlessly. "It was wedged behind the sink."

He hands it to me, and I heave it up on to the table. Together we gather the items and lay them in the pot.

"Now we need Marmalade Chowder Glue," Phoenix says, sounding out each syllable.

"That is kind of a weird concoction," I say, grinning. Phoenix goes back into the kitchen, and I check the shelves. Marmalade Chowder Glue, where are you?

I open cabinets and drawers. No Marmalade Chowder Glue. I find a closet with a wooden door and yank it open. Inside are shelves and shelves bursting with jars and items and weird things. I spot a can of dead worms. Gross. There are also blue candles with mermaids on them. I find a purple clam shell and open it. Black ink pours from it. Ew! I snap it shut. My fingertips are dotted with black ink. I notice a pair of rusty scissors, a bracelet made of emeralds, a coconut, a pair of sandals with wings on them, a yellow robe with red numbers on the sleeves, and lots of other peculiar items. I shove a can of raspberries to the side to discover a small jar with a label that says, MARMALADE CHOWDER GLUE. Yes!

"Found it!" I holler.

Dashing back to the kitchen, I unscrew the lid. The inside is filled with a goopy orange substance that feels like jelly and smells like my garage and vanilla at the same time. A very weird smell, but I kind of like it.

Phoenix grabs a spoon, and I dump the goop into the pot. It oozes from the jar and covers over the items. Immediately, I hear the items sizzle and watch them disintegrate before my eyes as the glue drowns them. I take the spoon and stir. I can feel the magic sizzling and popping under the spoon. This is so crazy.

"Okay, one problem: I don't know how to design and create a pen," I say.

I glance down at the pot. The orange goop is now turning to white goop. The white goop fades to lavender. I glance at Phoenix. He shrugs.

"I don't know either," he says.

"But your grandfather does," Noah cries.

"Yeah, but he's not here," I say, watching as the glue darkens to a deep shade of violet.

Noah clomps his hooves against the floor and towers over us, "Yes, indeed that is so, but when your grandfather first came here, he had a whole binder full of drawings and sketches of pens and the Portal Pen. I'm sure it's here somewhere." Noah clomps into the other room, and I hear him trample up the stairs, the wood creaking under his weight.

I keep on stirring and groan, "We have to do this for a whole hour. We'll need to take shifts stirring."

"I'm fine to take a shift whenever," Phoenix offers.

"Oh my goodness," I say.

"What? What's happening?" Phoenix runs to look into the pot.

"No. I forgot one of the things Papa B said: 'three triangular-square leaves.' They aren't in here yet."

"I can help with that!" Ginger offers, running outside to gather the last thing we need.

I keep stirring. The glue begins to become a lighter shade of purple, and then slowly blends into blue. Noah scrambles back a moment later, a faded gray binder clutched in his teeth, paper fluttering out and all over the place.

Phoenix takes the binder from Noah's mouth and flips it open. "Thanks!" I say.

Ginger returns with the three glass leaves, dropping them into the pot. They dissolve right into the mix. I sigh with relief. That was too close. If I hadn't remembered the leaves, this wouldn't have worked. "Thank you, Ginger!" She rubs her head into my hand, and I give her ear a scratch.

Phoenix intently studies the pages of the binder Noah gave him, flipping one at a time and examining each. "Eva, come look at this," he says.

I hand my spoon to Ginger, who clutches it in her paw and takes over the stirring, and I walk over to Phoenix. There are sloppy sketches of pens, all labeled. The writing is in pencil, which has smudged.

"Look!" Phoenix points to a small slip of notebook paper. I can barely make out the title: BUILDING A PEN. It shows the steps and materials needed.

Noah walks over and stretches his long neck to study the paper. "Oh! Wait! I know just the thing!" he cries, scrambling up the stairs once more.

We study the page until Noah slowly steps down the stairs with the edge of a box tightly gripped in his teeth. I rush up the stairs and grab the box from him. It's full of different pen and pencil supplies. There's a plastic bag full of lead, erasers, bottles full of ink, tops of pens, metal and plastic pieces, and so on.

"This is perfect!" I cry as I examine the page. "And this box contains all the things we need!"

Together, Phoenix and I rummage around through the dusty materials and grab everything the page calls for. Then, very, very slowly, we follow Papa B's pen-making guide. Thank you, Papa B! We learn how to screw on the top, and make sure everything is tight and secure, and we also learn how to carefully place the ink into the clear container. Now I know how to put erasers on pencils too!

About an hour later, Phoenix and I work to slip the perfect amount of ink into the container. Ginger is taking turns using both of her paws to stir.

"Uh, Eva? You might wanna come see this," Ginger says, peering down into the metal pot.

I wipe my hands on a kitchen towel and jog over. "What?" I ask.

Ginger points into the bowl, "I can't stir it anymore. It kept getting thicker and thicker, and now it's hard and crunchy."

I glance into the bowl. Oh wow. The goop is now a brilliant turquoise color, and it's no longer goop. But the goop absorbed all the items except for the piece of Tiki's wood. Instead, it laid itself upon the wood and hardened. Turquoise Wood! This is the result of the recipe!

I squeal, "We did it! We actually made Turquoise Wood!"

I pick up the single piece of Turquoise Wood and examine it in my fingers. It feels a little pasty. I hug Ginger with my free hand and bring the piece of Turquoise Wood over to Phoenix.

"Look!" I cry. "We did it!"

Phoenix high-fives me and plucks the wood from my hand. He says, "Okay, so now we just need to . . . "

Phoenix flips the pages of the binder until he lands on one. It says, NOTES FOR APPLYING WOOD. "See," he says. "It's different for the Portal Pen—instead of building it around and inside, we lay the piece of wood on the top of the pen, place the pen on a piece of wax paper, and stick it in the oven for twenty minutes at exactly 350 degrees."

Phoenix wipes his ink-covered hands on a paper towel and hurries into the kitchen. I love Phoenix with a plan. He bends down and quickly opens a drawer. There's a neon yellow box inside along with blue boxes. Phoenix scoops up the yellow box and opens it up. Inside is a half-full roll of wax paper. Phoenix tears a strip off and sticks the box back into the drawer. He scrambles over to the tiny oven and turns it to 350 degrees.

He searches around until he finds a baking sheet he can place everything on. Finally, he finds one in a cabinet so he places the sheet of wax paper on the baking sheet and then lays the newly created pen on top of it. Gently, he takes the piece of Turquoise Wood and balances it on the top of the pen. Then, he places this in the oven, closes the oven door, and brushes himself off. He's huffing and hurrying, and I can tell he's stressed. He turns to wash his hands, but I grab his shoulder.

"Phoenix," I say calmly. Phoenix turns. His hair is all scraggly, beads of sweat cling to his forehead, and his cheeks are rosy. He's breathing hard.

"Yeah?" he says breathlessly.

I raise my head a little. "Take a deep breath," I say. Phoenix smiles weakly and throws his head back, heaving in a big breath and letting out a big sigh.

"I can tell you're stressed," I say. "And I am too. But we need to be calm and prepared."

Phoenix nods. "I know," he says. I grin at him and let him go. "Oh, hey. Do we have a timer?" he asks.

"Oh. Yeah. I've barely used my phone. I'll see if it still has a charge," I say. Thankfully, it does, and I set a timer for the alarm to go off in twenty minutes.

We walk back to the main room and collect the papers, materials, boxes, and binder. Ginger is curled up on the wooden couch in the living room sleeping. When we're nearly done, Noah comes in with two trays balanced on his back. Once we put everything away, we plop down on the couch next to Ginger. I stroke her fur. It's super soft—not too scraggly and not too sharp. She purrs softly as I run my fingers through it.

"Tea, anyone?" Noah cries, setting the trays down on the table.

"Yes, please!" I cry, grabbing a warm mug from the tray.

Phoenix holds a cup of tea in his hands. "Okay, so we need a plan," he says.

"Well, first things first, we probably want to write a story that frees my grandfather," I say. "And next, we'll need to write a story freeing everyone in this world from any curses at all. And then, free any innocent prisoners and people that Romi captured," I explain.

Phoenix nods. "Good idea," he says. He stares into his mug. "But what about Romi herself?" he asks.

Good point. "Well, we'll have a Portal Pen, and she'll have a Portal Pen, so . . . " My voice trails off. What will we do then?

Phoenix stands up. "We'll use *this* Portal Pen to steal *that* Portal Pen," Phoenix cries.

I jump up, clapping my hands. "Yes! Perfect!" I cry.

"Then, we'll say goodbye and bring Romi back with us to the real world. And, to do that, we'll write a story that opens up the Portal," Phoenix explains.

"And I'll write a story creating a box holding the Portal Pens with a password that only I know," I grin. "So that no one will ever steal or use them again. Only me," I say.

Phoenix nods. He grabs a cookie and takes a bite out of it. I tap my chin. "So, once this Portal Pen gets out of the oven, we'll just write a story that magically takes the Portal Pen from Romi's hands and puts it in ours?" I ask.

Phoenix shrugs and nods. "I guess," he says. I grin and take another sip of my tea.

Pretty soon the oven beeps, and we rush over to see. Phoenix opens the oven, and smoke pours out. Oh no. A burnt smell fogs up the air, and we all cough and sputter.

Phoenix pulls the baking sheet out and blows on the Portal Pen. Despite the burning smell, the pen is perfect. It's as beautiful as my old one. Or, the one that Romi is using right now. Phoenix hands it to me, and I run my fingers along it.

"The only problem is, it's not smooth. It's still kind of chalky. Is there any way to fix that?" I ask Phoenix.

Phoenix takes the pen from my hands and nods. "Of course!" he cries.

Rapidly he rushes back over to the wooden table and grabs the binder from the shelf. He flips open the binder so quickly that loose pages flutter and fly all over the place. He rummages around in drawers until he finds a hot glue gun, which he instantly plugs in.

Anxiously, I tap at my mug. The tea sloshes around. I'm so nervous. So many thoughts are running through my mind: *Will this work? What if we can't get Papa B back? Will we get the pen from Romi? What if this pen isn't another Portal Pen? What if, what if, what if.* I swallow the lump in my throat and try to calm my anxious heart. I sip my tea, hoping it'll take away the heavy rocks sitting at the bottom of my stomach.

As the glue gun heats up, Phoenix runs to the kitchen to find a spoon and a glass cup. Once he does, he runs over to the sink where he fills the cup with hot water before walking back to the glue gun. Then he squirts some of the glue into the glass of hot water before grabbing the spoon and spooning the hot sticky glob of glue and water onto the pen. He sloppily spreads the glue stuff all over the chalky part of the pen. Then, he smooths it out with a knife and comes over to sit by us while it dries.

"I know what you're up to," a voice suddenly rings out through the little wooden tree house. The little tree house trembles slightly, and the thick curtains covering the cracked windows whip around anxiously. We huddle together a little tighter.

"Romi? Is that you?" I growl.

The voice laughs. "Yay! You remembered me! How lovely. But yes, it's me, and I know exactly what you're up to."

I frown. "Then why are you letting us get away with this?" I ask.

There's a pause in the air until Romi cries, "Because for three generations, the McFullys have been trying to grab, take, hunt down, find, and have the Portal Pen to ourselves! But noooo. It never worked. So, I decided to play the old 'Good Friend, Bad Friend' trick with you. And, oh, how easy you fell for it."

Tears sting my eyes. I knew it this whole time. She used me.

"Once your second Portal Pen is done, all that's left to do is battle to the finish. Then, I'll have more power than ever! *Two* Portal Pens!" Romi giggles. "And, I can't just let you guys go to waste. I want to fight! Rub it in your face that the McFullys finally get what they deserve!"

The house abruptly lights up with a neon green glow. I shield my eyes. "So, see you at the battlefield!" Romi cries.

Suddenly, all is silent again. The glow disappears, the curtains stop struggling, and Romi's voice and presence are gone.

"A battle? We can't win a battle against *her*!" Noah cries.

I put a finger up. "Ah, ah. She may seem all evil and powerful, but without that pen, she's just a regular, helpless girl. Plus, we have a Portal Pen too," I say.

Noah nods but then says, "Or ours might not work."

Ginger kicks his cheddar-yellow side with her paw and he yelps. "Try to be positive, Noah."

"Speaking of Portal Pens, I think ours is done," Phoenix says.

He gets up and goes over to the table. Sure enough, the sticky, hot glue goop is perfectly melted into the pen, giving the Turquoise Wood a smooth, shiny texture.

"It's perfect," I whisper. I hold up the pen to my face and examine it. It's so beautiful. I bite my lip with excitement.

"Okay, now we just have to make a wish that the Turquoise Wood will grant," Phoenix says.

I stare down at the beautiful pen. "I wish that all of the stories you will write will magically appear in this world," I say. Immediately I feel a tingle of magic run through my body. I shiver with excitement. "Should we try it out?" I whisper.

Phoenix gestures toward my backpack, and I scramble to it and pull out my notebook. My hands shake as I turn the pages. I flip to a blank one and lead the tip of the pen to the very top line.

"What should I write?" I ask. Everyone shrugs. I think. What should I write about? "How about some delicious dinner?" I ask. Everyone cheers and agrees. My stomach is growling. And the tea didn't exactly fill me up much anyway. "Okay," I say.

I slowly and carefully write. Everyone stares at me, eagerly waiting. I write, *Once, Eva Mason and her friends were hungry, so they were all served a large dinner feast with yummy foods of different kinds.* I look up anxiously. My hopes slowly begin to plummet. I hang my head. Everyone frowns. But then, out of nowhere, a single plate appears on the table, startling us. It's a large plate, heaped with golden spaghetti noodles, caked in tomato sauce with meatballs buried inside. It looks yummy, but it's not a feast. I guess it doesn't work very well.

Until . . . more plates appear. Phoenix quickly clears off everything that's on the little wooden table to make room for all the plates and bowls and cups that are piling onto it. There are bowls with buttery rolls, plates with warm ravioli, trays with little veggie-square bites, steaming bowls of white rice, giant plates with deep brown steak, bowls of dumpling soup with onions, and tons of other options. This is amazing! It actually works!

"I can't believe it! It works!" I cry. I let myself close my eyes and laugh with joy. It works! It really, really works. Everyone digs in. I grab a greasy breadstick with a thick garlic smell and dip it into a small bowl of dumpling soup. Mmm, so good. Phoenix munches on a turkey sandwich with mayo oozing out of the sides. Noah is nibbling on a veggie spring roll, and Ginger is trying to rip a piece of steak to shreds. I smile.

After we stuff our bellies until we can't stuff them anymore, we settle down for the night. Noah sleeps in his little nook, Ginger curls up by the fireplace, Phoenix sleeps on the couch, and I sleep in Papa B's bed. He crafted the bed himself a long time ago, taking a bunch of bamboo sticks and strapping them together into a sturdy bed holder. Then, he sewed cotton together to make his mattress. It must have taken a lot of cotton. It's really cozy though.

Papa B's bedroom is super small, and there's no straight wall because it's curved into an oval shape, with barely enough room to squeeze in a bed and a desk. The open window lets in a chilly breeze and droplets from the never-ending rain slip in through the window and splash onto my face. I cringe and pull the thick curtain over the window tighter before I bury myself under the fur blanket and try to sleep. Everything is quiet except for the faint chirp of buzzing crickets and the crackling of the fire in the living room fireplace.

I can't sleep, though. I toss and turn all night. I'm half asleep the whole night, confusing dreams with reality. My head begins to pound and my mouth is dry. I'm *so* tired, but I just can't fall asleep. At one point, I sleep for about fifteen minutes, and when I wake up, it's still dark out, but the sky is slowly getting lighter. Rubbing my eyes, I throw off my blanket. Might as well start the day I decide as I slip into comfy traveling clothes, a mint-colored shirt with shorts, and put my hair into two long, red braids flowing down my shoulders. I open the small wooden door into the tiny living room. Ginger and Noah are still sleeping, but Phoenix is up and trying to fry an egg in a sizzling pan. I walk into the kitchen. He turns up the heat of the stove, and the fire flickers with blue flames.

"Couldn't sleep either?" I ask, noticing the dark bags sagging under his droopy eyes. He's slumped and shuffling around with such tiredness. But when I speak, Phoenix practically jumps out of his skin. Then he grins tiredly and nods. I bet I have big, black bags under my eyes too.

Phoenix finishes making his fried egg, and we sit down on the couch next to Ginger. I sigh.

"Are you ready for all of this?" I ask.

Phoenix chuckles slightly. "No, I am not," he smiles.

I laugh softly. "Yeah, me neither."

I stare at the flames of the fireplace. Phoenix stares at them too. Phoenix then turns toward me.

"But we're gonna still do this anyway," he says.

I smile and nod. There's my Phoenix! We high-five. Then I get up and grab the Portal Pen. I can feel it's magic power surging from it and through me. Ginger slowly stretches and gets up. Noah yawns.

"Morning," he says.

"You guys ready for this?" I ask.

Noah and Ginger nod. "Oh yeah!" she cries. We gather our things, and then we all head outside and hop on Misty.

Misty soars into the air. I write fast.

Once, Eva's grandfather (Papa B) was freed, and they were reunited. Suddenly, Papa B himself pops up in the back of Misty.

"Eva!" he cries.

I smile, tears welling up in my eyes. "You're back!" I cry. This Portal Pen does work! And quickly!

Next, I write, *Once, Eva stopped this terrible ongoing thunderstorm.* Suddenly, the dark clouds clear and the rain stops. The sky is a bright blue, and there's not a single cloud in sight. Then, I write, *Once, all the imprisoned people of this world were freed.*

Suddenly, people appear everywhere. Thousands of them. We can see them showing up all over the place below us as we fly by. They're confused at first, but then they cry out in joy and hug and kiss each other. Lastly, I write, *Once, all the curses in the world were broken.*

All of a sudden, a huge wave of golden light ripples over the tops of the forest like a giant wave.

"Okay, now, the next step," I say. I scan the ground below us. Spirit Forest is stretched out for miles and miles, but beyond that, I can see a mini-desert with Romi's large, silver factory. I can see her climbing onto Midnight. Wait, I also see like, a thousand more Midnights! Oh no.

"Okay, everyone!" I cry. "Suit up!" I write in my notebook: *Eva, Phoenix, Papa B, Misty, Ginger, and Noah all had on protective armor that can block anything during battle.* Out of nowhere, we're instantly dressed in stiff but secure purple armor, the color of Misty. We have helmets that cover our foreheads, chest plates, swords, and even shields. Misty is equipped with head gear too. In that moment, all the evil dragons turn toward us. All of their eyes glow red. Then, Romi turns toward us.

"Okay guys," I say. "Let's win this thing."

Chapter Twenty-six

The Battle Zone

"Fly, Misty!" I cry.

Misty lets loose a terrifying roar and zooms toward the hundreds of dragons, who then lift up into the air and race toward us. We bowl into them with such force, but it doesn't faze them at all. Neither does it faze Misty when one chomps on her side. This is going to be a long battle.

Romi soars above all the rest of the dragons. "Think you can beat me? Well, you're so . . ."

But I'm already scribbling something down. I don't care anymore about her and her remarks. She comes here to brag about the race, but I'm here to win it. Suddenly, Romi is wrapped in ropes that are tied to Midnight and binding the dragon's wings. The two scream and roar as they plummet toward the ground. We swoop down, but the Portal Pen is still in Romi's hands. She manages to write something down on her paper, and soon the ropes snap and she's up in the air again.

She scribbles something down as I scribble something down, and soon we're both tangled in ropes with our hands tied behind our backs. I fall off of Misty and scream as I sail toward the ground. My stomach tingles as the gravity of falling makes me cringe, and the ground is getting closer and closer to my face. I squeeze my eyes shut. But I don't hit the ground. I hit something slick and slippery. There's a pair of swift hands untying the ropes. I open my eyes and look over. Romi is struggling in the grass, trying to write something down but failing, and her dragons patiently waiting for the next command.

I look up and notice a face that looks baked by the sun with wild eyes and scraggly, dark red hair and a ragged zebra dress. "Dakota!" I cry.

Once the ropes are untied, I scramble up and hug her tight. I notice that the slick and slippery thing I landed on is Dagger's back. He turns his huge head to show me his deadly fangs. I laugh nervously. Dakota helps me off. She has a deep cut on her arm with dry blood clinging to the edges.

"You okay?" I ask.

Dakota nods briskly. "Yeah, just trying to fight that one." She points a thumb over her shoulder at Romi, still struggling in the grass. "We thought you might want some backup," Dakota grins.

I look around, and we're surrounded—by the friends we've made in this world. Captain Seaweed rides his giant ship over to us and swings a sword around. His pirates yell and shout. The mermaids of the Blue Bay burst through the water with their queen holding her trident. All the mermaids flick their tails and bow at us. Suddenly, a stampede of Spirit Animals come crashing through the forest and halt, each and every one crouched and battle-ready. Misty roars and thousands of colorful dragons swarm the sky. They all dip their heads low at me. The remaining Cloud Council floats down on a cloud with an army of cloud men. The ladies of Lovely Valley soar through the sky on a clump of flowers with Majesty standing in front, looking determined and ready.

Looking to my right, I see that the trees from the forest aren't just trees. They all have wooden faces— and Gloria and Tiki are in the front with magic billowing around them dangerously. Then, the council from Pixie Grove shoots through the sky and lands with a cloud of pink mist. This is so amazing! There's so much more too. I spot an army of bronze soldiers from the Jewel Kingdom, a large group of people with rakes, knives, sticks, and torches with Miss Amelia the Fortune Teller in the front. There's also the BigFoot and the Yeti, growling and clutching giant clubs. My eyes fill up with tears for the millionth time.

"Of course I could use the help!" I cry. I hug Dakota once more.

Unfortunately, Romi manages to scribble something down, and she's instantly back up on her dragon. The evil crew of dragons' eyes glow red, and they all roar at us.

"CHARGE!" I scream.

Immediately, everyone rushes toward the dragons. The mermaids of the Blue Bay create a huge tsunami wave for Captain Seaweed. His giant ship rocks and sways as they soar over the wave. Figures in black jump onto the ship, and the two sides break out into a sword and knife fight. The Cloud Council breathe in one huge breath and let it out, sending a gigantic gust of wind at the dragons and blowing some of them backwards. The evil dragons slowly start to gain on us.

"Get the pen!" I cry. "Get the pen!"

Taking my words as direction, everyone begins to engage closer to Romi. Tiki suddenly grows very tall and starts shooting wisps of magic at Midnight, which causes a big blow every time. With one of the hard blows to Midnight's side, Romi slips and tumbles off of the dragon. I scribble something down and she's trapped inside a net. The pen has fallen out of her hands and is now lying in the grass. Miss Amelia shoves people out of the way, determined to get the pen, but just as she touches it, a figure in black swoops down and grabs it. Ugh!

"Come on!" I cry. "You can do this!" I write something down, and the magic increases. Dakota scurries up her snake and leaps into the air. She lands on Midnight, who begins to plummet. Meanwhile, Romi rips through the net and jumps onto another black dragon that's resting on the ground. She grabs the Portal Pen from the figure in black, and her eyes glow green as she writes something down. Out of nowhere, we hear sounds like jets. Loud, soaring jets. Everyone stops to look up. I gasp. Dakota gasps. Phoenix gasps.

Oh. My. Gosh. This is not happening.

Five giant planes shaped like dragons burst through the sky. They are gigantic—ten times bigger than Dagger, and Dagger is the biggest creature here. Little plates open up on the bellies of the planes, and then a wave of figures in black pour out from the planes. They have jackets with fabric wings sewn between the arms and the waist, causing them to soar through the sky and land safely. They look like little black bugs falling from the sky. When they do land, the ground is absolutely covered in figures in black.

I scribble something down that causes magic to surge through everyone on my side. Dagger's giant body slithers up as his head lifts to the sky. He opens his giant mouth and begins squirting venom at the planes. One of the planes glitches from the venom and plummets. It hits the ground and explodes. Fire and ash erupts everywhere, and smoke begins to fill the air. Dakota slides down Dagger's back and begins to karate-chop figures in black. A figure in black rapidly slices the air with his sword, barely missing her every time.

Romi writes something down, and suddenly, I'm on Midnight. She beckons for me to give her the second Portal Pen. Never. I write something down, and I'm instantly standing back on the ground. I write something else down to fill all my dragons' mouths with blue fire. They begin shooting it down at the ground in big balls. Figures in black duck and dodge. The good and bad dragons begin to fight in the air.

Romi lands in front of me and writes something down. Then, she opens her palms and sparks of magic fly out. One hits my arm and I yelp. It burns! I write something down to make balls of red fire shoot from my hands. I take a shot at her. We go on like this for a little while, shooting and dodging and writing and firing. I see Phoenix fighting off figures in black. He's getting more and more surrounded. I turn and run, and Romi runs off as well. I hide in a talking tree and quickly write something down. A giant bubble appears around Phoenix, and when the figures in black try to stab it with their knives and swords, it doesn't work. Yes! Then, I see Papa B riding on Silvie the Unicorn's back.

I spot Romi writing, and Silvie suddenly stumbles and goes limp on the ground, leaving Papa B exposed and vulnerable. I quickly write about him being armed with spiky-covered bombs, and it happens right away. Papa B pauses, looking at what's in his hands, and he takes off like a lunatic, chucking bombs this way and that. I look back at Romi, who's writing something that causes Phoenix's bubble to pop. But before I can put it back up again, he falls from his bubble and into a swarm of figures in black. They carry him up to Romi, who writes something down that makes Phoenix disappear into thin air.

"NO!" I scream. Romi catches my eyes and grins. She writes something, and all the figures in black turn to me. I'm staring at them. They're staring at me. They break into a sprint, right at the talking tree I'm sitting on. I quickly write something down, and suddenly, a magnetic force plucks the Portal Pen from Romi's hands and into mine. Ha! I have both of them!

But the figures in black are still running toward me. I wasn't quick enough to write myself into safety! I'm pulled from the tree and thrown down on the swarm of the figures. I scream. I lose one of the pens and begin to cry. *This is not happening!* Suddenly, an elbow hits my head and everything goes black.

When I wake up, the battle is still going on. I can hear it. I can hear the muffled yelling and shouting and the muffled high-pitched wisps of magic and the muffled boom of explosions. I also notice that the other Portal Pen isn't in my hands. "Oh no! Where did it . . . ?" I search my pockets. Nothing. Which means now, Romi has both of them. Arghgh! I'm sitting on a cold floor. I look around to figure out where I am. Romi's factory. Brrr, it's freezing in here.

I'm also tied to the ground by ropes. I struggle and pull. I feel a knot. If I can just untie the knot . . . I try to use my fingers to pull on one rope, but it doesn't budge. I pull on another—this one begins to slip and get loose as I pull. Yes!

I slowly pull it looser and looser until it unravels, and my whole left arm is free. I reach over and untie the knot. Both arms! Then I untie all the knots. I scramble up and look around. I'm in the main part of the factory, near the entrance. I run around to find a way out, but the doors are locked. I turn and run down a hallway and check all those doors. Ugh.

But I notice a pink light seeping out from under one of the doors. I push the door. It doesn't budge. I push it harder. It still doesn't budge. I pull on it. It swings open with ease. Wow.

I gingerly enter the room. Everything is dark accept for a giant, pink, oval-shaped bubble with Phoenix inside! He seems like he's in a coma. I search the room for something sharp, and I find a shovel leaning against the wall. I quickly grab the shovel and drag it over to the pink bubble. Oof, it's super heavy. I use all of my strength to heave the shovel and and pull back. Then, with all my force, I stab the shovel into the oval bubble, and it begins to crack like an egg. Then, it bursts open and glass flies everywhere. Syrupy pink goop oozes from the bubble. It covers the ground and begins to make the room much hotter. Steam rises up. We gotta get out of here.

When all of the pink goop has oozed out, Phoenix stops floating inside the bubble and crumples to the floor. His eyes flutter open, and he gasps for air. His forehead is drenched in sweat, and his shirt is damp. His eyes are wild, and his cheeks are flushed. It must have been so hot in here. I feel myself begin to sweat as the pink stuff heats up the room even more.

"Phoenix!" I cry. I rush over and hug him.

He stands up. "Where am I?" he asks, looking around.

I study his face. Something's not right. "Romi had you put in some sort of pink bubble thing that's heating up the room as we speak. We need to get out of here." I begin to tug his arm, but he yanks it out of my grasp. Whoa.

"Who's Romi?" he asks.

I blink. "What? You know Romi! She's taking over this world right now! We have to stop her," I cry.

I grab his hand again and drag him out of the room. This time he follows. I throw open the doors to the hallway. Immediately, cold air hits us. But then, Phoenix picks my fingers off his wrist.

"Wait, stop!" he cries. His eyes seem angry.

"What do you mean? We have no time to lose," I say wildly. Oh, wait. Oh no. "Phoenix? What's wrong?" I cry.

"I don't even know who you are!" he cries.

I gasp. Oh. My. Goodness.

Chapter Twenty-seven

Foggy Thoughts

My hand flies over my mouth, and my eyes fill with tears. Romi erased his memory.

"Oh no," I mutter. I put my hands up to his face.

"And who's Phoenix?" he cries. "And where are we?"

"You're Phoenix. I'm Eva Mason, and I want you to follow me, okay?" I say, a big, warm tear trickling slowly down my cheek.

He cocks his head and sticks out his lip. "Why are you crying?" he asks.

I bite my lip and squeeze my eyes shut. "Because . . . because I . . . " I wipe away my tears. "Let's just go, okay? It isn't safe for us here. And I know you don't remember me, but I need you to try to trust me."

Phoenix puts his hand up to my cheek and rubs away my tears with his thumb. "Please don't cry, Miss Eva. Then I might cry too."

I choke on a sob. I nod furiously. "Okay," I whisper. Phoenix lets me take his hand. "So, Romi, a mean girl who has dragons and is trying to ruin this entire world, has us locked up in this factory," I explain sadly. I can't believe she would go this low, erasing Phoenix's memory. It's too much. "And she also has two magical pens with her that we must get," I say. "After we get the pens, you let me do the rest."

Phoenix nods. "Whatever you say, Miss Eva."

He has a very kiddish presence to him. I don't like any of this one bit. We run through the huge factory. Every single door is locked. I bang on the doors.

"There has to be some way out!" I cry. I bang on the doors more. Phoenix just stands there.

"What do doors do?" he asks. Oh my goodness. "Are they what lock us in?" He cocks his head.

I bang on the doors super hard. "Yes, Phoenix!" I cry. I get that his memory is gone, but he still sounds very dumb. Does he really remember nothing, even normal things like what doors do? It makes me even more angry knowing that he can't help it. Suddenly, Phoenix runs off.

"Where are you going?" I scream. My voice echoes all throughout the factory and bounces back to me.

I hear doors unlatching and closing. I hear drawers opening. I hear running. "Phoenix?" I ask. No reply. I run down the hallway that he ran into and find him cringing as he scoops up the sticky pink goop.

"What are you doing, Phoenix?" I ask.

"This goop will melt metal." Phoenix grabs more with his sticky pink fingers.

I spot a box on the desk in the room and run over, grabbing it and running it back to him. "Here!" I cry. He dumps the goop into the box. "How do you know that this will melt metal?" I ask. Phoenix shrugs.

"Somewhere in the back of my head . . . I just sorta know, I guess," he says.

I smile. Of course. Of course Phoenix would know something like that. I guess Romi didn't take away his whole memory after all. Oops. Wait. "Phoenix! If it melts metal, should you be touching it? Will it burn through the box or your fingers?!"

He keeps calmly grabbing the gunk and putting it in the box. "Nope. It only melts metal. It doesn't melt things like cardboard. Or fingers," he says, gesturing toward the box. "Also, who's Phoenix?"

I roll my eyes. "You are, Phoenix. We've been over this."

When he's got enough, we scramble to the main metal double doors. "Okay, ready?" I ask. He nods and tilts the box. The pink goop oozes out of the box and over the handles of the double doors. The handles melt and crumble to the floor. I push open the doors and they creak, but they open! Squealing, I hug Phoenix, but draw back when he gives me a weird look. We run out and hide behind a bush nearby.

The battle is still going on. Romi is now using both pens, and the sky is swirling with green clouds. Everything blows in the wind, and my hair whips around crazily. It seems like my side is losing. There are even more giant planes with tons of figures in black pouring out of them. A wave of them attacks Dagger and drags him down, his tongue flicking around angrily. Dakota's on top of Midnight, trying to fight Romi, but Romi dodges and writes something down. Immediately, Dakota's wrapped up in a net and starts plummeting toward the ground. She hits the top of Gloria, who gently sets her down nearby.

"We have to get those pens," I whisper to Phoenix, pointing to Romi, who's now holding them up in the air and laughing. Phoenix nods. "But we have to get on her dragon without her seeing us."

"Like a surprise attack!" Phoenix adds.

"Yes, I guess," I say.

We make a run for it and sneak over to the patch of talking trees. Figures in black come at them with swords, and the trees do their best to swing at them with their branches. Misty is kicking a blue dragon's nose.

The blue dragon snarls and flies off. Misty turns and sighs happily when she sees me.

"It's okay. I'm here now, girl," I say.

Phoenix steps back in alarm. "It's a d-dragon," he whispers.

I roll my eyes. "Yep," I say, and climb onto Misty's back and reach out my hand to Phoenix. He doesn't seem so sure, but then he gingerly climbs up as well, shaking a little in nervousness. "Okay, get as close to Midnight as you can without Romi seeing us, okay?" I whisper into Misty's ear.

Misty nods and flies up into the air. She swoops down and flies low behind the trees. She flies over to the factory and then behind it. Romi is at the top, fighting Captain Seaweed and his crew.

"Fly up, Misty," I say. She slowly swoops up until we're at the top. I climb off and gesture for Phoenix to do the same, but he sniffs and shakes his head.

"I don't even know her!" he cries.

I swallow the sadness in me and put my hand down. "Fine," I say. "Misty, fly away."

I turn and watch as Misty flies off with poor, forgetful Phoenix cowering on her back. Then, I creep up over the roof of the factory. I creep closer and closer until I'm close enough to jump on Midnight's back and grab at Romi's hand. Romi shrieks and turns to swat me away.

"Stop it, Eva!" she cries.

She writes something down and Captain Seaweed's ship sorta deflates into the water. The water dies down, and the ship tips onto its side. Crew members are flung out of the ship and land in a heap on the sand. Some swim out from under the ship, gasping for air. Luckily, no one is hurt. His crew gets up slowly, and they draw their swords. Romi writes something else down, and their swords disappear into thin air.

"No, you stop, Romi!" I cry, grabbing her wrist. She struggles and elbows me in the side. Ow! I crumble and grab my side. "Look at what you're doing!" I yell. "Is this what you really want?!"

Romi's eyes glow green. "Of course this is what I want!" she cries. But I see a hesitance.

"Is it though?" I ask.

Romi puts her hands down for a split second. Her eyes flicker, and tears roll down her cheeks as she stares at me. "I . . . "

But out of nowhere, lightning cracks through the sky and hits Misty. Misty goes tumbling down and collapses. Phoenix stumbles off and hides under her limp right wing.

"NO!" I scream.

Romi's eyes go green again. "Yes, Eva. Now get away from me!"

Romi writes something down, and suddenly, I'm dangling off the building. There's a little ledge on the roof, and my jacket is barely hanging on it. My arms and legs are draped in layers of thick and heavy chains, and I'm very high off the ground. I scream in horror. Romi turns to look at me. The evil magic is blinding her.

"I'm too good for this world, " she says as she writes something down, and up in the sky, a swirling portal appears.

"Romi, no!" I cry. "Don't you dare!"

Romi grins. "So, I'll let you stay trapped in here while I finish off this horribly magical place." she laughs. Midnight drops, and Romi levitates in the air. "Bye, bye!" she cries.

She flies up and up and up until she's sucked into the portal.

Then, it closes, leaving nothing but the sky.

"No!" I cry. "No, no, no!" I look around. Everyone is still fighting, and my team is losing. The mermaids of the Blue Bay try to summon sharks and dolphins, but there are evil sea creatures swimming toward them. When they notice, the mermaids swim off in fear. The talking trees are slowly backing up. There's literally a cliff behind them that drops off into the ocean, and the forest is on the other side. Fairies swoop in, using their little wands, but figures in black reach up and snap the wands in half. The fairies back away and fly off. Captain

Seaweed is on his own. He's trying to fight with a sword, but a figure in black is doing better. Suddenly, the figure in black cuts a deep gash in Captain Seaweed's arm, causing the old pirate to scream in pain. Then, the figure in black chops off his wooden leg, and Captain Seaweed collapses.

I let my tears fall to the ground. I can't believe it. We've lost. This is the end for me. For all of us. This world that my grandfather and I created is being destroyed by evil.

Evil.

Ugh, I hate that word. My friend secretly betrayed me and is a McFully, my best and only friend has lost all memory of our friendship, and I'm hanging off the roof of the factory about to fall at any moment. We're stuck here. Plus, there are swarms of dragons and figures in black who never cease coming. At any second, I will fall from this roof, hit the ground, and be swallowed up by Romi's army. I shake my head.

Oh, Romi. If only you could truly see all the damage you're causing right now. If only, if only. But she doesn't. And she never will. She'll never apologize, she'll never change, and she'll always have those two magic Portal Pens with her. And we'll always be here—in this world of betrayal and swords and running and fear and evil. I guess I was wrong. I guess she really does have *everything* through evil magic. I should have known.

And suddenly, the chain slips and I fall. Off the roof. This is the end!

I scream.

But I don't hit the ground. I land in the leaves of a talking tree, a branch stabbing my face. Immediately, a cut forms, and blood trickles down my cheek. I can taste it. I close my eyes. And wait. Wait for the army of figures in black to come at me with their swords and knives. I just want it to be over so there can be no more pain for me. Ugh, I wish there was no more pain for anyone ever.

But I hear a strange noise. It sounds like fireworks. I open my eyes to see the portal back up in the sky. I gasp. Wait, what?

I see a single, little stick-thing fall from the portal. The portal immediately closes up. But the falling thing glimmers in the sun, and I see a rainbow keychain and a flicker of turquoise. I gasp again. It can only be . . . I sit up and scramble down the tree. As it hits the ground, all the figures in black turn and begin to rampage toward it, tearing and shoving things out of their way. It's my Portal Pen!

CHAPTER TWENTY-EIGHT

Saying Goodbye

I bolt after the pen. It lands in the grass, out in the open and completely exposed. I run fast, but the figures in black run faster. I run through the talking trees, dodging roots and bumps. I turn to look. I'm not gonna make it! I run faster but it's no use. Just as the figures in black reach it, Papa B swoops in hanging from a rope on a tree. He grabs it!

"Go, Papa B!" I cheer. The figures in black tumble into a giant heap, kicking and pushing to free themselves. My armor is heavy. I throw my head mask off, letting my hair out and run to Papa B. He hands it to me.

"For you," he says. I take it and grin. I turn to look at everything, and I see more planes dropping thousands of figures in black. They run in different directions, up mountains, over hills, and into the Spirit Forest. Some even jump off the cliff, their parachutes puffing out as they land in the water, and they swim to another patch of land to invade. All of the story creatures scatter. The council of Pixie Grove and the Cloud Council fly away. No, no no! Captain Seaweed scoots up onto his ship, along with his injured crew, and sails off. Gloria gives me a sympathetic look as the talking trees stomp off. Dakota hops on Dagger, and the giant snake slithers away. Now it's just me, Phoenix, and Papa B. More waves of figures in black come and more dragons. Dragons swoop down, their giant teeth showing.

"We gotta get out of here," I whisper to Papa B. I pause. "We need to go home now." Papa B tenses up, but nods. "But our stuff is at your tree house," I say.

"Then let's go!" Papa B cries. He turns and takes off running into the Spirit Forest.

Phoenix runs up to me, out of breath. "Miss Eva! I've been looking all over for you!" he pants. Phoenix looks at Papa B and cocks his head. "Who's he?" he asks.

"He's the person we need to follow," I explain. "Now let's go!"

I take off running with Phoenix hot on my heels. Armies of figures in black come billowing behind us, their swords and knives shimmering in the sunlight. We dodge around glass trees, but the figures in black just destroy them. As we run, all different kinds of colored mist swirl and swoop and flutter around us. Animals transform and scurry behind bushes. I see a raspberry-colored groundhog dart into a hole in the ground. A yellow monkey scurries up a tree, but it's soon knocked down by the stampede of figures in black. As I'm running, I spot a cave just outside of Spirit Forest.

"Phoenix! Lead all the Spirit Animals into that cave over there!" I direct.

Phoenix looks confused for a moment.

"All the colored mists that turn into animals. Lead them into that cave," I explain. Man, I miss the old Phoenix.

But he seems to understand now because he nods and runs off. As he whistles and whoops, all the animals are drawn to him. "Follow me, Spirit Animals!" he cries, running off, and all the Spirit Animals turn and race off with him. I almost get trampled by a tiger with stripes the color of blue raspberry flavor. Papa B and I keep running.

"There it is!" Papa B cries.

"The Curly Tree!"

We throw open the door and dash in. I slam it behind me.

"Grab the stuff!" Papa B cries, grabbing his big backpack and slinging it onto his back. Then, he grabs a black bag and starts stuffing items and trinkets and things into it.

"What are those for?" I ask, grabbing Phoenix's bag too.

Papa B sighs. "Well, I'm never gonna see this place again so I might as well take everything I want and need with me," he says, shoving a golden time glass into the black bag.

All of a sudden, we see a wave of darkness through the windows, and immediately, figures in black bang on the door and begin to smash the windows.

"Okay, we gotta go!" Papa B grabs his bags and I do too. We run to the door but figures in black smash the door to bits and point swords at us.

"Uh, back door!" Papa B cries. We spin around and run to the back door, but figures in black burst through that door too.

"We're surrounded," I say.

Papa B glances around. "Quick! Up to the balcony!" he cries, running up the wooden spiral stairs behind the kitchen.

I stomp up the stairs after him. "But there's no way out," I say.

Figures in black invade the house and begin smashing everything.

"That's not true," Papa B says.

He shoves open the wooden door leading out to the balcony and slams it behind him. We stare out. All the glass trees are broken and shattered.

"Oh, goodness," I whisper.

I look over. There's a rope attached to the straw roof of the tree house, tied to a hook. Figures in black scurry up the stairs after us and bang on the door. Papa B rushes over to the rope and unties it.

"Grab the rope," he instructs. "And then jump off the balcony."

I do a double take. "Wait, what?!" I cry.

The old wooden door moans and creaks as figures and black shove it. A sword stabs through the wood door and begins to cut it. Ahhhh!

"Just do it!" Papa B cries.

I grab the rope and grip it tight. Then, I close my eyes and jump. I scream as I swing over the ground. But then I swing into the leaves of a nearby tree. I cheer and throw the rope back at Papa B. He grabs it and hollers as he swings. He bursts through the leaves next to me and grins, sticks and leaves sticking out of his beard. We can see the figures in black burst through the door and pile up on the balcony.

"Let's get out of here," I say.

I step on a branch and scramble down the tree as Papa B follows. We bolt through the glass pieces of what used to be the Spirit Forest. One almost cuts my knee. We run over the hills and into the mini-desert clearing. The dragon planes have moved on from the clearing and are spread out all over the land. Clumps of figures in black are still pouring from the planes and cover the land. It's now thunderstorming outside. Misty is still limp in the sand, and we rush over to her.

I quickly whip out my notebook and write, *Eva makes a magic bubble around her and her friends so no one can touch them.* Out of thin air, a clear, shiny bubble forms around us and we float up in the air. Then, I write, *Eva woke Misty up from her coma and healed her injuries.* Misty's eyes flutter open and she grins, her purple tongue sticking out happily. Then I write, *with a simple wave of her hand, Eva cured all the curses in the land that were just created, healed all the injuries, and got rid of all the figures in black, dragons, storms, and any sort of evil in this land.* I wave my hand in the air, and all the figures in black instantly disappear—as well as the planes, evil dragons, and the storms. White, fluffy clouds begin to litter the sky as it clears. The smashed pieces of glass promptly piece themselves back together into glass trees.

I smile. There.

Then, I turn to Phoenix, who's scratching his head in confusion, and write, *Phoenix's memory returned, and he remembered everything that had happened in his life.* Phoenix flutters his eyes as if he was just in a deep sleep even though he was already awake. He rubs his head. Then, when he spots all of us, he cries out in joy.

"Eva!" he shouts, dashing over and hugging me. He pecks me on the cheek then blushes. He pats Misty's purple head and gives Papa B a friendly pat on the back.

"Are you okay?" I ask Phoenix.

He grins. "Yeah, that was weird though. I was sleeping, but then when I woke up, I just couldn't remember anything, not even my own name," he explains.

"Yeah, I witnessed that," I chuckle.

Phoenix smiles. I pop the bubble, and we all step down to the ground. I hand him his bags, which he takes gratefully. I swallow the huge lump in my throat.

"We did it!" I practically whisper in awe.

We three take a moment to look around at the peace and calm that's returned to this world.

After this time of quiet, I remember just how ready I am to get home. "We need to say goodbye to everyone," I say, sighing with the mixed feelings of sadness and joy. I've made so many friends and seen so many things here, and I've almost gotten used to it. I'm really gonna miss this place.

Papa B and Phoenix nod. I write something down, and all of the kings and queens and creatures and people pop up. Even the king and queen from the Jewel Kingdom are here.

"Hi, everyone," I say. "We've done what we came to do, and it's time for us to go home now," I say.

Out of nowhere, the entire crowd begins to cheer for us. My eyes sting with tears. When they stop clapping, I continue, "I guess. I guess we have to say goodbye."

I feel so sad. I wish I never had to say goodbye. But I miss my family, and I know we can't stay here. Everyone rushes toward us in a big hug. The mermaids of the Blue Bay flop around so I lean down and give some of them hugs. Gloria and Tiki wrap their branches around all of us, and Gloria's pink leaves brush my face.

"I already miss all of you!" I cry.

I hug Ginger and rub her fur, and hug Noah's tall neck. I hug the Cloud Council, even though it feels like hugging a wad of chilly air. Dakota walks up to me, and I throw my arms around her. She smells like salt water.

"Thank you again," I say. "I don't think we would have made it without you."

Dakota tries to hide her grin. "Hey, I may look intimidating on the outside, but if a friend is in need . . . " Datoka backs away and winks at me. "I will always be there." She turns and climbs onto Dagger before his giant body slides away through the trees. I try not to cry. I made so many friends and memories here. Captain Seaweed shuffles up to me, two crew members helping him walk. He gives me an awkward pat on the back.

"Hey—you're a tough cookie," he says.

"Thanks," I grin.

Captain Seaweed nods. He then leans closer to me and whispers, "Also, I never really wanted your Spirit Animals. I was just testing you to see if you'd actually give them up. I let them free afterwards." He moves away, and by the time I'm about to reply, he and his men are already boarding their ship.

Suddenly, big hazel sticks are brushing my cheek, and I turn to see Gloria's beaming wooden face, smiling down at me, her pink and golden leaves dancing in the breeze. "Eva, you are one inspiring teenager," she says.

I let her hollow breath tickle my cheek. "Oh, Gloria, I'm gonna miss you," I say, trying not to let the tears fill my eyes.

Gloria sighs. She looks out at everyone. A chilly wind ruffles her leaves. "You feel that?" she asks.

"Feel what?" I ask.

"The wind . . . it's much more calm and peaceful now."

I smile. "It's because of you," she says.

"Me?" I ask.

"You saved this place. Everything is peaceful again thanks to you."

I close my eyes and let the wind tickle my face. Then I hug Gloria's wooden body one last time. Gloria waves and turns to join the other trees, where Tiki is waving and beckoning her. She turns and beams at me, and I usher her to go join him.

"Goodbye, Eva! I can't believe that a person I healed would be the person to save this world!" a little high-pitched voice says. I turn to see Majesty, her magnificent butterfly dress billowing behind her, the sun shining on her black hair. She raises a perfectly arched eyebrow and shoots me a warm smile. I turn to hug her. The butter-flies fly off her dress and flutter around me in swarms.

"Girls! Do not fly all over Eva," Majesty says, and her butterflies quickly flutter and adjust themselves back on her dress. "Good job, Eva," Majesty says. "I'm really, very proud of you."

My eyes fill up with tears so fast and soon, and for the millionth time, spill down my face until my eyes are pink and my cheeks are blotchy, and I'm crying happy tears in Majesty's arms. "I'm going to miss this place so much," I sob.

"We're going to miss *you* so much," she whispers back, her soft breath warming my cheek. I pull away and force myself to say goodbye for the last time.

We all wave goodbye sadly, and I write something with the Portal Pen to make everyone disappear back to their kingdoms and villages and homes. Then, I turn to Misty.

"Oh, girly," I say, tears filling my eyes and sneaking onto my face. Misty coos at me and her long, black eyelashes tickle my face. "You've done so much for us and . . . we wouldn't have been able to do this without you—like, at all," I say, tears blurring my eyes. Misty gently peeps out her tongue and licks my cheek. I laugh. "Thanks," I say. I stroke her cool scales. They feel so nice and soothing. I stare into her beautiful eyes.

"I'm going to miss you so much," I say sadly. Misty blows a puff of air at my face. I stroke her cheek. "Okay, girl, see you later," I say. Misty's eyes sadden, and I choke on a sob. Then, I back away and Misty turns and flies off. I turn around so that I don't have to watch her fly away.

"Okay, everyone ready?" I ask.

Papa B and Phoenix nod.

"I'm more than ready!" Phoenix shouts.

Papa B gives a slightly sad smile, looking back over the world he created—the world he's lived in for nearly 40 years. "Yes," he says finally. "Yes. I'm ready."

"Okay," I say. My hands shake as I carefully write something down. *Once, Eva, Phoenix, and Papa B all went home.*

CHAPTER TWENTY-NINE

The Return of Billie Mason

Suddenly, we all begin to float up into the air. Our purple armor disappears, and I feel like I'm as light as a feather. I've gotten super used to this place. I've gotten used to riding Misty daily and sleeping in huts and tree houses and hotels. I've gotten used to seeing fairies and dragons and trees made of glass and purple clouds and floating kingdoms. I've gotten used to all of this. And just when I get used to it, we have to leave.

I look up and see the open portal swirling above us. All I can see is darkness inside of it, with wisps of rainbow and twinkling stars. We float closer and closer. I wonder what Romi is doing right now. Probably fuming. Then a thought hits me. Romi's the only one with both pens, so she had to be the one to drop it into the portal. Was it an accident?

Then, I put all of the connections together. How she hated it when we called her McFully, and the look of jealousy and sadness on her face when all my friends came to back me up. And the way she looked at me when she thought I wasn't looking. How sad she was when I told her we weren't friends. *She still wants to be friends.*

What . . . ?

But my thoughts are suddenly smeared and slurred as we're sucked into the portal like a magnetic force. I feel like I'm on a roller coaster. I can feel the gravity of the portal close up underneath us. As I squeeze my eyes shut, I wait for this uncomfortable feeling of shooting upwards to go away. Wind cuts my face and stings my eyes. It's freezing cold and boiling hot at the same time. I cringe.

Then, all of a sudden, we're sitting on the dusty wooden floor of the storage space of Mrs. Creamer's Coffee Shop. It's the middle of the day, probably around lunch time. Orange sunlight streams in through the cracked windows, and everything looks as if it was in a deep sleep.

And that's when my body and mind remember my overwhelming lack of sleep. I hunch over and my eyes droop. Ugh, I'm so tired. We all shake our heads and stand up. Papa B's eyes are wide. Sweat drips down his forehead and into his beard.

"I . . . I remember this place," he whispers. His eyes fill with tears. "So many . . . years ago."

We watch as his face seems to crack, his mouth curving up into a smile as salty tears pour down his face. His eyes are filled with such wonder. I can't even imagine all the emotions running through him right now. Sadness. Happiness. Joy. Maybe even a little fear or even anger. Or all of them—jumbled into a heap.

I smile and rub Papa B's back. Phoenix awkwardly steps closer to him and pats his shoulder. I turn and glance at the portal. Cold air is pouring out of it. I feel like I've grown so much from when we traveled into the portal. It felt like so many years ago—like we were so young and innocent when we entered—and now, coming out of it, I feel so much more older and mature.

I glance at Phoenix and Papa B, but they're just colorful smudges right now because of my tears. Smiling, I let the tears flow. There was so much sadness and pain and resentment and hurt in this trip . . . but there was also joy and friendship and strong bonds and love and new beginnings. And all of it was good.

I walk over to the portal. Oh, that beautiful portal with it's magical creatures and fairies and lands and secrets and amazements. I watch as my tears drop from my face and into the portal. I smile and sniff. Then I stand up. Phoenix has blotchy stains running down his cheeks from crying. Without saying a word, we gather in a group hug and embrace all of this. *Everything.* We have everything. This right here is *everything*. I open my eyes. We're all hugging each other—broken girl, broken grandpa, broken friend. Yet, we have so much love for each other, and we're all family. I rub their backs and then pull away.

"Come on," I say, rubbing my nose. "Let's cover this portal up." I grab the old blanket and drape it over the portal. Phoenix and Papa B lift the table over the blanket, and Phoenix and I clip blankets to the sides of the desk. We smile at each other from under the table.

I whip out my phone and call Grammy. Grammy. I didn't realize how much I missed her until now. Her blue car that spits and sputters smoke. Her wacky sense of fashion. Her love of driving out in the middle of nowhere. Oh, I miss her so much. And my parents. I miss them really bad. I miss my deep discussions with my mom, and my dad and I just enjoying outside on the back porch. And Marty. My sweet, caring brother Marty. I miss him so much too. I miss everybody. I even miss school.

I tap on Grammy's name in my contacts and wait. I haven't used my phone practically at all, and I honestly feel refreshed. Grammy answers almost immediately.

"Eva?! Eva!" Grammy cries. I cringe as Grammy screams into the phone with joy.

"Hi, Grammy," I laugh.

"How did it go? What happened? I need answers! Did you get the Portal Pen back? How about . . . "

I shush my anxious grandmother. "Grammy, we're out of the portal and here at Mrs. Creamer's Coffee. Can you come pick us up?" I ask patiently.

"Yes, of course I can! Getting in my car now!"

I snicker. She sounds super excited. I bet everyone's waiting anxiously for our arrival.

"I'm driving out of your neighborhood right now, honey bun. Be there in a little while, okay?" Grammy says. I hear the tired grumble of the car engine in the background.

"Okay, Grammy," I say. "Bye."

"Bye, baby!" Grammy cries. I hang up.

"So . . . now what?" Phoenix asks.

"Now, we wait for Grammy to pick us up," I say.

I pull out my notebook and read through my stories. Wow, there are so many of them. Phoenix comes over and sits by me. Papa B can't seem to sit still. He paces the room, then sits back down, tapping his foot, then gets back up and begins to pace again.

"Hey, you okay?" I ask Papa B.

Papa B runs his fingers through his beard and shakes his head. "No, I'm not okay," he cries, kicking a box, which slides across the floor. "I . . . I don't think I can do this," he says quietly.

I stand up. "What do you mean?" I cry. "We've come all this way, and you were so excited."

"I know, I just . . . it's been so long. So, so terribly long. And I'm just . . . " Papa B puts his head in his hands, then looks up at me with scared and pleading eyes. "What if Georgia doesn't want to see me again? What if my son is angry at me? Oh, Eva, I'm so confused. I'm starting to think that I made a huge mistake going through the portal in the first place," Papa B complains.

I rush over to him and put a hand on his shoulder. "Papa B, I think that it's so amazing that you went into the portal. And I get why you did. I wanted to see my stories alive there too! But I also think that there's nothing to be scared or worried about. I think that my dad will be so excited to see you, and so will Grammy. You were stuck there, Papa B. You didn't have the Portal Pen to get back," I explain.

"But. Wait. You knew how to make a Portal Pen. Why didn't you do it so you could get home?" Phoenix asks.

"By the time I wished to know how to make a Portal Pen, I was so lost in the story world. It just replaced my memory of this world until you reminded me, Eva," Papa B says.

We're quiet for a moment, then Papa B's eyes widen. "Oh, and that's right! Georgia's your grandmother!" he cries. "See? I've been gone too long! There's too much catching up to do!" He throws up his hands.

"Papa B! You can stay at our house with Grammy until all the catching up is done," I say gently.

Papa B slumps back in his chair. "Okay," he says finally.

A little while later, I look out the window to see a rusty blue Corvette speeding down the highway and do a U-turn into the town square. My heart leaps with joy. It's Grammy! The blue car screeches as it swerves around the fountain, gaining speed as it races up the road. It swerves to a stop, and the one and only Grammy herself—with a pink hawaiian flower in her hair, a flowing mint-colored top, and a beige skirt—climbs out of the car and races into the building.

"She's here!" I cry. "She's really here!"

Papa B, who's calmly reading, gasps and throws down his book. He backs up into the corner.

"I can't!" he cries. "Too long! It's been too long!" Sweat drips down his face, and his eyes are wild with fear. I walk up to him and take his hands.

"Papa B, stop. I know you're scared, but please, trust me. There's nothing to fear at all. Can you trust me on this?" I ask, peering into his eyes.

Papa B stares at me for a long moment, then finally gulps and nods, "Okay, then let's go."

We grab our stuff and thump down the stairs into the sunshine outside where Grammy is anxiously scrambling out of her car.

"Grammy!" I cry.

"Eva!" she cries. Grammy and I hug each other tightly. "Ugh! You know how long it's been?"

"How long?" I ask, giggling.

"Three weeks!" she cries. My smile fades.

"Wow. We were gone a really long time," I say nervously.

Grammy squeezes me harder. "And we all missed you so much!" she says as she gives me a kiss on the forehead and steps back.

Then, she dashes over to Phoenix and hugs him too. "Phoenix!" she squeals.

She looks around. "Where's Romi?" she asks.

I smile weakly. "Well, long story short, she uh, she betrayed us and stole the pen, and we had to make another one—so that's why it took so long," I say sheepishly.

Grammy frowns. "Did you get the pen back?" she asks.

"Well . . . sort of," I answer. "We have the original, but she has the second one, and I guess she felt bad and dropped this one into the portal so we could get it, but we still need to get the second one back from her," I explain.

Grammy nods and raises her eyebrows. "Why did she betray you?" Grammy asks.

"Because she's a McFully," Papa B answers.

In that moment, Grammy looks up and notices Papa B for the first time. Their eyes lock, and it feels like the whole world is suddenly frozen. Grammy looks so very vulnerable, standing there, arms hanging limp at her sides, not doing anything. Same with Papa B. Then, Grammy whispers something so softly that we have to strain to hear: "Billie?"

Papa B stands there for a moment, and then gives the smallest nod I have ever seen. Grammy gasps. "It's you!" she cries. Tears fill her eyes and fall down her face like salty waterfalls. She stomps toward Papa B. Papa B backs up.

"I know, Georgia. I'm so sorry. It was all my fault and I . . . " But he can't say anymore because Grammy marches up to him, grabs him, and kisses him on the lips. Papa B's eyes go wide, and then he kisses Grammy's back and hugs her. Grammy's tears stain his shirt as they embrace.

"You have no idea how much I've missed you," she whispers.

"I've missed you terribly too," he whispers back.

Grammy kisses his face over and over again and squeezes his hands. She smiles at him. She looks at all of us. "Well, come on then! Let's go home!"

We all pile into Grammy's car, with me and Phoenix in the back, Grammy driving, and Papa B in the passenger seat. We begin the long trek home once again. The whole time, Grammy and Papa B talk. Papa B tells her about when he fell from the portal, and how he met Noah and about his tree house and so on. He tells her about his adventures with Captain Seaweed, and Grammy gasps or smiles or frowns. But the whole time, she seems so fascinated by all of his adventures. Grammy tells Papa B about how she raised my dad, what they did, her job, his friends, his school, where they grew up, and so on. She tells him some things about my dad that I never knew. Turns out my dad was born four weeks early, he played basketball in seventh grade, and loved math. She tells him about herself too. It almost feels like she's reading him an essay on her own life.

Phoenix and I just listen the whole time. I love hearing them catch up. Grammy even tells Papa B about me. How I would write stories pretty much all day, every day if I could, how I play the harp and make earrings, and other weird stuff about me. But I love it all. Every second of it.

Papa B even tells Grammy about our adventure— how they almost had to give me up for a piece of leather from Captain Seaweed, and how the legendary Misty of the Dragon Gate was drawn to me and got us places ever since, and how I used the second Portal Pen to battle Romi, and how all of the story characters took our side and helped us.

I feel so amazing in this moment because of the way Papa B is describing it. His eyes are filled with joy as his hands fly around in big gestures, creating and animating the story.

Grammy nods and smiles the whole time. She seems so happy. There's a rosy glow to her cheeks, and her mouth has been curved up into a smile the whole car ride. Instead of hunching over the wheel like she usually does, she's sitting straight up—her whole body seems filled with joy. It's amazing.

After about two hours of driving and catching up, we begin to pass familiar areas of Colorado. We pass my school, and the little playground that rests on a patch of land. The sky is clear and the sun is hot. We pass the road leading to Romi's neighborhood. Ugh, Romi. I need to get the second Portal Pen back.

"And Phoenix, your parents told the school you came home from a two-week vacation and then came down with a cold," Grammy says.

"Okay!" Phoenix says, looking right at me. My cheeks go slightly pink.

Soon, we're driving on the main highway with the bunched trees and the CONSTRUCTION sign that's been there for almost three years now. We drive ahead into Phoenix's neighborhood. I don't think I'll ever look at Phoenix the same again. He's brave and smart and . . . still nerdy, but he has my back and I have his.

I walk Phoenix up to his front porch. "Eva, I just want you to know, I loved that big adventure," he says. I beam.

"Me too. Thanks for being there for me," I say.

"Thanks for being there for *me*," he grins.

We give each other an awkward hug and then super cheesy smiles. It's hard to think of something small to say when we've been through something so huge together.

"See you at school, Phoenix," I say, walking out to the car.

"Can't wait to beat you writing a better story!" Phoenix calls.

"Not if mine is even better!" I call back. Because, I mean, not to brag, but my stories are actually living and breathing in another dimension.

I hop back into Grammy's car with a smile on my face.

"What was that hugging and stuff about?" Papa B asks. Grammy raises a curious eyebrow in the rearview mirror. My cheeks heat up and turn rosy.

"Nothing, we're just hugging cause we're best friends," I say, my heart swelling.

Ten minutes later, we pull up into the slanted entrance of my neighborhood. Oh my goodness, we're just about home. I miss that word so much. It's like an old friend that I finally get to see again. *Home.*

Grammy takes a left into the extension with the townhouses and drives until she takes a right, and there's my red brick townhouse with dad's car parked in the driveway and the "Hey, good-lookin'" pillows on the chair. I missed those pillows. Dad and Marty are playing football in the front yard and mom's planting petunias. *Mom! Dad! Marty! I'm home!* I'm so excited. My heart is beating wildly.

Grammy pulls up into a parking spot across the street and all three of us scramble out. When my parents hear a car door slam, they look up and literally drop everything.

"EVA!" they scream, dashing toward us.

"Mom! Dad! Marty!" I cry, rushing into their arms. It's one big group hug, and I'm getting squeezed, but I love it.

"We're so, so sorry that we doubted you," they say.

I smile. "It's okay," I say.

Mom kisses my forehead, and dad squeezes my shoulders.

Marty gives me a friendly fist bump. "Hey, I already knew you could do it from the very beginning," he half-grins.

I elbow him playfully. "Oh, shush! You did not!" I scoff.

"Did to!" He smirks, elbowing me back. We laugh and hug.

"Did Phoenix get dropped off with his family?" Mom asks. I nod.

"And where's Romi?" Mom asks.

I scratch my head. "Well . . . we'll explain it all inside, but uh, she kinda, sorta secretly is a McFully and stole the Portal Pen and took over the world, so we had to stop her," I explain.

Mom's eyes go wide. "Um . . . well okay then," she says, her lips moving like a fish, as if trying to say so many things but not knowing where to start.

Mom and Dad both look up at Papa B, who's kicking an acorn around awkwardly.

"And, uh . . . who's this?" Dad asks.

Grammy giggles. I start to giggle too. Mom and Dad and Marty all turn their heads back and forth between us, their faces flashing with utter confusion.

Finally, Grammy says, "Gavin, this is your father."

My dad stares at Papa B for a moment, and then it sinks in, and his eyes get shiny with tears and he tenses up. "Wait . . . what? But, how?" he asks.

Papa B's eyes get shiny too. "My son," he says.

Grammy takes my dad's hands and explains, "You know how we told you that no one knew what had happened to him? Well, we just wanted to protect you, but really, he wanted to visit his world of his stories, and he got stuck there without the Portal Pen to get back. But Eva found him. And now he's home."

Papa B nods. My dad steps forward to Papa B. He flings his arms around his neck and hugs him like a little boy hugging his dad. Well, technically he is hugging his dad—it's just that he's not so little anymore.

My mom steps forward and wraps her arms around both of them.

Papa B looks up and gasps. "Is this the beautiful wife and mom Karen I've heard so much about?" he cries.

My mom laughs and nods. "That's me," she says.

Marty shifts uncomfortably. Papa B smiles at him. "And this must be Eva's older brother, Marty!" he exclaims. Marty nods and grins.

Mom pulls away. "Now, let's all go inside and relax. It's hot outside, and I'm sweating. How about we chat over lemonade and watermelon slices?" Mom asks.

We all cheer and go inside. Our little family piles into the living room and sits down. Mom brings over glass cups with delicious yellow lemonade with ice cubes bobbing around in them. Then, she brings over a bowl of watermelon slices. Mmm, I love watermelon.

"First things first, Eva, you have a lot of homework to do," Mom says, shooting me a stern look.

"I know, I know." I put my hands up. All of us laugh.

"So, let's start from the very beginning. What's all this crazy talk about a Portal Pen?" Dad asks.

Grammy explains, "Well, here's an easy way to say it: Once, in a time long long long ago, magic collided with our world. But then, when this world and the magical world were separated, and magic became its own thing, pieces of magic were left all over our world in the shape of Turquoise Wood. When Billie was a boy, he and his family took a trip to Mount Everest, and there, Billie discovered the last piece of Turquoise Wood existing on Earth. But Turquoise Wood can grant wishes. So, since Billie loved writing stories, he took the wood home and turned it into a pen. Then, he wished that all of his stories that he wrote with that pen would become real in another world."

Dad and Mom both nod and exchange several glances with each other.

"Look! I even have the proof right here," I say, taking out the Portal Pen. I hand it to Mom and Dad, who've seen it before but never touched it or known its power.

Mom gasps slightly as she feels it. "It feels so . . . alive," she whispers.

"That's the magic," I whisper back. She looks at me with such wonder in her eyes. I smile and I feel like my face is glowing with pride.

"Shall I continue?" Grammy asks.

Dad gestures. "Of course!" he cries.

"So anyways, Billie would write stories, and every time he did, it would magically form in another world. But, then, he and I got married and soon I was pregnant with you, Gavin."

I take a sip of my lemonade. It's so cool to hear the story from Grammy's point of view, and she gets to tell it all to my parents. Even Papa B seems a little intrigued.

"When Georgia was pregnant, I suddenly realized that I'd never visited my stories, and writing was my life. So I decided that I wanted to create a new life there," Papa B explains.

Mom and Dad's eyes look so fascinated.

"So then what happened?" Marty asks.

"So, I asked Georgia if she would come with me and raise Gavin there, and we'd be a family in that magical place," Papa B explains.

"And I said no, because I knew you'd never be the same if I raised you there, and you'd never truly know what the real world was like," Grammy explains.

"And you made the right decision," Papa B says, taking Grammy's hand in his hand.

"So, I went into the portal, but I'd left the Portal Pen with Georgia so I couldn't come back, and I made a life for myself there ever since. I mostly forgot about this world until I saw Eva. Something sparked in me. And when she told me who she was . . . it all came back!" Papa B says.

Marty grins. "What was it like there? Where did you live?" Marty asks eagerly.

Papa B laughs. All of us lean forward in our seats. None of us really know what it's like to live there. Phoenix and I were there for three weeks, but that's just a long visit. Papa B is the only one.

"It's amazing," he sighs happily. "I built my own tree house, made my own trades with the market, traveled all over, battled enemy ships with Captain Seaweed (which was one of the stories I wrote), had my own Spirit Animal buddy," Papa B explains. "His name was Noah, and he was a giraffe."

"I had a Spirit Animal too while we were there!" I cry. All eyes turn to me.

"Really? What was it?" Dad asks.

"Her name was Ginger, and she was a wolf with green fur," I say, remembering her silky green fur. I miss her.

"Wow," Marty gushes.

"And, Gavin and Karen, all of this is true, you know," Grammy says.

Mom smiles. "Yes, we know," they say.

Grammy takes a watermelon slice. "But, the phone and the doctor and . . . "

Dad squeezes Grammy's hand. "We knew you were right the whole time because we could see it in your eyes, and we could see the creativity in Eva's eyes too. We knew deep down, but we just didn't want to accept it," Dad explains.

"So, how did the portal get created?" Marty asks.

I explain: "Well, when Papa B was young, one day, he used the Portal Pen to write a story about a portal, which became the entrance to his world of stories, and the way he later went into it. But in school one day, I, coincidentally, wrote a story about a portal. And every time I write a story with the Portal Pen, I've always felt this inner rumbling in my body when I finish the story . . . which I found out was the story coming to life in the story world . . . but, anyway, that day I wrote about the portal, the rumbling didn't stop for a whole day. Turns out, I had reopened the portal to the magic world of Papa B's stories that Papa B had created so many years ago!" I exclaim.

Gasps fill the room. I hear myself gasp too. It *is* pretty crazy.

"Whoa," Marty breathes. "Where is it?" he asks.

"It's under a table covered in blankets in an old, abandoned coffee shop in Wyoming," I explain with a smirk. "You never would have guessed that place."

"So, why did you end up going into the portal?" Mom asks.

"Well, we were debating, because Grammy told me about Papa B and I thought that maybe I could find him. But then I accidentally dropped the Portal Pen *into* the portal—so we kind of didn't have a choice," I say with a sheepish smile. Everyone chuckles slightly.

"So how did it go?" Dad asks.

Everyone is looking at me with eager eyes. "Well, it was such an awesome and scary adventure at the same time," I say.

"I bet," Mom says.

"We met so many people and went to so many places. We even trained a dragon named Misty, who got us to every place we needed, pretty much the whole trip!" I exclaim. "We asked everyone if they'd seen our pen, and they said that only a man named the Adventure Man could have something like that. So, we journeyed to find the Adventure Man, and surprise, surprise, the Adventure Man was actually my grandpa, Papa B!" I cry. The word *grandpa* doesn't fit quite yet. It feels weird and out of place when I say it. I guess I have to get used to it!

Everyone turns and looks at Papa B with curious smiles. "We got the pen back, and we were about to go back home. But we found out that Romi was a McFully, and she stole the pen and betrayed us," Papa B explains.

Mom sits up. "I remember hearing stories about the McFullys. Mean, selfish, and horrible people," she says.

Grammy nods. "And, Sparrow McFully, turns out, used the Portal Pen and accidentally cursed himself and his family to hate us Masons and get the Portal Pen," Grammy explains.

Mom and Dad gasp. I suddenly realize something.

"Grammy?" I cry.

"Yes, honey bun?" Grammy asks.

"Right before we left, I wrote a story undoing all the curses. That means that the curse of the McFullys is broken too!" I exclaim.

"Oh! You're right!" Grammy cries.

I smile weakly. I don't know if I should be disappointed or excited. But there's a tiny hope that's tugging my heart and saying, *Maybe that's your chance to be her friend again.* But I quickly shove it away as Papa B continues, "So, then, I realized that we had to make another Portal Pen to stop Romi and her army, so we had to go on this long quest to collect a bunch of stuff to make Turquoise Wood for the Portal Pen. And we made it, but it took a lot of work."

"Yep! There were lots of dangers, flying, getting hit by venom, making a kingdom collapse by accident . . . " I begin.

Mom holds up her hands. "Wait, who got hit by venom?!" she cries.

I point to myself, and my mom looks like she could faint.

"Mom! Don't worry! I'm cured, and it's all better," I say. Mom sinks back down into the couch, relaxing.

"So, we made the second pen, and there was a huge battle and then we stopped Romi and she flew off leaving us in the cursed magic world. But we got out and all is well," Papa B says dramatically.

"I can barely believe you two kids did all of that. I guess it's kind of like you aren't really kids anymore," Dad says.

Dad's right. He just echoed what I'd been thinking. I feel like I've been through so much. Before traveling into that magical world of stories, I was just a regular girl with homework and a regular life. Now, I feel like

I've grown up so much. I went through a portal, rode a dragon, swam with mermaids, saved the world, talked with trees, became friends with a jungle woman and a giant snake, and . . . met my long-lost grandfather!

We keep talking for about two more hours about the trip, answer tons of questions, hear lots of cries and gasps and cheers, and there are even some tears too. But in the end, we end up pretty much telling them every little detail. We look out the window. It's dark outside.

Mom stands up and wraps me in a hug. "Well, you have no idea how proud I am of you!" she cries, her eyes shimmering with tears.

I smile. "Thank you, Mom," I say.

Dad and Marty get up and hug us too, and soon all of us are in one group hug in the middle of the living room. We all separate from each other.

"Okay, guys, it was a very busy three weeks. I was so excited and scared and angry and worried for you," Mom says honestly.

Oh wow. I can picture Dad trying as hard as he can not to call the police, and mom biting all of her nails off and rambling and pacing the floor.

"Well, now we're home so now there's nothing to worry about," I assure her.

Mom nods. "I know, honey. Okay, so, Grammy and Papa B can sleep in the guest room," Mom says to everyone. We all nod.

Mom turns to me. "Eva, I told the school about three weeks ago that you had gone on a vacation with your grandfather," Mom says, winking at me. I grin. I mean, it's not entirely a lie. I did go on a vacation with my grandfather. "But, that doesn't mean you don't have any homework. I want you caught up completely on studying by next Monday. Got that?" Mom demands, but she still has a sly edge in her voice.

"Yes ma'am!" I say. I can't believe I'm saying this, but I've missed the rhythm of things, including my nightly homework.

"Okay. And you can take tomorrow off, but you'll be going to school the day after." Mom kisses my forehead.

I'm almost excited to go back to school. I miss my teachers and my classes.

"Alright, now everyone get some rest," Mom says. She turns out the lamp in the living room, and all of us part ways to our rooms. I throw open the door to my room. It smells fresh, like a new room in a new house. I guess it's supposed to smell like that since there hasn't been a body here in three weeks! Everything is exactly as I left it. The covers are thrown to the side, and the bed is wrinkled from when I got out of bed three weeks ago. The hamper in the corner is still filled with laundry that I need to put away, and my wooden floors are all dusty from not being swept every other day in three weeks!

I throw my stuff down on the floor and unpack it. I put all my dirty clothes in a pile in my closet. I throw away trash and put my shoes back in their cubbies. Then, I hang my backpack up on a hook in my closet and slip into my favorite pair of pajamas: the fuzzy gray pj pants and the mustard-yellow T-shirt that says HONEY on it. I throw my hair into a sloppy bun and brush my teeth and slip socks on. I shut the door and plop down on my bed. Were my pillows always this fluffy? Were my sheets always this silky? Was my black-and-white-striped blanket always this soft? I don't know, but they sure are now.

I bury myself under my blankets and close my eyes. It feels so nice to be back home, in my little neighborhood, in my small red brick townhouse, with its "Hey, good-lookin'" pillow and its petunias planted in the front lawn. I love my little room and my stuff and my friends and my family.

I suddenly think: *Can I be Romi's friend again? Can I forgive her? Is it even possible?* Maybe when I see her again on Wednesday when we go back to school, she could still be bitter and selfish and power hungry. Or she could be the complete opposite. She might desperately want to be my friend again and give up the second Portal Pen with ease. Who knows? But what I do know is that on our trip, I could see it. The loss in her life that she tried to fill with evil magic and power. But maybe all she needs is someone to be there in her corner and love her.

So, I think, *As I lie here right now, I'm going to go up to her on Wednesday and talk to her, and possibly forgive her. Maybe she won't want to be my friend, but I think I'm still going to forgive her.*

Chapter Thirty

Back Together Again

Oh my goodness! That was the best sleep I've gotten since—I have no idea when—but it was the best sleep I ever remember having! I wake up feeling refreshed and ready for the day. I notice I've slept super late. It's 12:06. Almost lunchtime already! I put on a white tank top, a mint cardigan dotted with pink flowers, and navy jeggings. I comb my hair and tie it up into a messy bun. Then, I march into the kitchen where Marty and Papa B are playing video games—Marty's teaching Papa B how to use the controllers. I can see Mom outside reading her book on the back porch wearing her hot pink sunglasses and her large sun hat with the sunflower on it. Dad's trying to perfect his strawberry cream cheese sandwich recipe. Grammy's outside with Mom wearing her gardening hat and plucking weeds from the ground.

"Morning, Eva!" Dad calls to me as I enter the kitchen.

"Morning," I say, plopping down at the table. I feel so happy. I'm in the perfect mood. Everyone seems so happy and content, and I feel like this is exactly where I need to be.

I eat up my strawberry cream cheese sandwiches and chug my apple juice, then I run down the hall into my room to get on the Writer's Circle. I scroll through people's stories and upload some fresh, new stories. I notice that Romi's posted a couple of new stories. These ones seem a bit happier. One is about a group of mermaids who explore an abandoned ship and free an octopus when one of his tentacles getting stuck under a treasure chest. They're kinda cute.

Later, my parents invite Phoenix and his family over for a little while before dinner. Immediately, Phoenix and I dash up to my room and plop down on my bed. We share a plate of strawberry cream cheese sandwiches—I've missed eating them so much—and scroll through the Writer's Circle.

"Should we use the Portal Pen?" Phoenix asks suddenly.

I turn to grin at him. We scramble onto my bed and flip open my notebook. I let Phoenix use the Portal Pen.

"What should this story be about, Eva?" Phoenix asks me.

I tap my chin. What *should* it be about? "How about . . . another pirate crew who are archnemeses with Captain Seaweed and the Tsunami Cruiser!" I cry.

Phoenix grins and nods. "Perfect," he says. He begins to write. My imagination kicks into action, and the gears in my head start turning. This happens every time I write a story. It's like my brain knows exactly where to go and what to do and how to start. I'm itching to take that pen and jot down all of my ideas right now. But I stay calm and eagerly watch Phoenix write.

"But, the captain should be a girl with a tough female crew," Phoenix adds.

I beam. "Yes!" I cry. He's super good at this too!

"What should she look like?" Phoenix asks.

I lean back on my bed. "She should have curly, bleached hair that's long and blond, and skin the color of dark chocolate," I describe. Phoenix nods eagerly and writes all of this down. "She should have piercing blue eyes and a sly expression, and she always has a way to outsmart Captain Seaweed," I explain.

Phoenix sits up. "Okay, my turn," he says. He hands me the pen and we switch places. "Her ship should be made of bright red wood with black sails the color of charcoal," Phoenix describes. I can see the gears turning in his head. This is so cool. We make a great team. "Her crew should be all female, and they are all sly and smart." I jot this down excitedly. His eyes are twinkling with excitement as he bounces slightly and looks around the room for inspiration.

"What should their ship be called?" I ask.

Phoenix pauses. "The Scarlet Fox!" he cries.

I squeal. "Perfect," I say.

"And they should have a big battle with Captain Seaweed, but secretly, they're friends," Phoenix explains. "And even though they have big battles and say that they steal each other's treasure, they really just exchange and trade their treasures to be nice," Phoenix says, chuckling to himself. I quickly scribble it down. We high-five.

"That was awesome!" I cry. Then, suddenly, I feel the rumbling inside of me, and Phoenix clutches his head and looks at me with worry.

"You feel it too?" I ask. Phoenix nods.

"This is what I feel like every time I write a story!" I say.

"So, you're telling me that when you write with the Portal Pen, and you feel this rumbling in the real world, that means the story you wrote is actually forming in the other world?" Phoenix asks. I nod excitedly. Phoenix's mouth drops open, "Whoa!"

Soon, the rumbling stops. Phoenix stumbles and steadies himself. I laugh.

"The world's not actually shaking, Phoenix," I assure him.

He swallows and nods. "I know," he says.

After two hours of chatting and writing and scrolling through the Writer's Circle and eating more strawberry cream cheese sandwiches, Phoenix heads home.

Later, I take a warm shower. Oh, the warm water and soap bubbles on my body and in my hair feel so refreshing. I rinse out my hair and wash my face. Once I dry off, I put on a soft, gray shirt, a silky mustard-yellow cardigan, and some nice jeans. I then French braid my hair and march into the kitchen, where everyone is getting ready to leave. Papa B has borrowed some of my dad's clothes and is itching his neck and trying to shift the tight collar. Marty is wearing an identical navy shirt with Dad's. Mom's wearing a fancy, sky blue denim romper with her hair styled in curls. Grammy's wearing a flowing purple top and a beige skirt. She's adjusting the white flower in her hair and applying bright red lipstick that pops with her outfit.

"Everyone ready?" my mom asks.

We all nod and pile into our van. We drive to a fancy Italian restaurant, and the food there is so delicious. I scooch into the seat next to dad and take a glance at the menu. There's a bunch of exotic-looking foods with spices and sauces that look strange, and the names of the foods are big and fancy and long. Then I spot something: Wild Mushroom Flatbread! I point frantically at the menu and try to get Papa B's attention.

"They had this in the Spoon Kingdom!" I cry. Papa B grins. We both order the Wild Mushroom Flatbread, and when it comes, it looks so delicious. It's warm bread toasted perfectly and with a nice crunch. On the top is buttery mozzarella cheese plastered over the bread with mushrooms and onions littered on the top. Steam fills the air, and I take a sniff. This reminds me so much of the Spoon Kingdom. I take a bite of one of the slices of the flatbread, and oh, it tastes so good. The buttery cheese makes my mouth water as I try to savor every bite. It makes me miss that magical world so much, but at the same time, I'm happy that we were able to go on that journey and come back to enjoy family and friends. I take another bite. Mmm, delicious.

The next day, I pack my backpack and say goodbye to my parents. Grammy and Papa B got up early and went out for coffee. Both of them seem so much happier since they reunited. I march to my bus stop and stand next to the sixth graders. I'm having serious déjà vu right now, even though it's been so long.

The big bus turns on to our street and roars as it sails through our neighborhood. As I climb onto the bus, the cheddar-yellow color reminds me of Noah so much. I can just picture his long neck stretching out of one of the windows, and his happy face peeking out at us. We climb onto the bus and I sit in my usual seat: the second to last row of seats anond the side with the broken window that's always open. It's not fun sitting here in the winter, but I like this seat and everyone on the bus knows that.

Everything's back to normal now. Our cranky bus driver with his gray mustache and squinty eye balls. The annoying hum of the broken air conditioning. The clueless sixth graders who sit in the front, shooting spitballs at each other and making trouble. The seventh graders in the middle rows talking loudly. And the eighth graders, which would be me, in the back. I usually do my homework on the bus, but today, I get out Papa B's old story notebook and read all of his old stories.

School is just the same. But in a way, I'm so happy to be back. I run through the doors and throw out my arms. I don't care about the stares people give me. I'm just so glad to be back. I find my locker with its streamers dangling from the top and the jammed door. I throw it open and hug my textbooks and notebooks. My long, red hair sticks to my rosy cheeks, and I march happily through school.

Then, I notice Romi farther down in the hallway. People I don't even know are running up to her and asking where she's been. Romi talks to them, but she doesn't really seem interested. Her smokey makeup and black-and-blue swirl dress are all gone, and she's back to wearing her signature red sneakers and plain sweat-shirts—though her hair is still dyed pink with blue tips. Other students rush up to me. Random people that I don't even know ask me questions:

"Eva, where have you been? We've missed you!"

"You have so much homework!"

"How was your vacation?"

"You were gone for three weeks!"

Luckily, the bell rings, so I turn my back on curious students and head to class. I see Phoenix across the hallway. He waves at me and heads to his separate class. I pass Romi as I head to history, and we lock eyes. But as soon as we do, Romi looks away, her curls bouncing behind her as she rushes off. As I walk into class, I keep thinking, *I need that second Portal Pen! I need Romi to give it back. But when?*

Phoenix comes to sit by me at lunch. I grin at him, my mouth full of mashed potatoes and gravy. His tray bangs against the tables, and his french fries leap into the air. Phoenix pecks me on the cheek, and I swat at him, my face beet red.

"Phoenix, stop it! Not at school!" I hiss, giggling my head off.

Phoenix grins. But then he turns and points. I follow his gaze to see Romi, eating quietly with Chelsey Hendrickson and Alexis Alec. Alexis has cut her hair into a bob, and Chelsey looks a lot taller. Man, it feels like decades ago when they stole my notebook and I had to snatch it back from them.

Phoenix nudges me. "When are you gonna get that pen back?" he asks.

I stand up. "Right now," I say, confidentially.

I march over to their table. Chelsey and Alexis look up and make faces at me as I come over here.

"Where have you been?" Chelsey snaps.

I ignore her and keep my gaze on Romi. Romi pretends like she doesn't notice me. I put my hand on her shoulder, and she tenses up.

"I forgive you" is all I say.

Romi shudders under my hand. She slowly turns to face me. "But . . . why? After all I did to you! I destroyed kingdoms, I put terrible curses on people, I damaged everything that was yours, I . . . "

I hold up my hand. "I know, but I still forgive you," I say. Romi's eyes look so confused. "And I know you still want to be my friend, right?" I ask.

Romi lowers her head and nods sheepishly. "Yes, I did. And I do," she whispers.

"Romi. I know it wasn't all your doing. I know your family was cursed. And I could see in you when you tried to fight that curse, but it was just too much for you. Besides, you were the one who dropped the Portal Pen into the story world so we could end the battle, right?" I ask.

Romi nods, so I say, "You still want to be friends. And besides . . ." I take out my Portal Pen and hold it up. "I undid your family curse anyways."

Romi gasps and tries to hide her smile, but she's not doing very well. "Really?!" she cries.

I shrug. "Yeah," I say blankly.

Romi jumps up and hugs me. "But, maybe it wasn't just the curse—maybe it was the bond of friendship and love that overcame," Romi smiles.

We grin. "That was so cheesy, but so beautiful," I say.

She and I giggle. I almost want to burst out laughing at Chelsey and Alexis's confused faces. Oh, they have no idea. Romi lets go of me and digs into her pocket. She pulls out the second Portal Pen and hands it to me. I smile.

"Is it okay if I give the second Portal Pen to Phoenix?" I ask.

Romi nods furiously. "Yes! Please do! I'm horrible with that thing!" Romi cries.

Phoenix comes over. "So, did we make up?" he asks.

Romi and I nod. Phoenix wraps us in a group hug.

"Friends?" Romi whispers.

"Friends," I whisper back.

Later that night, I invite Romi and Phoenix over to my house, just like old times. We open up my notebook, and write stories, just the three of us. Suddenly, we all feel the rumbling. Romi squeals. It's the first time she's felt it writing something good—writing something with her friends. We all gather in one big group hug.

"Wait, what should we name our story?" I ask when the rumbling stops.

Romi taps her chin. Then she cries, "The Amazing Tales of the Portal Pen!"

I nod and write it down.

"Perfect!" I cry. "Absolutely perfect."

THE END